THE IMPERFECT MARRIAGE

L. STEELE

DEAR GOOD GIRL,
DOES YOUR SIGNIFICANT OTHER
KNOW YOU'RE IN LOVE WITH A
6" 3" TATTED SILVER FOX
WITH ICY BLUE EYES
WHO GROWLS: "MY WIFE"?

PRIMROSE HILL

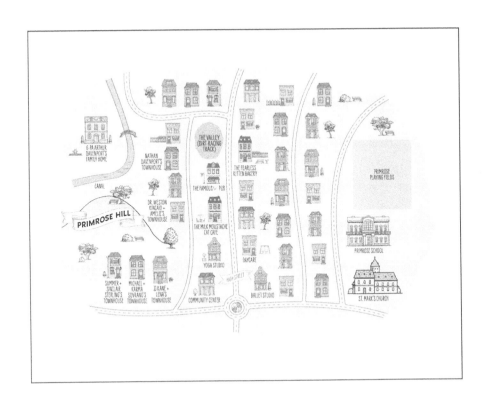

THE DAVENPORTS

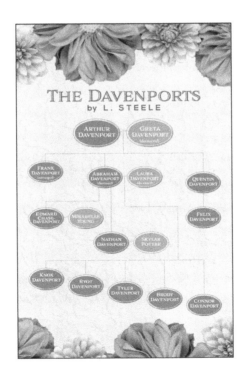

SPOTIFY PLAYLIST

Earned It – The Weeknd (Q's theme song)
    Red (Taylor's Version) – Taylor Swift
    Right Side of My Neck – Faye Webster
    About You – The 1975
    When Doves Cry – Prince
    Salted Wound – Sia
    Streets – Doja Cat
    Earned It – The Weeknd
    Cinnamon Girl – Lana Del Ray
    Afterglow – Taylor Swift
    I Feel Like I'm Drowning – Two Feet
    BABYDOLL – Ari Abdul
    Your Guilty Pleasure – Henry Verus
    Favorite – Isabel LaRosa
    Dangerous Woman – Ariana Grande (Vivian's theme song)
    I'll Do Anything For Love (But I Won't Do That) – Meatloaf

1

Vivian

I can do this. I'm doing the right thing.

Why didn't I think of bringing a bouquet? I take a step forward to walk up the aisle alone.

My heart leaps up into my throat. My fingers tremble. I lock them together in front of me and take a deep breath. Then another. The organist strikes up the opening chords of "Here Comes the Bride."

There. That takes the decision out of my hands. I take a step forward, then another, fixing my sightless eyes straight ahead. The crowd hushes. I walk down the aisle. Sweat trails down my back. My knees tremble, but I manage to stay upright. *Keep moving. Don't stop. You want to marry him. You do.* Why am I trying to convince myself? A little too late to turn back, isn't it? A shiver runs up my spine.

The fine hairs on the nape of my neck tighten. Beneath the scent of incense in the church are notes of woodsmoke and pine, and something evocative that reminds me of a forest I visited once when I was a young girl. I look to the side, and I meet the gaze of a man I've never seen before.

Those blue eyes are like sheets of ice. Thick, jet-black hair cut in a military style crew cut shows the shape of his skull and lends him a severe appearance. Threads of silver at his temples only add to his distinguished look. His jaw is square, his cheekbones sharp enough to cut diamonds.

That beautiful throat is corded with tendons, while his shoulders are broad enough to fill my line of sight.

Then there's his hooked nose, and that thin upper lip, which adds to the impression of his spartan nature... As for that plush lower lip—I swallow—it would be perfect to bite down on.

Whoa, what am I thinking?

His lips firm, thinning out that upper lip further. I drag my gaze back to his; to find he's scowling at me. The expression on his face is angry and confused, and yet, there's so much naked need. My nipples tighten, and my toes curl. My steps slow. It feels like I'm walking through quicksand.

What is this fluttering sensation in my belly? This shivering that grips me. This hesitation which churns my belly. Who is this guy? Why have I never felt like this before? Why is this stranger having such an impact on me?

Fighting my instincts, I walk past him.

As I pass my father, he wipes a tear from his face. My own threaten, but I don't give in. I stifle the ball of emotion that clogs my throat.

Keep moving.

I force myself to look forward and come to a halt opposite the priest who's going to marry us. Only problem?

What does it say about me that I didn't notice my bridegroom was missing until I reached the altar? I was too focused on gathering my wits, then on putting one foot in front of the other. And when I saw that scowling guy, all other thoughts flew out of my head.

I turn to the groomsman, who I recognize as my bridegroom's friend, Stan. "Where's Felix?" I ask.

"Err..." Stan's Adam's apple bobs. "Err... I... He..." He shakes his head, sweat beading his upper lip. *Why does he look like he's going to puke?*

Behind me, murmurs arise from the crowd. Then my father calls out, "Is everything all right, Vivi?"

I hold up my hand, and the conversations quiet down. I narrow my gaze on Stan. "What's wrong? Is Felix okay? Did something happen to him?"

"Err... He... Uh...He sent me this message." Stan thrusts his phone under my nose.

> Felix: Tell Vivian I'm sorry. I can't go through with it

He dumped me. What the—! My bridegroom didn't have the courtesy to tell me to my face that he was breaking up with me?

Heat flushes my cheeks. Embarrassment squeezes my chest, and I hunch my shoulders. Yet, my heart... My heart stays steady. And my brain whispers... *Thank God.*

A giddy sense of relief infiltrates my blood stream. My bridegroom stood me up, and while I am upset and angry, I also feel like I managed to avoid the gallows. *What does that say about me? Was I about to commit the biggest mistake of my life? And did my bridegroom save me by not turning up for our wedding?*

He did me a solid. Except, he dumped me in front of a church full of people, including my father. That sense of mortification tightens into a lump in my throat and spreads to my chest. My stomach heaves. Bile boils up my throat. I swallow down the acidic taste coating my tongue and draw in a breath, then another.

Someone in the crowd loudly asks, "Is the wedding off?"

He's greeted by a chorus of shushing and admonishments and what seems to be a thousand voices raised in conversation.

The dress, which had once felt so right, seems too tight for my body. I should sidle away so I'm no longer in the center of this shit show; only, my legs refuse to obey me.

"I am so sorry, Vivian," Stan whispers.

For some reason, the sympathy in his voice is my undoing. Tears squeeze out of the corners of my eyes, and I brush at my cheeks. *Why am I crying? This is so stupid. Why do I feel like I've really been ditched at the altar? Because you were ditched at the altar?*

Only, I didn't love Felix, and I'm grateful he didn't turn up. *So why do I feel so wretched?* I should get out of here and hide my face; pretend I wasn't subjected to the single most mortifying moment in my life, but... Nope, my feet seem to be cemented to the ground.

I lower my chin and stare at the floor, when someone steps up to stand in front of me. Someone who has big feet, going by the size of the polished black formal shoes he's wearing, and who can afford a tailor, as evidenced by the pants that cling to his powerful thighs. Also, that bulge between those thighs which hints that he's not lacking in that department at all. Huh? I have no business noticing a stranger's junk, when I've just been dumped by my bridegroom—*who you didn't want to marry.* One who left me stranded in front of this crowd.

That's when I realize, the murmuring and shuffling around me has faded away. Silence surrounds me. My heart rate spikes. The hair on the back of my neck rises, and when I draw in a breath, I smell woodsmoke, pine and wild open spaces. I know it's him, even before I raise my gaze to his chest and realize it's so wide, it blocks out the sight of everything else. I know it's the man I saw in the pews as I walked up the aisle before I tilt my head back, then further back, until I meet those silver-blue eyes. I'm almost not surprised it's him; not at all.

When our gazes met earlier, I knew I was going to see him again... There was this connection that almost stopped me in my tracks. But I pushed it aside and, feeling a sense of obligation, I continued forward toward my non-existent bridegroom.

Of course, it would have to be like this. A sense of destiny settles around my shoulders. And when the stranger leans in and lifts up my veil, I don't flinch or protest. A gasp runs through the crowd, but I ignore it. My gaze is caught and held by this enigmatic man who something in me recognizes.

It's him. Him. Him. My blood sings in my veins. Electricity fires up my nerve-endings. *He's the reason it felt wrong with Felix. He's the reason I knew marrying Felix was wrong. But I never thought I'd meet him; not in this lifetime. It's why I almost married Felix. Thank God, he pulled out.*

Some of my thoughts must be reflected on my features, for there's an answering flash in his eyes. His jaw firms. He seems to come to a decision because he lowers his hand to his side, then drops to one knee.

My gaze widens. My pulse rate spikes. *What's he doing? He can't be. No. No. Way.* He looks up again and locks his gaze on mine.

I see the question in his eyes and know what my answer is before he growls, "Marry me."

Another gasp runs through the crowd. It fades away, and then there's silence. The blood pounds at my temples. My heart seems to swell until I'm one thump from exploding into a ball of smoke—*poof*—I'll be gone. No one will know I'm here. No one will pass judgement on me. No one need know I almost agreed to marry him in church when he proposed because I'm so attracted to him.

I open my mouth to whisper my assent but what comes out is, "It's often impossible to hum while holding your nose."

The man blinks slowly.

"Also, most people find it impossible to lick their own elbow." I nod, then wince. This is when he stares at me like I'm crazy, like so many others have when I begin to spout weird facts in a bid to cover up my nervousness.

I begin to turn away, when that stern mouth of his twitches. "Is that right?"

Did he smile? He *almost* smiled. *What if I could make him smile for real?*

"It's physically impossible for pigs to look up into the sky." I peer at him from under my eyelashes.

One side of his lip lifts. His eyes light up with amusement. *Yes!* I resist the urge to fist pump.

"And you must be aware, I can't say yes to you..." *no matter how much I am tempted.* Spouting that inane trivia bought me a little time, and I realize now, even contemplating marrying him is insane. I don't know him. And he's much older than me. Nope, it's wishful thinking that he's my knight in shining armor come to rescue me from this horrible situation.

"Why?" His gaze grows intense. "Why can't you say yes?" The silver in his eyes flares. Everything else around me fades. My senses light up as my vision focuses on him. All I can see is his features. *Him.*

Also, that's a good question. *Why can't I marry you, even though every cell in my body insists I should?* And my instincts scream I should do the right thing, ignore how it seems to the world, and follow what feels right for me.

I clear my throat. "Firstly, there's the fact that I don't know you."

"That can be rectified." His voice is confident.

I gape at him, then begin to laugh. "You can't be serious," I say between gasping breaths.

"I never joke," he says with such vehemence, I know for a fact, he's telling the truth. I want to say something about how he could do with some laughs in his life, but who am I to say anything when my entire life has turned into the stuff of party conversations?

My own laughter dies. I stare at him, and he peruses my features with an intensity I've never been subjected to before. An intensity which turns my nipples into pinpoints of desire, and causes my belly to flutter, and my pussy to clench in on itself.

How am I so drawn to him? I should be crushed my bridegroom did a runner. Instead, all I can think of is how much I want this stranger. This is wrong, no matter which way I look at it. Something of my resolve must reflect on my face for he nods, then straightens to stand back up.

Once more, I have to tilt my head back to see his face. Once more, I'm struck by how tall he is. How broad, how big and solid and dependable. How he invites trust. How... He'd never leave me stranded at the altar... How he definitely would not break up with me through a text message sent to his best man.

My scalp tingles. All the air in the room seems to have been sucked out. The voices around us fade. I want to look away from him, but I can't.

I feel discombobulated, like I'm watching this scene unfold from far away. *Is this an out of body experience?*"

"This is real. I am here. So are you. And you're going to marry me." His voice rings with conviction.

I shake my head, open my mouth to speak, when—

There's a clattering in the vestibule, then Felix races up the aisle toward us. "Wait! I'm here."

My jaw drops. *Felix? What's he doing here?*

A gasp runs through the crowd. I catch sight of my father watching me with worry in his eyes.

Felix barrels to a stop. Chest heaving, sweat dripping down his temple, he bursts out, "I'm sorry, Vivian. Sorry I sent that message. But I'm here now." He takes a step in my direction, but I throw up my hands.

"Don't come near me!" I cry.

"Vivian—" He swallows. "Please, listen to me."

I clench my fists at my sides. The anger that I've been struggling to hold back rampages through my veins with the force of a tornado. "No. No way, do you get to speak with me now. Not after you didn't even have the decency to tell me to my face. You broke up with me at the altar. And through a text message? To your friend? And you have the nerve to turn up and apologize?"

Pressure builds behind my eyes. My heart threatens to snap through my ribcage, the blood pumps in my ears, and I can barely hear myself speak.

"Why did you return?" I turn on Felix. "What gives you any right to come here and ask me anything? Haven't you hurt me enough?"

"It's not like that, Vivi—" Felix takes a step forward.

I stumble back. "Don't you dare call me 'Vivi.' And how dare you try to explain things? Do you realize what you did? Do you?" *And why am I grateful for it? And why am I so angry, when I realize now, he was all wrong for me, and I didn't want to get married in the first place?* "Oh my god, why is everything so complicated?"

"But I have to… I …I. Please, Vivi. Please, let me explain."

"Nope, no way, not happening. I should have realized how wrong this was." I motion to my gown, to him, and to the space between us. "I never should have accepted your proposal in the first place. I'm almost glad you dumped me. Hurtful as it was, I'm relieved. You stopped me from making a huge mistake."

"Vivi." His gaze widens. The color fades from his cheeks. He seems taken aback, then he shakes his head. "No, please don't say that." His chin trembles. "I... I didn't mean to hurt you." His Adam's apple bobs as he swallows.

"Are you kidding me?" I clench my fists at my side.

He runs his fingers through his gelled hair, which stands up on end.

He seems so young. We might be the same age, but I've always felt this compulsive need to take care of him. *Is that why I agreed to marry him? I thought it was to save money but maybe it's because I miss taking care of someone since my younger sister moved away to attend ballet school. And while I do help my father, it's not the same as having her around. Was I looking to fill that hollowness inside me with his need for me? Why didn't these thoughts occur to me before I accepted his proposal?*

He must see the conflicting emotions on my features, for his own crumple. "I'm so sorry." A tear runs down his cheek.

"No." I stab my finger at him. "You don't get to be the injured party here. You don't get to cry."

"Please Vivi, please. Can't we speak, at least?" he asks in a beseeching tone. There's so much sadness in his eyes that some of my anger fades, and I feel pity.

Not only was I looking to fill the emptiness left behind by Lizzie, I chose someone I could mother. I wince. *Nice. I should have realized that before I rushed into marrying him.* I bite down on my lower lip.

"There's no point in discussing what happened. We never should have planned to get married. Although, figuring that out in such a public fashion"—I wave my hand at the surroundings— "is not how I thought this day would turn out."

"Me neither." Felix lowers his chin. "That's the thing. I thought everything was fine. Then I walked into the church and—"

"You had second thoughts?" I ask dryly.

He nods. "I thought it was the usual pre-wedding jitters, until I saw the crowd... I knew then, I couldn't go through with it."

"Are you listening to yourself?" I throw up my hands. "That is not an explanation. Couldn't you have thought this through before you proposed to me?" I chuckle without humor. "You'd think *I* could have figured out we were wrong for each other, before I agreed to marry you."

He hunches his shoulders—so thin, in comparison to the stranger.

I glance sideways at the man who decided to prolong the mockery of the situation by proposing to me. *Why did he do that? Was it because he felt sorry for me? And am I seriously considering his proposal?*

My heart somersaults into my throat. The blood pumps in my ears so loudly, I can barely hear myself think. It's good manners and the tightness of my wedding dress that keep me from fleeing down the aisle and away from this place. Marrying him? Marrying a complete stranger? That would be crazy... right?

But what's wrong with being crazy? I was jilted at the altar. That's crazy enough. But having a wild, sexy stranger propose to me directly afterward is even crazier. What if I do the craziest thing of all? What if I don't run away screaming? But instead, say yes. Agree to marry a man I've never met before. A man who's older than me. A man who looks fully capable of wringing pleasure from my body with his beautiful mouth and thick fingers and the equipment he's packing.

Felix blinks, then follows my gaze to the stranger. His gaze widens as if he's noticing the stranger for the first time. A weird light flares in his eyes.

"What are you doing here?" He glares at the older man. "I didn't invite you to my wedding."

They know each other?

"No way was I going to stay away. And I'm especially glad I didn't, after you decided to turn into a runway bridegroom," the older guy growls.

Felix winces. His gaze narrows, and he sets his jaw. "I don't have to listen to this from someone who's been an absent father most of my life."

"Father?" I gape at the stranger whose proposal I nearly accepted. "You're his father?"

2

Quentin

I should step back. I should walk away. I can't let my life be marked by this one move; I don't need to do this. There are other women I can marry to fulfill Arthur's condition, and without hurting my son further. It doesn't have to be her.

It has to be her. No one else but her.

She looks from me to Felix, then back at me. Her gaze widens in surprise before she firms her lips. Her eyes flash. "What made you think it would be a good idea to propose to the woman your son almost married?" she spits out.

Felix reels back. "Y-you p-p-p-proposed to her?" he sputters.

"I'm trying to set right *your* wrongs," I say in a low voice. *And for the first time in my life, I'm following my heart.* Not since Felix's mother left, have I felt this overwhelmed.

"'Tis some visitor. Tapping at my chamber door, only this and nothing more," I say without taking my gaze off her features.

"You're quoting Poe?" She blinks.

My son makes a rude noise. "Of course, you're quoting Poe. Always did have a nonsensical verse when you had no other excuses to offer."

"I didn't mean to hurt you." I hear the words and cringe. *Isn't that what Felix just told her? And am I directing those words at her, or at my son?*

My aunt shoulders her way through the onlookers, none of whom have yet left the church. They came to see a wedding and were awarded with the spectacle of something far more interesting. When she joins the group, there's a look of trepidation on her face.

Among the crowd in the pews, I catch sight of my nephew Knox. He's staring at me with a look of shock on his face.

An older man rolls down the aisle in his wheelchair and comes to a halt next to the woman I proposed to.

"What's going on?" He scowls at me. "Did you propose to my daughter?"

My aunt's face pales. She opens and shuts her mouth, as if she is having difficulty forming any words.

I turn away from her accusing stare and draw myself to my full height. "It's true, I asked—" *Shit. Shit. Shit.* I don't know her name, but given Felix called her Vivi... "Vivian to marry me," I say, as if I've known it all along. Going by the lack of surprise, I know I'm right. "No title defines something so pure. By any name, the feelings endure," I murmur.

Her forehead furrows. "Shakespeare," she whispers.

"Fucking Bard. You always did think you could use a verse to get away with anything," my son says in a bitter voice.

"Poems have no influence on me." Vivian tips up her chin.

"Then how did you know who I was quoting?" I allow my lips to twitch.

Her features grow mutinous.

"And I'm not trying to excuse my actions." I turn to my son. "I'm not trying to show you up."

Felix scoffs. "I don't believe you. Never have. Never will. You're a selfish bastard. You only think of yourself."

I wince again. "I deserve that, and all your anger. I did not mean for this to happen, believe me. It was... Something beyond my control. I couldn't stop myself."

"That's your excuse?" He levels a look filled with so much scorn in my direction, that I feel my cheeks redden.

"The one thing I laid claim to. The one thing I wanted to make mine. And you couldn't resist screwing it up?" He spits out.

I see Vivian stiffen at his words.

"You're the one who screwed it up, when you did a runner on your own wedding."

My son's face grows so red, I'm sure he's going to have a cardiac event.

"Felix, please—"

"Fuck you, Quentin." The next second, he throws himself at me. I see him coming and could step aside but choose not to. I deserve his anger and his hate, and it's better he takes it out on me than keep it inside.

He slams into my chest. I take his weight without flinching. My son, however, lets out an anguished yell. He grabs his shoulder and, with pain-filled eyes, glares at me. "You're an arsehole."

"I am."

"I told you not to come. I told you I didn't want you here. I knew you'd send everything tits up." His chest heaves.

I open my mouth to point out it was he who, in fact, started the ball rolling in that direction, then wisely rein myself in.

"Did you hurt yourself?" I reach for him, but he steps back.

"Don't touch me. I don't want anything to do with you," Felix yells.

"How dare you, father and son, play with my emotions?" Vivian stamps her foot. "How dare you embarrass me like this? It was bad enough what you did." She jerks her chin in Felix's direction. "Then you"—she trains her gaze on me—"make it a thousand times worse. Did you think you could make up for what Felix did by substituting yourself? Did you think I'd be so relieved to be getting married to someone—*anyone*—I'd jump at your offer? I'm not some pawn or possession for you to stake a claim to. I'm not the prize in some twisted competition."

"Vivi—" Felix begins.

"Vivian—" I say at the same time.

"Will the two of you keep quiet?" She plants her palms on her hips, and glowers between us. "I have had enough of the both of you."

"But—" I take a step forward, and she shakes her head.

"Haven't you done enough for one day? Will you please leave me alone?"

She spins around and walks down the aisle. The crowd of people part, and head held high, she glides away. I make to go after her, but her father rolls to a stop in front of me. I pause, torn between stepping around him to follow her and standing here, letting her go.

He looks me up and down. "What are your intentions toward my daughter?"

She stalks to the door. In a flash, I see my future slipping away from me, and I know I have a choice to make. "Vivian!" I call out.

3

Vivian

"Another." I slide the empty shot glass of tequila toward the bartender. He obliges me. When he's filled it to the brim, I throw it back.

The alcohol sets off a trail of heat in its wake as it slides down my throat. When it hits my stomach, the warmth shakes loose to my extremities. It's my second shot, and already, my head feels light. It feels like I'm floating. It's not a bad feeling for someone who, right about now, should have been a married woman. I glance at the empty ring finger of my left hand. Felix dumped me. Which is a relief, but also means I'll have to move out of the flat I share with him. I stiffen. *Oh, my god. How did that slip my mind?*

Felix insisted on paying the rent for our place. At first, I declined. But he told me he doesn't have a father and sister to take care of, like I do. So, I gave in. I insisted on paying for the groceries and the utilities, but it meant I could save the money I needed to help my dad with his treatments.

Now, everything is back to square one. I'll have to move back into the cramped apartment with my three previous roommates—assuming that's still available—and even if it is, it means, once more, no space for Lizzie to spend her weekends. Also, I'll have to cover the rent of wherever I move next. *Ohmygod. How am I going to manage this?* What's worse, I'm also the woman who was stood up... At the altar. My pulse rate spikes. My heart begins to boom in my chest. I throw back my tequila, then slap the shot glass onto the counter.

You can plan all you want, but when you least expect it, something happens that teaches you, things were never within your control. I thought I was being smart accepting Felix's proposal. Turns out, I was on the wrong track. I grip the edge of the bar counter and squeeze.

I told myself, the kind of love written by my favorite poets didn't exist in real life. Besides, I was focused on taking care of my father's medical needs and paying my sister's tuition. Which meant I had to work many hours to pay the bills. I didn't have time to meet men, let alone the kind who'd sweep me off my feet. But don't I deserve to feel the kind of passion outlined in those poems? Am I not worthy of a love as deep and as all-encompassing as Pablo Neruda wrote about? I never wanted to let myself believe in it, but clearly, I do.

I down another tequila and shake my head at myself. My sister is right. I need to be more spontaneous. *But spontaneous enough to marry a stranger?* And hopeful enough to believe his proposal was genuine? *Can I allow myself to dream that a man who proposed to me out of the blue is going to sweep me off my feet and give me a chance to feel like the heroine of my own love story?*

How can I contemplate a life with someone I never met before, who also happens to be my ex's father? What madness is it that I'm thinking about him, instead of the ex who ditched me?

I shove the train of my wedding dress away. Yep, I got into the car that was parked outside—the car I rented and drove over, to which Stan affixed a "Just Married" sign, which I didn't pause to tear off. Luckily, my purse was in the glove compartment and the car was unlocked, with the key fob in the ignition, so I made a quick getaway.

I drove the car out of there and kept driving until the tears knocking at the back of my eyes threatened to overflow. And I was not going to let myself cry.

So, when I found a neighborhood pub, I pulled over. I'm, maybe, twenty minutes from the church, but this is far enough away that no one will find me. I stomped in here.

It's early evening, and the clientele is light. I scowled at the couple staring at me open-mouthed from across the room, until they looked away.

Then, I glared at a man with a half-full mug of beer in front of him at another table. He hastily brought the glass to his mouth. I ignored them after that and marched up to the bar. I plonked myself onto a barstool and asked for a tequila.

Now, the bartender tops me up again.

I contemplate the golden liquid in the shot glass. The dim light picks out sparks at the bottom. Sparks that remind me of those in his blue eyes. Sparks which... I should ignore. I should be thinking of my almost-husband, instead of his hot-as-Lucifer, father.

Argh. That sounds gross. Not Lucifer. But the thought that the man I'm lusting after is my now-ex's father. It's enough to make me want to get completely drunk.

I throw down the shot and slap the glass on the counter. "Another, please." I nod at the bartender.

He flashes me a smile, grabs the Jose Cuervo, and tops me up. "Everything okay?"

I scoff, "But for the fact I discovered my latent weakness for silver foxes—or rather, one silver fox in particular—and I might be suffering from Daddy issues, everything is peachy."

I toss back the glass of tequila and slam it back on the counter, wiping the back of my palm across my mouth.

"Worse, he's put me in a situation that seems impossible but might be the solution to all of my problems." My shoulders droop. "Also, I'm running from the fact his son left me standing at the altar."

"Oh?" He raises his eyebrows in surprise.

"One in four Americans overshare on social media, then regret it," I respond.

"Is that a fact?" he exclaims.

"It is." I half laugh. "And before you ask me how I know that, you should know, my brain stores up these facts without my trying. Weird, right?" I pop a shoulder. "Kids in high school thought so, too. Combined with the fact we moved to the UK from the States when I was five, it means I got picked on a lot. It was enough to turn me into an introvert. Try as I might to fit in, I haven't lost my American accent completely." I frown. "It doesn't bother me now." *Having to worry about paying your bills will do that for you. Also, that tequila sure makes it easy to spill my thoughts.*

"I'm sorry you had a hard time in school. High school is the worst, amirite?" He chuckles, then lifts the bottle of Jose. "Just for that, you deserve a free drink, but... I think you've had enough."

"Aww." I pout. "Please, please, please? I want to forget this shit show of a day, you know?"

He hesitates.

"Pl-e-e-e-ease?" I flutter my eyelashes at him. Anything to forget this stabbing sensation in my chest. Anything to forget a pair of blue eyes with silver sparks in their depths. Anything to forget the fact I could have said yes to a hot, handsome stranger and let him carry me away to his lair and have his way with me. "Pretty please?" I spoil the effect by hiccupping.

The bartender sighs. "Last one, and then I'm calling you a cab." He spills more of the golden liquid into my shot glass.

I reach for the glass, but it's snatched up by someone else.

"You've had enough," a dark voice growls.

I turn to find Quentin sliding onto the stool next to me. The breadth of his shoulders, the way he blocks out the sight of everything else, the way his gaze sears me, sends a burst of heat up my spine. My thighs clench. My panties dampen. My nipples harden into bullets of need that take aim at him. It's as if I manifested him from my thoughts.

Our gazes meet, and it's as if I've been hit in the chest with a bolt of lightning. My heart slams into my ribcage. My breath hitches. Then he smirks, and indignation follows on the heels of the heavy lust that's stuck its claws into me. *What is he doing here? How dare he follow me here? Can I not wallow in self-pity for a few seconds without this tall, dark, sexy stranger, once again, sweeping into my life like he owns it?* I need to take back control.

"Gimme that." I swipe at the shot glass he holds in his hand, overbalance, and fall into him. I hit his arm—his very strong, hard arm—and it feels like I've hit the side of a building. But only if the side of a building were to be covered in warm muscles that ripple and move like there's a current of electricity running underneath.

Oh wait, that's me. That's the zip of sensations running up my arm, to my heart, and down to my core. My chest hurts. My belly quivers. The bud between my pussy lips threatens to bloom. *Nope. Not happening. Not now. Not after how he embarrassed me in front of everyone.* I push away from him and right myself on my stool. "Give me. My. Drink," I choke out.

"Not happening." There's a finality in his voice, a resoluteness that slices through the thoughts in my head. It pushes something in me to bend and obey, a-n-d...

No. Absolutely not. I set my jaw, turn to the bartender and scowl. "Another drink, please."

"You will not give her another drink." My ex's father pulls out his wallet and throws a few notes on the counter.

The bartender seems taken aback. He looks from Quentin to me, then back at Quentin. A look of comprehension comes over his features and he scoops up the notes.

"Hey!" I try to get his attention, but he's already moved away.

Fine, I can help myself. I reach over and grab the bottle of Jose from under the counter, but Quentin snatches it from me.

"Gimme that!" I attempt to grab it.

He holds the bottle out of reach. "You're leaving."

"No, I'm not," I argue.

"Yes, you are," he says in a slow, patient voice that brooks no argument, but which also makes me feel like I'm younger than him. And I *am* younger than him. In comparison to his age and experience, I'm a novice. Damn him for highlighting our age gap. For bringing home that he's the father of my now-ex, and it's a pipe dream to think we could ever have anything when it's forbidden and all wrong.

"You can't tell me what to do," I seethe.

"Sure I can." He nods slowly.

Anger suffuses my guts, floods my chest, fills my blood, and spurts out through the pores of my skin. "Who do you think you are?" I snarl.

"Your-husband-to-be."

4

Quentin

"What the... WHAT?" She throws back her head and laughs. Then straightens, all mirth wiped from her face. "You have some gall, saying that to my face."

I allow my lips to twitch. "As I recall, you didn't seem averse to the idea of marrying me when I proposed to you."

She scoffs, "And if *you* recall, I said I *couldn't say yes* to you because I didn't know you."

"And you should know, your father is not opposed to this marriage." I place the bottle of tequila on the other side of the counter and away from her.

"Excuse me?" Her eyes flash. "You have some nerve bringing my father into this conversation."

"I'm old-fashioned that way."

"Don't you mean old?" Her words are laced with sarcasm.

Dammit, she's right. I continue as if I didn't hear that. "I wanted to get his blessings on our union."

"Excuse me?" She gapes.

"I would have chased right after you, but your father deserved to know my intentions were honorable. He gave his blessing, you know?"

She snaps her mouth shut. Stubbornness settles across her features. "It doesn't make a difference. I'm not marrying you." She folds her arms across her chest.

You will. She has no idea how persistent I can be. *She's mine.* I won't give up until I possess her. "I promised him I'd take care of you, and that you'd want for nothing. I also told him I knew it was unorthodox, the way I went about proposing. Not to mention, you're my son's ex. But I knew we were meant for each other as soon as I saw you."

She stares at me, surprise in her eyes.

"The awkwardness of the situation is not lost on me," I say gently.

"And what did my father say?"

"That he was pissed-off with my son and he needed proof that I wouldn't do the same to you. I told him I'd have married you right then, if I could've, but since that wasn't happening, I gave him my word—"

"Y-your word?" she sputters.

I nod. "A gentleman's word is everything, and I promised him we'd be married as soon as you agreed to my proposal."

"*You* promised—?" Color smears her cheeks. "You *promised?*" Her voice rises toward the end of the statement.

"I did the right thing, didn't I?" I say it, knowing full well it's going to anger her, and she doesn't disappoint me.

"You dared talk about me when I was not in the room? Like I am some... Some... Bit of chattel?" she spits out.

"It was a man-to-man conversation." That, too, is aimed at riling her up, and once more, she rises to the challenge.

"About me!" She curls her fingers into fists. "How dare the two of you decide my fate when I wasn't in the room? What do you think this is? Regency England? I didn't realize you were *that* old."

I suppress a smirk. "It was simply my way of putting your father's fears to rest. I realized he wasn't well, and he felt helpless that his daughter's wedding had fallen apart. He knew you were hurt, and he couldn't do anything about it. This was my way of handing some of the control back to him."

"Oh." She deflates a little. "You're right; he was upset about what happened. What father wouldn't be? The last thing I would've wanted was for him to witness my humiliation, but"—she points a finger at me—

"how dare the two of you discuss things that could impact me, and in my absence?"

"It's totally up to you to decide, of course."

"Why, thank you for letting me have a say in my own future," she snarls.

I tilt my head, pretending not to hear the scorn dripping from her tone. "You're welcome."

She thrusts out her chin, frustration inherent in the way she holds herself stiffly. "You're a chauvinistic pig."

"I've been called worse," I agree.

She stares at me, frustration etched into the lines on her face. "I think you should leave."

"Only if you leave with me."

"You wish." Once more, she reaches for the bottle of tequila, but I use my body to prevent her from getting closer to it. Going by her flushed cheeks and feverish gaze, she's had enough to drink. Any more and she'll be sick.

Has she even eaten anything today? It hasn't been an easy day for her. The stress of the wedding, then Felix standing her up, followed by my surprise proposal. That's a lot! Her emotions are, no doubt, all over the place, and the alcohol is not going to help.

She overstretches, the stool tips over, and she begins to slide. I grab at her shoulder and steady her. She rights herself and shakes off my hand. "Don't touch me."

"Is that any way to talk to your future husband?"

She makes a gnashing sound with her teeth and looks like she's about to throw herself at me, not that I wouldn't welcome that. And when she purses her luscious lips, they form a moue, and all I can think of is having them wrapped around my cock. I shake my head. *Nope, don't go there.* This is not about sex... Well, not only.

I admit, from the moment I saw her, I couldn't take my eyes off of her. Not even the fact she was going to marry my son stopped me from wanting her. And when I realized Felix had stood her up, I seized the opportunity. At my age, you don't wait for the right moment. You know that these feelings come around but once in a lifetime; so when you feel this strongly about a woman, you don't hesitate. *You claim her, and keep her, and worship her, and take care of her, so she never wants for anything. It also means, you protect her with everything you have.*

I glance around the room, making sure to look every asshole who's looking at her in the eye. They promptly look away. Losers. None of them deserve to set their gaze on a goddess like her.

"Did you just growl?" Her eyes widen.

I don't reply.

"You growled." She draws in a breath, and her spectacular bosom rises and falls. She juts out her chin, and her defiance is so fucking cute. So endearing. So... Adorable. A-n-d, I need to get her out of here before I say or do something that could spoil the chances of her accepting the proposal I have for her.

She folds her arms across her chest. "If you think you can stake your claim by acting all possessive—"

"That was not acting possessive." I unfold my length and straighten, so she has to tilt her head back to look at me. "This is." I bend and scoop her up in my arms.

"What the—!?" She begins to struggle in my grasp. "What are you doing?"

"Getting you out of here to somewhere we can talk."

"Put me down." She slaps my chest. "You can't be this... This..."

"Overbearing?"

"Arrogant," she hisses.

"Don't you mean dominating?"

"Egoistical." She begins to struggle in my arms.

"I am all that, and more."

"You're drawing attention to us," she snaps.

"No, *you* are. Hush now. Stop struggling, and everyone will assume we're married and I'm carrying you off to our honeymoon."

She stills, and when I glance down, I find her features pinched. There's a look of anger and helplessness in her green eyes. She must be remembering what happened at the church earlier. She lowers her chin, her lips are curved down, and goddam, but I don't want her to look this unhappy, this defeated. I want her to fight back at what happened.

I want her to fight me. I want her to show her mettle. I want her to stand up for herself. If I push her, she'll react. That way, I'll know what she wants. That way, I can give her what she needs. But she's got to have fire in her to make it worthwhile for me, and to make it satisfying for her... Because she could be the perfect submissive.

Is this why I'm so drawn to her? Did I sense the hidden need in her to submit to the right master? Did the dominant in me take one look and know she was it? Is that why I proposed to her as soon as I saw the opportunity?

As if she senses my thoughts, she tightens her hold about my shoulders. Instinctively, I cradle her closer. Her weight feels perfect against my chest. I could hold her like this forever.

"I'm sorry, I shouldn't have said that," I say in a low voice.

When she doesn't reply, I blow out a breath. Felix may have been the one who stood her up, but I feel responsible for his behavior. I need to make it up to her. Need to put things right with her. "What happened at the church was unpardonable. He shouldn't have done that."

"And what about what you did?" She scowls at me.

I hesitate. "What if I tell you I don't regret it?"

She frowns, and I sense she's digesting what I said.

I carry her out of the pub and to my car, then lower her to her feet. A gust of wind blows the tendrils which have come loose from her hair around her face. She sways, and I keep my arm about her.

"I'm not drrr...u-nk." She spoils the effect by slurring her words, then giggles. "Oops." She takes a deep breath and tries again. "Guess, I *am* drunk, and embarrassed."

"I'm sorry. It wasn't my intention to embarrass you, but I want to speak with you in a place where we don't have an audience."

"And I *don't* want to speak with you." She sets her jaw.

"Give me a chance to outline what I have in mind," I plead.

"And if I don't care?"

"I think you'll want to listen to my offer before you decide."

"Offer?" She frowns.

In response, I pull open the car door. "Get in."

5

Vivian

"There are many reasons why you should say yes to my proposal," he rumbles.

"Oh?" I wriggle around, trying to make myself comfortable.

The gown I'm wearing is a Karma West Sovrano original. It looked elegant and sexy on the hanger in the charity shop—which is the only reason I could afford it. It was meant for walking down an aisle, not for sitting down and having a tête-a-tête with the father of the man I was supposed to marry.

We're in the living room of his townhouse in Primrose Hill with sweeping views of the city. It's amongst the poshest neighborhoods in London. I know he's rich, but being here brings home how out of my reach this man is.

I handed over the keys of my rental car to him, and he arranged to have it returned. He's so in control, it's tempting to hand over all of my problems and have him find a solution. To lean on him and have him make my decisions.

I've had to depend on myself for so long. I've had to stay strong for my family. Then, along comes this man who seems to have the answers to my problems.

It's so tempting to hand over the reins of my life and have someone else drive for a while. It so happens, the man who makes me want to lean on him is older than me. And he's my ex's dad. This is so wrong. Worse? I haven't stopped thinking about his proposal. And here I am, in his house.

He's so charismatic, I have no doubt, given the chance, he'll convince me to marry him, too. He'll be so persuasive, I won't be able to say no. And I can't do that. How would Felix react to that? He was once my best friend. I can't walk all over his feelings. Even if he did stand me up at the altar.

Strange as it sounds, I really don't think he intended to hurt me. Maybe he didn't think it through. But I'm thinking this through, and I don't want to intentionally hurt him.

My fingers tremble; I lock them together. "I... I shouldn't be here. This was a mistake."

I jump to my feet, take a step away, and trip on the train of the gown. I pitch forward and throw out my hands to stop my inevitable face-plant, only an arm around my waist halts my descent. The next moment, I'm set back on my feet.

He holds me in place, the warmth of his touch setting off frissons of excitement which travel to my core. I squeeze my thighs together. The movement is so slight, and yet, he seems to notice it, for his gaze sharpens. That woodsmoke and pine scent of his, laced with healthy male sweat, teases my nostrils. My nipples bead. My scalp tingles. *I want him so much. Why does that make me feel like such a slut? And why do I not care that it does?*

The heat from his broad chest slams into mine, and I sway toward him. His grasp on me tightens. He stares at my mouth. The pulse at his temple beats in tandem to the racing of my heart. He lowers his face, and his breath heats my cheek. My throat dries. *Bam-bam-bam.* My pulse rate goes through the roof.

Waiting. Waiting. This is it. He's going to kiss me now. His lips are so close. His nose bumps mine. And his eyes... Those silver sparks are joined by golden flares, which I thought I must have imagined seeing earlier. But no. There they are. Gold and silver in the midst of a storm of feelings. My eyelids flutter down.

The next second, cool air hits my front. The weight of his hand is gone from my waist. Without his support, I sway forward.

This time, he doesn't catch me. I find my footing and look around to find him striding out of the room.

Huh? For a few seconds, I stand there, dazed. I already miss him. I want to follow him, to please him, to seek his approval, and to follow his orders. And goddam him, I don't want to resist it, either. *Is that wrong? And so what if it is?*

I've lived my life carefully, and look where that got me? Dumped and disgraced. I'm done with the safe, scared me who planned for the future and wouldn't do anything until she'd taken care of everyone else. *I'm going to think of myself. Put my needs first.*

And right now, I want someone else to make the decisions for me. Someone to take command and tell me what to do. I'm tired of being the responsible one. Tired of people always leaning on me.

What if I let myself lean on him? He's seen more of life. He knows what he wants and doesn't hesitate to go after it.

I want everything implicit in the promise of his smoldering glare. I'm turned on by the expert way with which he handles my body. I'm drawn to that confident manner of his which weakens my knees and appeals to that part of me which wants to submit... to him.

Without allowing myself to examine my thoughts further, I pick up my skirt and the short train, and trail after him. I walk through the hallway, past a conservatory, and into the kitchen. Late afternoon sunlight pours through the sliding doors which lead out onto a deck on one side. He's standing by the sink, filling a glass of water.

He turns, walks around the island in the center, and places it on the corner closest to me. "Drink," he orders.

I find myself reaching for the glass of water without conscious thought. *What the—!? Apparently, there's no not obeying the command in his voice. And I love it. And hate it. And I want more of it.*

And if I don't obey him? What would he do then? A thrill of anticipation unfurls in my core. *And would I like what he'd do to me?*

I already know the answer to that. It's why I tighten my fingers around the glass, lift it, and fling the water in his direction.

I must catch him by surprise, for he doesn't move. Water drips from his chin and wets the front of his jacket and shirt. *Oops.*

His lips thin. The tips of his ears grow white. The air between us zings with tension. He curls his fingers into fists at his side. I'm sure he's going to yell at me or, maybe, shake me by my shoulders. This is it; I've pushed him too far. I brace myself for the inevitable explosion.

He chuckles. The sound is unused, gravelly, and so rough. So sexy. My nerve-endings spark. That itch between my thighs deepens. I swallow and watch as he wipes the mirth off his face. "Next time, I won't be so forgiving."

"Because there won't be a next time." *Yes, there will be.*

He knows it. I know it. But I have to defy him. I have to push him to the edge. I have to cleave through that icy control of his so I can face the full brunt of his dominance. *Dominance.* I blink. *He's a dominant?* And there's a name for what he turns me into with that hard, deep, bossy voice of his. *Submissive.*

I quiver. My core clenches. I've read about this lifestyle. And also gotten off to it. Most women use vibrators to bring themselves to orgasm. For me, it's been stories where he dominates her and commands her to get on her knees and suck him off before he bends her over and uses her as his own personal fuck toy.

I swallow. I've never dared say the four-letter word aloud, but I've read it plenty in novels. And yes, I've seen videos on Pornhub. But I never thought I wanted it for myself. Correction, I never met anyone who brought out that craving within me to be dominated. *Is that why I'm so drawn to him?*

Because this man... There's a confidence at his core. An assurance which confirms to me that he'll know what I want and give it to me. There's a coldness to his demeanor which signals he'll use my body to satisfy his urges... And that... Oh, my god. That turns me on so much.

"Are you hungry?" he asks.

"What?"

"Food. When was the last time you ate?"

"Food?" I shift my weight from foot to foot. *Did I eat this morning? Nope. Last night? That would be another no.* "Uh, I had breakfast," I offer.

"This morning or yesterday morning?"

I flush, then stiffen my spine. "None of your concern." I spoil the haughty tone I was striving for when I hiccup. Ugh! I should have accepted that glass of water, instead of throwing it at him, and no doubt, he's going to point that out to me with a knowing smirk.

Only, he doesn't. Without comment, he fills another glass with water and, heading back, places it in front of me.

"Thank you." I hand the empty glass in my hand to him and bring the one with water to my lips.

He heads to the refrigerator and pulls out a casserole in a microwave-proof dish.

I can't keep my gaze off of his solid figure. Can't stop tracking each movement of his, which is so precise, it gives away his military background.

He heats it up in the microwave, puts the food on plates, then walks back to the island and places it there, before grabbing some cutlery.

"I should clean the water on the floor," I murmur as I prepare to take my seat.

"I'll do it." He nods to the plate. "Eat."

He mops up the water on the floor, washes his hands, then walks over to take the seat opposite me.

I watch him take a bite, watch his jaw move as he chews, the tendons of his throat flexing. That itch in my core spreads, until I have to squirm around in my seat to try and relieve it.

Once more, he senses that little movement and tilts his head. "Everything okay?"

"Why wouldn't it be? I got ditched at the altar, then the father of my now-ex proposed to me, and I'm sitting opposite him in his house having dinner like nothing is wrong with my life."

"Everything is about to turn out fine in your life," he says in a confident tone.

I narrow my gaze. "If you'd had to fight to put a roof over your head, and food on the table, and take care of your family like I have, you wouldn't take anything for granted. It's your privileged background that gives you the luxury of being so assured about your future." *Or maybe, it's also his experience?*

He puts down his fork, and his features, once again, settle into neutral lines. "You know about my background?"

I play with the food on my plate. "Felix told me his grandfather started the Davenport Group and that his family was well off. He also mentioned he was estranged from his father."

It's one of the few bits of information Felix revealed about his relationship with his father. And having met Quentin, I understand how difficult it must have been for Felix to measure up to him. Quentin's confidence in himself is enough to shake any other man's self-assurance, and Felix didn't have much to begin with.

Breaking away from the family fortune was Felix's way of finding himself. But Quentin is a possessive man. The brief encounter in the bar, and the way he made sure everyone there knew I was his, proves it.

I mean, think *that I was his. Which I'm not. Right? Right?!?*

"What else did he tell you?" Quentin's features have an almost-bored look, but his gaze is sharp. He's interested in finding out more about his son.

"He didn't talk about you, or his mother, for that matter."

Quentin's expression doesn't change, but the light in his eyes dims a little. I feel sorry for him. And I don't know why. "He was angry with you. He felt you did him wrong."

"And he's right." Quentin runs his fingers over the short stubble on his scalp. The gesture reminds me of Felix messing up the considerably longer hair on his head every time he was anxious or upset about something. Ugh, I'm not sure how I feel about that.

It's one thing to contemplate marrying your ex's father, but this resemblance between them makes the situation downright uncomfortable.

"I'm not going to sugarcoat the situation. Fact is, after Felix's mother left us, I was quick to hand over the responsibility of child-rearing to my aunt."

"What about his mother?" I blurt out. I've never been curious about her before this, but having met Quentin, I have a burning need to find out more about the woman who bore him a child. A woman he was interested in enough to have a relationship with.

"She left." His voice is flat. "The only times I saw her after that were when she'd show up to ask for more money."

"What did you do? Did you send her the money?"

He stares at me with something like disdain. "Do you think I wouldn't? I'm not heartless. I knew I was partly responsible for her leaving us. I wasn't there for her when she was a new mother, struggling to take care of Felix. I put her on an allowance until Felix turned twenty-one."

Surprise and something like warmth coils in my chest. I wouldn't have expected him to do that. Especially since, he comes across as all stern and grouchy, almost bordering on mean. "That was generous of you," I suggest.

"She was the mother of my son." He snorts. "No matter that she wasn't interested in meeting Felix or finding out how he was doing."

I stare at him in shock. "That's horrible."

"Not to mention, stressful. Over the years, she's had a knack for turning up whenever anything big happens in my life. The only thing that made her go away was more money." He runs his fingers through his hair. "At least we weren't married. Saved me the bother of divorcing her."

He must see the consternation on my face, for he smirks. "Have I shocked you?"

"Not particularly." I pop a shoulder. "Maybe a little. But who am I to judge? I'm pissed off enough with what Felix did to wish I'd never met him."

His features tighten. "I'm sorry he did that to you. But also, I'm not." His gaze grows intense. "We wouldn't be sitting here, otherwise."

That warmth in my chest turns to sparks which zip down to my pussy. Gah, one look from him, and I'm wet. Correction: I've been wet since I first saw him at the church. I squeeze my eyes shut.

"We... shouldn't be doing this. I shouldn't be here. You're Felix's father. This is so wrong."

When he doesn't reply, I open my eyes to find him staring at me with an inscrutable look. "I understand the situation is unorthodox," he says slowly.

"That's putting it lightly," I snort.

"But if there's one thing I've learned, it's that, no matter what you do, there'll be someone who disagrees with you. You need to follow your instincts. So what, if no one else understands your actions? They're not in your situation. They don't know what you're going through. Only you can decide what's best for you."

I search his features and find honesty. He's not trying to sell me a load of bullshit. He means what he says. Guess there's some benefit to having more life experience?

"How... how old are you?" The words are out before I can stop them.

"I'm forty-nine," he says without hesitation.

"You're twenty-six years older than me," I whisper.

"Does that bother you?" His stance is relaxed, his gaze alert.

I consider his question carefully, then shake my head. "Honestly, no? I've often felt older than my years. And I've met people older than you who act like they never grew out of their teen years." I laugh. "I'm aware age has nothing to do with maturity."

His eyes gleam. He's pleased by my response, and that sends a flush of heat curling in my belly. *Why is his approval so important?*

"What's keeping you from accepting my proposal?" he asks carefully.

I cross one leg over the other, then uncross them. "Umm... Felix." I don't need to say anything else, for his jaw tightens.

He wipes all expression off his face. "You're right to be concerned about him. I am, too... but—"

"But?" I ask through my suddenly dry lips.

"It doesn't change the fact that he didn't want to marry you."

That's true.

"You're a single woman, am I right?"

I nod.

"And you can choose who you want to marry?"

I nod again, slowly.

"And I won't give up until you agree to marry me"—he looks between my eyes—"which you will."

I can't stop the surprised laugh that wells up. "That's awfully confident of you."

He curls his lips. That's his response. That wicked smirk. And damn, but his arrogance turns my stomach inside out. Butterflies fan their wings through my blood. The tension between us stretches. The air grows thick and presses down on my shoulders. My nipples harden.

This man is lethal. Any minute now, I'm going to climb him like a tree and cling to him like I'm a koala bear. I glance away and rack my mind to say something to break the growing silence.

"You were saying—" I clear my throat. "You were saying, you brought him up on your own?"

His features tighten. Guess leading the conversation back to Felix wasn't the best diversion? But he's Quentin's son, and I do want to know more about their relationship.

His chest rises and falls, then he smooths out his forehead. "It was my aunt who brought him up." He shifts his weight on the bar stool. "I was busy setting off on yet another tour of duty, or so I told myself. I made sure I wasn't emotionally available for my son. I wasn't ready to be a father and deal with the emotions it triggered inside me. I never did bond with Felix."

His jaw hardens. "I made sure he never lacked for anything material, but emotionally, I was absent. Didn't help that I suspected his mother'd had an affair while I was away on tour, either."

A pulse throbs at his temple.

"It's one of the reasons I stayed away from her and, consequently, my son, for long periods of time. It never felt like I had a home to come back to. My team became my family, and being on tour became my reality. Fighting a known enemy seemed more manageable than fighting the unseen devils haunting my family life."

Oh, wow. That's quite a lot to take in. Definitely hadn't expected him to reveal so much. My heart goes out to him. After my mother died, I was thrust into the role of caregiver for my sister, and later, my father. It wasn't a responsibility I bore happily. While I didn't turn away from it, I withdrew into myself. I didn't socialize as much. Instead, I read a lot, discovering my love for poetry and later, painting.

We've both had to find ways to cope with emotional turmoil. He, with the loss of his family life. And me, with the loss of my youth and friendships when I had to step into my mother's shoes. Perhaps we're not that different?

A soft sensation squeezes my insides. I realize I feel sorry for him. Not what I expected to feel for this larger-than-life alpha male.

For a few seconds, we stare at each other again. Then, as if aware of what he's revealed, Quentin rolls his shoulders. "You seem surprised that I shared that with you, but if we're getting married —"

"That's a big *if*," I remind him.

"—it's best for me to be open so you can understand me better."

Is he that serious about marrying me? Does he intend to go through what I was sure was a moment of madness that made him propose to me without knowing who I was?

If he senses my confusion, he doesn't show that. Maybe, that's what he intended all along. To throw me off balance?

He nods at my plate. "Eat," he says in that voice that insists I obey.

On cue, my stomach grumbles. It's been more than twenty-four hours since I ate. And I do want to eat, but a part of me can't help but wonder what he'd do if I refused? What would happen if I challenged him, hmm?

When I don't respond to his command, his eyes smolder. "You realize, I won't let you get away with defying me, Ms. Wells?"

Ooh, his dark tone turns my pulse into a drumbeat of arousal. The triangle between my legs grows heavy. My heartbeat spikes, and I can barely stop myself from panting. "What... what would you do if I did?"

His gaze turns canny. He thinks for a little then nods. "I could spank you for your impertinence —"

"What?" I squeak. *Why do I find that so hot?*

"But I'll settle for feeding you." He scoops up some of the casserole from my plate and holds the fork out in my direction.

My stomach rumbles again. My mouth waters. The food smells sooo good. *Fine, fine.* I lean in and close my mouth around the tines of the fork.

The creamy textures, combined with the savory rich umami flavors of the casserole coat my tongue in a warm, homey blanket of comfort.

When I look at his face, he's watching me closely. The skin is stretched tightly across his cheekbones, making them seem more prominent. The look in his eyes is both tortured and hungry, but it fades away so quickly... Perhaps, I imagined it?

"Did you make this?"

"Would it surprise you if I said I did?"

"Would it surprise you if I said I don't believe that?" I widen my gaze.

He half laughs. "You're right, I didn't. My housekeeper made it. It's one of my favorite dishes. A chicken casserole packed with water-chest-nuts, celery, onions, and bell peppers, seasoned with curry powder, and held together with cheese sauce."

I send him an incredulous look. "So, you *do* cook?"

"I like being able to provide for myself." He scoops up some of the vegetables and holds the fork to my mouth. I take my time licking the tines. Once again, something sparks in his eyes; and again, he banks it.

When he resumes eating from his plate, I take it as a sign to polish off the rest of my food, then sit back with a sigh. "That was so good. It beats having pizza for two meals a day." I half laugh.

His expression grows stormy.

"You eat pizza every day?"

"Perks of working at a pizza parlor. Speaking of" — I point at my empty plate — "you can pass on my appreciation to your housekeeper."

"You can do so yourself."

I sigh. "I'm not moving in with you, and I'm not marrying you. This situation is bizarre. I shouldn't be here. This is all wrong."

"Not if I pay you a million dollars.

My fork clatters onto my plate. "Excuse me?" I choke out. "Did you say —"

"I'll pay you a million dollars to marry me."

Is this guy for real? I manage to pick my jaw up from the floor. "You're offering to pay me a million dollars?"

6

Quentin

"Is it not enough?" I scan her features.

There's surprise and disbelief on her face. *Is she the kind of woman who's impacted by the number of zeroes in a figure?*

"I'll pay you two million dollars." Before I can stop myself, the figure is out. I'm not surprised when her gaze widens. The color fades from her cheeks. She seems to have trouble digesting the number, which was my intention. But there's also a sinking sensation in my chest. Is money the answer to everything? Can anything and anyone be bought by money? *Prove me wrong, please. Show me you felt the connection when we met?*

And yet, why should she? I'm a stranger to her, as she's pointed out. So what, if it feels like I've known her forever? So what, if it feels like my life would be incomplete without her? She's the woman my son almost married.

I'm going to hell for coveting her. And that's nothing new. I've killed enemy soldiers. I've committed mistakes, which have cost my own men their lives. So what, if I'm adding another sin to the litany that features under my name?

"If that's not enough, how about —"

She holds up her hand. "Let me think… please."

I rise up to my feet, head back to the kitchen counter, and grab a jug of water. By the time I return and pour her a glass, she seems more composed. She takes a couple of sips of the water, places her glass back on the table with care, then folds her hands in her lap.

"Why?" She tips up her chin. "Why would you pay me to marry you?"

"Because I already asked you, and you haven't replied." I take my seat.

"So the solution is money?"

"Isn't it?" *Please say it's not. Please say you don't want the money. Please show me you're not another pretty face swayed by dollar signs. Please.*

She twists her lips to the side, a contemplative look about her eyes. "I'm not saying I don't need money."

A-n-∂, I rest my case. Money has an impact. It's the sad truth.

The idealist in me, the one who enlisted in the Marines and was proud to fight for my country; the one who believed in the power of doing the right thing, that man would have said money didn't mean shit. It was intent that mattered. It was your ability to do good, to believe in a better future, which was most important. I should have known better.

"The impact of a dollar upon the heart smiles warm red light…" I murmur.

Her forehead furrows. "Did you quote Stephen Crane?"

I blink. "Not many people would recognize that."

She hunches her shoulders. "I remember all kinds of trivia. It's how my mind works. It's how I developed a love for poetry."

I'm taken aback. "So you can match a line from any poem to the poet who wrote it?"

"Mostly," she says in a cautious tone.

"That's incredible."

She looks at me with suspicion. "Are you taking the piss?"

I chuckle. "I am not."

"And you're not going to fire off lines from some obscure poet to test me?" Her forehead furrows.

"Why should I? You've already demonstrated you're a fountain of knowledge."

"Largely useless knowledge." She shrugs.

I scan her features, taking in the flush on her cheeks and the strands of hair that have escaped her chignon to frame her beautiful features. "Clearly, you have a high IQ and are extremely bright. What are you doing working in a pizza parlor?" Then, I hear my words and manage not to wince. "Not that there's anything wrong with working in a pizza parlor. But why didn't you study further?"

"Wasn't interested in academics. I wanted to paint but"—she looks away, then back at me— "my mother died."

"I'm sorry." My fingers tingle with the need to touch her. To hold her and pull her into my chest and soothe her. To take care of her. A surge of protectiveness squeezes my chest. Why do I want to kiss her lips, then cup her face and hold her close—before I carry her up to my bedroom and fuck her until she can't walk straight? *Get a grip!* I shake my head, focus on what she's saying.

"Then my father fell ill, my sister gained admission to ballet school. And I—"

"Decided to put your ambitions on hold to take care of them."

"I did what needed to be done, and I don't regret it for one second," she says fiercely.

"I know you don't. But you want to follow your dreams."

"Who doesn't?"

"And you can, if you marry me."

"And be a kept woman?" She tosses her head. "No thank you.

I swipe my thumb under my lip. "You'd be *my* wife."

Her pupils dilate. Does she realize how responsive she is to the possessiveness in my tone?

"Not to mention, the contacts you'd have access to from being married to me..."

A furrow forms between her eyebrows. "What use do I have for your contacts?"

My phone vibrates with an incoming message. Just in time. I pull it out of my pocket and read the message. A burst of anticipation pinches my veins. This is what I was waiting for. Let's see what her answer is now. I place the device face-down on the table.

"Your father could benefit from a revolutionary new treatment which might slow the onset of his ALS and let him, not only live longer, but also walk again."

Her features pale, and she grips the edge of the table. "How did you find that out?"

"I had my investigator get a hold of your father's records from the hospital where he's being treated."

"How did you manage that?"

I stare at her meaningfully.

Her lips tighten. "Right, you threw money at the problem."

"Something like that."

"But to find out all of these details in such a short time?" She rubs at her temple.

"It took a couple of hours—longer than I expected. I also have him investigating you," I confess.

"What? Why?" Her voice rises an octave. "Why would you do that?"

"I had to find out who you are." I raise both of my hands. "I'm going to marry you; you can hardly blame me for that."

"I still haven't said yes."

You will. "I can get your father into a trial at Johns Hopkins that could improve the quality of the rest of his life."

She stiffens.

I touch the tips of my fingers together. "Then, there's the fact I know the president of the Royal Ballet School."

She firms her lips. "Do you realize how crazy everything you're talking about seems?"

"Not as crazy as the connection I felt with you. Tell me you don't feel it."

When she stays silent, I nod. "That's what I thought. I admit, my methods have been unorthodox, but that's because I couldn't let go of this opportunity. Not when what we have is so unique."

She grimaces. "This is when you use the fact that you're older than me to your advantage." But her tone is unsure.

Yes, she's thawing. I have to push my advantage. "You know what I'm saying is right."

She purses her lips. "What you're saying is going to hurt Felix."

"I'll find a way to make it up to him. I just have to figure out how," I murmur.

Her frown deepens. "You think he'll come around, after how you publicly humiliated him?"

"My asking you to marry me had nothing to do with him."

"I rest my case." She rolls her eyes.

"It's not ideal, but it is what it is. You can't deny that from the moment you saw me, you wanted me."

She opens her mouth, then shuts it. The guilt on her face confirms what I already knew. "You sense the connection between us. You felt the physical impact when our gazes first met. You knew... It was wrong to continue up that aisle—"

"But I did."

"And here we are." I flatten my hand palm-up on the table between us. She stares at it but makes no move to take it. Trust. She doesn't trust me yet, but she will. I am going to win her over. I am going to marry her. I am going to make her my wife. "You are the woman I've been looking for my entire life."

Her features soften. "How can you be so sure?"

"Place your hand in mine," I order.

She instantly slips her hand in mine. When our skin touches, a flurry of heat zips up my arm from her touch. As for her? Goosebumps dot her skin. Her lips part. She tries to pull away, but I close my much bigger fingers about hers.

"Look at me, Raven," I say softly, but with a slight edge of steel.

She raises her gaze to mine, and whatever she sees on my features has her blushing a deep red. She swallows, then lowers her eyes, as if she's unable to hold my gaze any longer. Her breathing is ragged. I know she's turned on. I know, if I asked her to get on her knees and open her mouth so I could use it for my pleasure, she'd do it.

Her downcast eyes indicate she's a natural sub, and the way she hurries to obey me confirms my theory. I can teach her. I can please her. I can control her orgasms. I can take her to the edge over and over again, so when she climaxes, it will be the kind of pleasure she'll never know again with anyone else. I know... Exactly what it will take to have her screaming my name. *Mine.*

I am not letting her go. I'll do everything in my power to bind her to me. Fuck the age gap. Fuck the forbidden nature of our relationship. I need her. I want her. I'll do anything to have her. *And Felix? Fuck!*

I have to convince him she was never his. The evidence is in the elevated pulse of her wrist, the blush which stretches to her décolletage, the hard nubs of her nipples outlined against the material of her wedding gown, the way she keeps her gaze steadfastly lowered and her shoulders erect. The fluttering of her eyelashes as she anticipates my next command.

I can take her to the edge. But first, she needs to know that I am going to take care of her.

7

Vivian

When I raise my gaze to his, his blue eyes smolder. His jaw is set. There's frustration on his features but also, resolution.

He releases my hand, and I miss his warmth at once. A shiver zips up my spine. I wrap my arms about myself and rub my lace-covered arms.

His gaze narrows. "Are you cold?"

I begin to shake my head, then stop when he stalks out of the kitchen. He returns a few seconds later with a throw that he wraps about my shoulders.

"Thanks," I murmur.

Without a word, he gathers up our used plates and cutlery.

"I can help." I begin to stand, but he touches my shoulder and says, "You rest up; it's been a long day."

I sink back into the chair and watch as he stows the utensils in the dishwasher. His movements are easy, like he's spent enough time here to know his way around. Which shouldn't be a surprise. After all, this *is* his home.

He flips on the kettle, and when the water boils, brews the tea and brings it over to me.

The scent of peppermint rises from the cup. I wrap my fingers around the warmth and allow it to percolate through my blood.

"Where did you get that?" I point to a scar above his eyebrow.

"On a mission." He firms his lips.

I wait for him to share more, but he doesn't. He's a master at keeping secrets, this man. But that makes me more curious. I want to find out more about him. If I'm going to consider his proposal—which I am not... *yet*—I need to understand this motives, right?

"What do you get from this marriage?" I tip up my chin. "Why are you offering me so much money?"

His forehead clears. Apparently, this is an easier conversation for him than sharing about his past.

"When I retired from the Marines, my father wanted me to join the family business and take over as the CEO of one of the Davenport Group companies." He takes his seat opposite me.

"Sounds like a good deal. You turn up, and just like that"—I snap my fingers— "you have a job waiting for you."

"Ah, Arthur wants his pound of flesh. I'll get my due, provided I give him what he wants."

"Which is?"

The muscle at his jawline flexes. "He wants me to find a wife and settle down."

I blink slowly. "Wow. Rich people live in a different world. He demands you get married, and you offer me money if I agree to your proposal."

"It's not like that."

I stare at him, and he has the grace to flush.

"Not only." He rubs the back of his neck. "I admit, his putting down that condition meant I had marriage on my mind. And then I saw you, and something clicked."

Warmth floods my veins.

"Once my role as the CEO within the division is confirmed, I stand to inherit a lot of money." He leans forward in his seat. "It's fair you get a percentage of it. One million when we tie the knot within the month. Another when we complete a year."

The warmth fades away, and once again, a chill invades my skin. I pull the throw around my shoulders.

"And then, what? We walk away from each other?"

A strange look comes into his eyes before he manages to hide it.

Wearing that cool, distant mask I'm coming to recognize as his default expression, he raises a shoulder. "If that's what you want."

Huh? "Isn't that what you want?"

"I want... whatever makes you happy."

"How is paying me money in return for my marrying you going to make me happy?"

"It's going to pay for your sister's education and for your father's treatment. I assume that's one reason you would be."

"There are more reasons?" I can't stop myself from asking.

A sly look comes into his eyes. "One specific reason."

"Oh?" I frown.

"Exactly."

"I'm sorry, I don't understand."

He holds up his hand as if he's taking a pledge. "I solemnly promise to give you so many O's, you won't want to leave when the year is up."

I flush, all the way to the roots of my hair. No one has ever talked to me this way. Worse, how can I be so turned on by his filthy talk? I squeeze my thighs together, then tip up my chin. "You're uncouth."

"I also promise, I'll be honest with you." He leans a hip against the table.

"You're my ex's father."

"Q."

"Excuse me?"

"You need to practice calling me by my name."

I huff, "Your name's Quentin."

His eyes flash. "Say my name again."

"I won't."

"What if I say please?"

"Being polite won't change anything."

He strokes his chin and looks at me with a contemplative expression. "Because you don't want a polite man."

I make a rude noise. "Awfully presumptuous of you to arrive at that conclusion when you don't even know me."

He smiles slowly, an edge of cruelty in the curve of his lips that has the effect of making me lose my breath. "What I do know is"—he leans forward—"you need a man who'll command you. A man who'll make you submit to him."

An electric frisson of sensation pinches at my nerve-endings. When his gaze drops to my mouth, I realize I've parted my lips, and my nipples are tight, and the triangle of flesh between my legs is dripping. I lean in, unable to take my gaze off of his, caught in the promise inherent in his words.

"A man who'll take care of your needs, so you can entrust him to do what's right for you —"

My toes curl. My breath hitches. A thousand little hummingbirds seem to flutter under my skin, but he doesn't stop talking.

His gaze narrows, and his eyes gleam. "—A man who orders you to do his bidding, so you can give yourself up to him, confident that you will be pleasured."

Oh, my god. That sounds like the end of all my feminist ideals. But also, hot. So hot. I bite the inside of my cheek.

"A man who ensures you never want for anything. A man who treats you like the goddess you are. A man who pleasures your body, fulfills your soul, and feeds your mind. And your dirtiest, filthiest urges." He drags his gaze down my flushed features. "A man who sees through your defenses, senses your deepest, darkest desires, and brings them to life without you having to ever give voice to them. A man who brings you to orgasm over and over again."

A million tiny sparks zing my blood stream. A bead of sweat runs down the valley between my breasts. Heat licks up my spine, and I feel like I've dived into a vat of lava.

"So, you see"—he drags his thumb under his lower lip—"I think we'll do very well together."

His gaze, his voice, his presence... It's too overwhelming. My skin feels too tight for my body, and my chest feels like it's pushing down on my ribcage. I arrange my thoughts into some semblance of logic and clear my throat. "From the outside, it's going to raise a lot of questions that I broke up with my ex, only to marry his father."

"First of all, you didn't break up with him. He jilted you at the altar."

My face must reflect some of my hurt because he winces.

"I'm sorry; I didn't mean for it to come out like that. What I'm trying to say is that he was a fool." He spears me with a look that almost makes me melt. "But it doesn't matter, Vivian, because I don't care about anyone else's opinions."

"Easy for you to say," I grumble. "You're a man. Taking up with someone younger than you will enhance your reputation."

He smirks. "And being associated with the CEO of a Davenport Group division will enhance yours."

I chew on my lower lip. He's right. It's not only the money. His connections will open a lot of doors for me. I would definitely find a platform for my paintings. He probably knows all of the rich folks in town. The kind who'll be interested in buying my paintings. Not to mention galleries who'll be receptive to exhibiting my paintings.

And if I take him up on his offer, I'll no longer be an artist who paints to interpret the human condition, but someone who entered a marriage of convenience to find a platform for her art. I'll be another in a long line of materialistic women before me who married for money.

So what? I need the cash, for Lizzie's tuition and to extend my father's life. I curl my fingers into fists.

If only he weren't so ridiculously sexy, and macho, and dominant, and every freaking thing which appeals to me. With his brooding good looks and the hint of 'tortured poet' in his eyes, he's everything I've ever hoped to meet. He's everything I was sure I could never have. The chemistry between us feels like too much. Too real. And that makes resisting him so very difficult. "What if your family guesses our arrangement is... uh... not real.

"They won't, because of the attraction between us. You feel the connection between us, don't you?"

I want to say yes, but that would be admitting this marriage of convenience makes sense, and I don't want to do that aloud... Yet. When I stay silent, he bends his knees and looks into my eyes. "I'm not going to hide what happened from my family. I'm going to be open with them that I saw you and wanted you, and when my son decided to leave you at the altar, I came to your rescue. It enhances—"

"Your status as a knight in shining armor and me as the helpless woman who had no choice but to marry you?" I ask drily.

He shakes his head. "Let's get one thing straight. You own the power in this."

"You're not making sense." I hunch my shoulders. "After all, wouldn't I be dependent on you?"

"And I, on you. Remember, I need you to fulfill my father's condition. We need each other." His gaze turns smoldering. "Besides, it had to be you."

My heart leaps into my throat. A pulse flares to life between my legs. "Wh... what do you mean?"

His lips curve. "As soon as I saw you, I knew it had to be you. The connection between us ensures anyone who sees us together will believe our story. So, you see... It couldn't have been anyone else. That's why I need you."

He looks deeply into my eyes and, oh my god, the heat of his gaze turns my blood to lava. The pulse between my legs intensifies. He hasn't even touched me, and I am so turned on.

He must see the reaction on my features, for he nods. "Of course, it's up to you how you spin this for yourself. Either you can play the victim of your circumstances, or —"

"Or?"

"Or you can claim this as an opportunity." He peruses my features, his tone confident. "With my money and influence, you can pursue your aspirations. Surely, that's invaluable?"

He's right. And that makes it worse. I wish he didn't make sense. I wish he weren't so persuasive. I wish I weren't so drawn to him, enough to override every sane thought in my head. The seconds stretch. The air between us sizzles and grows heavy. Every cell in my body is aware of his bulk, his solid presence, his broad shoulders, that force of his dominance, which seems to wrap around me and pin me down... in a good way.

When he straightens, I draw in a breath, and the rush of oxygen makes me realize I forgot to breathe.

He surveys my features. "Do you need more time to make up your mind?"

Fact is, I'm wavering. He makes a good argument, but... this is my life. And this decision will impact me in so many ways and for the foreseeable future. *Surely, I need to think it over some more?* "Yes," I square my shoulders. "Yes, I do."

He wipes his thumb under his lower lip. "I'll give you a week to think it over."

"A week?" I gape at him. "That's too short; I need more time."

"Ten days, then?"

Is he kidding? How can he expect me to make such a life-altering decision in that short timeframe?

A gleam of mischief enters his eyes. The playfulness is so surprising, it makes me stare. *So, he wants me to negotiate, huh?*

"Three months," I jut out my chin.

"Two weeks," he retorts.

"Two months," I scowl.

"A month, and that's my final offer," he snaps in that bossy tone. A shiver squeezes my spine. I want to say yes right away, but I make myself pause and pretend to consider his offer.

"A month," I finally agree.

"Good." He nods in a decisive gesture. "But know this. I get what I want."

8

Quentin

"What are you doing here?" Knox spins a chair around and straddles it. Whether on purpose or by chance, he makes sure to keep his face in shadow.

"Last I checked, this was a weekly poker game where all Davenports are invited." It's not my first choice of where I want to be. But when not even work can distract me from thoughts of her, I decided to accept Arthur's invitation to join the poker game.

"Thought you'd be at your woman's place."

"Woman?" Sinclair Sterling, a business associate turned friend whose home I've been to for dinner many times, looks between us. "You have a woman?"

"Or should I say, girl?" Knox twists his lips. Which causes the scars on his features to bunch. Combined with his larger-than-average height and a physique honed by his military stint, as well as his regular workouts, I wouldn't like to meet him in a fight. He's one scary-looking motherfucker. No wonder he likes to keep his features hidden as much as possible.

"Girl?" Sinclair frowns. "What am I not getting here?"

"What Knox is trying to point out is that she's younger than me."

"More than two decades younger." He smirks. "And she's his son's ex," he adds.

I expect Sinclair to do a double-take, but instead, he appears thoughtful. "She's your *son's* ex?"

"He stood her up at the altar."

Sinclair whistles. "I assume that means your son is no longer interested in her?"

"About that—" I shuffle my feet. "He apologized to her, and it didn't look like she wanted anything to do with him, but it means—"

"It means, it's a bloody shit-show," Knox drawls.

"Why her?" Sinclair looks at me with curiosity.

"Why not her?" I growl.

When he stays silent, I sigh, then loosen the tie around my neck. My mind's not in the right place... And is not going to be until I convince her we belong together. It's less than twenty-four hours since I met her and there hasn't been a minute when I haven't thought about her. I rub the back of my neck. I need her in my life.

"Quentin?"

I glance at Sinclair. "Have you ever looked at someone and realized exactly what was missing in your life? Have you seen her and known you'd do anything to be with her? To have her in your life... by any means necessary?"

Sinclair seems taken aback, then his features soften. "Like that, eh?"

Knox chortles. "No idea what you two are talking about but take it from someone who's never felt that way and who never plans to feel that way, it seems like a load of crap."

Sinclair smirks "Don't say that too loudly. Fate has a way of creeping up on you and pushing you to do things you swore you'd never do. "

"Not gonna happen." Knox grabs a cigar from the humidor and offers it to me. When I refuse, he shrugs, passes one to Sinclair. Then he takes one for himself, snips off the head and lights up.

Sinclair and I exchange looks. "The more confident they are, the harder they fall," he murmurs.

"What-fucking-ever. Meanwhile, I'm happy to follow along with the drama, also known as your life." He nods in my direction.

"The drama is a distraction. Nothing can change the fact that she's mine."

Sinclair puffs on his cigar. "Does she know it? More to the point, does she accept it?"

"She will."

"And your son?"

I shake my head. "When Felix's mother left, I knew it was my fault. I couldn't stop her, but I told myself I'd make it up to my son. Each time I left on a tour of duty when he was a child, that was my intention, but I never made it back for more than a few days at a time." I look down at my hands. "I assuaged my conscience by making sure my aunt was there as his caregiver, so he never lacked for the necessities. He got the best education money could buy. When I couldn't make it to his graduation ceremony because I was leading another mission, I sent enough money to cover the celebrations for him and his friends. I told myself I'd compensate the time I didn't spend with him, but... I never did."

"And now?" Sinclair holds the cigar in between his fingers. The ash builds before I speak.

"Now? I've hurt him in a way I'm not sure our relationship will recover from. It hurts, and I know it's wrong, and yet"—I lower my chin — "I'm compelled to push through with my decision to marry her. I've made a lot of mistakes in life, but when I met her... It feels like I've been given a second chance. And this time, I'm not making promises I can't keep. Not to him; not to her, not to myself. This time, I'm going to reorient my life so that I can keep my word to the people who matter most to me."

Sinclair looks like he's about to speak, when Ryot, my other nephew, stalks in. He spots me and hatred spreads across his features. He spins around and is about to leave, but I jump up. "Stop!"

I head after him, shoot out an arm to grab his shoulder, but he turns, knocks it aside, and throws up a fist. I feel the breeze whistle past me, not because I ducked, but because he stops mere millimeters from connecting with my face. He clenches his jaw, muscles pinging at his cheekbones. His eyes dart anger at me. And it's justified. What happened isn't exactly my fault, but he holds me responsible.

"I understand now," I offer.

He frowns.

"I understand how it is to lose the woman you think is your soulmate."

His gaze widens. The anger fades, and in its place is regret and sadness, and a tortured wistfulness that tells me how much he misses her. How much he yearns for her. How much his life is not worth living anymore, now that she's no longer in it.

Twenty-four hours ago, I wouldn't have understood the full extent of his agony. But having met my 'one', having felt that instinctive connection with her I know won't come with anyone else, I have a better understanding of why Ryot is so livid. If I were in his shoes... I'd be... Heartbroken and want revenge. I'd want to find a way to take out my anger on the person I thought was responsible for her death. I'd be maddened with grief and pain. I'd need an outlet. One I could provide. I allow my lips to twist.

"A fight," I offer.

The fold between his eyebrows deepens.

"You and me, in the ring?" I incline my head.

Ryot glares at me, then turns to Knox. Something unsaid passes between the brothers.

Knox stiffens. He seems like he's about to say something, then nods in his brother's direction. "Can you give us a second?" Without waiting for his reply, he pulls me out of earshot. "Have you lost your fucking mind? Not only are you not going to be able to defeat him, but he's going to pulverize you."

"I'm aware"

"Are you?" Knox regards me with skepticism. "He's fast *and* he's built like a tank. He's got at least twenty pounds on you, most of it muscle. You realize, he won the Royal Marine's flagship boxing tournament three years running? If he hadn't joined the Marines, he might well have competed professionally. You, on the other hand —"

"—fought in the finals and won the title one year, but never made it past the semis again," I state.

Knox looks at me closely. "You realize, you can't win? In fact, you're setting yourself up to be injured."

"Good," I say under my breath.

"The fuck?" He scowls. "What are you up to, old man?"

"The fuck does it matter to you?"

"It doesn't. In fact, it's better for me if you're out of commission. It sends a message to Arthur that I'm more reliable than you when it comes to taking on a position of responsibility in the company. But it seems, not even *I* can stand by and allow another man to plan his own funeral. Apparently, I have a sliver of conscience left that insists I point out the inevitable injuries that will follow this offer."

When I stay silent, his gaze narrows. "Unless..." He snaps his fingers. "That's your plan... To have him beat you up? You want to give him a chance to get some of his antagonism out of his system?"

I bark out a laugh. "You think?"

He nods slowly. "You'll never be able to make up for your actions that got his wife killed. Apologizing for it can never be enough. But you can offer him the chance to beat you, fair and square. A symbolic defeat in a fight which might go some way toward helping him find some resolution…"

"It's the least I can do." I raise a shoulder. "I always thought of what happened to her as collateral damage. I made the choice to prioritize the lives of thousands over that of a few. It's the way of war. But it doesn't lessen the personal impact of my actions. She died because of the decision I made. I have to live with that on my conscience. And he must live with a broken heart." I look past Knox's shoulder to where Ryot stands. His shoulders are tense, his fingers curled into fists at his side. His gaze is locked on the two of us.

"Does this have something to with the woman you proposed to?"

I jerk my attention back to Knox's face. "What do you mean?"

"You're competing for the love of someone decades younger than you. Perhaps you want to prove a point to her, and to yourself, that you still have the mojo?"

"Don't be stupid. I don't need to prove a point…" my voice trails off. *Or maybe I do?*

Knox nods knowingly.

I rub the back of my neck. "Perhaps you're right. But that's not the only reason to take on this fight."

"Pray, explain that to me, Einstein." Knox smirks.

"It was my actions which indirectly caused Ryot's wife to be killed in action. It's why he's angry with me. I've tried to speak with him about this, but he refuses to engage in conversation. If this is the only way to communicate with him then I'll take it." *If this is the only way to get some kind of redemption, then I'll take that, too. I deserve to be beaten up by Ryot for the grief my actions caused him.* "It'll force a conversation, at the very least."

"There are better ways to build bridges with Ryot."

"But none that will give him a chance to get some of the frustration out of his system."

Knox begins to speak, but I brush past him and toward Ryot.

"You're going to lose," Ryot's voice is gravelly from un-use. Since his wife's death, he's retreated into himself. He's taken to speaking only when absolutely necessary. I'm responsible for that. My heart seizes up. My stomach pitches like I've been caught in an automobile pile up.

"Ryot." I curl my fingers into fists at my sides. "I'm so fucking sorry for what you went through."

"Yet, you maintain that you wouldn't take back your order for anything?" he snaps.

"I had to make a split-second decision between saving a few lives and saving those of thousands. You'd have done the same if you were in my position."

"Don't compare yourself to me. We are nothing alike." His gaze turns venomous.

"Fucking hell!" I grab the back of my neck and squeeze. "It's why we need this fight. You need to take out your grievance against me—"

"I'll kill you." There's a note of finality in his tone, which sends a chill down my spine.

"Probably,"—I set my jaw—"but I'm willing to take that chance if it helps clear the air between us."

He scoffs.

"You're right, probably unlikely, but I have to try." I take a step forward, he growls. But for the first time since his wife died, a gleam comes into his eyes. Some of that despair in his gaze fades.

He looks me up and down. "You're old."

"That your excuse?" I taunt him, not because I want to sharpen his pain, but because I need him to fight me.

He bares his teeth. "It's your funeral, asshole. Pick a date and time."

"How about tomorrow night?"

9

Vivian

"You need help packing?" Lizzie asks from the phone screen.

"No, thanks. Though, I'm beginning to forget you exist outside of a device!" I waggle a finger at her. "If I accept Q's proposal, I'll have a space for you to come visit me."

'You're considering it?" she cries.

"I am," I confess.

Her forehead wrinkles. "Have you seen Felix since the uh... wedding?"

That was three days ago. "I haven't seen him at work. He hasn't been home, either." *Not that I'm complaining.* I pop a shoulder. "He paid the rent for the rest of the month on this place. Now that our wedding is off, there's no way can I live here." I came home today and realized I had to start packing.

Ideally, I'll be out of here before he returns. But I've been so exhausted, I haven't been able to muster the energy to get my stuff together.

"Where are you going to move to?" Lizzie's question makes me sigh.

"I'm not sure."

There's silence on her end. When I glance at her on the screen, it's to find a worried look on her face.

"Honey, don't worry. I'll figure it out." I paste a smile on my face, but I don't think I'm fooling her because her frown deepens.

"Vivi, where will you go?" she probes again.

"I... uh... could look up some of my friends from high school?" I wince.

I wasn't ever that popular. Lizzie's the one who had a lot of friends. I preferred the company of colors and my canvas, or poems, to real people. Not much has changed now that I'm grown up. Unless you count watching Pornhub or reading spicy romances as a hobby.

"Hmm"—she frowns—"you sure?"

No, I'm not. "By the way, there are trials being run at Johns Hopkins near Washington, D.C. for ALS. If Dad got onto one of them, it would be experimental, but at least it would extend his life expectancy and improve his quality of life." I say it, hoping to distract her, and I'm rewarded when her features brighten.

"That sounds amazing, but wouldn't it be expensive?" Her shoulders sag.

"It would." I nod. "Except Quentin already got him accepted for it and has agreed to foot the bill."

"He has?" Understanding dawns on her face. "Oh Vivi, I see your reasoning behind considering his proposal now, but—" She purses her lips, "— is this what's best for you?" Her forehead furrows. "You agreed to marry Felix because you thought it'd help you save money and look what happened."

I wince. "It won't happen again. Quentin won't stand me up at the altar." *Given a choice, he'd consummate the marriage before the wedding night. I'd agree to that, too...* No way I'm telling her that.

"But you don't know this guy. You only just met him," she protests.

"I know enough. I know he's trustworthy and that, as his wife, I'll have access to money, which we need badly."

"I can't let you sacrifice yourself again, Vivi. I can't!" Her chin trembles. "You're young. You should be going to university and studying for your degree in fine arts," she bursts out.

"Degrees are overrated. Besides, I got to paint the interior of the pizza shop, and the operations director of the company loved it and promised me I can paint the interiors of the other shops, too," I offer.

"Not that he paid you anything extra for it." Her scowl deepens.

"I... Uh... Plan to talk to him about it." I hunch my shoulders. "You don't have to worry about it or anything else." I shove the rest of my clothes into my suitcase and straighten. "I'll figure it out Lizzie, I promise."

I head over to the kitchen and pour myself the last of the boxed wine. I take a sip from the glass, then wince.

"That bad?" she asks sympathetically.

"It's not vinegar... yet."

She snickers. The intercom buzzes, and she frowns. "Were you expecting someone?"

I shake my head and press the button on the device. "Hello?"

"Vivian?" a woman's voice asks. "Vivian Wells?"

"Yes?" I say cautiously.

"I'm Summer Sterling, a friend of Quentin Davenport."

"Okay?"

"I know this is a surprise, but do you mind if we come up?"

"We?"

"Hello," another woman chimes in, "I'm Zoey Malfoy. Also, Quentin's friend. We would love to speak with you, if you have a little time?"

"Is Felix's father's name Quentin?" Lizzie whispers loudly.

I throw her a look, then speak into the intercom, "Did Quentin send you?"

"Yes, but only because he felt you'd be on your own and might need a bit of company," Summer answers.

"I promise, we are legit. We'll show you our ID and everything. We're here because he's worried about you, but he knows you don't want to see him... Yet," Zoey adds.

"Also, we have wine."

"Wine?" I say slowly.

"A very good 2009 Merlot." Summer's voice is persuasive.

"A 2009? That would taste better than the vinegar you were having earlier," Lizzie exclaims.

I scowl at her. "What do you know about wine?"

She coughs. "Anything would be better than your boxed wine."

"Hmm."

Before I can reply, Zoey chimes in, "Also, cupcakes and tacos."

Tacos! I exchange glances with Lizzie again.

"Keep me on the line, so I can make sure they are who they say they are," she insists.

"No, absolutely not, you need to get back to practice."

She sighs, "You're right, but—"

"I'll message you after."

"Message me in ten minutes, and let me know you're fine, else I'm coming over to join the party."

I roll my eyes. "Okay, grandma." I disconnect the call, slip the phone into the pocket of my jeans, and buzz them in.

A few minutes later, there's a knock on the door. I throw it open to see a pretty, pink-haired woman with a big smile on her face. She's holding onto a pram with a sleeping baby in it. Behind her is a taller woman with blonde hair pulled up into a tidy knot. She's wearing glasses and a skirt suit and has a satchel in her hand. It looks like she came here directly from work.

The pink-haired woman beams at me. "I hope you don't mind us coming by. I'm Summer, by the way."

I hold out my hand. "I'm—"

"Vivian. Quentin's told me all about you." She eschews my hand, steps around the pram and throws her arms about me. Her excitement at meeting me is infectious, and I find my lips curving. She steps back and her smile grows broader.

The other woman waves at me. "I hope you don't mind our gate-crashing like this?"

"Quentin called me this morning and gave me a quick overview of the situation," Summer offers.

"Situation?" I'm unable to keep the suspicion out of my voice.

"He explained you were special to him and that it would help if we dropped by to keep you company," she adds.

"Did he now?" I can't keep the skepticism out of my voice.

Does Q know I don't have that many friends? Is this his way of ensuring I didn't start overanalyzing things in my head like I want to? But that's not possible; he barely knows me.

And yet... When my gaze locked with his that first time, it felt as if he were seeing straight through to my insecurities and my deepest desires.

Like he knew me better than I know myself. And I felt like I already knew him, though I'm positive it's the first time I saw him.

"If you're not comfortable, we'll leave." Zoey scans my features.

"It's not that. I'm just..." I raise a shoulder. "I'm surprised he'd reach out to you. Or that he'd have the time to do so, given we met three days ago."

Zoey opens then shuts her mouth. "I didn't realize —" She coughs, then shoots a sideways glance at Summer, who's looking at me with shrewd eyes.

"Q mentioned the circumstances of your meeting were unorthodox." She rolls the buggy back and forth without conscious thought, in the way mothers often do when they soothe their child. "But he didn't tell us the details, so you know."

I'm not sure what to say. It's not like I know these women. Though, I suppose I appreciate Q looking out for me.

"Q is friends with my husband Sinclair Sterling. It's how I met him. He struck me as someone who's a loner, by choice —"

"So of course, Summer goes out of her way to make sure he's invited home for dinner every chance he gets." Zoey rolls her eyes.

"Often, it was me and Sinclair, and my sister Karma and her husband Michael, and then there was Q. My husband met Q after he retired from the Marines and joined the Davenports. They became friends very quickly, and that's unusual for my husband. Sinclair doesn't trust people easily, nor does Michael. But they both trust Q, enough to ask him to join us for dinner. I'd like to think it was my husband and Michael who convinced Q there's life after the Marines," Summer adds.

"Karma... You don't mean Karma West Sovrano, the designer?" The name Karma is unusual, so I venture a guess.

Summer nods, and her features shine with pride.

"Oh, my god, I love her style! I found one of her originals in a charity shop, which was the only way I could afford it at my wedding —" I stop. "I mean, my almost-wedding."

The baby yawns and stretches. He opens his eyes and looks at me in the way little kids have, when they're fascinated by what they're seeing. He blinks, then holds up his arms. And that's it, I'm a goner.

"Aww, you're a cutie." I glance at Summer. "May I?"

She nods and smiles, then bends and picks him up. She kisses him, then hands him over. I cuddle the baby, who continues to stare up at me. He smiles suddenly, and my heart melts further. "What's his name?"

"It's Matthew, but I call him Matty." She beams.

I carry the kid inside and the women follow with the pram. "Hey, baby, you're such a cutie pie." He blows a bubble, then raises his hand and tugs on my hair.

"Oh, Matty, don't do that." Summer walks over and tries to disentangle my hair from his little fist, but I laugh.

"It's fine, really." I sit down in one of the armchairs and continue to gaze into Matty's startling blue eyes. They are clear in the way babies' eyes can be. He pulls on my hair again, and when I lower my head, he bats at my cheek with his other hand. He gurgles, and a wave of love overpowers me.

I rub my cheek against his hair and breathe in his fresh baby smell. Baby powder and milk and that indefinable something that's innocent and intangible and yet, so evocative.

"He likes you," Summer says in a soft voice.

I glance up to find the two of them are standing. "Oh please, sit down. Sorry I didn't ask you to make yourselves comfortable. Little Matty distracted me."

"You're good with kids." Summer takes a seat on the settee.

"I took care of my sister, after my mother passed," I murmur.

"I'm sorry; that must have been difficult for you." Her tone is sympathetic.

I shake my head and slide my finger into Matty's little fist. "It was a long time ago."

"Where is your sister?" Zoey wanders around the apartment. Most of the furniture was left by the previous occupant, and the rest of the stuff belongs to Felix. Except for the paintings on the wall and the overloaded bookcase I rescued when my neighbor threw it out.

"She's at the Royal Ballet School."

"She must be very talented," Summer says with a smile.

"She is." I tickle little Matty's stomach, and he laughs. I can't stop myself from laughing with him.

"This is striking." Zoey comes to a halt in front of the painting on the wall next to the bookcase.

"Thanks," I murmur.

She shoots me a glance over her shoulder. "Did you paint it?"

I nod. "I created it in one night."

Zoey gasps. "That's incredible."

"Not really. I like to mull over the ideas in my head, until one day, I know it's time to put it on canvas. Then, I can't stop until it's done." I bounce Matty on my knee, and he giggles. "I don't get much time to do that though, because of my job at the pizza parlor."

"It must be difficult to work a day job and also paint," Summer says.

"It is." I hand Matty to her. "At least I'm not a waitress anymore, so that's something." I shrug.

"Managing a team isn't easy," Zoey adds without turning around. She seems to be entranced by my painting. A flush of pride squeezes my chest. I'd forgotten how good it felt to have someone respond to my art.

"It isn't. Most days, by the time I finish, I'm emotionally drained. I end up coming home and falling into bed, then getting up the next day and doing it all over again. It's the nature of the job." I choke out a laugh. "Sorry, I don't mean to overshare."

"Oh, you're good." Summer smiles up at me.

Lizzie is my closest confidant, but with her, I'm in the role of her bigger sister, the one who takes care of her and pays her bills. I can't allow myself to show weakness with her. I need her to know she can depend on me and trust that I have everything under control. Then, Felix entered the picture, and he was my best friend. He's the only one who knows about the money issues I have. And now, I'm not sure where I stand with him.

I've never had a strong circle of girlfriends. Looking from Summer's sympathetic face to Zoey's engrossed one, I realize what I've missed.

Zoey turns enough that she can meet my gaze. "I'm a book editor; I get to meet a lot of authors. And many of them work a day job while writing at night, and I've seen, up close, how difficult it can be to juggle both."

"It is." I nod. "And I'll be the first to admit, I haven't been painting lately." Of late, I haven't been able to look at my paints and my canvases without feeling sick to my stomach. The more time that passes between painting sessions, the harder it's getting to find my muse. It's like some muscle inside of me is weakening with disuse. "I've often wondered if there isn't an easier way to earn enough to pay my bills"—and take care of my family— "while keeping in touch with my art."

I stand up and join Zoey to take in the abstract she's turned back to. "That's the last one I did."

"Do you have more?" she asks in a considering voice.

I nod. "A few."

"Enough for an exhibition?" She shoots me a sideways glance.

"Oh, no, no—" I laugh. "I'm nowhere near ready to exhibit."

"Would you mind if I took a picture of this and showed it to a friend of mine who runs a gallery in Soho? He's always on the lookout for emerging artists."

I quash my budding excitement and pretend a nonchalance I don't feel. "When I was younger, I'd send pictures of my creations to agents. I was so hopeful." I sigh. "Eventually, when I didn't hear back from them, I gave up."

Of course, that was before Dad's ALS worsened and any spare time was gobbled up with caring for him.

The baby becomes restless, and Summer rubs circles around his back. He calms, then begins to warble again. Then, he waves a hand in my direction.

Summer laughs. "He's trying to tell you how much he loves being with you."

"I love him, too." I walk back to her and kiss Matty's forehead.

Zoey takes a few pictures of my paintings, then walks over to stand next to us. "Are you coming to watch Quentin's match tomorrow?"

"Match?" I rub my fingers over Matty's downy-soft hair, then laugh when he wrinkles his nose at me.

"He's fighting Ryot, who happens to be an accomplished boxer, himself."

"And is Quentin a boxer, too?"

"He used to be but hasn't competed in a professional capacity in a while." Summer lays the baby down on the settee and pats his tummy. "Which is why my husband tried to talk Quentin out of it, but Q feels he owes it to Ryot."

"Why's that?" I glance up, my curiosity piqued enough that I tear my gaze off of the little mite to look at her.

"Oh, that's not my story to tell." Summer meets my gaze.

"I respect that." I look between them. I could do with some guidance right now. Maybe they can give me some insight into Quentin that'd help me decide on how to respond to his proposal? "Somehow, the fact that you won't share the details of his story gives me the confidence to share how he and I met."

Zoey sits down on the other side of the baby. "Why? Did you have an interesting meet-cute?"

"You could say that." I chuckle.

"Ooh, tell us, please," she begs.

I sit down in my armchair and cross my legs. I've just met these women, but something about them inspires confidence in me. They don't seem like the type who'd take advantage of my sharing with them. Also, my head's whirling from everything that's happened so far. Perhaps talking about it will put things in perspective. "I was supposed to marry his son, but he stood me up at the alter. Enter, his father, who offers to marry me." Hearing the words from my mouth makes it all feel real and also, so very unreal. *Can this be happening to me? Am I going to go through with this?*

"What?" Zoey looks at me wide-eyed. "You were going to marry his son?"

I nod.

"Now you're going to marry his father?"

"Oh, no, no, I haven't agreed to anything. Besides, this only happened three days ago."

"Three days?" Zoey bursts out. "You two have known each other for three days?"

I manage a small smile.

Summer's features take on a contemplative look. "When Quentin called me, it didn't feel like he'd just met you. In fact, he seemed very concerned about you."

"Not surprising, considering he and his son lowered a double-whammy on me in one day." I toss my head.

"Woman, all this happened and you're still standing?" Zoey rises to her feet. "Speaking of, now would be a good time to open that bottle of wine." She reaches for her satchel and pulls out a bottle of red.

I rise to my feet, head to the kitchenette, and grab the wine opener from the drawer. When I turn, I find that Zoey has followed me. She takes the opener from me, and waves toward the living area. "Go on, take a seat. I'll bring you a glass."

"You'll find them on the top shelf on the far right." Leaving her to deal with it, I return to my position on the chair.

"This must be a lot. First Quentin and his son, then us," Summer mutters in sympathy.

"I suppose..." I pull my feet up under me. "I should be freaking out more, but maybe... I'm numb?"

My phone buzzes. I pull it out from the pocket of my jeans and read the message.

Lizzie: I'm coming over!

Shit, I forgot to text her.

> Me: Noooo. Sorry. Sorry. I'm good. Summer and Zoey are sweet. I'm hanging out with them. Talk later
>
> Lizzie: *Heart emoji"*

I slide the phone into my jeans' pocket. The baby starts to fuss again. Summer takes him in her arms, then nods toward the pram. "Can you get me his sippy cup? It's in the bag hanging over the handle." I head over, fumble around in the bag until I find the cup, then walk over and hand it to her. She uncaps it, and the baby reaches for it and latches his mouth around the spout.

"Gosh, you're one thirsty boy, aren't you?" she coos.

"Here's *our* sustenance." Zoey hands me a glass of wine and places a glass of water in front of Summer. "She's the designated driver," she explains, then takes a sip from her own. She sighs. "I needed that." She sits down in the chair next to mine.

I take a small sip from my glass. The taste of plums, cherries, and a hint of pepper underlain with the tannic taste of red wine coats my tongue. "Wow, I've never tasted anything like this."

"It's from Sinclair's personal collection." Summer laughs. "After not being able to drink while I was pregnant, then breastfeeding this boy, he insists I drink the best."

"And since she's driving" — Zoey waggles her eyebrows at Summer — "I get to drink her share, too. But coming back to the subject at hand..." She turns to me. "How do you feel about everything that's happened so far?"

"Truthfully?" I rub at my temple. "I'm still making sense of it." I look between the women. "Also, I'm not sure I should be sharing all of this with you two, considering we just met, but —"

"Oh, honey, it must be so disorienting for you to be faced with such a decision." Zoey touches my shoulder. "I can only imagine how confused you must be feeling."

Tears prick the backs of my eyes, and I blink them away.

"I'm so sorry if our coming here upset you —" Summer begins in a concerned voice, but I wave her off.

"No, really. I am grateful you guys are here. My sister... I'd have loved to talk to her about this, but she needs to focus on her ballet classes.

And my father's unwell and"—I sniffle—"I never managed to form close friendships with the girls I went to school with. That's what comes of being a loner. I guess it's because I had to mature before my classmates. While they were acting like kids, I was already a mom to my sister." I pause. "And then... Felix came along, and he became my best friend. I made the mistake of agreeing to marry him. And now, I don't think we're even friends anymore." My eyes water and I look up at the ceiling to keep the teardrops at bay. "So, although I'm glad he pulled out before we got married, I feel like I've lost my only friend." I take a shuddering breath. "You think you don't need anyone, and when you realize you do, it's too late."

They exchange glances, then Zoey takes my glass, places it on the table, and takes my hand in hers. "It's not too late. We're here, and we want to be your friends."

"We do." Summer nods.

"Right, because I'm so pitiful. I'm thinking of marrying a man I met three days ago, and I don't have friends of my own, so I'm crying on the shoulders of perfect strangers, who are *his* friends." I swipe at the moisture on my cheek.

Zoey leans forward in her seat. "For what it's worth, I already know you're a badass. No one who paints like that"—she stabs a thumb over her shoulders— "isn't. Also, my instincts never lie. I already know we're going to be great friends, regardless of whether you marry Quentin or not. And full disclosure? I'd rather you *did* marry him."

I incline my head.

"What Zoey is trying to say is that Quentin not so subtly wanted us to come so we could convince you that he's right for you." Summer half smiles. "And for the record, I firmly think whether you do or not is your decision. But like Zoey, I already know we're going to be good friends because I like you, and"—Matty kicks at her arm, and she looks down at the baby with a smile— "and yes, so does Matty, as I already told you."

"Quentin sent you two to convince me of his merits?" I ask slowly.

Zoey shifts in her seat. "He never said it openly. Well, not to me, because he spoke to Summer, and Summer asked me to come along. And I was curious because... Well... In the little time I've known Quentin, I thought he was a grouchy bastard who seemed dissatisfied with most things, and to find out he wants to marry you... I was curious."

"And what do you think now?"

"That you're too good for him."

I chuckle. "Thanks."

"No, really, you are. You're taking care of your family, and working, and trying to carve out a career in a competitive, creative industry—"

"I haven't been painting much," I remind her.

She cuts her hand through the air. "You've been trying, and that's what matters."

"I've known Quentin since he returned from the Marines and joined the Davenports. He has his faults but"—Summer pauses to gather her thoughts— "but he's the kind of guy you can trust to have your back when the chips are down."

"Not long ago, Karma was unwell." Summer's smile dims. "My sister was born with a hole in the heart. The condition was exacerbated when she got pregnant... a second time." She swallows. "I was with her when she collapsed at my place, less than a month ago. I tried to call her husband, then mine."

Zoey gasps. "Oh, my god, Summer! I had no idea."

Summer nods. "When neither answered, I called Q. And this, despite the fact my husband has six other very close friends and business partners he went to school with. I've known them longer than I've known Q." Summer pauses to take a deep breath.

"Sinclair and his friends run a company called 7A Investments," Zoey interjects.

"I could have called any of them, but Q's the person I reached out to." Summer's voice grows contemplative. "Something about him inspires confidence, and it's not about his age. Well, not only. He feels so solid. Like he's seen life, and he knows what to do in an emergency, you know?"

I nod dumbly. I know what she means. It's the same feeling that gripped me when my eyes met his. Oh, there was lust, certainly. But also, this something inside of me that insisted he'd take care of me.

"He happened to be working from home that day. Luckily, he doesn't live far from me and Karma. He dropped everything and arrived at our place as she was being loaded into the ambulance. I got in with her, and he followed us to the hospital. He stayed with me until Sinclair and Michael arrived. If it hadn't been for him, I don't know how I'd have survived." She wipes a tear from the corner of her eye. "He and Karma have had a special relationship ever since. And her husband and mine trust him even more."

"That's"—I clear my throat—"quite a story."

"I'm not telling you this to influence you— Okay, maybe I am."

Summer laughs. "But I'm grateful for Q. I trust him. And if you want to marry him, I'd say follow your instinct."

"Okay, wow, I didn't know about that incident." Zoey stares at Summer wide-eyed. "It explains why he's so tight with you guys."

"All I'm saying is, don't judge him until you've given him a chance to share his side of the story." Summer smiles gently.

"I think you have a point. But"—I bite the inside of my cheek—"don't you find it weird that he proposed to me within minutes of meeting me, and that he's much older than me? Not to mention, I was going to marry his son."

"Maybe." Summer shrugs. "I admit, it seems impulsive. And I might add, out of character for him. But I think that's because he decided to follow his instinct and not waste time second-guessing himself."

I turn to Zoey. "And what do you think, Zoey? What would you do if you were in my position?"

She meets my gaze without flinching. "I think you're right to be suspicious. I would be, too, if someone walked off the street and proposed to me. But it's also dependent on the man—and I do happen to think Q is very personable. And hot"—she snickers— "so I'd get to know him better before making a decision. In fact,"—she snaps her fingers— "I have an idea. Q's participating in a fight tomorrow. Wanna come with me?"

10

_____

Quentin

The underground parking lot in Hackney where the fight with Ryot is about to take place, is a couple of miles from my Primrose Hill townhouse, but it might as well be in a different country.

I spent much of my rebellious youth here getting into scraps with the underground gangs that rule this area. I turned my back on Arthur and his money by taking on criminal elements, then thought I was leaving it all behind when I enrolled in the Marines, but life has a way of coming full circle.

It's a testament to how much I've forgotten that it's only when I park my refurbished Cadillac Eldorado next to the Kebab Shop near the lot that I realize I don't have a hope in hell of finding the car intact upon my return. I may have changed, but this area hasn't. To play it safe, I pay the guy in the Kebab Shop to keep an eye on it. For good measure, I incentivize the teens milling about around the corner to guard it.

In the less than half a block I walk to the lot, I pass a make-shift shrine at the spot where a knifing took place a week ago, a pound store, a corner shop with barred windows, and another which is shuttered.

I drop a hundred-pound note into the cap of a homeless man who grabs it, stuffs it under his torn bedding, then goes back to sleep. The air smells of rotting garbage and unwashed bodies.

If I close my eyes, I might as well be back in one of the run-down areas of the Middle East country where I was posted for a lot of my time abroad. Except the temperature here is cooler.

When I enter the car park, the scent of copper grows heavy. It's then it sinks in that I'm going to take on Ryot, not in a gentlemanly match at the 7A gym, but in a free-style boxing scenario.

When he told me to choose the date and time of the match, he left out the venue which he picked. Which is this—his home turf. Blood has been spilled here from previous fights and, possibly, gang run-ins before that. There are no cameras, either—I checked. The air is thick with the stench of imminent threat. The echoes of those hurt before me bounce off the walls.

I thought I was early but already crowds press in on the ropes rigged around the platform, which forms the temporary ring in the center of the lot.

I shoulder my way past the throng to where Knox waits for me with my gloves. He's agreed to be my corner man for the duration of the fight. He chin jerks in my direction.

Without a word, I strip off my T-shirt and drop it on the floor, then take a seat in the chair in front of him. I pull on first one glove then the other. He tightens, then tests them. No mouth guard or any other protective gear because those are the rules of this wannabe Fight Club match.

"You sure you want to go through with this?" Knox drawls.

I don't answer.

"He's going to kick your arse."

"Thanks for the vote of confidence," I grumble.

Around us, the crowd begins to chant. It takes me a few seconds to realize they're screaming, "Kill-er, Kill-er, Kill-er."

"Killer?" I scowl.

"Newsflash: they don't mean you." Knox snickers.

"Shouldn't you be joining them in supporting your brother?"

He chuckles. "I thought so, too. Until I realized he meant to meet you on his patch. He hasn't lost a match since he began competing in these wannabe Fight Club encounters."

My muscles flex. I shake out my arms, crack my neck. I didn't think I missed this part of my youth, but a part of me feels like I never left.

A ripple runs through the crowd. The chanting grows louder. The crowd parts for Ryot. He runs forward and bounds onto the platform. He's wearing a pair of boxing shorts, boots, and gloves. His torso is bare, like mine. Unlike him, I'm wearing a pair of jeans.

For the first time, I assess him, not as my nephew, but as competition. He's a little shorter than me, but his torso and shoulders seem to be hewn from rock. I know he's heavier than me. But seeing him without his suit on, I realize I misjudged him. The man is in peak physical condition. And unlike me, he doesn't have a single grey hair on his head, or on his chest. *Also,* unlike me, he carries the grief of a broken heart. One I caused—unwittingly and by carrying out my duty—but that means shit to him. He's suffering and I can give him an outlet, by letting him take out some of his rage on me. It's not going to hurt less, though.

Knox follows my perusal, and his expression grows sober. "He's going to beat you up."

And I welcome the absolution. "Maybe then, we'll be even." *At least, I hope so.*

He sighs. "I know you're going to let him thrash you, but for the sake of entertainment, try to last more than one round." He shakes his head. "That would be an improvement on the ones who went before you."

Fuck. I glance at his face to see if he's joking, and Knox shakes his head. "It's true."

Bloody fuck. Yes, I came here, ready to be beaten up. Doesn't change the fact that I'm a fighter. I'll have to curb my natural impulses to strike back.

Brody and Tyler scowl at me from the sidelines. Connor, who's standing next to them, gives me the bird. I'm not popular with the Davenport brothers, a.k.a. my nephews. I can't help but feel admiration for how they've rallied around their brother. They've grown into the kind of men I'd like to know better. But aside for Knox, who's taken a shine to me, the rest might well be strangers. *And whose fault is that? It was you who didn't take the time to get to know them when they were growing up.*

"I'm rooting for you, mate." Sinclair walks over to join us. "But then, I prefer to be on the side of the underdog."

He and the rest of the Seven started holding the fights on this parking lot when they were dissenting schoolboys. It became so popular, they opted to keep it running, with the caveat that any money raised goes to charity. Entrance to fight, as well as to be in the audience, is by invitation.

Sinclair pulls out his phone. His fingers fly over the screen, and

Knox's phone dings. Knox glances at the screen, and his lips curl. "At least you're a good loser, you wanker. Get ready to lose more money."

"Did you place a bet on me?" I snap.

Sinclair looks sheepish. "Couldn't pass up the opportunity of a fast buck. Just for shits and giggles, of course."

"Of course." I narrow my gaze on Knox. "And you've been collecting bets from your brothers, I assume?"

Knox's grin widens. "And the assembled crowds. You'll be glad to know the odds are one hundred to one against you."

"Thanks for the pep talk." I rise to my feet and brush past both of them, stalking in the direction of the ring. A series of boos greets me, but I keep going.

"I've asked Doc Weston to be on standby to treat you." Knox, who's on my heels, nods to where the doc is watching me with a sympathetic look on his face.

"There's an ambulance outside — "

I raise my hand.

Knox, mercifully, shuts up when I say, "I won't be needing it."

I don't need that ambulance. I don't. Maybe if I repeat that often enough, I'll convince myself? I bounce on the balls of my feet, then duck and avoid a blow. What was I thinking, taking on a man younger than me? Ryot's bloody good at this. And I'm a little rusty.

He bares his teeth, throws an uppercut which lands. The pain bursts across my jawline, but it's not enough to absolve me. I will never stop feeling guilty, even if I was only indirectly responsible for what happened to Ryot's wife.

Another hit. This time he sinks that barbell-sized fist of his into my side. Pain sears up my spine. Sparks flash behind my eyes. I stumble back. *Motherfucker.* He definitely bruised a rib or two. I shake my head to clear it.

"Again" I yell at him. "Hit me again."

Sweat pours down my forehead, stinging my eyes. He glares at me, eyes shooting darts of hate before he throws another punch.

This one smashes into the side of my head. Pain is a bullet that streaks down my spine. Fuck. I see stars. Feel myself sway, then manage to find my balance. Each breath I take sends a message of agony to my brain.

I shake my head to clear it, but that only sparks a fresh burst of torment in my bloodstream. Ryot glowers at me but makes no move to strike further.

"Do it! Throw another punch."

When he hesitates, I throw an uppercut and make contact with his chin. It's as if I've rammed into the side of a bunker as pain whizzes through my mind, but there's not a grunt from him. Or a cry of pain. The man's been silent. Grim. Not a single syllable escapes him.

He could be carved from granite, or from hurt. The kind of hurt that eats into you, slowly, surely, over the years, gnawing at you from the inside, eating up your flesh, settling in your bones, your teeth, until you taste it, smell it, see it in everything around you. Until it becomes you and you... become a shadow of your past, someone who sees a black hole in the future.

"Hit. Me. Arsehole," I bite out through gritted teeth.

He doesn't move. *Fuck. Can't he see I deserve every blow? Every bite of pain?* "I'm responsible for the suffering you're going through, or have you forgotten?"

An ugly look comes into his eyes. A growl rumbles up his throat. I can hear it over the screaming of the crowds. He bares his teeth, throws up his fist.

I dance out of reach. "That's right. It's all me," I spit out.

Tension coils through his frame. He rushes at me, but I step out of the way. When he turns on me, I throw up my arm to block his next punch. "I didn't know—" I block his next punch. "We had an informer—" I duck his next hit. "He colluded with our enemies—" I jump back to avoid his next blow. "Led your wife's team into a trap. If I'd known... I'd've stopped them." I force out the words.

His shoulders bulge. Knotted ropes of muscle flex beneath his skin, then with a roar, he swings at me; I step to the side, and his knuckles graze my arm. Pain pinches my nerve-endings, but I shove it into that dark space inside of me where I can't access it. The space I drew upon when I had to find my focus and give orders on a mission.

"I was the team leader," I pant, "I could have called off the strike."

A muscle works at his jawline. A vein pops at his temple. Hatred distorts his expression, and he rushes me.

He punches me in the torso. I grunt. "That's it. I deserve it."

Another punch to my chest. The breath wheezes out of me. "More. Hit me more." *It's because of me you're in pain. You need revenge for what I did to you.*

He buries his fist in my side. I bite down on my tongue to swallow my groan and taste blood. "I made the decision to bomb the space," I taunt, "knowing they were there."

Another noise, this time like the growl of a wounded animal, emerges from Ryot's throat. He rains blows to my sides, my stomach, my chest, in such quick succession, it feels like I've been struck by a hail of canonballs. *Fucking hell!* Sensations zing through to my pain centers in such rapid succession, I groan.

I'm pushed back until I hit the ropes, and still, he keeps coming. *Fuck, fuck, fuck.* At this rate I won't survive another minute. *I need to stay upright to get the rest of my confession out.*

I try to get in a counterpunch, but he dances away, only to land another one in my stomach. The air rushes out of me. I grunt, blink the blood out of my eyes, and with what feels like superhuman effort, I throw my arms around his neck.

I try to smother his punches to get some control over the proceedings, try to get my breath and my energy back. My nephew is bloody good at this.

I stifle the pride that coils in my chest, tighten my hold around him and place my mouth next to his ear. "Listen to me, boy—" He struggles to get free, but I rein him in. "They gave up their lives so many more could live. You'd have done the same in my place. They knew what they were getting into when they enrolled."

He makes a growling sound—half rage, half pain—in the back of his throat. For what it's worth, at least he's listening. "Nothing I say will ease your pain. I'll go through life with the death of your wife and her team on my conscience. Even knowing I did my duty; I'll never forgive myself."

He flexes his enormous shoulders and breaks through my hold again.

He pushes on my shoulders and uses the leverage to take a step back. He swings his rear fist up in a hooking arc position which connects with my temple.

Spit flies out of my mouth. The world tilts. My face feels like I've run into a tank—or Ryot... Same thing.

I crumple against the ropes. The fluorescent lights above waver in front of my eyes. I blink. Then Ryot's grim countenance fills my line of sight. This is the time when a referee should be there, counting down to see if I'll rise, but there is no one to help me. I deserve to lose this match. I deserve to lay here bleeding. I deserve the agony that threatens to overcome me. The darkness that closes in on me. Ryot loved her and lost her because of me. I've never loved in my life. There's no one waiting for me. No one I'd walk off this platform on my own strength for. No one—

"Quentin!"

Her voice reaches me. It penetrates the loathing that fills my mind. The hate for myself that I've drawn around my shoulders like a shroud. The helplessness that engulfs me and mires me in its swirling, dark arms.

"Quentin!" Louder this time; more drawn out.

My gaze is drawn past Ryot's shoulder to where she's standing near the ring. Fingers clenched, shoulders rigid, green eyes burning with hate —? *No, it's fear. For me?* A chip in the wall I've built around my heart loosens.

She draws in a breath, sets her jaw, and screams, "Quentin, fight!"

11

Vivian

His gaze locks with mine, and the force of the connection is like a gut punch. My ribcage squeezes down on my lungs. My throat closes. I'm caught in the magnetic tether that seems to lasso around me. I can't move, can't look away. The noise around us and the sight of the crowd fade away. It's him and me, and this primal link between us I sensed from the moment I saw him.

Then, his body shudders. The blood drains from his face. Oh, no, no, no, Ryot hit him again.

"Quentin, fight!" I yell.

An electric current seems to run through him. He tears his gaze from mine, swings, and catches Ryot with a hook to the right side of the temple.

Ryot seems to freeze mid-step. Then, he shakes his head and keeps going. Quentin moves so fast; he seems to blur. The grace, the agility with which he moves, the fluidity of his body as he follows with another upper cut to Ryot's cheek, then a jab to his shoulder, then to his side, a final one to Ryot's stomach... *Oh my god!* My pussy clenches. My nipples harden. *How can I be turned on when he's beating up another man?*

And why was I so upset when I saw him getting beaten? I couldn't stand by and let it happen. I couldn't understand why Quentin seemed to give up without a fight. I had to do something to get him to retaliate. I yelled out his name but didn't expect him to react the way he did.

Ryot shakes his head as if to clear it and throws another punch. I don't know a lot about boxing, but even I can tell that the big man is tiring. Quentin dances out of his reach, and with a litheness that lights a thousand fires in my bloodstream, he kicks Ryot's legs out from under him.

Ryot goes down with an earth-shaking thud. Without giving him a chance to recover, Quentin leans his knee into Ryot's throat. Ryot struggles to rise. Quentin presses his weight down into his stance.

The crowd around me boos. Seems these people are on Ryot's side. Time to even things out.

I cup my palms around my mouth and chant, "Quen-tin! Quen-tin! Quen-tin!" Next to me Zoey jumps up and down. "Go, Quentin!"

Quentin bends his head; his lips move. He seems to be talking to Ryot. Asking the giant if he's ready to give in? At least, I think that's what is happening. There's an imperceptible nod from Ryot, and Quentin rises to his feet. He holds out his arm to Ryot, who ignores it. The hulking man straightens, his movements slow. He rolls his shoulders, cracks his neck, then brushes past Quentin.

He heads to the ropes, ducks under them, and doesn't acknowledge the men standing there. A man who I assume is Ryot's brother, going by the facial resemblance, holds out his T-shirt. Ryot grabs it, without breaking stride. He walks through the path that emerges when the crowd steps aside. He walks past me and heads for the exit.

Clearly, the crowds were there to see him in action, for they begin to stream out after him.

From inside the ring, Quentin lifts his head, and when our gazes meet, it feels like all of my breath leaves me. He takes a step forward, another. His jaw is hard, his forehead furrowed. Only, his eyes are clear. Those blue eyes flare with cold fire. His gait is purposeful. His expression determined. He reaches the ropes, and I back away. He ducks under them, straightens.

Knox walks over and hands him his T-shirt. He nods his thanks, without breaking our connection.

Not bothering to wear it, he stalks closer. I take in his massive shoulders, the width of his chest with the tattoo of the beating heart dripping blood on the skin over his heart, and tiny black triangles which peek out on either side of his torso. It's almost like a serrated edge brackets his chest. Then there's the brick-like musculature of his abs, with his dog tags nestled in the demarcation of his pecs, the concave stomach with the trail of hair that disappears into the waistband of his jeans, the thick thighs which strain the fabric, and the bulge at his crotch which indicates the size of what this man is packing.

As he closes in on me, the scent of his sweat, mixed with the coppery tones of the blood splotched on his torso teases my nostrils. And below that is the pungent scent of woodsmoke and the freshness of pine, a confluence I recognize as uniquely Quentin.

When he comes to a stop in front of me, I tear my gaze from the part of him that has captured my imagination and meet his eyes. Oh my god! He's more injured than I realized. I saw him take the hits; now I notice the impact of Ryot's fists on his face.

Blood drips from a cut on his forehead, there's a bruise on his cheek, and one eye is swollen. Why does it add to his allure? Why does it make him seem more magnificent?

He could be a conquering hero or a knight returning from a joust to claim his spoils.

In this case, me.

He inclines his head. "Deep into that darkness peering, long I stood there, wondering, fearing, doubting, dreaming dreams no mortal ever dared to dream before." His voice is a harsh whisper scraping over my already sensitized nerve-endings.

"Poe." I swallow.

"Raven," he growls.

"You're bleeding."

"Not nearly enough." His lips twist.

"You're hurting."

Next to me, Zoey's gaze ping-pongs between Quentin and me.

He nods. "More than you'll ever know." The lines around his eyes deepen. "What happened is a part of me. I have to live with the consequences of my actions."

I frown. "Is this about... about... what went down between you and Ryot?"

"Uh, I'm going to head out. Glad you're, more or less, in one piece, Quentin." With a small wave, Zoey peels off.

Quentin nods in her direction, then turns to me. His features shutter. "What do you know about what happened between me and Ryot?"

"Nothing. None of the details. Only that... uh... There's a history between the two of you?"

Around us, the crowd thins further.

Quentin firms his lips. And when he glances away, it's clear he doesn't want to talk about it. I swallow down the disappointment that curdles my belly. Why did I think he'd unburden himself to me? After all, our relationship is superficial, at best. Still, this is the most vulnerable I've ever seen him. The anger in his gaze is aimed at himself, and it's tinged with helplessness and hurt.

I raise my hand to touch him, then stop myself. "You shouldn't be so hard on yourself," I murmur.

"It's the only way I know," he says through gritted teeth.

"Maybe I can show you otherwise?"

He jerks his chin in my direction. "Is that why you came here?"

"I came here because—" I bite down on my lower lip, and his gaze instantly darts to my mouth and stays there.

My body recognizes him, knows who its master is, no matter how my logical mind insists I'm crazy. How would it be to have him touch me, to place those thick fingers on the curve of my breast, to bury his face between my legs and draw his whiskered chin over my pussy lips? To have him squeeze my arse, and bite down on my nipples and suck on them? To have him cover my body with his weight and take me without showing any mercy? To—

"Because?"

"What?" I blink.

"You were saying you came here because—"

"I wanted to keep Zoey company." *Yes, that's it. That makes sense.* "I knew she was coming to watch the fight and uh... I decided to come take a look for myself." I bite the inside of my cheek.

One side of his lips twists. "Lying to me, Raven?"

I flush. "Of course not. It's the truth."

"So, you're here because you wanted to see me fight?"

I nod. Then shake my head. "No, no, not you... just... *An* underground fight. It could have been anyone fighting."

My cheeks are hot, and my heart is jackhammering away like it's going to cleave through my ribcage any moment.

"Only it *was* me," he reminds me.

And something shifted in me when I saw you getting beaten up. Something I'm not going to think about right now, because I have no right to feel that way. I have to stop feeling so much for him. Stop missing him when I'm away from him. Have to stop myself from wanting to throw myself at him and climb him like a tree. Have to stop myself from blurting out 'yes' to his crazy proposal. *OMG, don't you dare!*

I am so pissed off with myself; it's the only explanation for what I say next. "And Ryot." I jut out my chin.

His features darken. His eyes flash. He's angry, as I hoped he would be. His response propels a thrill of anticipation down the back of my throat.

"Why are you here?" he asks in a clipped tone.

His face has gone carefully blank, while a fine tension radiates from his body.

The lack of emotion in his voice sends a warning jolt up my spine. The hair on my forearms rises. *Did I push him too far? Do I dare stretch his control even more?*

"I came to see if you could hold your own against someone younger than you, of course." He's denied it's an issue, but c'mon, he must be conscious of the fact that I'm much younger than him, and his son's ex.

Or perhaps, it's *me* who's more conscious of our age gap, and that's why I drew his attention to the age difference between him and Ryot? Which is why I implied Ryot would have more stamina than him. Which would mean he could keep going longer, whether in a fight or in bed.

I wanted to make him uncomfortable. Now the words are out, and I realize, I've made myself equally uncomfortable. The space between us turns into a mass of pulsating emotions. An undercurrent of tension ripples through his demeanor. He hardens his jaw and narrows his gaze on me with such intensity, my chest seems to seize up.

"You're here to test my masculinity?"

His tone is casual, but it feels like a whip wrapped in silken threads curling around my body and pulling tighter. My insides quiver. There's a threat in his voice which warns me to shut up. *Shut up. Zip it, you idiot.*

But what if I push him all the way? A frisson of thrill pinches my nerve-endings. I want to see him unfettered. I want to goad him and watch him unravel. I want to find out what he does once he sheds that iron control he wears like chains. What will he do when he loses that iron grip on his emotions? What will he do to me? And why do I know that I'll like it?

"Not how I'd put it, but if you want to see it that way, sure." I raise a shoulder.

For a few seconds, his features turn into a mask of stone. Those blue eyes of his glitter with an emotion I later place as resolve.

And I know I've pushed him beyond the ability to think straight, for the next moment, the world tilts.

I yelp, for he's bent his knees, wrapped his arm around my thighs and thrown me over his shoulder.

My hair flows down, blocking out my line of sight, and when he begins to stalk forward, my breasts bump into the hard expanse of his back. My skirt rides up and cool air assails my upper thigh. *Ohmigod. Ohmigod. He's carrying me over his shoulder in front of everyone. Like he's some neanderthal and I'm the woman he's dragging to his cave.*

My cheeks feel like they're on fire. And it's not only from the blood which has rushed to my face. My scalp tingles. My skin feels too tight for my body. This is so embarrassing. So mortifying. But it's also primal and exhilarating and...

No, no, no, how can I think of it like that? I seriously can't be turned on, though my soaked panties say otherwise. This is the antithesis of every feminist principle I've ever believed in.

"What are you doing?" I cry.

He doesn't answer. Just keeps moving.

My cross-body bag with my phone is caught between my stomach and his upper chest. I bury my fists into the unforgiving muscles between his shoulder blades, then hiss. Pain shivers up my arm. Incredible. It's like I'm beating my fists against a brick wall. Or the side of a mountain. The man's super-built. And the way his muscles flex under his skin, every dip and roll of which I feel against my own, it's as if we're already melded into one organism.

And the fact that I'm so intimately close to him, and that my blood feels like it's turned into a crimson tide of desire, and every cell in my body seems to have opened up and is absorbing his nearness, makes me so pissed off with myself.

I lock my fingers together, raise my joined-up fists and bring them down on the slope of his back.

He must feel something, for he tenses. Then, his big palm connects with my butt. A sharp pain squeals up my spine.

What the —! "Did you spank me?" I yell.

In reply, he smacks my other arse-cheek, and the first and the next. With each slap, my backside quivers, and the pain zooms straight to my cunt. Moisture drips out from between my legs, and I have to squeeze my thighs together. Then, he places a possessive palm over my butt and gently squeezes.

Instantly, the hollow sensation between my thighs curls in on itself.

A groan spills from my throat. I bite down on my lower lip to avoid making any further noise. How can I be so aroused? I should be worried I've lost every shred of pride I had, but I can't bring myself to care for that. All of my attention is focused on the throbbing heavy flesh between my legs.

My silence must satisfy him, for he keeps moving forward.

I assume the crowd dispersed, for he carries me toward the exit without stopping. The warmth of his big palm over my butt reminds me he hasn't removed it yet. It's a declaration of his possession to the world.

I sense him walking up the short incline which leads onto the sidewalk. When he comes to a stop, I open my eyes, just as he wrenches open the front door of his car. He throws me down in the passenger seat.

The man carried me nearly a hundred yards over his shoulder and he's not out of breath. And I'm not slim, by any means.

The blood rushes away from my face, and my head spins. It's a good thing I'm sitting. Or maybe it's because his scent of woodsmoke and pine is in my nostrils. I feel like I'm surrounded by his presence in this car.

Without looking at me, he pulls my seatbelt across my chest, and when his knuckles brush against my pointed nipple, I shiver. He fastens my seatbelt and straightens, then shuts my door.

Knox walks over and talks to him. I hear the low murmur of their voices, before Quentin walks around. He shrugs on his T-shirt, then opens the door and slides into the driver's seat.

I should get out of the car. I should leave, call Zoey, who I'm sure would be happy to come back and get me or call my sister. I should do anything but go home with a man who just carried me like a sack of potatoes. But as much as I'm furious, I don't want to leave. I want to fight him because it will keep me in his blue gaze.

I turn on him. "How dare you carry me out of there like that?"

He places those thick fingers of his on the steering wheel and stares at me.

"Nothing to say for yourself? Do you realize how humiliating that was?" I burst out.

He inclines his head. "If I touched you between your legs, would I find you wet?"

I gape at him. "How?... What?... Why?... Why would you say that?" I sputter.

"Answer the question, Raven."

I open my mouth, then shut it. I could lie and say I'm not. But somehow, I can't bring myself to lie. So instead, I point at my head. "I'm blonde."

He arches an eyebrow.

"You called me Raven. But I don't have dark hair."

"But there's a darkness in you that yearns to be let out."

I begin to speak, but he holds up his hand. "Don't bother denying it, when we both know it's true."

I swallow past the knot of emotion in my throat. How is it possible that this almost-stranger *sees* me when everyone else in my life sees what I portray for the outside world?

I hear a sound of distress emerge from my throat. He does, too.

He cups my cheek and somehow, his touch is soothing. "It's okay. It's okay to let go. You're safe with me. I'll never judge you, I promise. I want you to be true to yourself. To your emotions. To what you feel inside. To what you want to be. To explore what you feel. Your feelings. Your desires. Your deepest darkest needs. They all matter to me."

A bead of sweat runs down his temple. It's cold in the car but I feel like a million flames are trying to burst out of my skin. "I... I don't know what you mean."

"Sure you do. You liked it when I carried you out of there."

I shake my head.

"You loved it when I spanked you."

"No, no, no." I squeeze my eyes shut.

"You craved more of my touch when I massaged your arse. And knowing everyone was watching us only turned you on further. Your feelings of humiliation pushed you further in the direction of an orgasm.

"Oh, my god!" I slap my hands over my ears. "Stop, please."

When he does, I'm surprised enough to open my eyes and look at him and instantly realize, it's a mistake. There's empathy in his gaze, and understanding, and below it all, a thick, heavy lust coats his features. A need which touches a hidden part of me.

He sits straight, his military bearing hard, uncompromising. Precise, like the edge of a scalpel knife. He could cut me and hurt me, and damn him, but I'd enjoy the pain.

He reaches for me slowly, like I'm an animal who could bolt at any time, and when I don't flinch away, he cups my cheek. "You can trust me. I'll take care of you, I promise."

"That's what I'm afraid of," I whisper. To be honest, I don't understand where these words are coming from, or what exactly I mean by them.

But he does, for he nods. "I promise, I'll never do anything you don't want. You have the power in this relationship."

"Doesn't seem that way from where I'm sitting."

"You think I have the power because I have the money that you need, but you forget that you have something I need, too."

"Sure, you need to get married, so your father confirms you as the CEO of the company and you secure your inheritance."

"Not only." His lips curve, and his smile is a little sad. "I need you because you remind me of possibilities. You give me hope that there's more to life than what I've lived so far. You make me believe in everything that is good and beautiful; you're an antidote to what I've seen as a Marine."

I laugh self-consciously. "You're making me out to be something I'm not."

"I have no doubt that you're submissive."

I swallow. It's one thing for me to realize that for myself. But hearing it from him makes me feel exposed. Like I have nowhere to hide. I've never been this seen as with this man.

His gaze intensifies. "You give me a reason to focus my attention, something I am grateful for. And if you choose me to bring out your submissiveness, then it's an honor I will never take lightly. You hold the power...to say no. I have the prerogative to test your limits, so you learn more about yourself, but the final say in whether you want me to dominate you or not is up to you."

I clear my throat. "Am... I... Am I supposed to know what you're talking about?"

"Do you expect me to believe that you don't?"

Answer a question with a question. Typical. Also, damn him. How does he know I'm aware of what he's alluding to? I look out of the window. "It's a fact, I'm curious about the BDSM lifestyle. Enough to watch porn featuring role play." It was one way to feel less lonely when you didn't have friends or boyfriends. "But I never thought I'd have a chance to experiment with the lifestyle."

"But you wanted to."

He's right again. How annoying. I turn and scowl at him. "Doesn't mean you can drive me to wherever it is you have in mind."

"Hmm." He taps a blunt fingernail against the steering wheel. He might as well have placed it against my engorged clit. One touch and I'd explode. I squeeze my thighs together. His shoulder muscles flex, and I'm sure he noticed my action, but he doesn't draw attention to it. "I am going to drive you out of here because it's an unsafe neighborhood. I'll also never mention this conversation again, if that's what you want."

I could ask him why I should believe him, but I know instinctively. If I asked, he'd never again bring up this possible exploration of a part of me I've been curious about. I could set it as aside as a brush with a lifestyle which intrigued me, but which wasn't for me or... I could indicate I was a willing partner in understanding what it means to be a submissive.

"Would it"—I clear my throat—"would it include whips and chains?"

There's surprise on his face, then he chuckles. "Not unless that's what you want. And if we both agree that it's in your best interest."

"My best interest?"

"Always, Raven."

"So you think marrying me is in my best interest?"

"I think you're too good for me. But I'm selfish enough to want you for myself."

"Oh." My heart flutters.

"I also think you're a brat who needs to be spanked."

I gape at him. "Did you call me a brat?"

"You trying to deny what you said back there wasn't designed to get me angry enough to punish you?"

The hard edge of his voice sends another spurt of liquid heat through my veins.

When I don't reply, he nods. "That's what I thought."

I glance away, then back at him. "Is now when you tell me you're the one who's going to bring me in line?"

"I'd certainly enjoy doing it."

I look between his eyes. His gaze is an expanse of blue, which is so bright it could consume me.

"I still don't know you."

"You know me better today that you did yesterday."

"What are you saying?"

"Have you given more thought to my proposal?"

Of course, he answers my question with another of his own. This man... His arrogance should piss me off, and it does, but his assertiveness is also a turn on. "You always sound so sure of yourself," I murmur. Mainly because I don't want to answer his question. If I tell him I've been considering his proposal, then he'll probe for an answer, and I'll have to reveal I'm no closer to making a decision. I don't want to appear as being indecisive, in contrast to his self-assuredness.

Something in his eyes fades. "I've learned I may not always be right." He scowls through the windshield. His shoulders are locked. The tendons of his neck stand out in relief. Is he referring to a mistake he made in his past?

"Quentin—" I begin, but he cuts me off.

"Do you want me to make a decision for you? Is that it?"

"What do you mean?" I ignore the excitement that ripples under my skin at the notion of him deciding for me.

"You give me the impression that you want to agree, but your ego is stopping you, so let me spell it out for you, Raven." He turns to me. "You don't have a choice but to go through with this."

"I... don't?"

"You need the money."

Of course I do. And I'm not getting it anywhere else. It's not like I'm going to win the lottery overnight and tell him I'm not marrying him. More to the point, I don't *want* to tell him I'm not marrying him, because I find him hot, and way too attractive, and I know sex with him will blow my mind. And because I feel safe with him. It's my instincts, something deep inside me which says, this man... will never leave me wanting for anything.

He continues, "Also, you didn't answer my earlier question."

"Wh-which question?"

"The one I know you remember. Maybe you want me to find out for myself?"

I begin to shake my head. I should shake my head. But something inside me... Perhaps that darkness he recognizes... Or that brattiness he referred to... Or it could be the need to find out if I'm as submissive as he says I am coaxes me to part my thighs.

Without taking his gaze off mine, he reaches over, slides his hand under my skirt and cups my sex. The confidence in his act pushes the breath from my lungs. Thank God, I didn't wear my jeans. It's only my panties separating my pussy from his touch.

"If you want me to stop, you only have to say so. If you don't want this, you can leave the car, and I won't stop you," he snaps.

But do I open my mouth to say no? Of course not. Instead, I squeeze my thighs together, trapping his hand.

12

Quentin

The heat of her pussy sears my palm through the fabric of her panties and that of her skirt. She squeezes down with her thighs, and the feel of her muscles clamping around my palm, combined with the beat of the pulse at her core, turns me rock hard.

I widen the gap between my legs to accommodate my arousal. The action draws her gaze down to my crotch, and a blush reddens her cheeks. She's so fucking beautiful. My breath hitches. My pulse booms at my temples.

"Are you sure?" I force myself to say the words. I cannot let myself take things further, unless she confirms she's ready to go to the next stage.

She hesitates, then nods slowly.

"Say it for me, Raven. Say it aloud." I inked Poe's bird on my back as a reminder of the darkness inside me. I never expected my Raven would one day look me in the eye and say...

"I'm sure." Her voice is low but strong.

"What are you sure about?"

Her chest rises and falls. "I'm sure I want to feel your hands on me,

your fingers in me, your tongue, your"—she squeezes her eyes shut
—"your—"

"—my cock impaling you."

Her cheeks turn crimson.

"Say it," I implore.

"Your"—she swallows— "your cock impaling me."

Any remaining blood drains to my groin. *Fuck me.* Hearing her say
those filthy words turns my body into a mass of fierce need. My heart
swells in my chest. My pulse rate ratchets up. I close my eyes and draw in
a breath, then another. Drawing on all my training as a Marine to gather
my wits, to regain my focus. Drawing on my ability to compartmentalize
any pain I'm feeling from my wounds, tightly locked in that space I'd
shoved it in.

I've faced down enemy soldiers, dodged bullets, run the most
dangerous of missions with a cool head, but the first touch of her pussy,
and I fall apart. The sugary scent of her arousal fills my lungs. A fresh
burst of craving turns my belly to a churning mass of anticipation. But I
will not hurry our first encounter, not when I plan to give her so much
pleasure, she'll not be able to think straight for days. I wrench my hand
from between her legs.

She gasps. "Quentin, what are you—"

"I told you to call me Q."

She swallows.

"Say it, Raven."

"Q," she murmurs, and a fierce surge of satisfaction lances through my
body.

I put the car in gear, ease onto the road, then step on the accelerator.

"Take off your panties," I growl, as the car leaps forward.

When she doesn't comply, I lower my voice to a hush. "Do it, now."

Instantly, she slides her fingers under her skirt, lifts up her hips and
shimmies her panties down her thighs. Her cross-body bag gets in the
way. I pull it off her and from under the seatbelt, then let it drop to the
floor. By the time she shoves her panties down her legs and slides them
off, the anticipation in my belly has turned into a tsunami of lust. I
squeeze my fingers around the steering wheel until the skin across my
knuckles stretches white.

"Touch yourself," I bite out.

"Wh-what?"

"Do it," I bark.

Out of the corner of my eye, I see the movement of her forearms, and hear the sucking noise of her wet flesh give as she begins to move her fingers in and out of her pussy.

"Faster," I command.

The squelching sound is loud in the car as she obeys me. She throws her head back. "Oh, god."

"Oh, Q. God has nothing to do with how I'm going to make you come.

"Oh, Q," she moans. "Oh… Q…" Her tone grows frantic. "Oh, Q. Q. Q."

Ahead of me, traffic slows down. The taillights of the cars in front glow red as they step on the brakes. No fucking way am I going to get caught in traffic when she's so close to the edge. I swerve the steering wheel to the right. Car horns blare, brakes screech as I make a steep U turn, over the divider and into the oncoming traffic lane.

"You're crazy," she cries.

"No, I'm horny." I step on the accelerator, and the car leaps forward. "Did I give you permission to stop touching yourself?"

"N-no," she gasps.

"I'm going to have to spank your butt the next time you do so without my permission."

"It… It's not fair that you can ask me to do what you want, and punish me when I disobey, and I —"

"You enjoy every command. In fact, it turns you on to obey me, and positively makes you drip not to, because you know I'll discipline you, and you'll love it."

"Oh, my god!" She bangs the back of her head into the seat. "I shouldn't find that hot. Why do I find that so hot?"

"Because you're a good girl who knows I love to see you like this. Isn't that right, Raven? You want to please me, don't you?"

She lowers her gaze, and her eyelashes flutter. "Yes." She clears her throat. "Yes, I do want to please you."

"Don't stop playing with your cunt," I growl.

She shakes her head. "I should be upset with you for talking to me like that."

"I'll be a lot more upset if you don't obey me and shove all four of your fingers into your pussy."

By the way her upper arm moves, I can tell she's obeying me. A whimper spills from her mouth, "It's… too much."

"Not as much as how my cock is going to feel when I sink into your warm, wet cunt."

"Q." She writhes. "Please. Q."

A-n-d, that's it. The need in her voice pushes out all other thoughts in my head. I turn into the parking lot of a supermarket, drive to the farthest spot, as far away from the other cars as I can, then slam on the brakes.

I unbuckle my seatbelt and hit the lever so the seat reclines back to an almost horizontal position — I knew I drove my Cadillac for a reason.

I release her seatbelt, grab her around her waist and haul her over the center console so she's straddling me. She looks at me wide-eyed, her fingers caught inside her pussy.

"What are you doing?" she asks.

"What do you *think* I'm doing?" I squeeze my fingers around her wrist. I apply enough pressure that she has to follow my lead when I ease her fingers out from between her legs. With a sucking sound, her pussy lips release her digits. I bring them to my mouth and wrap my lips around them. The sweet-tangy taste of her essence sinks into my palate, and fuck, if I don't want to feast on her. I wrap my fingers around the swell of her hips, then haul her up so her skirt is bunched around her chest and her knees are on either side of my face. *Finally, fuck!*

"Q," she protests.

"Ride my face." I balance her weight, so she has no choice but to push her cunt into my mouth, but she tenses up and holds back.

"Place that sweet cunt of yours on my mouth so I can eat you out," I order.

Her eyelids flutter. "B-but I might smother you."

I look at her like she's crazy. "Are you fishing for compliments?"

"What?" She stares at me wide-eyed.

"Do you realize how perfect you are?" I search her features and spot the disbelief on her face. "The flare of your hips gives me enough leverage to hold on as I fuck you."

"Oh." She draws in a sharp breath.

"And that squishy roll around your stomach is the fucking cutest thing I've ever seen."

She squeezes her eyes shut. "I can't believe you said that."

"And if I die, suffocated by your thighs and with your pussy juice on my face, then I can't think of a better way of going."

"Oh, god." A shudder grips her, and when she looks at me again, there's a yearning in her gaze. "Someone will see us," she says in a small voice.

"I perform better with an audience."

Her jaw drops. "Why do you have to be this... filthy?"

"Just getting started." I smirk. "Do as you're told Raven, I'm starving."

"Oh, god. Oh god" Her thighs tremble. She tries to pull away, but I hold her in place. My ribs protest from the beating they took but I ignore it. No way am I stopping to get my wounds looked at. I don't care if my back hurts and my side throbs and my entire body aches from that beating I took. All my attention is focused on pleasing her. The only thing that matters is her.

I pull her even closer, then I stab my tongue inside her wet channel.

13

Vivian

I cry out, try to grab hold of the short strands of his hair, and when my fingers slip, hold onto his head, as he flicks his tongue in and out of my pussy.

What's he doing to me? How can I let him suck and lick and slurp on my core like it's the tastiest dessert he's ever eaten?

I'd been worried about people seeing me, but the heaven of his tongue inside my weeping slit overpowers my inhibitions. Who cares who sees us, all I want is for him to continue what he's doing.

I dig my knees into the back of the car-seat, and the reason I'm able to balance myself here is because he's holding me up, with seemingly no effort. He keeps going, without a break.

He drags his tongue up my cunt, then around the swollen nub of my clit, and I'm ashamed to say that's all I need to feel the first stirring of my climax. My orgasm shivers up my thighs, around my core, swells up my spine.

"Oh, god, Q." I throw my head back.

He thrusts his tongue inside my slit and twists it. That sends me over the edge. I cry out. The orgasm bursts through me, water gushing through a dam, overflowing the banks of a river, pouring down a waterfall. Sparks fire behind my eyes, goosebumps pop on my skin.

And still, he continues licking at me. He's scooping up my cum, and only when I slump, does he slide me down and into his lap. The curve of my hip bumps into the steering wheel but there's enough space for me to coil into his chest. I breathe for a moment and listen to his heartbeat. I savor the comfort of his arms around me as I recover from the orgasm. As I come back into myself, I become aware of the pressing hardness at his crotch, which throbs against my butt. "You're aroused."

"I'm always aroused when I'm near you." He chuckles. The sound vibrates against his massive chest and sinks into my blood, and it's strangely comforting and also, a turn on.

"Q..." I open my eyelids and look up into his. "What's happening between us?"

"Nothing we don't want to."

"But this... is all wrong." I look between his eyes. "Isn't it?"

"It's as wrong as we make it out to be. Or as right."

"You're Felix's father."

"I'm aware."

"And I'm his —"

"Ex-girlfriend."

"Who he almost married."

"Do you love him, Raven?" His gaze grows intent. "Do you?"

I look away, then shake my head.

"Did you ever love him?"

I shake my head again.

"So why did you agree to marry him?"

"I thought I'd save money if I could share a flat with him, enough to take care of my sister and my father—" I blow out a breath. "I know... My reasoning was flawed. I realized that the moment I was more relieved than disappointed that he didn't turn up for the wedding. But when he proposed..." I shake my head. "At that time, I... I didn't want to turn him down, because what if no one else found me attractive enough to propose to me again?"

"You agreed to marry him because you were scared of ending up alone?" He scowls.

"People marry for less." I'm sounding defensive, probably because he's right, but I'm not going to admit it.

"You're not *people*." He notches his knuckles under my chin, forcing me to look up into his face. "You're the most beautiful woman I've ever seen, and you deserve everything. You deserve all your dreams to come true."

I laugh. "You don't know me."

"I know enough."

"In only a few days?" I scoff.

"I know you're generous and kind. That you'd sacrifice your happiness if it means you can take care of your family."

"And you'd sacrifice your son's happiness by marrying me?"

His features close. A hardness creeps into his eyes. I curse myself. *Why did I have to say that?* But we can't tip toe around this thing that stands between us. *Can we?*

I press my palm into his chest for leverage and begin to move away. He winces. I pull my hand away and take in the blood stain on his T-shirt.

Oh no! I was so distracted by the chemistry between us that I forgot how hurt he was. "You should see a doctor."

"I don't need a doctor," he says in a dismissive tone.

"You took a lot of hits."

"And I survived," he scoffs.

"Why didn't you fight back?"

"I did."

"Not when I arrived at the fight. You were getting beaten up and making no move to defend yourself."

His features close even more. He grips my waist and lifts me over the console and back into my seat. The fact he can maneuver my body any way he wants means he can also do so to put distance between us when he wants. But I'm not giving up yet.

"When I yelled your name, you seemed to come to your senses and decide to fight back."

His jaw clenches. A nerve pops at his temple. He squeezes those thick fingers around the steering wheel and stays silent. The tension in the car skyrockets. Sweat beads my forehead. His shoulders swell; those biceps stretch the sleeves of his shirt.

A buzzing sound cuts through the space. I reach down and snatch my cross-body bag and slide my phone from it. I notice the missed calls —five of them, all from Zoey. She and I exchanged phone numbers before she left my place yesterday. Now, a message pops up on the screen.

Zoey: OMG. OMG. Are you okay?

Me: I think so

The phone buzzes with an incoming call from her. I decline it.

Me: I'm fine... Honest

Zoey: Are you with him? It seemed so intense between the two of you, I thought it best to leave. Are you sure you're okay? *Eggplant emoji. Sweat emoji. Hot face emoji.* I can come and get you wherever you are

Me: *Laughing face emoji. Rain emoji.* No, don't worry. I'm good. I promise. I'll call you later

I slide the phone back into my bag. "That was Zoey."

He doesn't reply.

"*Your* friend Zoey. She came to see me yesterday. With Summer. That's how I found out about the fight, in case you were wondering."

He stays silent.

"They're good people. I like them."

Some of the tension goes out of his shoulders. He angles his head in my direction. "I hope you don't mind I asked them to check on you and gave them your address."

I shake my head. "I don't. It was interesting to talk to them. They're lovely and so genuine. I enjoyed meeting them. It must be nice to have a circle of friends you're close to." A hint of wistfulness slips through my tone, and I cringe. That was unintentional. Enough with the woeful Orphan Annie act already. But once more, Q doesn't seem to notice.

"I met Summer's husband Sinclair during a work meeting, and we hit it off so well, he introduced me to Summer. She, in turn, introduced me to her sister Karma, Karma's husband Michael, and Zoey."

"She mentioned." I nod.

"When I returned from the Marines, I didn't have many friends left in London. My military buddies are from around the country. But thanks to Sinclair, I found a circle of people I get along with."

"You have your family," I point out.

He barks out a laugh. "You saw how Ryot and I fought. My family isn't known for their ability to forgive or forget," he says in a wry tone.

Seeing the opening, I have to take it. So I ask, "What... What happened between you and Ryot?"

Instantly, his features shutter. Guess it was too soon for me to ask that question.

He starts his car, does a U-turn and drives out of the parking lot.

I pull up my panties and set my clothes right. We drive in silence for a few minutes. I glance sideways at the cut on his forehead where the blood has dried. "You really need to see a doctor," I insist.

He falls silent once more and doesn't say a word for the rest of the half-hour drive. When we reach my apartment block, I turn to him. "Please, Q, come inside so I can, at least, clean your wounds."

He hesitates, then nods. He turns off the engine, engages the hand-brake, then gets out of the car. By then, I'm standing on the sidewalk. He follows me toward the main door, which I push open, then scowls. "There's no lock on this door?"

14

Vivian

"I have a lock on the door to the apartment," I demur.

He follows me up the stairs, which creak. The scent of food lingers in the corridor. The sound of a woman yelling reaches us as we pass the apartment on the second floor. We reach the third floor, and I fit the key into the lock and push it open. I walk in, and Q follows me. I drop my handbag on the breakfast counter and turn to find him surveying the paintings I've stacked against the wall.

He walks over to them, begins to peruse them, and it feels like he's touching my body. I didn't feel this exposed when Zoey looked at them. I wasn't worried she was cataloging my soul the way Q is.

My paintings are personal; each of them contains a bit of my soul, but not everyone can see that. I'm afraid he's one of those who can. He continues to glance through them, and when he doesn't say anything, I bite the inside of my cheek. *Don't say it, don't say it...* "What do you think?" I blurt out.

Without replying, he continues to survey the canvasses. When he's done with the last one, he turns to me. He gives my words careful consideration then nods. "They have potential."

I blink, wait, but he doesn't say anything more.

"That's it?" I stare. "That's all you have to say?"

"I'm no expert, but there are flashes of brilliance in what you've done. I think you could be better. In fact, I'm sure you'll get better the more you paint."

Why do I feel so deflated that he didn't effusively praise my work? I should appreciate his honesty. Especially since he's right. And his observation cut straight to the crux of what's been bothering me. Time. I need to carve out more time to paint.

The more you express yourself, the better you get. That's all there is to it. Again, he's right. And now, I am more pissed-off, both at him and myself. Why does he *always* have to be right? Is it because he's older than me and has more experience? Why does that make *me* feel unsophisticated? Ugh. I spin around and head to the bathroom, with him at my heels.

By the time I retrieve the first aid kit from the shelf below the sink and turn to him, he's perched at the edge of the tub. I grab the roll of cotton and the antiseptic. I wet a clean washcloth with hot water from the tap and walk over to him.

"Take it off," I nod toward his blood splattered T-shirt.

Only when the words are out do I realize how suggestive they sound. He notices it, too, for his eyes gleam. "Bossing me around, Raven?"

"And if I am?" I tip up my chin.

Our gazes connect again and I'm sure he's going to tell me off for taking the lead, but he must be more hurt than I realized for he doesn't protest further.

He pulls off his T-shirt, and I gasp. The area around his ribs has turned a mottled-green. Blood oozes from the wound. He must have been in pain all this time, but the ease with which he carried me... I never would've guessed.

Without meeting his eyes, I step between his legs. When I touch the cloth to his wound, the muscles bunch under his skin. And when I begin to clean the wound, he exhales sharply.

"Sorry, I... Did I hurt you?"

I look into his face to find blue fire in his gaze. The muscles at his jaw flex, and I know he's grinding his teeth.

"Are... Are you okay?"

"Just get on with it." His voice is terse.

Oh God, it must be hurting him more than I realized. I increase my pace, while also trying to be gentle. I dab the cloth around the edges of his wound, and he flinches. When he doesn't pull away, I continue to soak up the blood with the cloth. I lean in closer to get a better look, and his breath ghosts over my cheek. I shiver. My hair brushes over his torn skin, and he groans.

"Oh, shoot. Sorry, sorry, I'm going as fast as I can."

My hand slips, and his entire body jolts.

"Ugh, I'm such a klutz." I blow on the wound, and a low groan rumbles up his chest. Instantly, I'm wet. My nipples peak. *Shit, shit, shit.* The man is in pain, and I'm worried about him, but touching him, taking care of him, being this close to him, and knowing he's just as affected by my nearness spikes the air between us with an eroticism that escalates the level of horniness I feel to thermonuclear levels.

I follow the cuts and bruises to one that dips under the waistband of his jeans. It feels right to be on my knees in front of him, so I sink down, my skin on the cool tile the only thing keeping me from overheating as I run the washcloth across his torso. The noise he makes thrills me. I want him to make it again and again.

I slide the cloth under the waistband, and he swears. His thigh muscles ripple like there are waves trapped under his skin. Also, there's a boat between his legs. No, make that a cruise ship as big as the titanic, after it hit the iceberg and is now sinking in a vertical fashion. He's aroused, and it's because I'm touching him. Exhilaration dampens the triangle between my legs further. A giddy sense of power courses under my skin. That... that... thing at his crotch is nothing to sneeze about. If he... If he puts it inside me... Assuming it fits, I'm sure to feel it at the backs of my eyes. My pussy begins to weep.

The sound of him clearing his throat cuts through my reverie. Heat sears my cheeks.

"Are you done?" His voice is like gravel.

"Almost." I jump up to my feet, then raise the washcloth to pat at the cut on his forehead. This, of course, puts my face in front of his, my lips in front of his. Our noses almost bump. Our eyelids almost tangle. I'm aware of his gaze scalding me, but I don't dare look at him. A cloud of heat spools off his big body and tightens around me. Sweat beads my upper lip. His breath singes my cheek, and I almost moan. It feels like I'm touching a predator that, at any moment, might open its mouth and consume me whole. And oh God, I'd like that so much. I swallow hard, then I incline my head to get a better angle; his nose brushes my neck.

Goosebumps sprout on my skin. He takes a deep breath and I freeze.

"Did you sniff me?" I whisper.

"Fucking roses." His voice has dropped a few octaves. "Why do you always smell of roses?"

"M-my... body wash."

He makes a strained noise at the back of his throat. Then, he slides his hand between us and adjusts himself.

"Are you... Are you... aroused?" I squeak.

"You're standing between my legs with your tits pushed into my chest, and I can feel your bullet-shaped nipples straining to tear through your blouse and stabbing into my skin, so forgive me for not being very disciplined," he growls.

"My boobs are not—" I glance down to find my ample bosom is, indeed, squashed against the planes of his chest. I was so caught up in cleaning his wound, I didn't notice. Or maybe I did and didn't pull back because I wanted to be a brat and provoke him into reacting. Maybe it's because being able to provoke a reaction from him, knowing how affected he is by my nearness excites me even more?

I jump back and toss the washcloth into the sink. Then, snatch the antiseptic spray and hold it by his forehead with the nozzle pointed at the wound, my hand cupped around his eye to protect it from overspray. "Ready?"

When he doesn't reply, I squeeze down on the nozzle. A hiss of air escapes from between his lips.

"Oh, my god, did that hurt? Should I blow on it and make it better?"

I rise up on my tiptoes to do that, and he snaps, "Don't." Then he clears his throat. "I mean, there's no need to do that."

The brat in me makes me say, "No, really, it's okay. It'll make it better." I blow on his forehead, then do it again.

He stays perfectly still. Doesn't make a sound. I look down to find his gaze is fixed on my cleavage. A nerve pops at his temple. His fingers are curled into fists at his side. The tendons on his throat stand out in relief. A chuckle wells up, but I manage not to laugh. It feels good to hold the power, for once.

"Are. You. Done?" He bites out the words.

"Almost." I lower back to my heels, then mop up the blood from the wounds on his side. With the blood wiped off, the wounds are not as deep as I'd anticipated. His chest planes ripple. He grunts, but there's no other reaction from him.

I resist the urge to roll my eyes. "It's okay if you want to groan or cry out. It won't take away from your macho-ness."

I look up to find he's watching me with an intense look in his blue eyes. The kind that makes me feel he's gleaned all of my secrets.

"Is this your way of getting back at me because you weren't happy with my answer about your paintings?" He arches an eyebrow.

"What? Of course not. I would never—"

His lips quirk.

I scoff. "I walked into that one."

"You did," he agrees.

I set the antiseptic spray aside and grab a few bandages. I begin to dress the wound on his forehead, but he wraps his thick fingers around my wrist. "There's no need for that."

"It's either that, or I take you to the emergency room." I meet his gaze with a challenge in my eyes.

He searches my features, and one side of his mouth quirks. "Enjoying being in charge?"

"I have no idea what you're talking about." I flutter my eyelashes at him.

"You'll pay for that, you know?" he says in a mild tone.

The goosebumps on my skin transform into heart-eye emojis. *I'm counting on it.* Outwardly, I toss my head and tease, "I'm sooo scared."

A sly look comes into his eyes. "I hope so. I always follow through on my promises, baby."

Ooh, why does him calling me baby, feel both tender and erotic, and so, so, hot?

"So do I, *baby*." I lean in close enough that our mouths almost brush.

Then he swears, "Fuck."

"That, too, *baby*."

Both of us glance down to where I've slapped the sterile gauze over a wound on his chest—this one, right over his heart. Symbolic? Maybe.

Perhaps that thought crossed his mind, too, for we both fall silent. Then I step back and finish dressing his wounds.

"There, all done." I begin to move away, but he stops me with a hand on my hip. It's a proprietary grip. The kind that conveys he feels owner-ship over me. The kind I feel all the way to my toes.

When I raise my gaze to his, his eyes are heavy with lust, but his expression is one of tenderness. "Thank you." The tendons of his throat move as he swallows.

"You're welcome," I whisper.

He draws in a slow breath. "Ryot thinks I'm responsible for his wife being killed in action." He takes the roll of bandage from my grasp and sets it on the counter.

"What?" I gasp. "What do you mean?"

"Ryot's wife was on my team. I sent them on a mission that was compromised. I had to make a snap decision which ended with her being killed. They never found her body."

"Oh, my god." I press my knuckles into my mouth. "I'm so sorry, Q."

The band around my ribcage tightens. I forget, sometimes, that as a Marine, he's seen death up-close. It's a word that's not part of my daily parlance, like it would have been for him.

It brings home, once again, how much more of the world he's seen.

"I'll never forgive myself for what happened." He lowers his chin to his chest. His eyes are bleak. There's a coldness to his demeanor that signals he's withdrawing into himself. I can't let that happen. Not when he's begun to open up.

"But she was a soldier, too. She had to know it was a possibility that she might not return from the assignment."

He tilts his head.

"And surely, Ryot must know that when you run missions, the chance of losing your life is high."

"It's why there are checks and balances in place. We've managed to bring down the chances of losing someone on a mission. It's rare that it happens."

"But it *does* happen?"

He jerks his chin.

"And you go in, knowing there's a chance you won't return?" *Why is it so important that he believe me? Why am I trying to get him to go easier on himself?* I don't want to examine the answer to that too closely.

His features twist. "Tell that to their families."

I take in the tortured expression on his face, and my heart squeezes in empathy. "It must be difficult for you to go on, knowing you played a role in what happened," I offer.

He looks at me with an expression of surprise on his features.

"I imagine it was also trickier because she was Ryot's wife. She was family."

He winces, then squeezes the bridge of his nose. "I knew, when I gave the order, that I was sealing her fate, and that of her teammates, but I couldn't hesitate. It was either their lives or those of the many thousands of civilians back home. It was supposed to be a straightforward mission. Only, they were ambushed." His voice turns hoarse, as if it's physically painful to relive what happened. "They were taken to the headquarters of the terrorists. We knew the leader of the insurgents was there. They were confident we wouldn't take them out, as long as they had some of our team"—he swallows—"so I... I... "

"You had to capitalize on the element of surprise and take them out."

My voice seems to cut through his thoughts. He opens his eyes and stares at me. "I've never told anyone the entire story." He seems taken aback. Frankly, so am I. I hadn't expected him to share that with me.

"It must have taken a lot of courage to give the order."

He straightens his shoulders. "I knew what had to be done. I knew it would hurt Ryot and, likely, destroy my relationship with him, but I did it anyway. And you know what? Faced with the same choice, I'd do it all over again. It was the right thing to do. That was my role. My job. To fight for the safety of those back home. I had to do what was needed, regardless of the repercussions." He says the last few words with a touch of defiance. There's a challenging look on his face.

Does he expect me to run screaming because he revealed himself as someone who gave the order that killed people, including those within his own family? Does he expect me to... turn down his proposal? I shake my head. That makes no sense, unless... He's testing me? I thought I was pushing him to reveal his secrets. Turns out, he was pushing me, as well.

"I understand why you did it," I declare.

"You do, huh?" His tone is disbelieving.

"You did your duty. You were put in a position where you had to make tough decisions. The kind that could rip you of your humanity. Yet, you didn't back down. You didn't blink. You made that choice, to bear the repercussions of your actions, so people like me could sleep peacefully in our beds at night."

He searches my face, and must see something that reassures him, for his shoulders relax the tiniest fraction, "Thank you for understanding." He clears his throat. "That's the first time I've spoken to someone about it."

"Thank you for sharing, it couldn't have been easy for you to do that."

Our gazes meet, and hold. That old tension between us is back, with an added intimacy. Because he's had his tongue inside me. He knows how I taste, how I cry when I come. The air grows thick with unspoken emotions. The way he's looking at me, I'm sure he's going to close the distance between us and kiss me, and I wouldn't be able to stop myself from responding. Again. I need a little more time to process my feelings toward him. To understand why my body wants to obey his commands.

"So, that's why you were letting yourself get beaten up by Ryot? You thought you deserved it? You were trying to give him a chance at payback?"

He rubs the back of his neck. "Guilty as charged."

"But you didn't lose the fight," I point out.

"I didn't." He shakes his head. "I heard your voice urging me to fight. Turns out, I couldn't let myself lose and lose face, not when my girl was in the crowd watching."

A warmth pools in my chest... and also in between my legs. Oh, my god. That is the sexiest thing anyone has ever said to me. Do I have that much power over him? It's heady, and I like it. "Your girl, huh?" I murmur.

"Am I wrong in calling you that?" His voice drops an octave, taking on that hard edge which instantly sends liquid heat shooting through my veins.

"Let's not get ahead of ourselves, considering I'm still not sure if I like you." I sniff. *What a liar you are. Just because you say aloud that you don't like him doesn't make it true. Also, you don't sound convincing at all.*

"You don't like me?" He smirks. And of course, he called me out. Can't get anything past this guy, can I?

"No, I don't." I tip up my chin. I have no choice but to continue this pretense, which neither of us believes in the slightest.

His grin widens. "That's not the impression I got when you were wailing my name in my car earlier."

Once more, I flush to roots of my hair. "I... I wasn't wailing," I sputter.

"Funny, it sounded like you were positively screaming in pleasure."

I huff. "It's not gentlemanly reminding me of that."

"But I'm not a gentleman. In fact"—he leans in close enough for our noses to almost bump—"I'm sure you don't want a gentleman, do you?"

I swallow.

"You like the idea of a bad boy."

My lips part, and air whistles out between my teeth.

He nods. "Ah, yes. Look at you, being excited. Do you like the idea of being disciplined? Do you want to be punished when you're bratty?"

My stomach clenches. My pussy squeezes in on itself. My ass twinges from the memory of how it felt to be spanked by him. I cannot seriously be turned on by his dirty talking. Oh, but I am. I am so wet. And so horny. *Oh, god.* My nipples tighten, a pulse flares to life between my legs.

"Do you, Raven?" He stares into my eyes, and there's no escaping the desire in his. Or the way his chest seems to expand, and his shoulders grow bigger or— I risk lowering my gaze to his crotch and find it impressively tented. My entire body turns into one big throbbing ache.

"Don't you want to be with someone who knows exactly how to wring orgasms from you?"

Oh, my god. He said the O word. Why did he say the O word? I squeeze my thighs together, all thoughts of hiding my body's reaction gone from my mind. I want... relief from this gnawing, aching sensation that's clawing between my legs.

His breath sears my cheek. His masculine scent is so strong it feels like I'm bathing in it.

"I can do that for you, Raven. I can touch and suck and lick every inch of you."

My nipples pebble. My toes curl.

"I can take charge of your orgasms. I can eat out your pussy every night and make you come over and over again until you can't walk straight."

My scalp tingles. My breath comes in pants.

"This will be our secret."

I shiver.

"I can pleasure you, and take care of you, and show you how good it can be when you give in to those dark needs inside of you. Question is"— he searches my eyes— "do you want to?"

15

Quentin

Her pupils dilate, color smears her features, her neck, the creamy skin of her décolletage. Her lips are slightly parted, her eyes hazy with lust.

I tighten my hold on her waist. I'm this close to throwing her down on the bathroom floor and having her right here, but that would be all wrong. I've never wanted a woman as much as I want her. Nothing could have stopped me from walking up that aisle and proposing to her. Not when everything in my body had been pulled to her. It was a visceral reaction, a connection which has only grown stronger since.

Question is, does she feel the same way?

"Do you always say what's on your mind?" she asks, then shakes her head. "No, don't answer that." She tugs at her hand; I let her go.

She doesn't want to answer my earlier questions. That's okay. I can wait until she tells me she's ready to explore this part of our relationship further.

I reach for my T-shirt and am about to shrug it on when she nods toward it, "let me at least wash it and dry it for you first."

I scoff, "It's only blood and my own blood at that. Unless—" I shoot her a sly glance, "— unless the real reason you want me to keep my T-shirt off is because you want to keep admiring my abs?" I say it to get a rise out of her and she doesn't disappoint me.

"Whatever, be macho and wear the T-shirt stained with *your own* blood," she flounces off.

I allow myself a low laugh. Seeing her all riled up and shoot arrows at me with those gorgeous flashing eyes of hers is my favorite past time. I could get used to it. In fact, I very much want to be the recipient of all her emotions throughout the day. I rise to my feet. "Move in with me."

"What?" She pauses halfway to heading out of the bathroom.

"I noticed you were packing your things."

"So?"

"Clearly, you share this place with Felix and can't stay here." I brush past her into the bedroom, then glare meaningfully at the pile of men's clothes folded on a chair in the corner. No way was that my son's doing. "You do his laundry?" My jaw tightens.

She follows me in and wrings her hands. "Uh, sometimes."

Which means she *always* does it for him.

I drag my fingers through my hair. I know my son hasn't picked up after himself a day in his life. Which is my fault. I wasn't around long enough to discipline him. I wasn't there to help him set boundaries or help him self-regulate. I stayed away and let my aunt deal with him. And while she tried, she never managed to be strict with him. The result? Felix got away with a lot. By the time I realized what was happening, he'd already grown into a teenager. That's when I tried to be home more often. I tried to correct his behavior but that didn't help. In fact, it often made things worse. I stopped trying after a while, preferring to keep the peace.

"You have to move in with me sometime. Why not now?" I throw out casually.

"Hold on." She throws up her hand. "I don't recall agreeing to marry you."

"But you want to." I infuse authority into my voice. "You're stopping yourself from following your instinct, so let me tell you again that you don't have a choice."

Her pupils dilate. Her cheeks flush. Then she shakes her head, walks to the window and stares out. "It's not fair that you can back me into a corner like this. It's not fair that you have the money and—"

"—and you need money, while I need a wife to ensure I get my inheritance from my father. We can help each other, Raven."

She turns to face me. "It… it's not right."

"It's everything that is right. The chemistry between us confirms to my family that our relationship is not a farce."

"But it is," she spits out.

"No one seeing us together will ever doubt that there's a connection between us; not even Felix." At once, her features pale. *Fuck, I shouldn't have mentioned my son's name.* I move toward her, but she stiffens. I slow to a stop.

"Move in with me. Give us a chance to get to know each other, while we work out the details of the wedding."

"How can I, knowing it's going to hurt Felix?"

"I'll... talk to him. I'll ensure he gives us his blessings."

"You'd do that?" She frowns.

"I'll call him tomorrow." The idea makes my stomach drop, but that's okay. I am a man, and more than that, I am his father. I owe him this. "I want him to come to our wedding. I want to make sure I make peace with my son. If there's anything I've learned in the last few years, it's that life is short. And I intend to make up for my past misdeeds with my son."

"Are you sure he'll listen to you?"

That twisting sensation in my stomach intensifies. "I'm not sure, but I have to try."

"And how do you plan on doing that?" Her brow furrows. "I saw how he looked at you. How the two of you spoke to each other. He doesn't like you."

"He hates me" — I raise a shoulder — "but that's a start."

"What do you mean?"

"If he were indifferent toward me, I'd worry. The fact that he's not, shows he harbors some feelings for me. So, maybe they're negative. It gives me something to build on. It's better than having nothing to go on."

"Are you always this confident?" She half smiles.

"The only thing I'm confident of is that our marriage —"

"Fake marriage."

"—will be beneficial for both of us. And it won't be fake once we consummate it."

Blotches of color flare on her cheeks. "Do you have to bring every-thing back to sex?"

"When its such a strong link between us? Yes. I want you and you want me. It gives us a good base to build on."

"There it is. That arrogant, dominant, overbearing, highly inflated ego of yours, which is never far from making its presence known."

I shrug. "I don't hide what I am."

"Some of us haven't had that privilege. Some of us have had to fight our natural instincts so we can do what is right."

"There is a thin line between right and wrong; no one knows it better than me. I—"

The door to the apartment opens. She glances past me, and the way her gaze widens, I know who it is before I turn.

16

Vivian

I brush past Quentin and head toward his son.

Funny how I already think of Felix as Q's son and not as my ex. His shoulders are squared, he's pushed out his chest, and his jaw is set. He's almost as tall as Q and while he isn't as built, his wiriness has a certain appeal. He scowls at me, an accusing look in his eyes.

My steps slow. I begin to wring my fingers, then stop myself. He has no right to make me feel guilty about being seen with his father. He dumped me, so I can be with anyone I choose to be.

"Felix..." I put my hand on his arm; he shakes it off.

"Felix, listen to me, please." As I say it, I wonder why I'm the one begging him to listen now. If it were anyone else, I wouldn't bother. He left me at the altar, not the other way around. And yet, I feel guilty.

He continues to glower, first at me, then at Q. The band around my chest tightens. There's so much animosity in the room, it's making it difficult to breathe.

I don't need to look over my shoulder to know Quentin must be glaring right back at him. Neither of them is going to give an inch.

My cheeks heat. How embarrassing to be caught between father and son. I do not appreciate this being thrust upon me, at all.

"Felix, please." This time, when I touch him, he grabs my arm. I'm so shocked, before I realize it, he's pulled me into him.

There's a sinewy strength to his frame which helps him hold me in place. Not that I try very hard to escape. Mainly because I'm taken aback. Felix has never acted this... aggressive, this commanding.

And maybe, a part of me wants to see what Quentin will do when Felix presses his lips to mine. Perhaps, it's that curiosity which makes me stand without protesting and allow Felix to slant his mouth over mine.

The next second, he's pulled away from me. Quentin plants his bulk between us.

With his back to me, he pushes his finger into Felix's chest. "Back off."

I peer around Q in time to see Felix peel back his lips. "You don't get to tell me what to do."

"In this case, I do. She's my fiancée."

"I don't see a ring," Felix snarls.

"Easily rectified."

"Hold on, don't I get a say in this?"

How dare they talk about me as if I'm not standing in front of them? How dare Q, once again, make decisions for me without consulting me? How dare the two of them ignore me and focus on their stupid oneupmanship?

"She was my fiancée before she was yours." Felix's jaw flexes with anger.

"She's mine now," Quentin says in a low, hard voice.

Jesus Christ! Did he just say that? How dare he. And why am I unable to stop the tremor of excitement fluttering in my lower belly? Why is it that he has to say the 'mine' word and I'm ready to do anything for him?

I manage to get a grip on my emotions. I don't care how my body reacts to Q's overprotectiveness. I need to be a part of this discussion. I am the one who has a say over my destiny. No one, no man, not even one as macho and as dominant as Q, can make decisions on my behalf.

"She belonged to me," Felix declares.

"Too late. She belongs to me now," Quentin growls.

"Hey!" I put my fingers to my lips and whistle. It cuts through the tension between them. Both men look down at me. Felix blinks. Quentin scowls.

"Let me make one thing clear. I belong to myself."

"But..." Felix frowns.

"Raven—" Quentin begins.

I shake my head. "No, both of you need to listen to me. You cannot fight like this, and definitely not over me. Felix,"—I turn to him—"you broke up with me at the altar, with a text message sent to your best man."

Felix reddens, but he stays silent.

"As for you, Quentin—"

The furrow between his eyebrows deepens. No doubt, it's because I called him Quentin, and he wants me to call him Q. But this is my bid to hold onto what shreds of dignity I have left in this farce, so I'm not giving him the satisfaction of knowing I do think of him as Q in my mind. "—you don't know me, yet you proposed, knowing it'd put me on the spot. Knowing—"

"You couldn't say no," he completes my statement.

"—it's the worst kind of situation to go from wanting to marry the son to the father."

"Does it bother you what people think of you?" He inclines his head.

"Wow, just wow!" I slap my palms on my waist. "Way to minimize the issue, Q."

He flushes a little, then holds up a hand. "I apologize if you felt belittled in any way. I also apologize that Felix and I spoke around you. That was wrong of us."

"You think?" I huff. Some of the anger inside me nevertheless fades at his words.

He glares at Felix, who's watching our exchange with a look of disbelief.

"Felix?" he prompts.

Felix continues to stare at us.

"Aren't you forgetting something?" Q growls.

"What?" Felix shakes his head. "Uh, yeah"—he clears his throat—"sorry about that." He shifts his weight from foot to foot as if he wishes he were somewhere else.

It's a lame expression of regret, but whatever. "Apology accepted," I say in a cool tone.

Felix flushes further. He hunches his thin shoulders, then lets his gaze slide away. The tension in the room builds again.

Q clears his throat, drawing my attention back to him.

"For what it's worth, it was a genuine question," he offers.

"The desire to present a favorable image to others is thought to be a universal human motivation across cultures." The words are out before I can stop them.

Q seems taken aback, then his eyes gleam.

He doesn't seem annoyed by my penchant for spouting weird facts when I'm nervous. In fact, he seems to enjoy my ramblings. I pretend not to notice the appreciative edge to his features.

"Unlike you, I have to live among them. I don't have the money to put up a cushion between myself and what people are gossiping about me." I wrap my arms about my waist.

"They only have to see us together to know what we have is real," Q counters.

"Did you two already sleep together?" Felix's gaze widens.

And when I blush, he takes a physical step back like he can't bear to be in my vicinity.

"We didn't sleep together," I insist.

"We almost did," Q confirms in the same breath.

Felix looks between us, and an ugly expression twists his features. He stabs a finger in my direction. "You spread your legs for *him*? You—"

Quentin slaps him.

Felix gasps. His eyes grow bigger. He stares at Q, then anger suffuses Felix's features. He takes a step forward, then curls his fingers into a fist and buries it in Q's side.

I cry out, "Felix, stop!"

17

Quentin

It's because my ribs are already bruised, but when Felix slams his fist into my side, I grunt. Pain spikes across my nerve-endings. I feel the skin tear open further, and blood begins to drip down my side. He follows it up with an upper cut, which I don't avoid. I'm not going to hit my son — though, considering I already slapped him; the point is probably moot. But what I did was wrong. He's a grown-up, an adult... And I shouldn't have insulted him like that.

But I'm not going to fight with my son, especially knowing I'm stronger than him and could seriously injure him.

The fact I'm not defending myself seems to anger Felix further. He sets his jaw; his eyes flash. Then he pulls back his fist and lets it fly. The angle is such, I know it's going to connect with my jaw. I brace for it, but at the last moment, Raven slams into him with all her weight.

His fist whistles by my ear, the breeze cool on my sweat drenched skin.

"Stop it." She shoves at his shoulder. "Stop it right now."

Felix shakes his head, then he looks between us. He opens his mouth, as if to speak, then shakes his head again and stomps away.

Her features fall. She begins to go after him, but I curl my fingers around her bicep. "Let him cool off."

"But—"

Felix tears open the door, barrels through it and slams it behind him. The crash resounds around the apartment.

Her shoulders droop. "This is not good."

She's right. "I was wrong in raising my hand on him, but"—I jut out my chin—"he insulted you. He shouldn't have done that." I release her and drag my palm over the short bristles on my scalp. "It's my fault he's angry. My fault he grew up feeling abandoned. I wasn't there for him when he needed me most. I was too busy pursuing my own career. I put my interests before his. I might have made sure he didn't want for material things, but emotionally, I was unavailable to my own son."

She purses her lips. "And his mother?"

I feel that old resentment rising to the surface, feel my defensive walls going up again. "I don't want to talk about her."

Her features crumple. The light goes out of her eyes, and goddamn, if I don't feel like the worst person alive for doing that to her. She turns and begins to walk into the bedroom, but I stop her with a hand on her shoulder. "I'm sorry, that came out way harsher than I intended."

"That's okay. We're almost strangers and this whatever-it-is between us is all based on lies." She stares straight ahead. "I shouldn't have asked that question."

"You should have absolutely asked that question, and I know how your cunt tastes, so we're not strangers. Besides, nothing between us is lies."

She draws in a sharp breath, and when I walk around to stand in front of her, I see the red blotches on her cheeks. "You're filthy."

"And you like it." I take in the feverish look in her eyes, and I know I'm right.

"Can you not constantly refer to my—"

"Pussy?"

She squeezes her eyes shut. "Yes, that. Can you not bring that part of me into every conversation."

"How can I not when I can smell the scent of your arousal, and taste the honey of your cum, and see how your nipples are outlined against your blouse?"

Her eyelids snap open. Her pupils are dilated. The pulse at the base of her throat kicks up in speed. If I were to touch her now, she'd come in a heartbeat. No matter what other issues are between us, when it comes to our bodies, there's a bond that neither of us needs to fake. I understand her on a primal level, and she can't help but respond to my demands. We understand each other's unspoken cues. We were drawn to each other from the moment we met. I know how to make her scream and she... can reduce me to putty. She has so much power over me. Good thing she doesn't know it yet.

I'm not stupid enough to think I deserve her, but... I also owe it to myself to convince her that I'm right for her. It's that which makes me fold to my knees in front of her.

Her lips part. A look of surprise is on her face, which turns to lust when I run my hands up her calves, then continue up the backs of her legs, lifting her skirt with the momentum. I squeeze her ample butt cheeks, move up further, then move my hands over her hips and across her lower belly, working my way back down the front to her inner thighs. I go slowly, very slowly, giving her every opportunity to back away or stop me, but she does neither. Instead, she swallows, then parts her legs further, giving me better access. I slip my hand up and under the seam of her wet panties, and when I brush up against her slit, she shudders. And when I stuff three fingers inside her, she cries out and grabs at my head.

She tries to pull at my hair, but since I have a military-style crew cut, it means her nails scrabble across my scalp. A flash of pain stabs my neck. It clears my mind further. Turns my already rigid muscles to granite. My senses sharpen; my vision tunnels.

This... This is why I was put on this earth, to make this goddess come. To keep her happy and fulfilled and satisfied and ensure she's never goes a few hours without an orgasm.

I pull aside her panties with my other hand, then slide my palm around to cup her butt, both to stabilize her and so I can feel the give of her flesh. She's not skinny, my Raven; she's exactly how I like her to be. Curvy, sensuous, and with enough jiggling bits I can hold on to as I ravish her.

I weave my fingers in and out of her, and she gasps. And when I press my thumb into the nub between her pussy lips, she throws back her head.

"Q, please, please, please," she chants.

"Do you want to come?"

She nods.

"Good, because I want you to spray that sweet cum of yours all over my face." I pull out my fingers and replace them with my tongue and lips.

I use both my hands to squeeze her butt cheeks and angle her so I can flick my tongue in and out of her, in and out.

She whimpers, moans, and wails. I note, she wails *again*. I store the sounds in my memory, knowing nothing has sounded more erotic to me than the sound of her helpless gallop toward her orgasm.

I keep my gaze on the curve of her neck, the way she writhes and moves her hips, meeting every thrust of my tongue. The way she pushes her cunt into my face, knowing I can satisfy this hunger within her. I eat her out, and slurp at her pussy lips, and when I squeeze apart her butt cheeks, she moans. When I play with her forbidden hole, she gasps.

Her eyelids flutter open, and she looks down at me, with my thumb inside her back channel and my tongue inside her cunt. She opens her mouth, but no sound comes out. All the better, for then, I close my mouth around her swollen clit, while releasing my hold on her butt long enough to stuff four fingers of my other hand inside her pussy. And when I twist those fingers and touch her G-spot while stuffing my thumb past the ring of muscle of her back hole to stimulate her A-spot, she cries out and orgasms.

The gush of cum from between her thighs flows into my mouth. I lick it up, tasting it and swallowing every last drop. And when she sways, I straighten her panties and her skirt, then rise to my feet and haul her up in my arms. I stalk toward the doorway, pausing to scoop up her handbag on the way out.

She manages to crack open her eyelids and look up into my face. "Where are you taking me?"

"Home." I kiss her forehead. "I'm taking you home."

18

Vivian

I should protest and say I want to stay here. But I can't. I don't want to face Felix again today, and I don't have anywhere else to go. I could stay with Zoey, but I don't want to impose on her. Which leaves me with... Q's place, as the most logical place to move into.

"This doesn't mean anything," I whisper.

"It means everything." He smirks.

When I squirm in protest, he tightens his arms about me. "Relax, Raven. You need a place to stay as you've, no doubt, concluded, and I have more than enough space for the both of us. Besides, you're going to marry me and move in with me, so why delay the inevitable?"

I slap at his chest, not caring when he winces. "Here I was thinking, perhaps, you're not all ego—"

"But I am." He shrugs.

"—you say something that confirms you're the most obnoxious man I've ever met."

"I'll take that as a compliment." He pulls open the door, despite the fact that he's also carrying me, maneuvers us both through the doorway, then shuts it behind him, all without losing hold on me. Is there no end to this man's talents?

I feel his chest planes flex and the muscles of his hard stomach coil as he descends the flight of steps to the main door. I wrap my arm about his neck and allow myself to admire the beauty of his visage from this angle. Not to mention, that musculature of his shoulders and the tendons of his neck, which stand out in relief. Every inch of this man invites me to touch, feel, lick, cuddle, and trace the dips and valleys of his physique.

"Why do you have to be so handsome?" I scowl.

"I was born this way."

For a second, I'm taken aback, then I burst out laughing. "I can't believe you said that."

He grins. "It may sound corny, but it's the truth." He hitches a shoulder. "I am charismatic enough to get my way, and it's not something I try to hide."

He carries me out the main door of my apartment building and places me in the passenger seat of his car, before dropping my handbag at my feet. Seriously, he remembered to grab my bag—he gets brownie points for that.

He comes around the car and slides into the driver's seat.

"You're so bossy and take charge and confident and self-assured and —" I search my mind for the right word and fail. I settle for, "I've never met anyone like you. It's overwhelming--"

"And you like it."

"I do." I nod. "More than I'd have thought possible. When you order me to do something, I shouldn't want to obey right away, but—"

"You want to."

I scowl at him. "Am I that easy to read?"

He smiles, and when he turns to me, there's a softness around his eyes. "Only for me. And only because you're submissive." He turns to look at me. "You're *my* submissive."

The possessiveness in his voice makes me shiver. His words resonate with that hidden part of me—the one only he seems to awaken. I nod slowly. "I am." It's a relief to have it out in the open. The tension I wasn't aware of holding in my muscles fades.

His eyebrows draw down. "When we get married, there'll be rules."

I don't bother pointing out that the 'when' was in error. What's the point? He'd ignore it anyway. My curiosity is piqued enough to ask, "What kind of rules?"

"These rules are for your safety. So you know what you're getting into with me."

"Okay?" I'm still not sure what he's talking about.

"I will reward you for being good. I will own your every orgasm. You cannot come without my permission. It's up to my discretion when I allow you to climax. Your body is mine. Your cunt is mine. All of your holes exist for my pleasure. Do you understand?"

My head reels from the impact of his words. My nipples are so tight, I'm sure they'll slice through my shirt. My cheeks are flushed, my breathing ragged. His words do not leave anything to the imagination — they never do — and it should come across as obscene, but the way he delivered them — without emotion, in a cold, clinical manner like a doctor laying down instructions that brook no argument — is so very arousing. And so puzzling. None of the passion-drenched poetry I've memorized, or the spicy romance novels I've read, or the porn videos have prepared me for the reality of this confident man telling me how he wants to possess me. And I find myself nodding in agreement.

"Do you, Raven?" he asks in a voice that's impatient.

"Yes." I duck my head.

"I didn't hear that."

"Yes." I jut out my chin. "I understand."

"If I were to bend you over the hood of the car and take your pussy, what would you say?"

Oh my god! My belly trembles. My toes curl. I'm so turned on I can barely choke out, "yes. I'd say, yes."

"Yes, sir," he prompts me.

"Yes sir," I whisper.

"Good girl." There's approval in his tone which elicits a fresh burst of arousal between my legs. There's a touch of relief in his eyes, which confuses me. Did he think I would say no? Doesn't he know, I *can't* say no to him. Does he know I trust him not to hurt me? Can he tell I know it's inevitable that I'll marry him, even though I haven't said it aloud?

He searches my features, then nods, as if satisfied with whatever he sees. Then he eases the vehicle onto the road.

"Wait, what about my clothes and my stuff I was packing?"

"I'll have it sent to my place."

"Oh." I suppose that saves me the effort of doing it. Besides, I don't want to head back to that apartment and risk running into Felix again. So

I nod, then reach for my handbag—and pulling out the key to the apartment, hold it out to him.

He looks at it then nods toward his jeans pocket. "Slip it in, will you?"

I hesitate, then slowly reach over the center console between the seats. He arches up his hips, not that it helps. His thigh muscles stretch the fabric of his jeans, so I have to struggle to slip the key inside the pocket. The whole time, I'm aware of the bulge between his legs. My throat goes dry. I tear my gaze away from his package and sink back into my seat.

"Seatbelt," he reminds me.

I comply and strap myself in as he joins the stream of traffic on the highway. We drive for half-an-hour in a silence that's companionable. My eyes are drooping by the time he turns off onto a smaller road. We're entering Primrose Hill; I recognize it by the street signs. Then he's driving up to a townhouse at the end of a street. It's set in a cul-de-sac, and when he switches off the engine, silence fills the space. Before I can open my door, he's out of the car. He comes around, opens my door for me, then once more hauls me into his arms.

"I can walk," I protest.

"Humor me."

He heads for the doorway to a Victorian style building. It's typical of the other houses on the street. There's greenery everywhere, manicured lawns, cars parked in front of the other houses. Behind the house I can see the rise of Primrose Hill in the distance. He keys in a password into the keypad set into the frame of the door. The latch releases, and he shoulders his way through. I've been here before, but it looks different without the tequila coloring my vision. He heads through a living room, past doors that lead out to a conservatory, and toward a staircase. "Can you give me the grand tour this time?"

"When you're awake."

"I am not ready to slee—" I yawn so loudly, my jaw cracks. Damn him. It must be the suggestion of sleep that's making me feel so drowsy. He heads up the stairs, then across a landing and into a room.

I take in the super-king-sized bed, and beyond it, a door that must lead to the ensuite. There's another double door next to it which must be the closet. There's a fireplace opposite the bed. In front of it are two armchairs. On either side of the fireplace are windows, beyond which I can see the rolling slope of Primrose Hill. On the wall next to the door through which we entered are bookshelves. They are filled from floor to ceiling with books, with one of those wonderful rolling ladders to reach the top. I am too far away to make out the lettering on the spines, but the books look well-thumbed. Unlike Felix, who hated to read.

The most overriding thought was that I needed to save money. Money Quentin has. But that's not the reason I'm allowing myself to consider his proposal.

It's the fact that I feel safe with him. That I've gone from not knowing him to trusting him, in very little time. I like his depth, how his experience has molded him. The hurt he carries at his core from whatever he saw when he was a Marine, his sticking to his duty, despite knowing he'd have to deal with the consequences, and not backing down from owning it. The regret he has about the impact of his actions on Ryot... Even the fact that he asked Felix to apologize for disregarding me... All of it paints the picture of a man who's complex and unique and very sexy.

And I can't deny that I love how he worships my body. How he can bring me to orgasm. Marrying him is no hardship.

So tell him now. Tell him yes. Tell him you've accepted his offer.

I open my mouth to say, "I'll marry you," and end up yawning again.

He places me on the bed, and I push my cheek into the pillow. "You should get some rest," he says as he pulls the duvet up to my chin.

"We need to talk," my voice is slurred.

"And we will, when you wake up. You've had a long day. Sleep well."

My eyelids flutter down. I sense a touch on my forehead. Did he kiss me? Sleep claims me before I can answer the question.

The next time I open my eyes, sunlight filters in through the window-panes. I am on my side and facing him.

He's asleep next to me. The covers are pulled up to his waist, and his chest is bare. The tattoo of the beating heart dripping blood feels so life-like. As for those triangular tattoos framing his torso? They feel lethal, like they could cut into me if I touched them. His dog tags rest in the crevice dividing his pectoral muscles. I follow the path down to the hair that disappears under the covers.

My fingers tingle. I want to reach out and follow that happy trail to where the covers tent over his crotch. A thousand little sparks flare to life under my skin. The valley between my thighs grows damp. All the mois-ture in my mouth seems to have been pulled down to the flesh between my legs. Something causes me to raise my gaze, and I find his eyes are open. He looks at me steadily, and those little sparks grow brighter. My belly flip-flops. The pulse at his temples picks up speed. He's as affected by my nearness as I am by his. I begin to inch closer when his phone begins to vibrate.

19

Quentin

My fingers twitch. I find myself leaning into her when the phone on the nightstand next to me buzzes. She jerks, the cocoon of sexual awareness we've been trapped in broken. I could ignore it and reach for her instead, but instinct has me stretching out my hand to the phone and bringing it toward me. I tear my gaze from hers and look down at the device. She must do the same and sees the name on the screen, for she freezes. The tension in the room escalates. I bring the phone to my ear and growl, "Felix?"

"I am at the door." His tone is both petulant and stubborn. My heart rate spikes. My pulse booms at my temples. I've been putting off talking with him, if I'm being honest. Instead, I've focused all of my attention on her because, again, instinct. And yes, delay tactics.

I need to talk to my son. I need to make it clear it's not a competition between us. I need him to see things from my point of view—though I don't expect him to. I am the parent here. I should put my son's happiness first. Instead, I've set myself on a collision course with him.

He wanted to marry Raven. Even if he didn't turn up in time for the wedding, he must have feelings for her. And I walked all over them when I proposed to her. Once more, I prioritized my needs before his. Once more, I'm a terrible example of what a parent should be.

"Quentin, you there?" Felix's angry voice snaps me out of my reverie.

"On my way." I hang up on Felix, then push my legs over the side of the bed and stand up. I'm aware of her gaze following me as I walk into my closet.

Footsteps sound, then her scent teases my nostrils. She runs her fingers down the wings of the Raven etched into my skin. Its wings embrace me on either side with the tips of the feathers curling around to flank my chest.

"It's a—"

"Deep into that darkness peering, long I stood there, wondering, fearing, doubting, dreaming dreams no mortal ever dared to dream before," I murmur.

"—Raven," she names the poem correctly. "You like Poe so much?"

I reach for a sweatshirt and turn to face her. "He speaks to the darkness within me," *as do you.* "He puts a name to the fear I feel inside me."

"Fear?" She half smiles. "I can't see you being afraid of anything."

I'm afraid of losing you. But that won't stop me from the duty I have toward my son, this time. I want to tell her that, but something stops me. Perhaps, my fear that she might insist my duty to my son comes first? Something I know I should prioritize but which, God help me, I can't. I have to find a way to balance my role as a parent with these very real feelings I have for her. I can't let her go. I can't. But I also need her to want to marry me willingly. I need—my phone buzzes again.

I pull it out of the pocket of my jeans and disconnect it. My son never did have patience. I brush past her, resisting the urge to grab her and kiss her soundly before I head to the door, then stop. "Why don't you shower, and meet me downstairs?"

"I'm not going anywhere until you explain to me why you proposed to her." Felix throws himself into the chair next to the window in my living room. Then he slides around to hook his legs over one of the arms of the chair. He wriggles around until his back is supported by the other arm, then flashes me a grim smile. So much posturing. The father in me is happy my son has picked up the confidence to go toe-to-toe with me. I'd rather we have a direct conversation man-to-man to work things out. But also, the father in me cringes at the fact I have to explain to my son why I can't *not* marry his ex.

I hold up both of my hands. "This is your home. You are welcome here, Felix; you know that."

He seems taken aback, then schools his expression back into one of hostility. "How am I supposed to know that? How am I supposed to know anything when you've barely been around for me?"

I draw in a sharp breath. I'm aware of my shortcomings. Aware of the mistakes I made when I was younger. But to hear it from my son's mouth is sobering. "It must have been difficult for you to realize your mother had left without you. And even tougher to have a father who wasn't there for you."

He blinks. Emotions war in his eyes. A mix of anger and fear and loneliness. The kind I've felt myself when I think of my son. Not knowing how to forge a bond with him. Feeling resentful to have become a father when I wasn't ready for it. Unable to deal with his mother leaving me when I needed her the most. Unable to face up to my duties. Hating myself for it, but also, never courageous enough to embrace my responsibilities. And by the time I was ready, feeling like it was too late. Like I'd lost my son. Except I didn't. He's here now. And I need to find a way to... build a bridge with him. Perhaps, his once fiancée and my now wife-to-be can help us find common ground. Both of us care for her, after all.

"You have no idea what I went through," Felix snaps.

"You're right, I don't. But I want to try."

He scoffs. "A little too late for father-son bonding, don't you think?"

"You're here, aren't you?" I point out.

He sets his jaw. "And you know what I want!"

I draw down my eyebrows. "She's not a possession."

He scoffs, "Says the man who believes she's his and who'd hide her away from the world if he had the chance."

I rock back on my heels. "You have to believe I didn't have a choice in this. When I saw her, it was like a bolt of lightning had struck me. And then, you had broken up with her... I... I couldn't take how she looked standing on her own at the altar. She looked forlorn and lonely, and so very sad. I acted on instinct. I couldn't leave her there."

"So you did it because you wanted to what, swoop in and save her?"

I rub the back of my neck. "I did it because there was no way I could not have proposed to her. It was a compulsion I hardly understood myself but could not deny. I acted on instinct."

He juts out his chin. "You did it because you saw the opportunity to move in on what was mine."

"Felix, I thought you didn't want her." *And I was so relieved.* "It was your wedding, and you were nowhere to be found. You broke up via a text to your best man. Can you blame anyone for assuming you'd changed your mind? That you didn't want her?"

"Well—" He averts his eyes. "Why did it have to be you that showed up to rescue her? You wouldn't even know her if it weren't for me."

"That's true..."

"When you met her, she was mine," he glowers.

"No, Felix. And I need you to hear this"—he turns back toward me, and I continue—"when I met her, you had *already* stood her up. She *wasn't* yours anymore."

"I... You... She wasn't supposed to be yours!"

I can hear the pain behind his words, and my heart squeezes. I can't have him thinking I did this to one-up him. "This isn't a competition, Felix," I say softly.

"Isn't it?"

I shake my head. "It's not. And it's her decision who she decides to marry."

"But you asked her to move in so you could influence her mind," a whining note enters his voice.

"Guilty as charged. I won't deny that. Also, she wanted to move out of the apartment she shared with you, understandably. It would have been awkward for the both of you. I had the space, so I asked her to move in with me."

"You expect me to believe you did it out of the goodness of your heart? One you don't have, by the way?"

I sigh, then widen my stance. "You already know I want to marry her, and—"

"Stop it!" He jumps up to his feet. "Do you have any idea how obscene that is? A father wanting to marry his son's ex? Have you no shame? No guilt? No remorse for what you're doing? You—" He shakes his head, seemingly at a loss for words. "How could you do this? The one thing I want for myself, and you stride in and take it away from me."

"You dumped her. She's not your girlfriend or your fiancée," I remind him.

"But you want to make her my stepmother... That's... just indecent. For once, can't you think of my feelings? Can't you see how difficult this is for me?"

And for me—fuck!

My heart pounds in my chest. Sweat pools under my armpits. I knew this confrontation with Felix was coming, but nothing prepared me for the depth of hurt in his eyes. For the anguish on his face. For the remorse that courses through my veins and turns my stomach to stone.

"Felix, son—" I reach for him, but he shakes me off.

"Don't touch me. Don't call me son. You... You're doing exactly what I expected you to do. You're being selfish and looking out for yourself, not caring how much your actions hurt me."

I stiffen. He's right. I've been fooling myself by thinking I could gloss over the issues having Raven in my life raises with my son. He may have broken up with her, but his feelings for her haven't faded. Then, to see her with his father? That can't be easy for him to stomach.

His upbringing wasn't kind to him. First, his mother left him. Then, I was an absentee father. It's enough to have caused abandonment issues. Likely, his not turning up at his own wedding was a means to protect himself from hurt. Before Raven could abandon him, like his mother had and, to an extent, how I had, he abandoned her. I'm to blame for his inclination to self-sabotage. No way, do I want to hurt him further.

And yet, I can't not go through with my plan to marry Raven, either. She is mine. Just as much as he is my son. Only, I need to give her space to realize she belongs to me, and not because I tell her so.

As for Felix... He needs to draw the same conclusion, without my trying to explain the situation further to him. Anything I say or do will make it worse. I need him to understand the connection Raven and I have. I need him to recognize that it was inevitable that she'd marry me.

"You're wrong," I say softly.

His forehead furrows. "What do you mean?"

"It means I'm asking you to move into my place." When I retired from the military and accepted a position with the Davenport Group, I bought this townhouse in Primrose Hill. I decided to keep a suite for Felix, should he ever want to stay at my place. In my mind, my home has always been his and he's welcome here. Felix didn't take me up on that offer. Perhaps this is the opportunity to entice him to stay under my roof. Forced proximity is one way to try to forge a bond with my son. It may not be the most effective of ideas, but it's all I've got.

He gapes at me, but before he can react, her gasp of surprise reaches us. "What do you mean?"

Both of us turn to find she's standing at the entrance to the room.

20

Vivian

That cannot be what he said. I look from Felix, whose face reflects the shock I'm feeling, to Quentin, who's watching me carefully.

"Did I hear you right? Did you ask your son — my ex — to move in and stay here at the same time as me?" I burst out.

Quentin clenches his jaw. Then slowly nods. "I've allocated a self-sufficient apartment for him within the house. It's on the opposite wing from the main part of the house and has a separate entrance." He turns to Felix. "You'd have your independence and wouldn't have to run into me or Vivian."

He'd still be in the same house as me and Q though. I shake my head. This is insane. He can't possibly imagine the three of us could co-exist. Yes, Felix will be in an apartment in a different wing, but under the same roof? What a disaster. What's going on in that mind of his? What is he trying to plan here?

Of course, Felix has a right to be here. This is his father's home, after all. My head spins, and a tightness takes hold behind my eyes. *Why do I get the feeling I'm seeing what Quentin wants to show me?* So far, I haven't been able to look past his gorgeous face and his spectacular body, and the fact that he seems to be so taken by me. Enough to propose to me as soon as he saw me. Despite myself, I've been flattered by it. And the events of the last few days have begun to reveal the man behind the façade he wears. A man I've begun to like. A man I know doesn't share what he's thinking. But no way could he have the notion that inviting his son to move in while I'm here is a good idea. I'm furious. And heartbroken, and damn him, but I also feel betrayed that he put me in this position.

He must see the emotions running across my face, for he takes a step in my direction.

"Don't—" I shake my head, then pivot on my heels and hurry out and back toward his bedroom.

I stomp inside, then into the closet. I begin to unbutton the shirt, but before I'm halfway through, he walks around to stand in front of me.

"What are you doing?"

"What does it look like? I'm getting out of the shirt I borrowed from you."

"Leave it on. I like seeing you in my clothes," he orders.

"So you can use this as another opportunity to rub it in your son's face that we're together? You can't resist branding me as yours and flaunting our relationship in front of him, can you?"

A spasm of pain crosses his features. "This...is uncharted territory for me. You can't blame me for wanting to shout to the world that you're mine. At the same time, I'm aware how much it's hurting him, and that it might alienate him forever, and I don't want that. This is, likely, the last chance I have to mend fences with him. It's why I asked him to move in."

For a second, he looks uncertain and vulnerable, and my heart begins to soften, but I rein it in. "This"—I throw my hands up in the air—"you, me and him, in the same space?"

"Why not?"

I scowl. "Because seeing us together would make it clear to him there's chemistry between us. And that would only show him what he's missing."

"Or it might make him realize we're inevitable," he points out.

"While putting *me* in an embarrassing situation. How do you think it'll feel for me to see the guy who dumped me at the altar in the hallway as I'm going to the loo?"

I finish unbuttoning the shirt and when the plackets gape, his gaze is drawn to my exposed breasts. His eyes widen. His nostrils flare. And when I look at the crotch of his pants, the telltale bulge there gives him away. A surge of power courses through my veins.

This attraction between us is real. It's why he brought me here. It's why I came willingly. I wasn't thinking too far out into the future last night, not beyond the possibility of a marriage to him… Or the prospect of not marrying him when my month of consideration is up.

But the run-in with Felix has shown me a glimpse of the future. This awkwardness between the three of us is going to taint our relationship, no matter how much time passes.

"Q?" I prompt him. "Did you hear what I said?"

He blinks, then seems to wrench his gaze away from my body and to my face. "I hear you." He draws in a breath, then runs his hand over his head. "I understand how uncomfortable this situation is for you. It is for me, too." He chooses his words carefully. "The last thing I want is my son under my roof while I attempt to start this new phase of my life with you. The last thing I want is for you to be reminded of how much Felix hurt you. But I'm also aware of how pissed-off he is about this situation, and rightly so. I'm afraid that in asking you to marry me, I may have alienated my son forever. He's the only immediate family I have, and if I don't do something I'll lose him. And I… I can't let that happen. But also, I want… No, I *need* you in my life."

I'm sure he'll take my hand, but he seems to respect my need for space. Instead, his gaze bores into mine.

"I need both of you in my life."

His blue eyes turn almost indigo with emotion. Tension radiates off of him.

"Timing is everything, and if I don't do something to show Felix I'm committed to resolving our conflict, I will have lost my son. I couldn't live with that."

Neither could I.

He must sense me thawing, for he takes a step forward. Not enough to touch me, but enough for the heat of his body to envelop me. Enough for that spicy scent of his to deepen. And damn, but my entire body lights up. I should move away, but it feels so good to be near him.

"I need you with me, under my roof, Raven." He locks his gaze with mine. "You mean so much to me. But so does Felix. And the only way I can continue to have some kind of relationship with him is by having him under my roof for a short period of time."

His voice is so gentle, his tone so tender, the worry in his eyes is so real, my stupid heart melts completely.

"It's only for a little while; just until Felix and I arrive at some kind of understanding," he coaxes.

Oh, my god, am I really going to do this? Am I going to agree to live under the same roof as Felix?

Quentin could have used that bossy voice of his, and I'd have given in earlier, but he didn't. And he hasn't leveraged the chemistry between us to seduce me into agreeing, either. Maybe that's why I pull my hand from his and shake a finger under his nose. "Fine then. But keep him away from me. Can you do that?"

The tension drains from his shoulders. The fine lines around his beautiful mouth smooth out, and dang it, but a flush of satisfaction warms me. Ugh, I care for this man more than I realized. And I do want to see him happy. When did I begin to develop feelings for him?

"I'll do my best to make sure the two of you don't run into each other; you have my word." His voice rings with conviction.

I nod. It's not the same as not having Felix living in this house, but it's the best I can hope for, under the circumstances. I suppose. I shrug out of his shirt, then walk over to the laundry basket and pull out the blouse I was wearing yesterday.

"You can keep the shirt," he offers.

"I'm not sure I can accept it."

"You're going to be my wife."

I stay silent. In my mind, I know it's inevitable. Saying anything contradictory seems pointless. But my hesitation must come through because when I turn, it's to find he's watching me with a look of speculation on his face.

"I know what you're thinking."

"Oh, you do, huh?"

He ignores the sarcasm in my voice. "You're thinking that entertaining the idea of this proposal was stupid."

My gaze widens.

"And moving in with me was a mistake. And you're regretting that you're so attracted to me, that it's making it difficult for you think marrying me is a mistake."

Shock has me immobile. Am I that easy to read? Or is it that he's able to understand my misgivings without my spelling them out?

He must read the surprise on my features, for he nods. He pulls out his phone and his fingers fly over the screen.

What's he up to?

He looks up at me, a look of confidence on his face. The hair on the nape of my neck rises. Before I can ask him anything else, a buzzing sound reaches me. *What the—? Did he text me?* With a last look at him, I head out of the closet and toward the bedside table where I placed my phone. I snatch it up.

It's not a text. A notification from my bank's app fills the top of the screen. I tap on it, and it enlarges. The figure in my account takes my breath away. So many zeroes, more than I've ever seen on paper, or on a screen, and definitely not in my account. Shock holds me immobile.

I turn to him. "You did this?" I hold up my phone.

He nods without bothering to look at the screen. "Now you can pay in full for your sister's ballet course and get your father the best medical help in the world."

I swallow.

"You can also arrange to move him to a better facility with higher quality care. With better attention and medication, there's no reason he won't live a healthy life into a ripe old age."

"Wait, what? You transferred the money to my account."

He nods.

"But how did you get the details? I never shared them with you."

He continues to glare at me, and a slow anger builds in my belly. "Of course, your private investigator got them for you. I'd have thought banks have to respect confidentiality, but clearly, anyone can be bought. Including me."

He shakes his head. "Don't cheapen what we have. It's not like that between us."

A heaviness knocks at the backs of my eyes. At the same time, I feel like I can breathe. So strange. Until this moment, I hadn't realized how stressed I've been about my father and my sister. Seeing the bottom line in my account makes our agreement a cold, hard reality. It's a reminder of how much I need this money.

"This... this makes it very real." I swallow.

He stays silent, letting me process my thoughts, and for that, I'm grateful. He's simply come through on his part of the deal, as he said he would.

"You said you'd give me a month to think about it," I remind him.

"And you still have it. But you need the money, so I transferred it."

I nod slowly.

"I'm not pushing you to agree. And I don't want to pressure you into deciding. Though I'd be happy if you agreed to marry me right away, of course." He smirks, then his expression turns serious. "I want you to have the cash now, when you need it most. No strings attached."

"No strings attached?" *What's the catch? There must be a catch... right?* "I may not agree to marry after a month," I remind him.

"The money is yours, no matter what." His grin widens. "But you will."

That grin is so potent, my thighs clench. And his cockiness shouldn't be attractive, but it is, damn him. "I suppose this is a sign that you can be trusted to keep your promises?" I sniff.

"I do. I keep *all* of my promises." A wicked look enters his eyes.

I have no doubt he's referring to his promise of keeping me in orgasms, too. My cheeks flush, but I don't look away. Fact is, I've wanted to say yes to him from the moment he proposed, but it seemed so wrong. How could I allow myself to marry a stranger—however hot he is? But he's right. I need the money urgently. Now that I have it, I can use it to help my family. And I'm attracted to him. This marriage won't be a chore. Really, any which way I look at it, I can't lose in this arrangement. My financial problems resolved. I also get a husband I'm very attracted to. All I have to do is say yes.

I draw in a breath. "Okay." I firm my shoulders. "Okay, I'll do it.'

His gaze widens, his shoulders bunch, and then he seems to force himself to relax. "I want to take what you say at face value, but I must remind you again that you have the month to decide. Not that you need to use up all that time, of course."

I shuffle my feet. He's right. I can take my time to decide. Except, the more I analyze this situation, the more I look at the positives and negatives and mull over it, the more I know, I'll get cold feet. I could walk away, as he said... And then what? Help my sister and my father and then... Return to my empty life? Sure, I'll be able to pursue my career as a painter, but I'll have missed out on this opportunity to explore this attraction between us. To find out about that part of me which he sparks and brings to the fore. To learn about my submissive side at the feet of a master. *My master.* To have him hold me, kiss me, make love to me... To follow my instincts and live spontaneously. To... be me. I can do this for myself. All I have to do is... say yes.

"Yes," I whisper.

His entire body stiffens. I expect him to be triumphant, but what I see on his face is an intense need. One that turns my blood hot and my pussy into an answering miasma of want.

"Say it." He searches my features. "Say that you'll marry me."

The command in his voice resonates with a primal side of me. My nipples bead. My scalp tingles. A bead of sweat slides down my spine. This is it. Say it aloud, and there's no turning back. Say it aloud, and you might get to experience the passion you've only read about. That this man would turn my life upside down is a given. Would I be able to cope with it? I *have to* cope with it. I *can* cope with it.

"I'll marry you." I say with a surge of confidence that takes me by surprise, but which also feels so right.

He holds out his hand, and when I place mine in his, he tugs me close. The heat of his body warms me. His blue gaze smolders. There's a serious look on his features. An intensity that holds me immobile.

"You're so fucking beautiful. It screws with my head every time I see you, every time I—" He lowers his head until his nose is millimeters from the curve of where my neck meets my shoulder. He takes a deep sniff, but I'm the one who feels lightheaded. It feels like he's inhaling me, storing up my scent in his lungs. Committing my very essence to the memory in his cells. It feels more intimate than having his lips on my cunt. It feels so intimate, so erotic, so compelling, I almost throw myself at his feet and beg him to fuck me. His eyes blaze, he leans in closer, then seems to get ahold of himself.

He straightens and that burning gaze of his turns cold again. "My son is not ready to let you go... yet."

I swallow. "I know."

"And this time, I'm not going to avoid the issue." His voice is resolute. "I know how tricky it's going to make this for you, but I can't run from this. I need to resolve the issues between us." He runs his thumb across the sensitive skin of my wrist, and my pulse leaps.

The ice in his eyes cracks and silver sparks flare. "I have to try. You understand?" His voice is hoarse and vibrates with an emotion that touches me on a primal level.

"I do," I croak through the ball of emotion that's taken up residence in my throat.

The left side of his mouth quirks in that half smile that, I swear, I can feel all the way to my toes. He's so potent, so ridiculously male, so yummy

I want to climb him like a tree, then proceed to lick him all over. As if he senses my thoughts, his smile widens.

"I'm not saying I have the answers. But what I know is, I'd rather have him here so I can communicate with him and explain more of where I'm coming from—which should, hopefully, help." He half laughs. "At the same time, I... *We* don't need his approval."

We don't? I don't say it aloud, but he must read my thoughts from my expression for he shakes his head. "He's my son, and I will try my best to make him see reason. But my decisions don't need his blessing."

"And me?" I hunch my shoulders. "Felix is... *was* my friend." After what he did, he doesn't deserve my friendship. But it can't be easy for him to see me with his father and I can't help feeling sorry for him.

"And he decided not to marry you. If we're happy, he'll realize we're right for each other, and he'll understand."

"I envy your confidence. I wish I felt half as assured as you in this." Though something in me tells me to trust him on this.

"I can only follow my instincts in this," he offers.

"The way you followed them when you proposed to me?"

"And you see where that got me. We're getting married in less than a month."

"Less than a month?" I gape at him.

"Will that be a problem?" he asks in a mild tone that, nevertheless, carries a ring of authority.

It's a little quick, but since that day at the church, I've known I was headed toward this moment. I shake my head.

"It's settled then." He pins me with his soul-searching stare. "Of course, we won't be sharing a bedroom or sleeping together, as long as he's here. Unless—" He leans in until his mouth is over mine and his nose bumps mine. Until I'm surrounded by him. Those silver sparks in his blue eyes draw me in, and my head begins to spin.

"Unless?" I whisper.

"You come to me and ask me to fuck you. And even then"—he tucks an errant strand of hair behind my ear—"I might decide to sleep in a different bed and deny you your orgasms."

My heart sinks. But my pussy? My pussy feels so turned on, it's as if he's dancing the tango with it, and my stomach writhes in anticipation. How can I be so turned on by the prospect of his denial? How can I look forward to him manipulating my orgasms any way he sees fit? Why does this make me feel even more desired? And because I have to, at least, pretend to protest, I stutter, "B-but you promised me a zillion of them."

"And you'll get them, too." His lips curl. He bends his knees and peers into my eyes. "I guarantee, with the edging I plan to do, when you finally come, it will be with an intensity that's going to blow your mind and leave your cunt begging for more. It'll be the kind of pain you've never felt before, and the kind of pleasure that'll leave you flushed with endorphins for days."

21

Vivian

"It's you, your ex, and your ex's father in the same house?" From across the floor of the wedding dress shop, I see Zoey's eyes widen.

"Pretty much," I respond while glancing around the shop.

Karma West Sovrano opened a boutique on Primrose Hill's High Street, and when Quentin informed me that he'd made me an appointment for a fitting, I was so excited.

I'm not sure if he realizes I was wearing a second-hand creation of hers when he first met me. No way was I going to turn down the opportunity to wear one of her dresses tailormade for me. Of course, I'm aware this is another way Quentin is showing off his connections. The way he's able to pick up the phone and make a call, and the next moment, I'm walking into this boutique…

No doubt, he also did it to make clear, nothing's stopping us from getting married in less than a month.

"Felix moved in this morning," I mutter.

"Oh no, that must be so awkward," Zoey cries.

I sigh. "As Q promised, he's in another wing of the house, so I haven't run into him. I've also managed to steer clear of him at work, thank God!"

"Girl, that's tough," she says sympathetically.

"Of course, our colleagues know what happened. It doesn't help that neither of us invited them to the wedding." I roll my eyes. "The atmosphere's so frigid, the pies could freeze coming out of the wood-fired oven."

Zoey chuckles.

At least being measured for the dress is helping me take my mind off the disaster of the day.

My phone vibrates. I glance toward the bag I left on the couch earlier. "Zoey, could you get my phone, please?"

She walks over, grabs my bag and brings it over. I take the phone and glance at the message. It's a video message from an unknown number. When I touch it, it begins to play.

A woman's face appears on screen. She has dark hair and flashing eyes. There are circles under her eyes, but she's smiling.

I gasp, "Oh my god, it's Karma."

She doesn't look like the normal, polished woman I've come to expect from her social media videos and in photos from her fashion shows. Perhaps her illness is more severe than Summer let on?

"What do you mean?" Zoey leans over my shoulder.

"Hi Vivian, sorry for sliding into your messages unannounced, but when Summer told me you were marrying Q, I wanted to reach out to you, so I got your number from her." She coughs, then smiles again. "I'd have loved to have been there in person today, but since I couldn't, I wanted to reach out to you. I'm so happy you'll be wearing one of my creations for your wedding."

"Q is very dear to me, as Summer must have told you. He was a source of great comfort to me and Summer when I was rushed to the hospital earlier this year. If he hadn't been there that day, I'm not sure how I'd have made it through."

She wipes a tear, then fans herself with her hand. "Sorry about that, it's these post-natal hormones; they make me cry at the drop of a hat. But I wanted to congratulate you and tell you how happy I am that you're marrying Q. We haven't met personally, but I've heard so much about you from Summer, and I know you're going to be good for him. Q can come across as all tough and stern, but he has a heart of gold. You might have to wait a little for him to share more of his true nature with you, but I hope you won't give up on him. Just give him a chance, okay?" She coughs again. "I hope you don't mind my sending you this message. I didn't mean to unduly influence you but I have such regard for Q and I was so excited to find out he was getting married that I had to call you." A baby begins to cry in the background. "Oh, the baby's up, I have to go feed her." She smiles, then coughs again, before bringing it under control. "Big hug and I hope to see you soon." Then she disconnects.

"Wow." I continue to stare at the blank screen, digesting everything. "Karma sent me a personal message. I'm such a huge fan of her designs."

"That's such a Karma thing to do," Zoey agrees.

"I didn't realize Q made such an impression on her." I hand the phone back to Zoey, who steps back and out of the way of the bridal stylist who's been taking my measurements.

"I haven't heard her voice since she went out on maternity leave two months ago. You must really be special!" The young woman smiles up at me from where she's kneeling on the ground. "I'll send these measurements off right away." She rises to her feet, nods at me and Zoey, and leaves.

"I still can't believe Karma sent me a personal message." I shake my head. "Being in this shop is privilege enough for me, but to have Karma reach out—" To say I'm gob-smacked is putting it mildly. If Karma meant to make me look at Q in a more favorable light, she succeeded. Of course, I'm marrying him, and men often come across differently with their wives than with their friends, but still... The very fact that the designer I have a girl crush on advocated for Q means something to me.

Summer messaged me earlier to apologize that she couldn't make it because little Matty has been a little under the weather and she wanted to stay home with him. Zoey invited her friends Harper and Grace to the fitting. She called them on FaceTime and introduced us. Both congratulated me and said they'd have loved to join but couldn't. Turns out, Harper's putting in another long day at the restaurant where she works as a sous chef. Grace begged off, saying she was exhausted and had to be up at two a.m. to prep for her morning show. Zoey hinted about a surprise guest who might be showing up, but since Karma already called me, I can't imagine who it could be.

It seems like even friends of friends of Q have quickly included me in their circle.

In fact, Q has more friends than I've ever had. They're all so loyal to him, and somehow, it's made them loyal to me, too, which is a strange thought to have. Like Summer's friend Skylar who runs The Fierce Kitten Bakery up the street from the boutique. Summer told her I'd be here for a fitting, and she had one of her team members deliver a selection of desserts.

I was overwhelmed and unsure if I should indulge myself, considering I was being fitted and didn't want to mess up the measurements. But Zoey waved aside my hesitation. And when she bit into one of the cupcakes and moaned, my mouth watered, and I reached for a doughnut myself.

Now we hear the sound of a motorbike approaching. The pipes make enough noise that all three of us glance toward the front of the shop, where a woman in a motorcycle jacket and leather pants, dismounts from a Harley.

She takes off her helmet and the sunlight glints off the silver strands of her hair threaded through the brown and blue-colored ones. She turns toward the shop, sees us and waves through the frontage.

Zoey waves back with enthusiasm. "Oh, goodie, our surprise guest has arrived." She turns to me. "I hope you don't mind. My Granny Imelda's a hoot, I promise. I thought she might provide a welcome diversion."

The woman struts into the bridal shop, and heads for us.

"Gran... I mean Imelda!" Zoey throws her arms around the other woman. "I didn't think you'd make it."

"And pass up the chance for free champagne and Skylar's desserts?" She huffs, "No fucking way."

Whoa, this is not your average grandma. This is a shit-kicking, in-her-prime woman, who's living life the way she wants, and to hell with the consequences. Zoey was right. She livens up the place.

Sensing my perusal, she turns and flashes me a wicked smile. "You must be Vivian."

I begin to nod when she closes the distance to us and hugs me. I stiffen at first, but her hug feels so motherly, so warm, I find myself relaxing by degrees. When she releases me, I smile back. "Nice to meet you, too, Imelda."

Her face brightens. "Thank God, you didn't call me Gran. Not that I'm not a grandmother, but I also have an identity. One I'm beginning to explore." She steps back and surveys my features. "And what about you, my dear? How are you feeling about everything?"

"If you mean the marriage—"

"I do mean the upcoming nuptials, but more importantly, how do you feel here?" She taps her left breastbone. "Do you feel he's the right man for you?"

I blink. "I ah, I... Um—"

"Imelda, you're putting Vivian on the spot," Zoey admonishes her.

"Sorry, I didn't mean to make you uncomfortable," Imelda says in a voice that indicates she definitely did mean to.

I bark out a laugh. "You're wicked."

Imelda looks pleased. "I aim to be. At my age, you cut the bullshit and get to the core of the issue. Which, in this case is, are you in love with the man you're going to marry?"

I gape at her. *Doesn't pull any punches, does she?*

"That's a very personal question," Zoey scolds.

The bridal stylist who's been measuring me for the dress looks between us. "Uh, I think I have everything I need. Feel free to stay and enjoy the refreshments. Karma instructed me to close the shop to customers, so you'd have privacy." She half waves at us, then leaves.

Imelda, who's been watching me closely all this time, blows out a breath. "I'm sorry, dear. I couldn't help but notice the uncertainty lurking in your eyes, and that's what led me to asking the question. Perhaps I've become insensitive in my old age. I didn't mean to hurt you, in any way."

"You didn't." I step down from the fitting platform and walk over to the bottle of champagne set on a table in the corner. I pour myself a flute and take a sip, before turning to face Zoey and Imelda, who've followed me. "And it's a valid question." I take another sip. The two wait patiently while I look around for the correct words to frame my thoughts. "The truth is, I'm marrying him because it's the right thing to do at this stage in my life."

Imelda looks taken aback, then nods. "It's an appropriate answer. I'd have, of course, preferred to hear the L word, but a modern marriage of convenience which furthers your goals is a good second option."

It's my turn to feel surprised. "So... you don't think it's wrong that I'm marrying a man for—"

"—his money?" She laughs. "Oh, my dear, do I look like someone who believes in roses and hearts and unicorns? The best possible outcome of a marriage would be that you get something out of it which benefits your interests."

"Granny Imelda!" Zoey turns on her. "I had no idea you were such a non-romantic."

"Oh, *I'm* romantic, but when you have an arranged marriage like I did, and know your husband for three minutes before you marry him, it's a different kind of love." She shrugs. "It's the kind that you develop for your spouse over a period of time, out of necessity."

"Did you say three minutes?" I cough.

"About all the time I had to see my husband's face for the first time before the bishop pronounced us man and wife."

"Ah..." I'm not sure how to react to that. I've heard of arranged marriages being the norm, especially among wealthy families, but Imelda is the first person I'm meeting who's been through one. "And you were happy?"

She half smiles. "I didn't have a choice in the matter. I married him because it was the done thing. Gave him kids because... it was expected of me. I made peace with myself. But it was after my husband passed that I found the freedom to come into myself."

"Oh..." I swallow, not sure what to say to that.

Her features soften. "I'm sharing this so you realize we do what we have to do. I couldn't let down my family, either. Truth be told, it didn't even cross my mind to say no. I wouldn't say I was happy or unhappy. And maybe, I even came to love my husband, in my own way. You, on the other hand, seem to have thought this through and decided this is right for you?"

I nod. "It is," I say slowly. "The money was a factor in making me consider the arrangement, but as I got to know him, I realized he wants to marry me because he feels a connection to me. Of course, he does need to marry in order to secure his position in his father's company and gain his inheritance, but" — I look away then back at her — "but it's more than that. I mean, he could marry anyone if that's all he wanted. Plus, he gave me the option of leaving with the money, without marrying him, but I couldn't do it."

"You couldn't?" Zoe's eyes round. "Why am I hearing of this for the first time?"

I blush. "Because I'm only coming to terms with it myself. There's something more between us. A connection. And I find him attractive. Very attractive, actually. There's good chemistry between us. And when I realized it wasn't the money that was making me want to marry him, I realized" — I swallow — "I realized this is something I want to do. And not even the fact that it's going to result in awkward encounters with his son, who happens to be my ex, is enough to dissuade me."

"Wow, that's—" Zoey shakes her head. "I'm so happy for you, babe."

"A good sex life is the cornerstone of a good marriage. It's a good base to build your marriage on." Imelda lowers her chin. "Make sure you don't give up everything too easily. Keep a little of yourself from him. Nothing like a little enigma to keep the marriage interesting, know what I mean?"

I frown. "I think so."

My phone buzzes. Zoey glances at the screen then holds it to up. "It's Lizzie." She walks over and hands the phone to me.

I answer the call. "Lizzie, you should see my dress, it's incredible."

22

Vivian

"This is ridiculous." My voice echoes around the empty hallway in Q's home. The joy of being fitted for my wedding dress seems like so long ago, but it's been only two days. To say today was a disaster is putting it lightly.

One of the delivery drivers made an inappropriate reference to the broken relationship between me and Felix—while Felix was in the room. He then invited me out to the alley behind the shop where he said, and I quote: "I'll show you how your wedding night should have been."

Felix snapped and swung at him. The other guy ducked and sank his fist into Felix's face. Felix fought back with a ferocity I didn't think he had, until a final hit took him down.

I screamed, grabbed the closest weapon—a pizza pan—and threw it at the guy. For some reason, my aim was spot on. It hit him in the chest, and he crashed into a table, which collapsed under his weight. All the dough and the different toppings were thrown to the ground.

That's when the Head of Operations for the chain walked in. One look at the three of us and he fired Felix and me, while promising to report the issue to the delivery company.

Felix had, by then, staggered to his feet. Without another look at me, he took off.

I left with a sinking feeling in my stomach. I lost my job, my livelihood. I began to stress about how I was going to pay my bills. Only on my way home, when I checked the balance in my bank account, did I remember, I'm no longer broke.

After using some of the money Quentin transferred to pay for Lizzie's tuition and to cover the costs of my father's care, I have enough left over to not have to work for a long time.

Money worries have crowded my mind for so long, and now that they've faded, I can think clearly.

I don't have to go to a job I hate.

When I reach Q's place, the townhouse is empty.

Now, I shut the door, and the snick echoes around the empty hallway. I shake my head at myself in the hallway mirror.

"Ridiculous," I repeat.

It's taken this incident and losing my job to open my eyes; to realize I don't have to go to work anymore. I didn't have to suffer through the indignity of what happened today. In fact, I don't have to do anything I don't want to do. The sense of freedom makes me almost giddy.

I blow out a breath and roll my shoulders, trying to work out some of the knots.

The housekeeper, who comes in daily to clean up, must have left the lights on in the conservatory. I walk toward it, and when I glance outside, I see the hot tub on the deck. I admit, I've been tempted to use it before, but I opted not to. Mainly, because I've been on tenterhooks, wondering when I'll run into either Quentin or Felix, and that's kept me confined to my room. Three nights of not seeing either of them—not even in the kitchen, has given me the courage.

Given the emotional upheaval of today, I've earned it, haven't I?

I head straight for the deck behind the conservatory and switch on the hot tub. The jets begin to gurgle and flow, with steam almost instantly rising up from the water. I return to my room, get changed into a swimsuit, slip on a robe, and grab a towel. En-route to the tub, I grab a bottle of red wine, open it, and with a glass, walk back onto the deck. Then, I slip off my robe and get into the tub.

Pouring myself a glass of wine, I take a sip, then lean back and sigh. Looking up, I see the full moon in the sky. It's too cloudy to make out stars, but the radiance of the moonlight makes up for it.

Slowly, my muscles unwind. I take another sip, then place the glass aside. I place the rolled-up towel under my neck at the lip of the tub, then stretch out. I am in that floating, half-drowsy state when I hear footsteps approach.

I crack open my eyelids to find Felix standing on the other side of the tub. He's wearing swimming trunks and his torso is bare. He also sports a black eye. "Felix, you're hurt," I sit up.

He shakes his head.

"I'm good, really."

"You don't look... good."

"Thanks." He half smiles. "Mind if I join you?" He jerks his chin in the direction of the jets.

I pop a shoulder.

"If you'd rather I leave—" He turns to go, and I almost let him.

But then I remember how he came to my defense when that delivery driver came onto me. And despite the fact the other guy was much bigger, Felix didn't hesitate to launch himself at him.

It makes me feel a little kinder toward him... Or maybe the hot tub and the wine have worked their magic and I'm feeling magnanimous enough not to castrate him right away. "Felix, it's fine. You can... join me," I call after him.

He pauses but doesn't turn around. He hangs his head. There's a defeated look to his posture. He looks so pathetic I begin to feel bad for him. Yes, he acted like an ass, but also, it can't be easy knowing I'm going to marry his father. And while a part of me feels he deserves the discomfort this causes him, he was my friend once. And he was there for me when I was struggling for money and to take care of my family.

"I could... do with the company," I throw out.

He nods, then turns and walks into the tub. He keeps to his end, which is so wide, that when he stretches out, there's plenty of space between our toes. For a few seconds, the only sound is the gurgling of the jets. Then he tips his head at the bottle of wine. "May I?"

I grab the bottle, top myself up, then lean over and hand it to him.

"Salut." He raises the bottle in my direction and takes a sip. "Fuck, this is good."

"It is."

"The old man has good taste; I'll give him that."

I look away, then back at him. "Why did you do it, Felix? Why did you not… decide the day before or the morning of the wedding? And to break it off with a text, not addressed to me… That was—"

"—a horrible thing I did to you." He sits up straight. "I am so sorry, Viv. I truly am. I just… lost my nerve. I saw you before the ceremony, all dressed up in your bridal gown and I… I—"

"Had second thoughts? Decided it wasn't right? Went into a moment of panic?"

Felix shifts around, his gaze ping-ponging everywhere, but at my face.

"It's okay, you can tell me. It's not going to make a difference now, anyway."

He nods and lowers his chin to his chest. "I realized I wasn't worthy of you… yet. That I couldn't give you everything you needed… yet. I… I knew I needed to get my life into shape first, before I could become worthy of you."

I blink slowly. That is not what I'd expected to hear.

"You could have, at least, had the courtesy to message me directly instead of through your best man."

Felix swallows. "I'm so sorry, I… That was cowardly of me. I should have told you face to face, but I… I couldn't stand the thought of disappointing you. But I'll make it up to you. I'm going to fight for you now."

"Excuse me?" I widen my gaze. "What do you mean fight for me?"

He begins to inch closer in the tub. "We… You and I had something, right?"

Wrong. What we had was friendship… if that. I felt the need to take care of him, the way I wanted to care for Lizzie or my father. I met Felix and saw the poor, lonely, lost boy that he was. I empathized with him and mistook it as the foundation on which to build something more.

When I stay silent, his features fall. He looks uncertain before he squares his shoulders. "We had something. I know we did. And I'm going to win you back. Just you watch."

"Felix, please, I—" *I don't think there's a future for us. I'm attracted to your father. And much as I don't like things about him, the sexual tension between us is something I never had with you. It made me realize this is what I was missing out on. And whether I marry him or not… I know you and I are all wrong.*

"No, don't say anything." He looks at me with that pleading look in his eyes, which is why I first noticed him. "Just tell me you'll give me a chance."

"But—"

"At least, promise me you'll think about it? I know I'm not my father... But I'm better than him."

"You are?"

"I'd never walk away from a child. I'd never put my career first. I'd never... be emotionally unavailable for my kids."

I flinch. It's an unwelcome reminder of things I've been trying to avoid thinking about. Namely, my desire for children and what kind of father Q would be. But Q wants to make amends. He knows what he did to Felix was wrong. It's why he's trying to repair his relationship with his son. And something tells me Q won't screw up the second time around. If anything, he'll go out of his way to ensure he does things right.

Doesn't take away from the fact that Quentin hurt Felix. And now, he wants to hurt him further by marrying his son's ex. I shift around to find a more comfortable position. Q's, clearly, so overcome by emotion that he's not thinking straight.

He knows the effect it's going to have on Felix and he's going to do it anyway because... *That's the connection he feels with you. That's how much he wants you.* He also saw me as a convenient way to fulfill the conditions imposed by his father for him to consolidate his position as CEO. *But he could marry anyone to fulfill his obligations, and it would be a lot easier than this whole situation. There are women who would kill for this opportunity, and he chose you.*

Felix must see the doubts on my features, for he pushes his advantage. "One chance; that's all I ask."

"So you can stand me up at the altar again?"

He blushes. The red stands out against his pale skin and makes his black eye pop. The skin is more swollen than when I first saw him. I wince. That must hurt. He should put ice on it. I open my mouth to say so, then shut up. Why do I care about him when he's the one who left me stranded there at the altar? *He did you a favor. If he hadn't had the balls to bail when he did, you'd be married to him and already regretting it.*

I blow out a heavy sigh. It's only human to help someone in need. Also, it's clear nothing I say is going to shake him from his conviction that he has to try to win me back. The more I tell him it'd be a fruitless exercise, the more he's going to dig in his heels and become adamant about his intentions. So instead, I rise to my feet. "You need to ice that eye." I step out of the tub.

"Where are you going?"

"To get you a pack of frozen peas." I use my towel to dry myself off quickly, then shrug into my robe. I walk back through the conservatory and into the kitchen, pull the door to the freezer open, then grab what I need. I straighten, shut the door, then yelp. Standing there, scowling at me, is my soon-to-be husband.

23

Quentin

Her big green eyes widen. I take in her flushed features, the blonde hair piled on top of her head with strands escaping. A drop of water clings to one of them. It slides off and I put out my palm and catch it. She draws in a sharp breath. I bring it to my mouth and lick off the moisture. "Why are you wet?"

"What?" she squeaks. The tell-tale movement of her legs under the robe she's wearing tells me she's squeezing her thighs together.

"I didn't mean your pussy, but thanks for pointing that out to me."

Color flushes her cheeks. "I'm not, wet; not there."

"Liar," I say softly.

Her blush deepens. Another drop of water slides down the valley between her breasts. This time, I lean in and lick it off of her.

A moan spills from her lips. Goosebumps crawl up her décolletage. She shivers.

I straighten and peer into her features. "You're cold."

"No, actually it was too hot in the tub. Speaking of—"

I follow her glance and notice the packet of frozen peas in her hand. I was so captivated by her appearance, I missed it earlier.

"—I need to get this to Felix," she murmurs.

"Felix?" I frown.

"Uh, yeah, we were in the hot tub."

Something hot and nasty crawls in my chest. It's a new emotion. One I've never felt before. One that takes me by surprise. Jealousy, thick and acidic and biting away at the insides of my veins. "You were with Felix, in the hot tub?"

She nods.

I curl my fingers into fists at my sides. "Together?"

"At the same time, yes."

I grind my teeth so hard, pain shoots up my jaw. I wanted to make up for my past mistakes. I wanted to make an attempt to get to know my son better, to build a relationship with him as an adult. That's why I asked him to move in. And yes, also, so I could prove to him that what he thought he and Raven had, is nothing compared to the chemistry between her and me.

I was so filled with guilt and remorse for my past with Felix, and so overcome with the unnamable emotions I feel for her, I overlooked the most obvious outcome of my actions—they *could* get back together.

"Oh, please, it's not like that," she huffs.

When I continue to glower at her, she scoffs, "Whatever. Suit yourself."

She spins around and marches back toward the deck. I follow her. She reaches the tub and when she sheds her robe, all the breath leaves my lungs. I take in the curve of her shoulders, the nip of her waist encased in the one-piece swimsuit. It's cut high on the thighs and showcases the roundness of her butt cheeks, the lines of her calves, the delicate turn of her ankle. I never thought I had a butt fetish, until her. Nor a breast fetish, or a thigh fetish. I've never noticed a woman this acutely before. Truth is, I have a Raven fetish.

And while Poe inspires me, I've never quoted him so openly until I met her. Never felt the dark eroticism the poet embodied in his work until seeing her brought new meaning to his words. Perhaps I've been waiting for this woman to bring new energy into my life. To help me interpret the nuances of death, loss and grief—the three constants in my life—in a different way. For the first time, I feel there's a reason to my existence.

A lightness to my soul comes when I'm with her. I've never felt this way before. She settles into the tub, on the opposite side from him. And the look on his face—bloody hell. That softness around his eyes, the slackness to his jaw, the way his muscles are rigid, and in his eyes, hopes and dreams and confusion clash. It's an emotion I've often felt when I find myself watching her. When I think of her, I wonder how my life could change so quickly. When I know I'll do anything to have her... When I know, while I'll never give up on keeping her in my life, I have to... give her enough space to work things out.

The old me would have pressed all of my advantages home, so it'd be abundantly clear to her I'm the only one for her... But thanks to her, I know, I can no longer break my son's heart. I hurt him enough during his growing years. And perhaps, before I met her, I wouldn't have been this sensitive to the impact my marrying her would have on him. But since she swept into my life and past my barriers, I'm more attuned to the impact of my actions on others. Strange, right?

The very reason I'd burn the world down for her also makes me more attuned to the repercussions of my behavior. And next thing you know, I'll be discussing all this emo shit with my nephews. She's ruining me, and she's not even aware of it.

I pause halfway to the hot tub, and watch my son say something. I'm not close enough to hear the words over the sound of the bubbling water, but I can make out by her response that it's an earnest conversation. She shakes her head, then jerks her chin in my direction. Felix's lips turn down. That pouting expression is one I've been at the receiving end of for most of his life, and deservedly so. And once again, I've failed him. Once again, I've allowed my own needs to get in the way of being a good father.

Sure, I invited Felix to stay as long as he wants under my roof. After all, my home will always be his home, too. This could afford me enough opportunities to build a relationship with my son.

And yes, a part of me hoped that if she saw the two of us together, she'd realize I was the one for her.

But seeing them together in the hot tub, it hits me how close in age they are, how well-suited they could have been, if they'd had a chance to know each other without the pressures of money getting in the way.

So, I'm going to back away, right? I'm going to postpone the wedding and give her time to decide?

And if she wants him? Even after he stood her up at their wedding? What if she wants to give him a second chance? If she chose him over me, would I walk away?

No. I cannot do that. But I may not have a choice if I go down this route. I curl my fingers into fists.

Felix glances in my direction; his brows furrow. He purses his lips, an adamant look on his face. Anger flashes in his eyes. He's pissed off at me. I would be, too, if I were in his shoes.

As for her? Her gaze is wary, a cautious air about her shoulders. She looks from me to Felix, then back at me. She's gauging us. She's trying to understand where she stands. What the dynamics of this situation mean for her. It's why I asked Felix here, after all.

I school my expression into one of disinterest. Even manage a smirk, while my heart seizes in my chest and my pulse crashes against my temples. I can feel my blood pressure shoot up. *Fuck. Fuck. Fuck.*

My body leans in her direction. The need to walk over and haul her out of that tub, away from Felix, and throw her over my shoulder to carry her up to my room overwhelms me. The need rises to a crescendo, and my vision narrows to pin-points. All I see is her and me and the future we could have had together. The one I might have if… I walk away now.

Do I want her enough to leave? Can I afford not to? I draw on every reserve of energy from deep within, tear my gaze from her, then I turn and stalk off.

I hear a splash behind me as she jumps out of the hot tub. "Quentin, wait!"

24

Vivian

I felt that piercing blue gaze alight on my body when I stepped into the tub. Saw the conflict in the angle of his jaw, in the jut of his chin, in how he looked between Felix and me before he squared his shoulders and came to some kind of decision. The hair on the back of my neck rose. Without conscious decision, I straightened. He'd already turned and stalked off by then.

I call after him, but he doesn't stop. I follow him through the conservatory, knowing I'm dripping water on the wooden floor but not caring. "Quentin, please!" I trail him into the living room and to the bar in the far corner. He uncaps a decanter of whiskey, pours himself a glass, and tosses it back. By the time I reach him, he's downed a second glass and has poured himself a third. I place my palm on the snifter. "You've had enough."

"Don't dictate to me, woman." He squeezes his fingers around the glass with such force that the skin across his knuckles turns white. He glares at me with so much anger, so much conflict, so much of everything, I reel back.

Then he looks away, and when he glances at me again, all that emotion is gone. It's replaced by that familiar mask of indifference, which is worse.

"Don't do that," I beg him. "Don't hide behind that mask of indifference. Tell me you're jealous. Tell him you want me. Tell me what you're feeling. Talk to me, Q, please!"

He lowers his gaze to my palm which covers his glass, then back to my face. There's enough steeliness in his eyes that I find myself withdrawing my hand. He instantly throws back his third drink, then places his glass back on the bar with exaggerated care.

"So that's your plan? To get drunk."

"It's as good as any."

What the — ! This macho alpha male who's dominant enough that if he asked me to drop to my knees right now and suck him off I would; *that* man doesn't have the balls to face his own feelings? Well too bad, I'm going to make him.

"Thought you were a fighter, not a quitter." I throw that out to get a rise out of him. Not that it works, for his expression closes further.

"Not sure what you're talking about," he says in a tone that has icicles dripping from it.

Gah! I'm so frustrated, I want to stamp my foot, but that'd only feed into the impression that I'm much younger than him and immature, so I settle for firming my lips. "I'm talking about the fact you saw me with Felix, assumed the worst, and stalked out."

"He clearly, has feelings for you."

"I—" I hesitate, unsure how to explain that I, too, have feelings for Felix, but they're not the kind he thinks. I feel a responsibility for him. The kind that had me stepping into my mother's shoes after she passed away. The kind that has me wanting to take care of Lizzie and ensure my father's medical needs are met. The kind that makes me look into his eyes and discern the hurt lurking there.

"Quentin—" I begin again, but he holds up his hand.

"What I saw out there, between the two of you... There's unsettled business."

"Ya think?" I scoff. "We were best friends. It's a little difficult to forget that we were there for each other when we felt we had no one else in the world to depend on."

He winces. And I shouldn't feel sorry for him. I shouldn't feel so drawn to him, so empathetic, so understanding that he couldn't have had it easy after Felix's mother left, trying to bring up a son on his own while trying to keep his promise to his country in terms of his service career. There's also the fact that he saw the opportunity when Felix walked away from me and moved right in. All of it shows he doesn't care about societal rules. He goes after what he wants. So why... is there conflict on his features?

"I... I didn't mean to hurt you with my words," I murmur.

"You didn't. You were telling the truth. I failed him... And now, I'm going to fail him again."

I open, then shut my mouth. I'm not sure if I can say anything to help the situation. It's best I let him speak.

He pours his fourth drink, but instead of drinking it, he stares down into his glass. The silence stretches but I know it's best to not speak and let him think through the thoughts in his head.

"I've made it clear; I want you," he finally growls.

"No argument there."

His lips twist. "But seeing the two of you together, I realize... I realize, I need time to get Felix on board with the situation."

"You mean?"

"I'm saying," he looks up at me and there's a decisiveness to features. "I mean, I'm going to postpone the wedding."

"So that's a good thing, right? That he postponed the wedding?" Zoey's face stares back at me from the screen of my phone.

That's what I have been telling myself. I know Felix is not the man for me. As for his father? I have conflicted feelings where Quentin is concerned. I cannot ignore the powerful pull I feel for him. At the same time, I am stricken by guilt that I am so attracted to my ex-boyfriend's father. It's so wrong that I compare the two of them in my head.

Felix is younger, has less life experience. He is finding himself, as am I. While Quentin... He's finding himself in a different way. I sense the deep-rooted hurt in him, and not just from whatever happened between him and Ryot when they were in the Marines. It's something more than that. Something on a personal level. Perhaps something to do with Felix's mother? He never talks about her. Was he so in love with her, that when she left, he never got over her?

Felix, too, never talks about his mother. All I know is that she left when he was two years old, and he's never seen her since. Felix is convinced Quentin is responsible for her leaving. But I know a lot of Q's behavior was down to the fact that he was focused on his duty to his country and also that he suspected Felix's mother was cheating on him. It's not my place to tell Felix that though.

The situation is more complicated than what I envisaged when I agreed to marry Quentin. I knew I was attracted to him, but I hadn't accounted for my growing feelings for Q.

Or that I'd get to know the man behind that gruff exterior. Someone who cares about me. Someone who's struggling to reconcile his differences with his son. Someone who's remorseful about the incident that caused the death of Ryot's wife. Someone who does not regret his past as a Marine. There are so many facets to Quentin, and that makes him more of an enigma. It makes him complex and confusing, and I'd be lying if I said I don't want to solve the puzzle that's Quentin Davenport.

"Vivian?" Zoey's voice cuts through the thoughts in my head. "You there?"

"Yeah, sorry, I'm confused. I thought he needed to marry me in order to firm up his role as the CEO of a company within the Davenport Group."

"There is that." She nods slowly. "So, what's he going to do about it, you think?"

"I don't know." When I woke up this morning, the house was empty. Quentin must have gone to work. Not sure where Felix is... He's probably sulking that I left him to go after Quentin last night. After that declaration, Quentin went up to his room. I retreated to mine, took a shower and, despite thinking I wouldn't sleep a wink, I drifted off as soon as I laid my head on my pillow. And since I got fired from my job, I have nowhere to be.

"What are you going to do now?" Zoey searches my features.

I begin to pace. "I have no idea." Lizzie's on a tour with the ballet school. My father's on an outing with his new caretaker. Apparently, now that I have money, neither of them need my presence. Quentin was right. Time is the one thing money can't buy. Something that's sinking in now.

"You could... paint?"

I stop pacing and stare at her. "Paint?"

"Isn't that the one thing you said had suffered all these years? Now you have the space to do it."

"I... am not sure I'm in the mood for it."

"I'm not a painter, but I do deal with writers, and what I've learned is

that when you are at your lowest, is when you're able to create the best,"
she offers.

I half smile. She's right. The last few years, the only way I've managed
to survive is by channeling all of my angst into my paintings. Granted, I
didn't have that much time to explore my creativity, but whenever I
managed to focus, I was happy with the results.

Zoey looks away, then back at me. "I wasn't going to share this yet,
but given the circumstances, I think I should."

"What is it?" I frown.

"Remember the pictures I took of your paintings?"

I nod slowly.

"My friend, the gallery owner, loved your work."

25

Quentin

"Care to explain the rationale behind your decision?" My father glares at me from across the expanse of the teakwood table in his corner office.

Arthur might come into work a few days in a month, but he insists on maintaining his office space in the iconic Davenport-owned building. Situated on the banks of the Thames River, the offices boast views of the London Eye, St. Paul's, and the Tower Bridge, with the skyline of the Central Business District, also called the City, in the distance.

I've been putting off telling him about my decision, but I know there's no getting around it. Knowing he'd be in today, I stalked into his office. When I told him I'd postponed the wedding, he was pissed.

He's keen to get me and his grandsons settled and help him in growing the Davenport group.

I refuse to become another successful statistic of his schemes — but for the fact that meeting Vivian awakened the possessive instincts in me. I admit, Arthur's condition that I need to marry to lock down my position as CEO also influenced me. But if I hadn't met Vivian, I doubt I'd have acted so quickly to comply with his stipulation.

"You're making a mistake," Arthur declares.

"It's my life." I shrug.

He leans back in his seat. "That's where you are wrong. *I* gave *you* life."

"And it's *mine* to live."

"Not if you want to continue as the CEO of the info-communications division."

I curl my fingers into fists. Had I thought my father would try to understand my point of view? Why would I think he'd have an iota of empathy in him?

"You must realize that my bride-to-be is the woman Felix almost married."

"But he didn't," Arthur points out.

"I'm aware. Doesn't change the fact that my son harbors feelings for her."

Arthur arches an eyebrow at me. "Your point being?"

Of course, he's going to make me spell it out. "I want to try and mend fences with my son before it's too late. I want him on board before I marry Vivian."

Arthur shakes his head. "You're getting distracted. The point is, you need to marry—and quickly—in order to confirm your role as CEO."

"It can wait a little longer," I argue.

"No, it can't."

"What the devil are you talking about? Nothing's going to happen if I wait another month to marry Vivian, and it gives me time to build a rapport with Felix. In fact"—I stab a finger at him— "I recommend that you aim to forge a connection with your son, the way I am with Felix. Try it Arthur; you'd be surprised at how good it feels."

Ignoring my last statement, he places the tips of his fingers together in front of him. "I thought you had the balls to go through with this."

Of course, he has to call my masculinity into question because I happen to talk about feelings. Is it any wonder I'm emotionally stunted with this man for a father? All the more reason not to let this cycle repeat with *my* son.

"And I will." I set my jaw. "Just not now."

"It has to be now. Firstly, because I've already arranged for an announcement in the newspaper publicizing your engagement, and secondly—"

"What the fuck? Why would you do that?" The last thing I need is for Felix's mother to see the news and pop back into my life to make more trouble for me. She managed to make an appearance whenever I got promoted in the navy and was on shore leave. It took me a while to connect the dots, but I realized her appearances coincided with something of importance that was about to take place in my life. I'll bet it's a matter of time before she does so again, once news of my impending marriage reaches her.

"Language," Arthur warns.

"You and I both know you're used to hearing worse."

He sets his lips in a straight line. "As I was saying before I was interrupted... Secondly, I don't have much time left, I want to see my son and grandsons married before —"

"Bull-fucking-shit. You're not going anywhere soon; we both know that."

Tiny, Arthur's Great Dane, raises his head from where he's been reposing next to his chair and whines. He must sense the tension in the air.

"Sorry, ol' boy," I say in a soothing voice.

Arthur pats the dog. Once the mutt lowers his head onto his giant front paws, Arthur turns to me with a strange look in his eyes. "And what if I tell you my days are numbered?"

"What do you mean?" I frown.

For the first time in my life, a look of uncertainty comes over Arthur's features. "It's nothing." He swipes his hand through the air. "Forget I said anything."

"Spit it out. What are you hiding?"

"It's none of your concern." He shuffles the papers on his desk, and his hand trembles. *What the —!* Arthur Davenport never gets nervous. *So, what is he playing at?* When I continue to glower at him, he sighs. "You've made up your mind, and obviously, there's nothing I can do to sway it."

My frown deepens. It's not like Arthur to give up that easily. I came in here expecting a full-on fight with him, and in a way, I'm disappointed he didn't try harder to get his way. It makes me suspicious. "What are you up to Arthur?"

He stills his actions, and when he looks at me, that hesitation on his features has bled into his eyes. "I wish I could say that this is all part of a bigger nefarious plan, but it is not."

"The fuck you mean, old man?"

He hunches his shoulders and seems to shrink in size. Suddenly, the desk dwarfs him, and the office seems too overpowering for his presence.

He seems to have aged in a matter of seconds and looks every day of his eighty-two years.

"It's nothing," he protests again, but the fight seems to have gone out of him.

I rise to my feet and lean forward. "What are you hiding?"

"It doesn't matter. I don't want to cause more stress to the lot of you."

"A little too late for that. Besides, let me worry about that. If there's something you should be telling us—"

The door bursts open, and a woman storms in. She's wearing motorcycle boots, leather pants and a jacket. She's carrying a helmet under her arm and is panting. Her brown hair is interspersed with strands of grey and blue. I recognize her as Zoey's grandmother Imelda. But what is she doing here?

She stomps toward Arthur, then raises the helmet and throws it at him. With an alacrity that belies his years, Arthur ducks.

"You motherfucker!" the woman growls as she closes the distance to him. "You shit-eating wanker."

Tiny springs to his feet. He takes one look at the advancing woman, then wisely, walks around her, giving her a clear berth, and stops by my side. I pat his head, and the two of us watch as she comes to a stop in front of Arthur. The look on Arthur's face, though... I suppress a laugh. It's the first time I'm seeing him gob smacked. Another first for me.

"Imelda, now, I'm sure I can explain, honey," he murmurs.

"Honey?" It's my turn to be shocked. I pick up my jaw from the floor and stare as the woman slams a fist into Arthur's table. "You two-faced, loose-bottomed, sandy-balled twat."

I wince. So does Arthur. He begins to rise to his feet, but Imelda stabs a finger at him. "Sit the fuck down, you wanker."

Arthur sits. And I'm back to gaping. I glance down at Tiny to find he has his mouth open and tongue lolling, as well. Tiny meets my gaze, then huffs. Is the mutt chuckling? Nah, not possible. Tiny looks back at Arthur. So do I, in time to see Imelda's shoulders shake.

"Why didn't you tell me about the doctor's diagnosis?!"

26

Quentin

"He has stage three liver cancer?" Knox frowns.

I nod. "And he wouldn't have told me except that his girlfriend, Imelda, barged in and—"

Tyler spits out his whisky. "He has a girlfriend?"

"It would seem that way, yes." I shake my head. I'm trying to get my head around the developments from this morning.

I realized the importance of getting my nephews up to speed on the news. I also knew they'd refuse to meet me, so I accepted Sinclair's help in arranging this meeting.

We're at his home office in his Primrose Hill townhouse—which had been designated neutral territory by them. I owe Sinclair for getting all my nephews in one place in a few hours. Is it something to do with the fact that, since my father is unwell, I suddenly feel responsible for them? My middle brother was killed in a car accident, and as for my oldest brother... Not only is he estranged from Arthur, but I haven't spoken to him in years. Which puts me in the position of being the oldest member of the family with ties to my nephews. And fuck, if that doesn't make me feel my age... Again.

My father's illness was sudden. It reminds me of the need to accomplish everything I want to accomplish. Besides marrying Vivian, reconciliation with my nephews is high on that list.

But I never equated death with Arthur, despite his advancing years. Influenced by his strong personality, I'd created this narrative of him being an unshakeable force in my mind. I'd been convinced he was someone who'd keep going on forever, someone who could bend, even death to the force of his personality. But being witness to how things can change in the blink of an eye has made me realize I'd be a fool to ignore the passage of time. Or that my time on this earth, too, isn't forever.

I feel a sense of urgency, a need to do everything I've wanted to. A need to embrace my destiny, to not be hesitant about going after what I want. It's why I knew I had to get my nephews together, so I could speak with them.

"Her name is Imelda Whittington." I glance around the faces in the room.

Connor is the first to react. "Did you say Whittington?" His gaze widens on the screen on the wall. He's off on another of his research trips. Unlike my other nephews, Connor did not join the Marines. He also opted to use his brilliance to pursue a career in biochemistry. He heads up the smallest and most profitable arm of the Davenport Group, which produces life-saving pharmaceutical drugs. Along with running the business, he also produces research papers, which he presents at conferences to fellow scientists in different parts of the world. He's off on these field trips and opted to join our impromptu gathering virtually.

Ryot agreed to attend and stands glowering in a corner of the room.

"Whittington?" Knox says slowly. "So she's—"

"Toren Whittington's mother," I add.

"Is this the same Imelda who was at my wedding?" Nathan frowns. "She's also Skylar's friend, Zoey's grandmother."

"Indeed." I nod. "In fact, that's where they first met."

"I had no idea her surname was Whittington." He rubs his temple. "Not that it would have stopped me from having her at my wedding, considering she walked Skylar down the aisle."

"She doesn't have any connection to the Whittington family fortune, apparently. She walked away from it all after her husband died. Her son runs the Whittington Group of companies."

"So, she gave up her right to the Whittington fortune?" Knox's tone is disbelieving.

"Apparently, she doesn't want to have anything to do with his money. She has enough from a trust her parents left her; she lives off that. She's also part of a motorcycle gang."

Tyler chokes on his drink, again. "Isn't she old?"

"In her early sixties." I frown at him. "Doesn't mean she can't ride a motorcycle."

"That's not what I meant." He raises his hands. "It's just, you have to admit, she doesn't have the profile of the kind of girlfriend I'd have picked for Arthur. Not that I'd have picked any girlfriend for Arthur. I mean, can the man get it up anymore?"

Knox grabs hold of the nearest object, which happens to be a stress ball, and lobs it at Tyler. He ducks, and the object hits the floor and bounces toward the door. "Heard of the blue pills, arsehole?" Knox growls.

"Heard about not being disrespectful to your grandfather?" I glower at the two of them.

Tyler's features take on an embarrassed look. "Didn't mean to sound insolent, but hey, you have to admit to being curious about how he gets it up at his age. Unless" — his brow clears — "oh wait, you're taking it personally because you have to use the blue pills, too, is that it? I — " he bites off the rest of whatever he was about to say, for I've rounded the table, grabbed his collar, and hauled him to his feet. I pull back my fist before I spot the smirk on his features. Wanker's trying to get to me, and he almost succeeded.

"I can keep going long after you lose steam and collapse in a puddle, you knob-headed tosser."

He wipes the grin off his face. "Sorry mate, didn't mean to be insulting."

"Yes, you did."

He smirks. "And you walked into that one."

I blow out a breath. I did, and that's a first. First Raven, then my father. The combination of emotional blows has thrown me off kilter. I release him, then straighten the collar of his shirt. "You're a fuck-witted, mangy-arsed, wank-spangled dipshit."

"Ouch, don't think I warranted that."

I shove at his shoulders, and he sits down heavily. "Alright, knock it off old man."

"You bloody — " I raise my fist, but Knox grabs me and pulls me back.

"Hey, hey, chill out, you two."

I shake off his hand, then walk around to stand behind my chair. Knox looks at me with a furrowed brow. "You okay, ol' chap?"

"The fuck wouldn't I be?" I grip the back of my chair.

"No reason." He peers into my features. "It's not like you to lose your temper, is all. I understand that Arthur being unwell is not great news, but"—his brow furrows—"is there something else that's bothering you?"

"There isn't." I hesitate. Now is not the time to lie. Not when I called this meeting with a view to uniting the family. If I expect them to put aside their differences and come together, then I owe it to them to be honest. I owe it to myself to be honest at this stage. "Actually, there is something that's on my mind."

"The wedding?" Knox guesses.

"The postponed wedding—"

"You postponed the wedding?" Connor asks from the video screen.

"Not anymore, apparently."

"So you didn't postpone it?" Tyler frowns.

"Bet Arthur used his ailment to emotionally blackmail you." Knox smirks.

I shoot him a dirty look, and when that has no effect, I rub the back of my neck. "The old man seemed to think if I did, he wouldn't be around for it," I say with reluctance.

"Knew it. In fact, I'm sure Gramps came up with this condition so he could coerce you into not postponing the wedding," Knox bursts out.

I hesitate. "It's true that all of it came to light only after I mentioned my decision to put off the wedding, but remember, it's not he who told me. If Imelda hadn't barged in, then thrown her bike helmet at him..."

This time Tyler chuckles. "I need to meet this woman!"

The expression across their faces varies between admiration, surprise, and amusement.

"Maybe he timed Imelda's entry. Perhaps he arranged for her to find out before you met with him?" Connor offers.

A headache begins to drum behind my eyeballs. "Not even Arthur would fake a serious illness to get his way." I tilt my head. "Also, I confirmed with his doctor."

"He must have paid off the doc," Knox snorts.

It's sad that we have such a low opinion of the old man, but Arthur's previous machinations in getting first Edward, then Nathan married off, mean all his actions are taken with a healthy dose of skepticism by all of us. "I wish that were true, but I had Dr. Weston Kincaid reconfirm the diagnosis."

Tyler sits up straight. "So, it's true?"

I nod.

Knox places the fingers of his palms together. "The old bastard is unwell?"

"It would seem that way. He's on immunotherapy and is responding well, apparently. His prognosis is good, but it's definitely impacted his energy levels. Of course, at his age"—I raise a shoulder—"there's no telling how things will change for him. When he asked me to not postpone the wedding, I didn't have a choice but to agree. I—"

There's a noise behind me. The hair on the back of my neck rises. At the same time, Knox's gaze is fixed on a spot behind me.

I know who I'm going to see before I spin around and spot her at the doorway to Sinclair's study.

She firms her lips. "You decided *not* to postpone the wedding and didn't think to tell me first?"

I wince. "I was going to, but—"

She turns and walks off.

"Shit, I'm sorry, man. Summer messaged me to ask if you were here. Apparently, Vivian was looking for you." Sinclair walks over to me and touches my shoulder. "I gave her your whereabouts. Hope this doesn't fuck up things for you?"

"Not more than I did. Make sure this lot doesn't kill each other, will you?" I head out of his study and past his butler Jeeves.

"The young miss went that way." He points toward the front door. "She didn't seem happy."

"She's not." I pick up speed, reach the door and wrench it open. She's not there. *Fuck.* I race down the steps and down the path that leads to the road. Homes in Primrose Hill, like most of London, do not have gates and fences around them, in part, due to this being in a safe area of the city, but also, because no physical gates can keep out intruders. Instead, Sinclair, like other residents, has opted for virtual security in the form of drones and security personnel who largely stay invisible.

I race out of the premises and onto the sidewalk, look both ways, and catch a glimpse of her before she disappears around the corner. I run after her. "Vivian, stop."

27

Vivian

He could tell his nephews, but he couldn't mention it to me? Is that all I am in the grand scheme of things? An afterthought? To think, I missed him enough to track him down and come to the Sterlings' place in search of him. To think, I was going to reassure him, again, that there's nothing between me and Felix, and that he shouldn't stay away from his own home — only to find he's making decisions about my future again... Without telling me.

I hear him behind me. I speed up, then break into a run. Thankfully, there aren't that many people, nor vehicles, on the road. I turn another corner and make for Primrose Hill High Street. His steps sound closer. No way am I going to make this easy for him. I blow past the entrance to Primrose Hill and race toward home. My speed slows down, my breath coming in pants. Damn, knew I should be doing something to get in shape.

"Raven, please let me explain." His voice sounds so close, I squeak, then give it everything I've got. Which, sadly, isn't much. I make it a few more steps before he grabs my shoulder. I stumble, and he rights me, then applies enough pressure that I have no choice but to turn around to face him. I'm at eye level with his chest—his gorgeous, broad chest, with the planes outlined under his shirt. Unlike me, he doesn't have a coat on.

The demarcation between his pectoral muscles is visible in the opening between his shirt collars. I focus my gaze on that yummy expanse of skin, then curse myself when my nipples instantly perk up. The man exudes pheromones; that must be the reason every cell in my body is tuned into his presence.

"Let me go." I try to pull away.

"Not until you listen to what I have to say," he growls.

That harsh edge to his voice skitters across my nerve-endings. Pulses of sensation eddy down to my clit. A heartbeat flares to life between my thighs. *No, no, no, you cannot think of how empty you are right now, or that you've been dreaming of how his cock will look when you wrap your fingers around it and squeeze it from base to tip. Also, why the hell isn't this man more out of breath?*

A bead of sweat slides over his Adam's apple, then down the broad column of his throat, towards the open collar of his shirt. Before I can stop myself, I reach up and scoop it up.

I bring my finger to my lips and suck on it. His body grows still. It's as if he's turned into a block of granite—one wrapped in sinew and tendons, warm masculine flesh, and his complex male scent.

"I'm sorry," I say in a small voice.

"I'm not." He notches his knuckles under my chin, so I have no choice but to raise my head. My gaze collides with the deep blue sea of his. Flecks of green and grey twist in them. Turmoil, helplessness, lust and resolve. An unbending, unflinching, decision that reaches out to me and slams into my chest.

"Q"—I clear my throat—"no."

I'm not sure what I'm saying no to, but it feels imperative I claw back an inch of space, independence, freedom, an inch of something that'll make me feel more in control. Something that'll help me hold onto a part of myself that'll ensure I maintain some mystique.

Then he bends his knees and peers into my eyes, and I know it's an illusion. I was never in control. I'm not the one calling the shots. I am not… making the decisions. My fate was sealed the day I looked into that drugging, mind-blowing gaze of his and lost my breath, and my thoughts, and was propelled into his trajectory to helplessly be trapped in his orbit. I've tried to break away, but every struggle has brought me closer to this collision. He's a black hole who's going to draw me in, trap me, swallow me completely, and I'll gladly accept it. There is no escaping. None at all.

My entire life has led me to this moment. I swallow, and a tear drop escapes from the corner of my eye.

It's his turn to lean in and lick it up.

"Marry me," he whispers against my cheek.

A ripple of apprehension runs up my spine. And when he drops to one knee and takes my hand in his again, emotions crowd my throat.

"I'm so sorry I didn't come straight home and tell you about my conversation with Arthur and his insistence we get married right away. I'm sorry I decided to stop by the Sterlings' first." His throat moves as he swallows. "I never wanted to delay the wedding. But I was trying to do right by Felix. I felt so bloody relieved that the decision was taken out of my hands. Now, I don't need to wait before I can proclaim to the world that you're mine. Not even the fact that Arthur's dying could take away from the exhilaration I felt."

"Your father's dying?" I gasp.

His features grow serious. "Stage three liver cancer."

"I'm so sorry." I twine my fingers with his. The anger I felt earlier fades. "No wonder you weren't thinking straight. It's difficult being faced with a parent's failing health. I've been through it with my dad.

His features soften, then he seems to get ahold of himself. "His prognosis is good, but it means, the time I have with him is shorter than I thought. I can't say no to him. I don't *want* to say no to him." He brings our joined hands to his mouth and kisses the back of my palm. "I should have come straight to you. I'm sorry I didn't. I... needed to get my thoughts in order. Needed to make sure that, this time, when I proposed, I'd get it right."

I nod slowly. "And I wanted to say, you have no need to worry about Felix. I know that's why you stayed away the last few days and I wanted to reassure you, I don't feel that way about Felix, at all."

"These last few days have been hell." His jaw tics, and his expression turns tortured. "When I thought there was a chance you wouldn't choose me... When it felt like you were getting further and further away from me... When I saw you with Felix—"

"It meant nothing," I interrupt him. "You have to believe me, Q."

"I do." He swallows again. "I'm sorry my jealousy got the better of me. I'm sorry I'm not a better man. I'm sorry I can't level out the playing field for Felix more. I'm a heartless, selfish, arsehole who cannot—will not give you up. I'm the kind of insensitive, cold-blooded, self-serving, dominant who commands you to marry me." He brings my hand to his mouth and kisses the back of my palm. "Marry me for real, Raven, and make me the happiest man on this earth."

"What are you saying?" I whisper.

"Marry me, not as a marriage of convenience. Do me the honor of becoming my wife and give me the chance to make you my world. Give me the chance to meet your every need, to fulfill your every desire, to please your body and mind and soul, to ensure you never lack for anything. Marry me and allow me to make you the center of my actions, my passion, my devotion, my everything. Let me show you we belong together, that we were meant to be together. Marry me tomorrow—"

"Tomorrow?" I gape at him. "That's... too soon."

"Not soon enough for me."

I begin to shake my head, and his hold on my hand tightens.

"—give me one chance to show you we were meant to be together. One chance, baby, please."

My heart melts in my chest. A tsunami of heat licks up the walls of my pussy. My clit throbs. My nipples swell. Every inch of my body seems to come to life. The chance to be with this man, to be his wife. The chance to experience the connection I felt with him when he made me orgasm. The fact that it feels like more than a physical connection. That it could mean he understands me on an emotional and a spiritual level. That he could be *the one*. I swallow.

"What do you say?" Tension vibrates off of him. His tone is strained. A vein pops at his temple, and the skin over his cheekbones is stretched. He looks like a man at the end of his tether. Like a man who'd give anything to get what he wants which, in this case, is me. He wants me. He needs me. He'll do anything for me.

For the first time, it's not me wanting to take care of someone else, but someone else asking to take care of me. So, will I give him that chance?

28

Quentin

I knock on the door to Felix's apartment with the hand holding the two tumblers I'd grabbed on the way here. In my other hand I have a bottle of Macallan's. When there's no answer, I knock again. I have a key to the apartment but I'm not going to use it. Not when I'd promised my son privacy. Doesn't mean my patience is infinite.

A few seconds pass. Then I raise my hand to knock again, when the door is flung open. Felix stands there with a pair of headphones around his neck. He's wearing a pair of jeans with holes at the knees and a sweatshirt with the words, "Up yours,'" with the image of a middle finger on it. Very mature. I resist the urge to criticize his attire and clear my throat. "Can I come in?" I ask.

His jaw tightens. He spins around and marches inside. I follow him through the living room and into the bedroom. He heads to the desk pushed up against the wall on the far side and where a computer screen shows a frozen image of an animated soldier firing and the explosions filling the screen, I realize, he's playing a video game.

It's as if I've walked into a scene from my past—when I returned from a tour of duty to find my son playing Call of Duty in his room. Only that was at Margaret's place. And this is in my house and my son is ten years older.

Felix drops into his chair. He pulls on his earphones, grabs the game console and begins to play. I walk over and stand next to him. He stiffens but doesn't take his gaze off the screen. I wait there patiently. Five minutes pass. The first sparks of anger lick my nerve-endings. I bat them aside, then dip into the reserves of patience I have stored inside. The kind I drew on when I had to stay vigilant while staying hidden after setting a trap for the enemy. It was always about who blinked first. Who was going to reach the end of their tether and reveal themselves. I widen my stance and lock my fingers around the bottle of whiskey.

He continues playing for another ten minutes, until there's an explosion on screen. Droplets of blood splatter the screen and it goes fuzzy around the edges. Felix tosses his console aside and tears off his earphones. "The fuck you want?"

He sinks back in his chair and lowers his chin to his chest. His lips are pulled down at the edges, his thin shoulders hunched. He looks petulant and angry and more than a little confused. His thick hair flops over his forehead, and before I can stop myself, I've placed the glasses on the desk next to his computer screen, then leaned in and brushed the strands back.

He jerks his chin up and stares at me.

I meet his gaze.

In his eyes, surprise flares, and a hot sensation stabs my chest. My son does not expect to see any gesture of softness from me. That's how low his expectations are of this relationship. I'm to blame for it, of course. I'll never forgive myself for not having a relationship with him.

Still, I have his attention now, so I take my gaze off his features long enough to pour the whiskey into both the tumblers. I hand one over to him. He hesitates, then takes it from me. *Thank fuck.* I raise my glass. Once more he looks like he's going to refuse me, then clinks his glass with mine. Both of us toss back our drinks.

I brought Vivian home, then coaxed her to return to her room and go to bed. It's going to be an eventful next twenty-four hours, and she needs her rest. She refused, of course, until I ordered her to go. She wasn't able to disobey. Shooting a glare in my direction, she'd retreated, and I came to Felix's room. It's past midnight, but I knew he'd be up.

"This is fucking good." He holds out the glass and I top him up, then myself.

"Can you talk without swearing?"

"Says the man who uses the four-letter word like it's his personal talisman."

I deserve that. I clink my glass with his, then wait until he takes a sip. I land a hip against his table. "There's something I need to tell you."

"She's marrying you." He stares at his now blank screen as he says it. His features are blank, but for the sheen of tears in his eyes.

My heart squeezes in my chest. I am his father and I do care for him, but I haven't been very good at showing it. The responsibility was stifling. I promised myself I'd take care of him, but when it came down to it, I wasn't able to rise to the challenge of parenting alone. I took the easy way out by choosing to devote my life to my career. Nothing I do will ever make up for my past mistakes... But the least I can do is be upfront with him on why I'm marrying her.

"She's the one for me."

He scoffs.

"The other time I've felt this way was when I held you in my arms the first time."

"And look how good a job you did with that."

I wince. "I wasn't a good father."

"You were the worst." He scowls.

"I won't try to defend myself."

"Nothing you say is going to change my mind about you."

"That's not what I'm here for."

"Then why are you here? If it's to ask for my blessing—"

"I'm not asking for your permission, I'm telling you what's going to happen. I'm marrying her —"

"You told me already."

"—tomorrow."

"What?" His eyes widen. His features form into a look of shock. "That soon?"

"Arthur... Your grandfather... He's not well. He insists I marry her sooner than not."

"You and he are the same." He looks me up and down. "You only watch out for your own interests."

"That might have been true once, but not anymore."

"Which is why you're marrying my fiancée?"

"Your ex-fiancée. Also, I hate to remind you once again, but you didn't turn up for your wedding."

"I know." He squeezes his fingers around the glass of whiskey. "I'm aware of my faults, but at least I'm honest enough to admit to them, unlike you."

I toss back the rest of the whiskey in my glass, then search his features. "I'm sorry I wasn't there for you when you needed me. I'm sorry I wasn't a better parent. I'm sorry I couldn't stop your mother from leaving."

"She didn't want me."

"No, don't say that. She couldn't cope with being a mother; doesn't mean she didn't want you."

"I suppose I should be grateful you stayed." He gives me a considering look. "Even though you were an absent parent, you at least provided for the roof over my head. And I never went hungry. And you did make sure Great Aunt Margaret was there for me."

"I should have stayed. I should have resigned from the Marines—"

He laughs and it's the first genuine emotion I've heard from him in a long time. "You and not having a military career? You and I both know you'd have been miserable."

"Instead, I made you miserable—"

He shrugs. "I was too young to understand how important being a Marine was to you. You had a lot of your identity tied up with it."

"I was also a father."

"I did miss you, but Great Aunt Margaret was there for me." He places his empty glass on the table with a thunk. "I'm not saying I forgive you for your absences. There were many school plays where I looked for you in the audience. But I also knew you were where you could make a real difference."

I nod slowly. This is unexpected. I didn't think my son had matured enough to begin to differentiate the nuances of his growing up years. I didn't think he understood how important it was for me to be a Marine.

"Does this mean—"

"I can't forgive you for moving in so quickly on Vivian," he interjects.

I'm not surprised. "If I were in your shoes, I wouldn't, either." I square my shoulders. "So, this is not a truce, I take it?"

He shakes his head. "I... I don't think I'll ever get used to seeing the two of you together." His throat moves as he swallows. "Where does she stand on this?"

I begin to answer, and he shakes his head. "You know what? I don't want to know." He grabs hold of the bottle of whiskey, then reaches for his headphones with his other hand. "And I don't want to talk to you." He snatches up his console, and the screen comes alive with the start of another game.

I've been dismissed. Clearly, I'm no match when it comes to being at the receiving end of the contempt of my own child. Parenthood is the greatest equalizer. Watching the back of his head, I reach out to ruffle his hair, then stop myself at the last moment.

I know I haven't done anything wrong. He stood her up, after all. And yet, there's no doubt I'm crossing an unspoken line. One which I know I have to make up to him. I should be grateful that Felix has turned out to be more mature than I gave him credit for. The conversation I had with him is more than I expected. I snatch up my glass, then turn and head toward the door when he calls out, "Quentin?"

I pause, no longer surprised he calls me by my first name, and thankful he calls me at all.

He half turns his face so he's in profile to me. "I'll be moving out after the wedding."

29

Quentin

"So, this is it?" Knox straightens my bow tie.

I swipe away his hand. "I'm good."

"Are you?" Sinclair, my other groomsman drawls from my other side. We're standing in front of the wedding arch, which has been erected in the garden of his townhouse in Primrose Hill.

Given we decided to hold the wedding overnight, instead of waiting for a few more weeks, the problem of finding a venue was resolved when Sinclair offered it up. It's the same place he married, he said. And given how happy he is with Summer, I took it as a sign to say yes.

Summer reached out to Raven and confirmed that her sister would ensure the wedding dress would be delivered in time for the ceremony. As for the paperwork, I took care of it. Nothing the Davenport contacts and fortune couldn't sort out. I've spent my life running from my family name, only to find myself flaunting it in order to tie the most precious thing I've come across in my life to my side. There's an irony hidden somewhere in the situation, but I refuse to contemplate it. All that matters is that I'm marrying her, and I'm never letting her go.

"What makes you think I'm not?" I scowl at Sinclair.

"The fact that you've been muttering to yourself for the last ten minutes?" Nathan murmurs. He's my third self-appointed groomsman. I didn't ask any of them; I didn't think that far out, but they'd beat me to it. They turned up this morning and announced their intentions, and I didn't decline. It makes no difference to me. All that matters is her, and that she gets the wedding she deserves.

My son counts, too. Telling him the wedding was going ahead sooner than planned is the least I could do. The coming days and months aren't going to be easy, but I'm going to see it through. I'm not running away from the confrontation this time. I'm going to prove to my son that this is the right decision for all of us. I'm going to prove to her that I am the man for her.

I take in a deep breath, another. *Pretend this is another mission — a life and death one. The most important one you've ever been on — get your thoughts under control.*

I roll my shoulders, then crack my neck. Close my eyes and drop into that place inside of me, that part I accessed each time I needed to find the calm to take out enemy targets.

Only this time, what fills my mind is the image of her face, her green eyes filled with desire, her lips parted and glistening and waiting to be wrapped around my cock; the blush on her cheeks as I nip on her mouth, the creamy column of her throat, so untouched and ready to be marked by me, the curve of her shoulder, which I will bite as I mount her, her trembling breasts, the nipples ripe and ready to be plucked by my fingers; her fingers digging into my hair, the moans that swell her throat. The way I'll stare into her eyes as I breach her, the very moment she realizes we fit together as I place my hand on her chest, feel her heartbeat in tandem with mine, feel her pulse rate soar, the sweat clinging to the cleavage between her breasts as she realizes she's mine. *Mine. Mine. Mine.*

"—Quentin, get a hold of yourself."

Knox's voice slices through my thoughts. I force my attention back to his face. "What did you say?"

He searches my features, and a smirk twists his lips. "You're pussy-whipped."

"And I wear it as a badge of honor."

He blinks slowly.

"You didn't say that."

"As someone who's part of the same club, I concur." Sinclair grins.

"I second that." Nathan inclines his head.

"The three of you wankers need to mind your own business," I growl.

"Why should we, when it's so much fun to be all up in yours?" Sinclair chortles. "The look on your face, man—and to think, your journey into the far reaches of this rollercoaster is only beginning."

"Fuck you, too," I say without heat.

Knox looks at the three of us in disgust. "What the fuck am I doing here in the company of you wusses?"

Sinclair and Nathan exchange looks.

"You thinking what I am?" Sinclair drawls.

"That he's protesting too much?" Nathan smirks.

"Who bets he's up next?" Sinclair's grin widens.

Nathan pretends to think, then shakes his head. "Not taking that one."

"The fuck you two talking about?" Knox lowers his chin to his chest.

"I don't think you want to find out in a hurry. I—" an electric shock runs up my spine. My muscles stiffen.

I turn to find her standing at the bottom of the aisle. From the corner of my eye, I notice that my nephew, Edward, who's going to officiate the marriage, has joined us. The seats around me have filled up with our friends while I'd been busy trying to calm my mind. I spot Arthur and Imelda in the front row, they're holding hands.

Then I see my son step up to my bride. What the hell? What's he doing dressed in a tux and why is her arm hooked through his?

Is he going to give her away? That feels like a selfless gesture on Felix's part. It implies a maturity I hadn't thought he had. It implies a blessing of, or at least approval of, our marriage, something I have only dreamed off. In fact, this feels like the conciliatory gesture from Felix which I have longed for. My mind says to accept it for it is, an attempt at burying our differences. But something primal in me is unable to get over the fact that another man is touching her. So what if he's my son? And that he's doing this to show he's ready to move past our differences. She's mine and I cannot stomach any other male near her.

She moves closer, her gaze soft, her gait slow. Her eyes connect with mine, and in them, I see an emotion which calms the jealousy that's infiltrated every part of my body. There's also a pleading in them... She's asking me to play along, to not react. I scowl at her, and her gaze widens.

If she thinks she can lead me on this... She's wrong. I'm the one who sets the pace. If she wanted my son to walk her down the aisle, she need only have asked. If she wanted to stage a reconciliation between us, she could have shared her plans. Sure, I'd have shot it down, but that point is moot. She didn't tell me what her plans were knowing what my response would be. She knew how pissed I'd be, but she went ahead and did it anyway.

I glare at her, and some of the color fades from her cheeks. I promise her retribution with my gaze. I promise to spank her arse for this bratty gesture. My fingers tingle.

And almost as if she senses it, her gaze flicks to my hand, then back to my face. She flicks out the tip of her pink tongue and touches it to her lower lip. All the blood drains to my groin. Fucking hell, at this rate I'm not going to be able to last the length of the ceremony.

I school all emotion from my features, and when I set my jaw, she swallows. She raises her chin, and in that gesture, I realize I've underestimated this woman. She's ready to go toe-to-toe with me, even if it means I'm going to teach her never to defy me. She's stubborn and adamant, and fuck, if I don't fall for her in that moment.

30

Vivian

"Are you sure about this?" Felix slows his steps, forcing me to reduce my speed, when all I want to do is pull out of his hold, close the distance to the glowering man who's standing at the end of the aisle with his wide stance, his fingers clenched into fists at his sides, and his shoulders rigid, and tell him he doesn't have anything to worry about. That I asked Felix to walk me down the aisle to show Q he was giving up his claim on me. That by doing this, he's acknowledging that Q and I belong together.

I didn't expect Felix to say yes to my request, so imagine my surprise when he did. Honestly, him agreeing is quite a gesture. Despite all his faults, I can't deny that Quentin and I wouldn't have met, if not for him. So, it feels right to have him play a role at our wedding. Perhaps, I should have mentioned it to Quentin, but I didn't want to chance his refusal.

I'd rather do it and ask forgiveness later or... Going by the glower on Quentin's features, face the consequences of my actions. But he can't blame me for doing this. He mentioned he wants to forge an under-standing with Felix, but from what I've observed, the two of them aren't any closer to that. So, this is me, forcing things along, the way Quentin did when he transferred money into my account.

And m-a-y-b-e, I want to see what happens when he realizes I didn't tell him what I was going to do. It's going to bring out the dominant side of him even more strongly, and if he wants to discipline me for it... Well, I'm not complaining. I ignore the ripple of anticipation that tugs at my belly and continue down the aisle with Felix at my side. Q's gaze darts from me to Felix, then back to me.

His blue eyes turn into arctic glaciers, the kind which are so densely packed with ice, you can't see through to their depths. The kind that hints there's a whirlpool of emotions churning under the surface, which he's hidden from you. It's there in the pulse at his jaw, the vein which tics at his temple, his flared nostrils, the skin stretched over his cheekbones, the way his shoulders swell, and his chest expands, the tightly clenched fingers at his sides, the wideness of his stance, which stretches the material of the pants over his thighs.

Oh my god, he looks so handsome. He's hot and sexy, and so virile, and he's the man I'm going to marry. I'm so excited it's him. It had to be Q. I knew it from the moment I walked up the aisle a few weeks ago. When I passed him and realized he was in the wrong place. That he shouldn't be behind the pew but up there near the altar, waiting for me. And now, he is. I'm so excited, I feel giddy.

I'm here in my beautiful Karma West Sovrano original dress, I have friends in the audience who showed up for me and are smiling at me, and I have someone walking me up the aisle.

My sister couldn't make it back in time because she's still on tour, but she called to wish me well. She still isn't entirely convinced about my decision to marry Q, but when she realized how happy I was, she gave in. She promised to visit as soon as she returned.

Everything is different, and so perfect, unlike my previous almost-wedding. It's beautiful and lavish, and most exciting of all, my groom wants me. Said groom, who's glowering at me from under his thick eyebrows because he's pissed at me. And who's going to teach me a lesson, so I never defy him again. A lesson I can't wait for. I squeeze my thighs together.

As I near Q, the tension in the air thickens. My footsteps slow, and Felix flinches next to me. He swallows, then relaxes his shoulders as we reach Quentin.

I hear Felix gulp audibly, then square his shoulders and hold out his hand. And when he shakes Felix's hand, the breath I wasn't aware I was holding deflates my lungs. The two stare at each other, something unspoken passing between them.

"This doesn't mean I condone your actions," Felix says in a low voice.

Symbolically it does, dude.

"This doesn't mean I'm not pissed off at *your* actions," Quentin growls.

Umm, actually it does. I stifle a smile. Men and their posturing!

They continue to glare at each other, but all I can think of is how sexy angry Q is. And how that hard edge to his voice sparks off my nerve-endings. My nipples tighten in response; my clit throbs. How is it that the more he's enraged, the more I'm turned on? The air crackles with the emotions vibrating off the three of us. The static in the space raises the hair on the back of my neck. The atmosphere is so heavy, it pushes down on my shoulders, pressing into my chest.

Fine, fine, guess I'll have to urge these two to take that last step to making up. Also, I'm tired of them taking up all of my mind space. I want to get past this drama, so I can finally enjoy my wedding properly.

I loosen my hold on Felix's arm and hold my hand out to Quentin. Without hesitation, he takes it with his free one. He brings my fingers to his lips and kisses the tips. With his other hand, he's holding Felix's. For a few seconds, the three of us are joined.

Then Quentin releases his hold on Felix. "Thank you for walking her down the aisle." Some of the anger fades from his face.

Felix's Adam's apple bobs. He jerks his chin. "If you do anything to make her unhappy, you'll have me to contend with."

Quentin barks out a laugh. Felix seems taken aback, then he chuckles, too. The tension dissolves. Finally! Once more, I feel giddy, this time with relief.

Felix steps back. Quentin draws me forward into his side.

Felix looks between us. The expression on his face is tinged with regret, but there's also a thread of something else. Acceptance? Isn't that the first step to moving on? Perhaps the three of us will get through this situation intact. I smile at Felix and mouth, "Thank you." Any animosity I feel toward him is gone, replaced by an almost brotherly fondness.

He smiles back.

Then, Quentin urges me forward. I take my place next to him. For the second time in as many weeks, I'm standing at my own wedding. This time, with the man I'm going to marry squeezing my hand in reassurance. And oh god, I'm so ready for this. I should feel nervous, but I'm not. I feel like I'm at the right place, at the right time, with the right man.

My fingers feel small and delicate and cold in comparison to his thicker, stronger, warm grasp. Reassurance bleeds from his fingertips to mine. The solidness of his bulk, the breadth of his shoulders, the warmth from his body—all of it surrounds me, grounds me, and holds me in place.

I try to focus on the words the officiant—one of Quentin's nephews—is saying. I see his lips move, but don't hear the words, because of the excitement that fills me. All I'm aware of is that I'm marrying a man I'm wildly attracted to and have feelings for. That I have more money in the bank than I know what to do with. That my father is watching—I met with him briefly when he popped by the room I used to get dressed. That I have a circle of supportive girlfriends who I'd never have met, but for him. Zoey is here, as is Imelda, who's, apparently, dating Arthur—that's news I'm trying to get my head around.

Then there's Summer, who delivered the wedding dress designed by her sister Karma—who had rushed her team to put the finishing touches to the wedding dress. I'm so touched by how this group of women has folded me into their circle as one of their own.

Along with Zoey, Grace also made it to the wedding. Harper messaged to congratulate me. She also sent her regrets that she couldn't make it at such short notice. All in all, I feel like I've found my tribe. I couldn't be happier, but for the fact I don't know where I stand with my new husband. Yep, he's my husband, for the officiant is pronouncing us husband and wife. My head reels.

My husband turns to me. I look up into his face and my lungs seize. Indigo-colored whirlpools eddy in his eyes. There's something carnal, something unholy, something very intent-filled, something salacious and yet, also, worshipful—an expression that signals he's both the saint and the sinner in this relationship, and he's not waiting anymore.

He's not going to hold back. This is the moment he's been waiting for since he met me. This is when he makes me his, in every sense of the word.

He slides his arm under my arm and flattens his palm over the curve of where my waist meets my hip. The next second, I'm flush against his chest. I gasp. And he must have been waiting for that reaction, for he closes his mouth around mine, and kisses me.

I'd be lying if I said I don't feel it all the way down to my toes, and my fingertips, and the roots of my hair, through every cell in my body, and my individual eyelashes. Heat flushes my blood, bathes my skin, and fills my chest with a deep, needy want, the kind I've never experienced before.

There's lust and possessiveness, and all of it is tinged with a desperation that speaks to something inside of me. Something that makes me lean into the kiss and return it.

I lock my arms about his shoulders, tilt my head, and bite down on his lower lip. A growl vibrates up his chest, turning my breasts into heaving globes. I feel something hard against my lower belly, and that fire in my body turns into an inferno. Every part of me is filled with a ravenous, aching craving that only he can fill.

He must sense my desperation, for the next moment, he's torn his lips from mine. He stares into my eyes, his own the color of burned cobalt embers. The next moment, I cry out, for he's thrown me over his shoulder.

31

Quentin

She wriggles in my grasp, and I tighten my hold across the top of her thighs. I'm aware of Knox smirking, of Nathan staring with surprise. Sinclair takes a step in my direction. He's stopped by Connor, who shakes his head. The silent ones are those to watch out for. Connor must read my intentions correctly, for he nods at me. Without bothering to acknowledge his gesture—there'll be time for that later—I charge down the aisle with my bride thrown over my shoulder.

Is it wrong to behave like a caveman right after my wedding cere- mony? Yes.

Do I regret it? No fucking way.

Show me a bridegroom who has eyes only for his bride, and I'll show you one who secretly wants to kidnap their wife after the ceremony and take her to a place where it's the two of them, where they could do unspeakable things to her. Of course, they don't have the balls to carry through with their intention.

But I do.

As I pass Arthur, he gives me a thumbs up—which I register with mixed feelings. On the one hand, it makes me realize that we have something in common, after all. On the other, I'm not happy that we have anything in common with him. I shove aside any feelings of misgiving and pick up my pace.

I walk past her friends, who're looking at us with varying expressions of surprise, shock, and dreamy rapture. Past her father, who looks apprehensive , and past my father, who has a smug expression on his face.

I don't owe an explanation of my actions to anyone—except for Raven. And I'm counting on the fact that when I make love to her, she'll understand what she means to me.

As I enter the house, she continues to wriggle around in my grasp. I don't hesitate to bring the palm of my hand down on her behind. The resulting slap vibrates through her body. She instantly stills. Long enough for me to make my way through Sinclair's conservatory, cutting a path through his living room and toward the doorway.

His butler holds the door open. He's poker-faced, as usual. Trust a British butler not to show any surprise at the prospect of a bridegroom leaving his own marriage with his bride hoisted over his shoulder. I reach my car, where my chauffeur holds the back door open. Once more, there's no surprise on his face. There'd better not be, considering the salary I pay him. When I slide her in, she splutters. "What the hell do you think you're doing?"

I urge her to move over and climb in. The chauffeur closes the door, then walks around to slide into the driver's seat. "Let's go," I order him.

When the car begins to move, I press the button to raise the partition between our seats. The car glides forward.

She turns, shoves her veil out of her face, and raises her hand. I see the slap coming, but let her palm connect with my cheek. The sound echoes around the space. She takes in the flesh of my cheek and the pattern of her fingers, no doubt, outlined there. When her gaze connects with mine, she must see my intent, for she slowly shakes her head.

"No." She begins to back away.

I let her, because it's going to be so much sweeter when I get my hands on her.

"Quentin—" she swallows. "No."

"You asked Felix to walk you down the aisle without telling me. That counts as being very, very bratty, don't you agree?"

She swallows, then nods.

"I didn't hear you."

"Y-yes. Yes sir."

"You did it, knowing I was going to punish you for it. And you want it; you want it so, so much, don't you, baby?"

A low moan escapes her. "Yes Sir," she whispers.

I'm instantly hard. Hearing her call me Sir makes me want to deliver on the trust she's put in me.

"Choose a safe word, baby."

"Safe word?"

"So if you ever feel that you need to stop things, you can use it."

"Why would I do that?" Her forehead furrows.

"Because I'm going to test your boundaries, and I want to make sure you're always safe. Your well-being is paramount to me."

She nods slowly. "I don't completely understand what that means, but I have faith in you."

Warmth squeezes my chest. A hot sensation pours through my veins. *How did I get this lucky? What have I done to deserve this goddess in my life?* I'm going to ensure she has the kind of wedding night she'll remember for the rest of her life.

"Your safe word," I remind her.

"Meatloaf."

"Meatloaf?" I frown, then smoothen out my forehead. "You mean, the 'I'll do anything for love, but I won't do that'? *That* Meatloaf?" I hazard a guess.

She looks at me with wide eyes. "You know that song?"

I scoff, "Of course I know that song. Nineties Rock is my favorite. I'm actually surprised that you know it."

"He released it in 1993, but its sound and style are more characteristic of classic rock from the seventies and eighties, which is the era Meatloaf is most associated with — "

I glare at her, and her words trail off. "Sorry, I tend to spout trivia when I'm nervous."

She's adorable. "I love it when you do that, baby." I allow my features to soften. "And when will you use your safe word?"

"When I want you to stop."

"Good girl."

The pulse at the base of her throat speeds up. She flicks out her little pink tongue and wets her lower lip, and fuck me, but I almost come in my pants.

I sprawl back in the seat, and when I spread my legs further apart, her gaze drops to my crotch. Her breathing grows rougher, her gaze transfixed by the evidence of my arousal stretching my pants.

I pat my thigh, and she shakes her head. "I'm not doing that." She raises her eyes to mine. When I glare back, she loses some of the color on her cheeks. I continue to stare at her, the command inherent in my stance. She swallows, then, as if unable to resist, she inches forward. When she reaches me, she hesitates. I glance down at my thighs, then back at her face. She swallows hard, then she wiggles herself on her stomach over my lap with her pussy radiating heat over my thigh.

32

Vivian

He positions me more firmly across his knee, and I shiver. Then he slides my gown up the back of my thighs. His fingers graze my skin, and an electric current shoots up to my core. My center of gravity seems to have shifted to the space between my thighs, where a beat flares to life. My nipples tighten. I want this so much. I want him to punish me because I already know I'm going to love it.

Anticipation tightens my belly. Then, he tears off my panties, and I cry out. Cool breeze grazes my backside, and goosebumps crowd my skin.

"What are you doing?" I begin to turn around, but he throws a heavy arm across the small of my back. It effectively prevents me from seeing what he's up to, which only makes his touch more agonizing. And that only turns me on further.

If you'd asked me the most likely scenario in the hours following my wedding, I'd have said we'd be at the reception. I would not have, in a million years, guessed I'd be laid out across my husband's thick thighs, with what seems to be a baseball bat-sized arousal poking into my lower belly and his blunt fingertip teasing the forbidden hole between my butt cheeks. My pulse goes into overdrive. Oh my god, how can that feel so good? How can I want this so much?

All of my attention is concentrated on my backside, following his touch as he slips his fingers between my legs and grazes my slit.

"Jesus, you're soaking, and I haven't even begun."

"B-begun?" I squeak, then cry out when his palm connects with my arse. *Slap-slap-slap,* in quick succession—he alternates between the cheeks—again and again.

Each time he spanks me, my body moves forward. It feels like he's putting his bulk behind each hit.

Fire streaks up my spine, igniting my clit, the hollow behind my belly button, swirling around my breasts, circling about my nipples, connecting the pulse points at my ankles, my wrists, and at the base of my throat, until every cell in my body feels full and fiery and ready to burst into flames.

If this is how it feels to accept him as my master, then I want more.

If this is how it feels to have him discipline me, then I'm going to make him mete out punishment as often as I can.

When he stops, shudders zip through me. Little twitches of pain on the heels of which a fullness follows. My body feels heavy and light at the same time. I'm weighed down by coiled springs of desire, winding into themselves, tighter, tighter. He massages my backside, and little eddies of pleasure spiral out to my extremities. Another groan bleeds from my lips.

"Look at you, with my palm prints etched into the curve of your behind. You make me want to feast on your flesh. You make me want to lose myself in your tight little holes." He stuffs two fingers inside my pussy, and I shudder.

"Fuck, you're so ready, if I slapped your pussy, you'd come right here, wouldn't you, Raven?"

I try to speak, but all that comes out is a thin, needy sound that horrifies me. How can I sound so debauched, so greedy, so... unrestrained? I squirm around and my clit connects with the hard column of his thigh. Shockwaves of sensations travel to my brain. OMG, a honeyed sensation coils in my lower belly. I'm aware I'm humping his legs but cannot bring myself to stop. I coil my fingers around his ankle for leverage. He doesn't stop me as my movements get more frantic. Each time my clit connects with his thigh, the column at his crotch throbs. He's as aroused as me; that's my one consolation.

Moisture collects at my slit, and I dig my toes into the Manolo Blahniks which were delivered to me this morning. The note said, *"I'm going to fuck my wife in these."*

There was no signature, but of course, I knew who they were from. Now, when he runs his fingers around the edge of where the stilettos encase my ankles, I shiver.

He tugs and spreads my legs wide... Enough to show him my pussy.

"You've made a mess on my pants, little girl." He doesn't sound angry at all. In fact, he sounds proud, and a little awed.

Once more, I try to peek over my shoulder, but his arm across my body stops me.

"Do you want me to slap your pussy?" he asks in a low, hard voice. One which whips across my sensitized nerve-endings and makes the part in question throb. Do I want him to slap my pussy? And if he does, will I orgasm right away? And how much would I love that? I bet he knows that I would, which is why he's asking me the question. If I say no — would he punish me further? More moisture coats my slit at the thought. Wouldn't I enjoy that even more? *I would. Totally.* I can't wait to see what he'll do next. I shake my head.

"Hmm, we have much work to do here, don't we?"

"W-work?" I say in a high-pitched voice, then clear my throat. "I have no idea what you're talking about, I—" The rest of my words get stuck in my throat, for a strange buzzing noise fills the space.

"What's that?"

"You're going to find out when you're wearing it up your bum."

"Excuse me?" My eyes widen. Surely not. He... I... All thoughts drain from my mind when he pries my arse cheeks apart. The buzzing switches off. Then I hear the unmistakable sound of him spitting. Something slides down the valley between the cheeks. He spit on my back hole. What the... *what?* Then he draws the cum from my slit to my back hole. Oh! *Oh!* He's lubricating it. The thought barely strikes me before he eases something into my forbidden hole, then slips it past the ring of muscle of my sphincter, which holds it snugly.

"What did you do? You did not... Did you—"

The buzzing sounds again, and my body bucks. *Jesus H Christ*, he made good on his earlier words. He actually inserted a—

"A butt plug," he informs me.

"What the h-hell is that for?" I say through gritted teeth.

He pulls out his phone and his fingers fly over the screen. He must have touched an app which controls it, for that damned thing sets off a burst of vibrations inside me. "Oh my... Q!" I pant.

"Exactly," he says smugly.

Thankfully, the vibrations taper off, but the sensations continue to radiate outward and wind around my clit. I shiver. Then he pats my smarting butt, and hot twinges of pleasure-pain squeeze my lower belly. He rightens the skirt of my gown, before he clasps me around my waist and sits me down next to him.

"Oh god." The weight on my backside sends fresh sparks of pain shooting out from his fingerprints on my butt. I swear, I can feel each individual fingerprint of his fat fingers on my skin. That, combined with that vibrating plug in that forbidden part of me, which has no right being this sensitive, makes my eyes roll back in my head. *Is it pain? Pleasure?* A combination of the two that increases my pulse rate and makes my heartbeat gallop. I grit my teeth against the sensations streaking under my skin.

I must sway into him, for the next thing I know, he puts his arm around me and tucks me into his side, saying, "Relax." He kisses the top of my head. "The more you resist, the more aroused you're going to get, and I'm not going to let you come for a while."

"You sure have a way of boosting my confidence, don't you?"

He chuckles, and the rumbling sound under my cheek is strangely soothing. He rubs circles over the thin lace of my gown, which encases my upper arms. I shiver in response, yet it's also, weirdly, reassuring. Enough for me to tip up my chin and ask, "Why did you do that?"

"Do what?"

"Carry me out of our wedding like a neanderthal?"

"Because when it comes to you, I lose all sense. When I see you, all I know is that you're mine. And when I slipped my ring on your finger, I knew I couldn't wait any longer to bury myself in your soft throbbing cunt and fuck your hot pussy until you can't walk straight and bring you to the edge over and over again. So, when you finally come, you'll never think about anyone else but me, never want to wear any other man's scent on your skin but mine, never want to look at another man without remembering your husband is the only one who knows how to take your every hole and make you orgasm on command." He looks between my eyes. "You feel me, Raven?"

33

Quentin

"Orgasm on command?" She scoffs. "Is that a thing?"

"Are you doubting me?" I ask in a voice that sounds casual but has an undertone of steel.

She shivers. Despite her earlier protests, her pupils are dilated, and her breathing elevated, and when I press down on the control in my pocket, she jerks.

"Stop!" She digs her elbow into my side. "Don't do that."

"Are you using your safe word?" I scrutinize her features.

She shakes her head without hesitation.

I relax, then twist my lips. "In case you haven't gotten the memo, darling wife, you don't tell me what to do."

She pouts, and all I can think is how I'd love to see those lips wrapped around my cock. Not until I pleasure her first. I slide my arm down her side and squeeze the top of her thigh. "Your body drives me crazy."

She seems taken aback. "I have no idea why. It's not like I'm particularly good-looking or stand out in any way or—"

"Hush, that's my wife you're talking about."

A flush fills her cheeks. She likes it when I call her 'my wife.' Interesting. *What else turns you on, little Raven?*

As I hold her gaze, her blush deepens. "Stop looking at me like that."

"Like what?"

"Like you want to eat me alive."

"Given a choice, I'd have your pussy for breakfast, lunch and dinner, but for now, I'll settle for getting to know every inch of your tight little body."

"Jesus"—she shakes her head—"you have a filthy mouth."

"And you love it."

A look of worry threads her gaze, then she nods slowly. "I do, and I can't understand why."

"What's to understand. We are debased creatures, one step away from animals, who are more honest than us. They give in to their passions, while we pretend we don't want the things that are hardwired into our DNA."

Her forehead furrows. "You mean, your wanting to dominate me—"

"—and you wanting to be submissive to me—"

"—is the natural order of things?"

"I mean"—I lower my chin so I can stare into her eyes—"I've wanted to make you mine since the moment I saw you. I mean, it was inevitable that a consensual BDSM relationship would be at the heart of our marriage. I mean, all the experience I've gathered over the years ensures I'll make every time we fuck more memorable than the last for you. I mean—"

She swallows.

"—that before the night is out, you'll be my wife in every sense. And before the week is out, you'll realize you can't live without me. And before the month is out, you'll have forgotten about your life before me."

Her breath hitches.

"I'm not going to stop until you realize there's no escaping this bond between us."

"And if I refuse?"

"Do you want to refuse?" I search her features. "Do you want to deny yourself the chance to find out how far you could go in search of your own pleasure? The kind only I can grant you?"

She draws in a breath, then looks away. "You mean, the kind Felix would not be able to."

I tighten my hold on her hip, and when she winces, I release her. "Don't bring a third person into this relationship."

"We met because of a third person."

I set my jaw. "I'd have met you anyway. It so happens, the sequence of events worked out the way it did."

She blinks, and her features soften. "You don't strike me as someone who believes in fate."

"I don't; I make my own. And my path"—I notch my knuckles under her chin—"leads to you."

She bites the inside of her cheek. "I wish I felt half as confident when it comes to us. I wish I had the life-experience to have faith in my choices. I wish—"

"What?" I allow my lips to curve slightly. "What is it you wish?"

"I wish it were easier for me to acknowledge that part inside of me that loves to be dominated by you."

I drag my thumb under her lower lip. "So, you found what I said interesting?"

"Don't pretend you didn't notice that I did."

"I want to hear it from your mouth."

"I thought you had other interests for my mouth," she says coyly.

The flare of heat in my groin is instantaneous. My already erect cock extends further. "So bloody sassy and yet, so innocent. So curious and yet, so shy. So ready to be led and yet, so much in denial. You're so fucking full of contradictions, baby, it makes me want to throw you down and rut into you right now, but I won't."

Her features flame.

"You're a submissive in every curve and dip and hollow of your body, in how you come across to me, in how you lower your eyes whenever I walk into a room. All you need is permission to accept your base nature."

"And you're the one who's going to give me permission, I suppose?"

"You already know the answer to that." I wrap my fingers around the nape of her neck.

She holds my gaze, "I won't give in without a fight."

"And that, my wife, is what will make your submission even more delicious." Could she be any more perfect?

Whatever she reads on my features has her lowering her own. "I'm on the pill"—she swallows— "and you already have my bloodwork."

"And you have mine." I had her go by the doctor as soon as we first set the date for the wedding and emailed the results of my latest tests this morning. Thank God, I was thorough. It means, there need not be anything between us.

Her thoughts must be along the same lines because the color on her cheeks spreads to her neck. "This feels like it's happening too fast."

"I understand." I lower my arm and put a little distance between us. "I promise, I'll go easy on you… the first time."

"Um… thanks?" Some of the tension seems to drain out of her shoulders. "Though it certainly didn't feel like that when you spanked me earlier."

"That was to remind you never to go behind my back and indulge in a stunt like you did earlier."

"You didn't have to put a plug up my butthole for that."

"Speaking of…" I pull the phone from my pocket, and when I touch the app on the screen, she sighs.

"You stopped that thing from vibrating."

"Because you're ready."

"Ready?" Her gaze widens. "Y-You mean—"

"I mean, you're not getting out of anal anytime soon." I smirk.

"A…nal," she squeaks.

"Thought you millennials preferred to skip the basics and go for the forbidden hole directly?"

She tosses her head. "I'm Gen Z, and I get the impression you say half the things you do just to shock me."

Damn, she caught me there. "I admit, I enjoy seeing that wide-eyed expression on your face when I say something that's out of your comfort zone," I say slowly.

She doesn't seem surprised. "Is that why you decided to use a butt plug on our wedding night?"

"No, that's because *I* have a preference for anal"—I hesitate— "and m-a-y-b-e I wanted to see what your reaction would be if I used it. Not to mention, I figured I might as well pull off the kid gloves and show you how depraved I am."

She tosses her head. "It takes more than a butt plug to shock me."

I stop myself from smiling. She's perfect, my wife. So spunky, so able to put me in my place. I couldn't have chosen better. And if I'm not careful, I'm going to fall in love with her, and I can't afford that. I want her in my life; and sure, I feel a connection to her. Doesn't mean I'm going to make myself completely vulnerable.

Once more, in a bid to change the direction of my thoughts, I cup her cheek. "Wait until I tie you up spread-eagled and pinch your exposed clit."

She flushes crimson. Her pupils dilate. "Jesus, how can you be so... so..."

"Explicit? Dirty? Salacious? Vulgar?" I smirk.

She shakes her head. "I was going to say upfront."

"My front will be up yours soon enough." I waggle my eyebrows at her.

She bursts out laughing. "That was such a NSFW dirty dad joke."

It's my turn to stare. "Did you refer to my pun as a dad joke?"

"A *dirty* dad joke."

"And what does NSFW mean?"

"You mean, you don't know it stands for Not Safe For Work?" Her eyes round. "How do you not know that? Oh, wait—" She snaps her fingers. "I forgot, you're old."

"Old, hmm?"

She giggles. "Ancient, actually."

I grab her hand and place it over my crotch. "Does that feel ancient to you, little Raven?"

34

Vivian

No, it doesn't. The thick rod under my palm feels angry, hard, and eager. It feels too big, too much, too everything. It feels full of life. It feels like it wants to fill me up and impale me with such force, I'll feel it at the back of my throat. It feels... Immense and overwhelming, and also, strong and devastatingly forceful. It feels like him. It feels like it's going to hurt when he tries to fit that monster cock inside of me. And how I'm going to enjoy every bit of that burn. How I can't wait to give him my virginity.

I can't wait any longer to be his completely, and yet—a shiver of apprehension runs through me.

"Make sure you don't give up everything too easily. Keep a little of yourself from him. Nothing like a little enigma to keep the marriage interesting, know what I mean?" Imelda's parting words echo in my mind.

Once I give myself to him, once I submit, will I find myself again? Will I lose my identity and everything I am to him?

I begin to move my hand away, but he lays his palm over mine to hold it in place. The warmth of his fingers bleeds into my skin, and it's reassuring. Which is strange, because the thickness under my palm is anything but. He leans in and, but for where I'm touching his cock with his hand on mine, we're not touching at all. His breath sears my cheek.

I lower my gaze to his mouth—that mouth which is more often than not in a straight line meant to convey his displeasure, that finely sculpted upper lip which hints at an austere nature, the illusion of which is shattered by that puffy lower lip. The one I want to sink my teeth into.

My intent must show in the way I'm staring at his mouth for he lowers his voice to a hush and growls, "Do it."

Constellations of desire pinprick under my skin. Without allowing myself to think, I close the remaining distance and bite down on his mouth. He doesn't flinch. Not even when the coppery taste of blood fills my palate. I look up and into his eyes. Our fingers intertwine, and he moves my palm down the length of his hardness. He grows bigger and wider, if that's possible. Heat sears my skin. My throat dries.

"See what you do to me, Raven?" He rubs his nose against mine. "You make me feel like I'm a teenager who's going to blow his load in his pants."

"But you're not."

"I'm not. Because I'm not letting myself or you come. Not until I've taken you to the edge many times over." His dick throbs as if to punctuate his words.

I swallow. "Sounds painful."

"Oh, it will be." There's an evil glint in his eyes.

"Are you trying to scare me off?"

"Am I succeeding?"

I want to say yes, but honestly, I'm dripping. And his veiled threat heightens my need for him and turns my core into a mass of quivering anticipation.

I shake my head.

This time, his lips twist in a smirk that causes those constellations in my body to glow brighter. Moisture bathes the flesh between my legs. My breasts hurt; my scalp tingles. I'm a mass of burning need. The car comes to a stop—thank God! He pulls his hand out from under mine, pushes the door open, and steps out. He helps me to my feet, then sweeps me up in his arms.

"Whoa!" I wrap my arms about his shoulders and, because I can't stop myself, I bury my nose in the curve of his neck. I should protest, but there's something very romantic about being carried bride-style by my husband up the steps of his townhouse— Wait, it's not a townhouse, it's a Victorian-built manor that wouldn't look out of place in Downton Abbey.

I look around the unfamiliar rolling gardens that surround the house. As far as I can tell, there are no other buildings around us for miles. Only a tree line in the distance, and beyond that, the gates through which we drove. He distracted me so well, I didn't notice we were headed toward an unknown location. The car that dropped us off begins to turn down the driveway. "The driver's leaving?"

"He is." My husband reaches the door, where he manages to key in the code while holding me in his arms, then he shoulders it open.

"B-but it looks like we're far from anywhere."

"That's the idea."

"Are we in London?"

"We're in the countryside, actually."

The door snicks shut behind us and he stalks across the grand foyer and toward a large double staircase that sweeps up to the second floor. I have a fleeting glimpse of stained glass high above us.

"I thought we were heading to your place."

"This *is* my place."

"Oh!" This is incredible. I take in the soaring ceilings, embellished with intricate plasterwork, a striking chandelier hanging above, and gleaming wooden floors below. Rich, wood wainscoting lines the walls, lending an air of warmth and sophistication.

Plush sofas and wingback chairs are upholstered in jewel-toned fabrics. They encircle an impressive fireplace that's almost as tall as him in height. Large bay windows frame views of the manicured gardens outside. On the walls are paintings—all of which, I have no doubt, are originals.

On one side the living room leads to a conservatory, and through an open set of pocket doors on the other side, I can make out a formal dining room with a long trestle table surrounded by high-backed carved chairs.

Whoa! The overall impression is both intimate and sophisticated. There's a feeling of elegance and grandeur, but underlying it is a hint of austerity. This place is so Q. I'm so grateful he brought me here. It's like getting a peek into his psyche without words.

I cuddle into his chest as he takes the steps two at a time. Whoa! He's carrying me, and I'm not particularly thin.

I tend toward the curvy side, but the way this man carries me, I might as well weigh nothing. His biceps tauten under my touch, and his heart beats steadily. He reaches the landing and walks down a corridor. We pass a few rooms, and when he reaches the double doors at the end of the corridor, he shoulders them open. He steps inside and into a large, carpeted room. He walks toward the center of the room and sets me down.

I take in the soaring fireplace, which takes up a big part of one wall. There's a rug in front of it and a sofa on one side. On the opposite wall are French windows, beyond which is the view of the sweeping countryside.

"The view's amazing."

"It is."

I glance sideways to find him staring at me.

"I meant the view from the window." I blush.

He watches me with interest, and that turns my cheeks fiery. "Stop looking at me like that." I brush past him and head toward the windows. I can't help but sneak a peek at the massive bed which dominates the room. The sheets are white, as are the pillows and the duvet cover. There are iron rings set into the posts... *and into the wall above the headboard. Also, are those ropes wrapped around the posts? Huh?* I realize I've stopped and am staring. He walks over to stand next to me.

"The number of times I've dreamed of having you here in my bed, tied to those rings, so you're spreadeagled, with your pussy bared for my ministrations, you have no idea."

The pussy in question squeezes in on itself. Tingling sensations run up my spine. "I wish you weren't so unfiltered in your words."

"When you've seen what I have, you learn to speak your mind."

I turn to him and find he has a pensive expression on his features.

"Was being at war difficult?" I hear my words and wince. What a stupid thing to ask. Like he's going to tell me, no, it was fun. Not to mention, it's not quite the conversation I envisioned on my wedding night —and with a plug up my butt—but the bleakness in his eyes hints at a vulnerable side of him. One I haven't seen before, and I don't want to miss this opportunity to find out more about my husband.

I'm sure he's going to brush me off, but to my surprise, he answers me.

"Seeing friends blown to bits and being unable to do anything about it was."

I wait for him to say more, but he opts to walk past me and to the windows looking out. Of course, this must be a difficult topic for him. I don't want to push him; he can tell me when he's ready. His spine is stiff, his shoulder muscles bunched. There's a sadness etched into every sharp angle of his body I didn't notice before. He's hidden it well... Until now.

I reach him and, sliding my arms about his waist, press my cheek into the firm wall of his back. Closing my eyes, I breathe in that pine and woodsmoke scent of his. He places his palm over mine.

For a few seconds, we stand there. I soak in the strength of his presence, the resilience of his muscles, the way I feel so delicate in comparison, the sheer security of being with him. Something coiled deep inside of me loosens.

When he turns and pinches my chin, I'm already rising on my tiptoes. He lowers his face and closes his lips over mine. His mouth is hard, but the kiss is tender.

I melt into him, and when he licks into the notch between my lips, I part them. He slips his tongue inside my mouth, and heat suffuses my lower body. My toes curl; my fingertips tremble. I dig them into his shoulders as he ravages my mouth.

The kiss seems to go on and on. Then suddenly, he wrenches his mouth from mine, sinks to his knees and, pushing up the skirt of my dress, he presses his nose into my pussy. He draws a deep breath, and I gasp.

Something warns me that if I follow his lead, it's going to be a long time before I come to my senses again. This entire experience with Q has been intense. It's making me feel emotions I haven't felt before. I need time to process it. I need... just a moment to regroup. "The science of kissing is called philematology." I burst out.

My stream of consciousness has the intended effect, for he freezes.

"Kissing can burn up to twenty-six calories per minute, depending on the intensity and duration," I add.

He looks up at me from between my legs, and there's something very erotic about seeing this powerful man on his knees with his fingers gripping the tops of my thighs. I snapshot the moment and store it away, sure it's going to inspire a painting. I continue to scan his features, committing the expression in his eyes to memory.

"What is it?" His tone is tinged with impatience. "Do you want me to stop?"

I shake my head. "No, but I'm aware you're deflecting."

"Deflecting?" His features are devoid of emotion, but his eyes flash. "What do you mean?"

"You started telling me about your past, then stopped yourself. And now, you're running away from your demons by focusing on giving me orgasms."

"Damn right, I'm going to lose myself in your tight, hot cunt as a way to escape my memories." Without taking his gaze from mine he licks up my pussy lips.

"Oh…" I breathe through the anticipation that bubbles up my throat.

His lips curl. "You mean, 'Oh Q,' don't you?" With that, he urges my legs further apart, then thrusts his tongue inside my weeping slit. My heart seems to drop to the space between my legs, until it feels like my entire body, my life, every part of me and all I am, is concentrated in that throbbing triangle of flesh. Then, he closes his mouth around my clit and sucks, and I cry out.

Quentin

Her cry arrows straight to my groin. All the blood has drained to my crotch. My cock is weeping to be let out of the constraints of my pants, but not yet.

First, I need to devour my wife's sweet pussy. I lick up her slit, and she shudders. And when I stab my tongue inside her wet channel, she groans. "Q, please, please, please—" She bites off the next word, for I've shoved two fingers inside her cunt. "Quentin," she screams and writhes, and I weave my fingers in and out of her, in and out. She tugs at my hair, throws her head back and pants. And when I hit the button on the remote controlling her butt plug, her body jolts.

"Omigod, omigod," she pants and warbles.

When her legs tremble, I rise to my feet. Holding her upright with one hand on her shoulder, I turn her around and undo the buttons on her dress. It falls to her ankles in a pool of white. I pull out the pins in her hair and the blonde strands fall in a cloud of gold around her shoulders. I shrug out of my jacket, undo my bow tie and toss them both aside. Then I walk around in a slow circle surveying the dip of her waist, the curve of her hips, the fleshy thighs which I can't wait to mark, the wiry hair on her unshaven pussy lips, which I adore.

This is the first time I've seen her naked, and she is everything I imagined. And more. Without taking my gaze off that triangle of flesh between her legs, I undo the button of one shirt sleeve and roll it up to my elbows, then the other. Something prompts me to look up at her face. She's staring at my forearms with something like fascination. I flex one, and she draws in a sharp breath.

"Everything okay?" I smirk.

She nods slowly. "Do you think I could make love to your forearms?"

Of all the surprising things to say— I plant my palms on my hips. "Let me get this right, you want to hump my forearms?"

"They're freakin' sexy, is all."

"If I'd known all I had to do was show off my forearms, I might have done it a long time ago."

"Specifically, your forearms with the sleeves rolled up to the elbows." She sighs.

Warmth suffuses my chest. A rush of pride engulfs my veins. One compliment from her, and I'm floored. I've got it bad, all right.

I want to say something blithe to deflect from the fact I'm halfway to blushing. A first for me, because... As much as I want her to submit and gain my approval, it seems... I want hers, too, and that's never happened before.

She flushes under my scrutiny. "Ignore me. Clearly, I have a forearm fetish."

It's too easy an opening, and I take it, because the alternative would be that I deal with these awkward feelings, the kind I've never faced before. I jerk my chin in her direction. "Time to find out what other fetishes you have. On your knees."

"What?" She jerks up her chin.

"On your knees, baby."

She hesitates, then complies.

I walk over to sit at the foot of the bed. "Now crawl to me."

"What? Why?" There's a note of horror in her voice. Yet her pupils dilate, and a ripple runs through her body. Her breasts seem to swell, the nipples hardening into pinpoints.

"Are you saying you're not turned on by the prospect of obeying me?" I drawl.

She swallows, then shakes her head. I confess, it's a test to find out how willing she is to submit. And when the pulse at the base of her neck kicks up in speed, I know she's ready. So ready. She needs that push, that permission to give in and enjoy her proclivities.

I glare at her, and the color slips from her features. She places her palms on the floor, then moves forward.

My blood thrums in my veins. Satisfaction fills my chest. "Good girl. You're perfect," I praise.

As she crawls, the globes of her breasts sway, the flesh of her thighs jiggles in a manner that makes me want to squeeze them and put my mark on the creamy flesh. And when I touch the app on my phone controlling the butt plug, a full body shiver grips her. She reaches me, and when I widen the space between my legs, she comes to a halt between them. "Do you want to suck your master's cock? Do you want me to fuck your face and use your mouth for my pleasure?"

A moan bleeds from her lips. Her pupils are so dilated, there's only a ring of green around the irises. And when she nods, fire zips down my spine. My shaft expands further, and I take several deep breaths to stop myself from coming in my pants. "Unzip me," I order.

She does it at once, and since I'm not wearing boxers, my cock springs out. She swallows. Her eyes grow round as she takes in the length, the vein running over the back of my shaft, the drops of precum that dot the crown. I squeeze my dick from base to crown and she licks her lips. "Want to taste it?"

She nods.

"What do you say?" I growl.

"Y... yes Sir. I want to taste it, Sir. Please."

"Such a good little submissive, wanting to suck her Sir's cock." Satisfaction crowds my chest. "Greedy, aren't you, little girl?"

She nods again, almost panting in her excitement. "Yes Sir. I am, Sir. Please, please, I want to take you down my throat, Sir."

The satisfaction in my chest grows until it resembles a tsunami of desire, which hardens my groin and extends my shaft further. "Open your mouth," I snap.

When she does, I wrap my fingers around her neck and press hard enough for her breath to falter. Then I urge her close and slide my cock over her tongue. When I hit the back of her throat, she gags. "Relax your jaw," I order. She does. And then, without being told, she hollows her cheeks.

The hot, tight suction on my cock lights a fire in my veins. Her mouth is sheer heaven. And the fact that she's my wife, flashing green sparks at me from under her lashes as she lets me stuff my dick down her throat, elevates the experience to something nearing nirvana. My heart rate accelerates. My pulse drums at my temples, at my wrists, even in my fucking balls. I increase the pace, begin to pump into her mouth.

Watching my cock disappear between her lips is something I've fantasized about since the moment I laid eyes on her lush lips, but nothing could have prepared me for how incredibly perfect it feels.

Tears squeeze out from the corners of her eyes, drool drips down her chin. Watching her fall apart tightens the knot at the base of my spine. "I'm going to wreck you," I promise her, meaning every word. "I'm going to break you down and put you back together, and every cell in your body is going to have my name etched into it."

I pull out, then reach down to slide a palm between her legs. "You're drenched. Even more, if that's possible."

I rise to my feet, forcing her to rise with me, then grip her hips, turn around, and drop her on the bed. She bounces once, then lays there, her hair in a golden halo around her face. The creamy skin of her neck is exposed, her breasts, the valley between her parted legs—all mine for the taking.

I reach behind me and pull my shirt up and over my head. When I step out of my pants and straighten, her breathing quickens. She stares at my upright cock, slight fear mixed with fascination on her features.

"Talk to me; tell me what you're thinking, baby."

"I..."—she swallows—"I was thinking that's too big to fit."

"You let me worry about that," I murmur. Doesn't stop me from preening a little and squeezing my dick from base to crown. I am human, and that look of trepidation mixed with anticipation on her face is enough to make me feel like a god.

"What if it hurts?" she croaks.

"I'll make sure it does."

"What?" She jerks her chin up and locks her gaze on my features. When she sees the humor in my eyes, she pouts. "You're an asshole."

"Guilty as charged." When was the last time I played around with a woman before fucking her? When did sex become as much about having fun as about domination?

Since I met her. Since this gorgeous woman came into my life. Sex with her is not casual. I can tell myself it's about making her submit to me but really, it's about my wanting to take care of her needs. To ensure she has the most incredible experience ever.

A hot sensation squeezes my ribcage. The slanting rays of the setting sun kiss her skin and turn it into burnished gold. Everything feels real and true, like I'm on the verge of something important.

I can't be falling in love with her. Can I? Nope, that can't be it. It's because she's my wife and I'm about to consummate our marriage. That's the reason for this melting sensation where my heart should be.

"Touch yourself, baby."

She instantly slides her fingers between her pussy lips, and a whine spills from her mouth.

"Now thrust your fingers inside."

She works three fingers inside her cunt, then moans.

"How does it feel?"

"It... it's not enough." She squirms. "I... I need more. So much more."

"And I'm going to give it to you. It's going to feel so good; I promise." My heart feels like it's going to burst out of my ribcage. The need inside me balloons until it weighs down every part of me. I climb onto the bed and between her legs, forcing her to part them wider to accommodate the width of my shoulders. I lick my way up one inner thigh, then the other before licking the crease on either side of her pussy. She writhes and pushes her pelvis up, and I laugh. "Not that soon, baby."

"Fuck you," she pouts.

"I intend to."

I pull her fingers from her pussy and lick them off, then replace them with three of my own, and she cries out. And when I curl them inside her, she bucks, squeezes her eyes shut, and lets out a long, low groan. As she continues to writhe, I reach over and loosen one of the ropes tied to a post and hook it around her ankle. Then replace the fingers with those of my other hand while I reach over and hook the rope from the other post to her other ankle. Then I squeeze her thighs apart and work out the butt plug. "How does that feel?"

"I feel stretched and empty there." Her eyelids flutter down.

"Not for long." I throw it aside before I slap her pussy.

"Jesus," she yells, and her eyes fly open. "What was that for?"

"Making sure I have your attention."

I slap her pussy once more, and she throws her head back and groans. She pants, and when she opens her eyes and stares at me, her gaze is heavy with lust. She tries to sit up, but the restraints around her ankles make it difficult, and she subsides. An expression of apprehension touched with excitement fills her features.

"All right, baby?" I run my fingers down her thighs and squeeze gently.

She nods, her throat moving as she swallows.

"How do you feel?" I scan her features closely.

"A little scared; but also, excited."

"You're a natural, and I promise, you're going to enjoy every moment of what I'm going to do to you."

Her shoulders relax.

"Anytime it becomes overwhelming, you only have to ask me to stop," I say in a soft voice.

She jerks her chin, and when she raises her gaze to mine, her eyes glitter with anticipation.

"What are you going to do now?"

"Now?" I allow myself a small smile. "I'm going to eat you out."

35

Vivian

He licks my slit over and over, until I'm wheezing and trembling and panting. I try to pull away from that wicked tongue of his, but he holds me in place. Besides, I can't close my legs because he's tied me down. *How did he know this would add to my arousal? How could he know my body so well when we're still strangers on so many levels? And what does it say about me that I want more?*

The moisture between my leg's drips down my inner thighs, but he laps it up as quickly. It's messy and filthy, and I love it. Gah! He's tapped into that slut inside of me who I've kept hidden so carefully. With him, I don't feel the need to censor myself. I can be free, knowing he won't judge me. He wants me to be uninhibited. There's a freedom in letting go like this. It makes me want to submit to him... It also makes me want to resist and not give in so easily. I grab at his ears and tug. My intent is to hurt him because I'm pissed that he can read me so well. But instead of being hurt, he laughs.

The vibrations against my pussy travel to my extremities, and that turns me on further. He shoves three of his thick digits inside my cunt, while he circles my clit with his tongue. And the combination of that, along with how he squeezes my arse, sending pain shooting out from the abraded skin from the spanking, coalesces in a perfect storm behind my clitoris. It swells and blooms until it seems to reach my chest, then my throat.

And when he sucks on my clit while twisting his fingers inside me to hit that spot which no one else has touched before, my climax screeches out from my center.

Instantly, he pulls out his fingers and crawls over me. Bracing his arms on either side of my shoulders, he presses his mouth to mine. I can taste myself on him and can't stop the whine that leaves my lips. He kisses me firmly, understanding my frustration. "Not yet, baby."

"But I almost came," I whine. "Please, please, let me come, Q."

"And you will."

"So you'll let me come next time?"

The bastard's lips curve against mine. "If you're a good little girl, perhaps."

Frustration stiffens my shoulders. What a sadist. *And why does the fact he's holding back my orgasm turn my insides to mush? Why, oh, why does he know which of my buttons to push? And why do I love it? And am I going to give in to him completely?*

Not yet. I love baiting him even more. I relish this play-acting, where I pretend to resist him and pretend to hold back consent. I swallow. Jesus... That's the first time I've admitted it to myself. I want him to hold me down and overpower me and take me without giving me a choice in the matter. It took Quentin Davenport to bring the depth of my filthy fantasies to the surface and give me the freedom to embrace this kink.

When he slides his tongue over mine, I bite down and taste blood. He pulls back, and a silver spark gleams in his cold eyes. "There you are. Can't wait to channel all that passion into our fucking."

"In your dreams," I spit out in mock anger.

"As long as I'm the only one you dream about." He notches his cock against my slit, and I shudder.

"Do you want it, little girl? Want me to bury my cock inside of you and bring you to orgasm?"

I make a growling side deep in my throat, the fake anger turning into real passion. I can feel the blunt crown of his dick cleave my pussy, can feel my insides clench in anticipation. Can feel my breasts tingle, my scalp

hurt, as every cell in my body waits for him to push inside. *Wait. Wait...*
That's when my stomach growls.

He freezes, and I could cry in frustration.

"Guess you're hungry?" Something unholy glints in his eyes.

"Don't you dare stop," I begin, but he's already pulled back. He sits
back on his haunches, that monster cock of his jutting up against his stomach. It has to be painful to be this erect for so long, but you wouldn't
know judging at the look of satisfaction on his features.

"But you're famished. Can't have you weak with hunger, can I?"

"Come back here and finish what you started, asshole," I hear myself
and realize how exasperated, and needy, and desperate I sound, but I'm
past caring. Somewhere along the way, I've forgotten I wanted to take a
stance and not submit that easily. I want him to ignore my growling
stomach and stick that big dick of his inside me and use me and take his
pleasure and give me mine. I want him. "I want the orgasms you promised
me," I burst out.

"You mean, you want this?" He squeezes his cock from base to crown,
then again. The veins up the side grow more pronounced. My mouth
waters, while my slit already hurts.

"Yes, yes, I want it. Take me, Q. Fuck me. Make me come. *Please,*" I
plead without taking my gaze off his weeping dick.

"And *I* want you to come, baby. And you will. I promise." He rubs his
thumb across the liquid which clings to the crown of his cock, then he
reaches over and rubs it across my mouth. I lock my lips around his digit
and wipe it clean.

His gaze intensifies. His shoulders bulge. He stares at me with so
much desire, I'm confident he's going to fuck me. Then he pulls back his
hand and shakes his head. "Food. I need to feed you first."

My pussy clenches; my back hole feels hollow. There's a growing
emptiness inside me. I scowl at him, exasperated that he's taking this
entire holding back the orgasm from me to the extreme.

At the same time, I find it even more arousing that he cares that I'm
hungry—enough to pull back a second from penetrating me to get me
food.

'Course, it's one way of making me wait further and driving me a little
crazy with desire, but you have to give it to the man.

He knows this 'being a Dom' business really well.

He slides off the bed. "Don't move." He points a finger at me.

"I couldn't if I wanted to," I reply in a sulky voice.

He turns and stalks off, and once more, I see the tattoo of the raven on his back. The undulation of his muscles gives the illusion of the wind beneath the bird's wings. It's magnificent and completely suited to him.

Minutes pass, and I wonder what he's doing. I try to relax my muscles, but I'm too aroused. Then, there's the fact my legs have been pulled apart and tied to the posts. It's not uncomfortable, but it makes me very conscious of the fact that when he walks back into the room, the first thing he's going to see is my exposed pussy. Which was probably his intention, the bastard. Why couldn't he have made me come first? The minutes pass, and I must doze off, despite my very revealing position, for when I open my eyes, he's standing at the foot of the bed.

He's still naked, with his cock still standing to attention. If I was worried that my older husband would have trouble keeping it up, I needn't have. He has a tray on which there's a plate with a sandwich, another plate with cake on it, as well as a bottle of wine with one glass. He climbs onto the bed, places the tray next to me, then assumes his position between my legs. Leaning over, he places the sandwich against my lips.

I take a bite. The zing of tomatoes, the sweeter taste of pickled relish and the briny undertone of something that resembles oysters and finally the buttery flavor of fries rounded off with the bite of vinegar and the crunch of pomegranate seeds, fills my palate. "What is this?" I moan.

"I call it the fuel-before-sex-with my-wife-sandwich."

A chuckle threatens, but I swallow it down.

"You're definitely building up the sex part, but considering you haven't fucked me… I'm wondering if you intend to consummate this marriage on our wedding night?" And when I hear my words I realize, this is it. All that tension boiling up inside me is going to get an outlet. My husband is going to make love to me very soon. My heart gallops in my ribcage. My mouth grows dry. *Will it hurt when he penetrates me?*

He promised it will, and to be honest, that scares me a little, but also fills me with a strange sense of anticipation. *What does it say about me that it turns me on further to think of him impaling me with his massive cock?* My thighs tremble. I swallow around the thickness in my throat.

He also promised he'll bring me to orgasm. Not ashamed to say he'll be my first. *Will he know that he's my first? I should tell him, right? And bring home our age-difference? Worse, it might make him decide he needs to go even slower and not fuck me today. No way. That's not going to happen. I'm tired of waiting for my orgasm. Tired of waiting for him. I want to feel him inside me. I want him to fuck me today.*

Some of my eagerness must show on my face, for a wicked gleam fills his eyes. Without responding, he feeds me a few more bites of the sandwich. When I tell him I've had enough, he finishes the rest in a few big bites. Watching his jaw move as he chews, then the column of his throat flex as he swallows it down, is more arousing than watching a live sexshow.

He pours some of the wine into a glass, then he takes a sip. Then he leans over me and dribbles some of it on my mouth. I lick it off, and when I open my mouth again, he trickles more of the liquid. Some of it spills onto my chin, then my neck. Each time the liquid threatens to spill onto the bed, he licks it off my body.

By the time we're done with the glass, I'm wearing the wine on my mouth, my chin, my throat, my chest, and my breasts, where he sucked my nipples in between licking off the wine. Also, I'm so wet, I'm dripping.

"I'm going to spoil your bedspread," I moan.

"I won't let that happen." He lowers his head and licks up the inside of first one thigh, then the other.

By the time he licks up my pussy lips, my body feels like it's on fire. "Quentin, please," I moan.

In response, he slides off the bed and places the tray with the cake on the floor before he gets on the bed once again. With his head cushioned on my thigh, he trails his fingers around my clit. I'm so sensitive there, shockwaves radiate out from my point of contact. I grab at his head, my fingers slipping over the short hair on his scalp, and I end up holding onto his ears. "Oh, my God, that feels soo good."

"It's going to get better." He sets to work, licking and sucking with that sinful mouth of his, and when he adds his fingers inside my pussy and twists it, shockwaves cascade from my core.

My knees tremble, my entire body jolts, and I cry out, "I'm so close."

He hitches his shoulders under the tops of my thighs, uses his fingers to spread apart my pussy lips and when he licks me from my clit to my forbidden back hole, I'm so shocked, I freeze. He proceeds to lick me there while finger-banging my slit. Once-twice-thrice, and when he adds four fingers inside me, I instantly orgasm. The climax slams into my chest, locks my throat, and explodes behind my eyes.

I'm dimly aware of him untying the restraints from around my ankles.

Then I'm being lifted and carried. I open my eyelids and realize we're in the bathroom.

He seats me on the counter, then scans my features. "You okay?"

I nod. "A bit high from the orgasm, but I'm slowly coming back to earth."

He chuckles. "I'm just getting started, baby. "

36

Quentin

I kiss her firmly on the lips, then move toward the bathtub. I run the taps, making sure to add something that fills the air with the scent of roses. I hold my fingers under the tap, then nod. Just the right temperature for my wife.

I return, scoop her up, then step inside the bathtub and sink down. I cradle her against my chest. With the hot water lapping around us, I slowly relax. Steam fills the room. I wrap my arms about her and soak in the warmth.

When the water reaches the level of her nipples, I reach up with my foot and shut off the tap. Making her come is the greatest feeling ever. I can't wait to give her more orgasms. The thought sends the blood draining to my groin. Nope, I need to let her rest and recover. Unfortunately, my cock doesn't get the memo, for it extends and insists on settling against the cleavage between her arse-cheeks. I've never felt this young, this alive, this turned on, this hopeful about the future as when I'm with her. I hold myself still, not wanting to disturb her, content to watch as her eyelids shutter down and she melts into me.

Her blonde curls stick to her forehead from the steam, her lips turned up slightly. That flush on her cheeks is not only due to the hot water; it's the orgasm I gave her that relaxed her completely. She looks so serene and sweet, and so well-fucked in my arms, it seems like a pity to wake her. No matter that having her curves pressed up against me has given me a raging hard on. I want to bury myself in her pussy, I want to squeeze the plumpness of her fleshy thighs, I want to mark the perfect swell of her bottom, then bend her over and fuck her arse. I want to lick and suck and possess every hole of hers.

I want to make her come so hard, she forgets every man who came before me. My thoughts send the blood draining to my groin and tighten my balls. I want to be inside her so badly, but hearing her sigh and watching her parted lips and the softness of her features, I don't want to rouse her. We could spend the rest of our lives in this bathtub with her in my arms, and I wouldn't complain. My dick, sadly, has other plans.

She draws in a sharp breath, and I know she's back with me.

I cup her pussy, and a whimper escapes her. And when I push aside her hair and drag my stubble across the curve of her shoulder, she shivers.

I trace my fingers up the cleavage between her pussy lips, then down to play with the rosette between her butt cheeks. She gasps, then spreads her legs, giving me more access. When I bring my fingers back to her clit to trace the swollen bud, she writhes and rubs up against my erect shaft.

I have been erect since the first day I saw her. And this, despite wanking off every opportunity I've had. Nothing's going to compare to being inside of her. And I'm not letting myself take her until I've ensured I've made her come enough times.

I pause.

I've never been as concerned about satisfying a woman before this. I've never wanted to care for someone else like this before. Never wanted to protect anyone else from the world—except for my son, but that's a different emotion. This, what I feel for her, is dangerously close to something I've never felt before. It's the kind of love that would make me want to burn down the world if it would make her happy. The kind of love where I wouldn't hesitate to give her anything she wants and stop anything or anyone from ever hurting her.

The kind of love that heats my blood and makes my heart stutter. And ties my insides up in knots.

I freeze with my fingers inside her pussy.

She squirms against me, and when I don't react, she turns her head and looks at me over her shoulder. Her lips are parted, her breath coming in pants, but when she peruses my features her eyebrows knit, "What's wrong?"

I stare deeply into her eyes, taking in the naked emotion in them. A mixture of need and lust, and a yearning so strong, it hits me in the chest like a steam roller. I want to tell her what I realized. That despite my best efforts not to, I'm falling for her. That I've never felt this way about anyone else.

I open my mouth to tell her, but nothing comes out.

"Q?" She pulls away, then turns around so she's positioned on her knees between my legs. "Is everything okay?"

I will never be okay. I'll never go back to being the person I was. You're already changing me. Out loud, I say, "Why wouldn't I be?" I manage a smirk. "I was simply thinking how I can't wait to fuck your arse."

She flushes, then firms her lips. "I want to believe you, but something in your eyes tells me it's more than that."

She searches my features again, and I resist the urge to look away. This woman sees me, and it strikes a chord of fear in my heart. I feel like I've bared my soul to her. Another first.

It's taken a woman less than half my age to bring me to heel. She's one of the most caring women I've ever met. Someone who feels responsible for her family and lives up to those expectations of herself. Felix's mother destroyed my faith in humanity when she left her child, but my wife is beginning to restore it, brick by brick.

"Baby"—I cup her cheek—"you're one of the few people who sees through my bullshit."

"I *am* your wife, after all." She snorts.

"And there's no one else like you." No one else—not my fellow Marines, not my father or my brothers or my nephews, and definitely not my son's mother—can look past my facade, to the sentiments that lurk underneath.

She blushes further, then bites down on her lower lip. I can feel the tug all the way to the crown of my cock. I can't stop myself from bending my head and covering her mouth with mine.

Her taste is drugging, and evocative, and the stuff my dreams are made of. It shifts something in my chest, then turns my thighs to iron and my balls into obsidian.

When I tear my mouth away, both of us are panting.

I search her eyes. Can she tell what she already means to me? That my life will never be the same again. I'm no longer Quentin Davenport. I'm first and foremost, my Raven's husband. Her protector. Her defender. Her lover. Her dominant.

She must sense something of my thoughts, for her eyes widen. Her lips curve in a soft smile. She dives in again for a kiss, but I evade her mouth.

I can't tell her what I feel for her. It's too much, too soon. It makes me feel too vulnerable. But I'm so grateful to have her in my life, so grateful that she's gotten me in touch with my emotions again, the least I can do is make her come. So what, if I'm avoiding talking about feelings by making her orgasm, I will tell her what I feel for her. Just not yet.

"Q, please —" she begins, but I grip her hips and lift her up. Thanks to our height difference, I'm able to position her over my face. She balances her knees on my shoulders, clutches my head for support, then stares down at me. "Wh — What are you doing?"

"I'm contemplating my wife's cunt; you have a problem with that?" I stare at her glistening pussy, and her stomach muscles clench. I press soft kisses up one thigh, then down the other, before I pull her close to my mouth. "Ride my face."

"What?" The shock in her voice makes me chuckle.

"Press that sweet little slit into my mouth and let me lick it until you come."

"You already did that," she squeaks.

"This time, I won't use my fingers."

When she hesitates, I apply enough pressure, so she has no choice but to bend her knees and bring the flesh between her legs close to my lips. I instantly latch onto her clit and suck.

She cries out, throws her head back, digs her fingers into my shoulders, and tugs. A burning sensation sparks down my neck, my spine. My cock jumps in anticipation. I growl against her cunt, and her thighs quiver. I slide my hands down until I'm cupping her butt cheeks. I squeeze them, and she whimpers.

The sounds she makes form the symphony of my life. Her lips, her pussy, her fingers, the touch of her skin on mine, the sound of her voice, her scent, the way she smiles, her little moans when she's aroused, the way she doesn't hesitate to go toe-to-toe with me, how she cares for the people in her life, how she embraces her submissive side and doesn't hesitate to open herself up to new experiences — all of it has chained my heart and locked it, and she has the key.

I'm hers. Does she realize that? Can she sense it in how I handle her body? And she is mine. She belongs to me.

That fire under my skin turns into a blaze. I begin to lick between her pussy lips, around her clit, then down to her slit, where I stuff my tongue inside her warm, wet channel. She whines and squeezes her thighs around my face, and fuck me, but this is heaven. Between her legs, with her thick thighs suffocating me. I slide my fingers down the valley between her butt cheeks and play with her back hole. At the same time, I curl my tongue inside her and her body bucks. She curves her back, throws her head back and screams. Moisture bathes my mouth, drips down my chin, and she convulses as she orgasms.

When she goes limp, I bring her down to my chest, where she curls in.

We stay that way until the water begins to cool. Her shoulders twitch, and she snoozes. I don't want to wake her up, but I also can't stop myself from trailing my fingers over the curve of her shoulder. I bend and sniff her throat, inhaling the scent of her body now infused with the notes from the rose-scented bath salts especially for her. For her, I'll allow myself to smell like flowers.

I push the hair from her face, then bend and kiss first one eyelid, then the other. I kiss the tip of her cute little nose, her lips. She parts them, and I slide my tongue inside, then stop when she stirs.

I don't want to wake her. She deserves to rest. She must be tired. I take full credit for her orgasms. I allow myself a small smile. I wore her out, and her muscles are so relaxed, she's almost comatose. It's been a long day, and no doubt, her emotions have been all over the place. I draw back slowly and wait until she settles, and her breathing deepens.

I rise up and step out of the tub, holding her in my arms. I manage to dry her and bring her to bed, where I tuck her under the covers. Then I deposit the tray of food back in the kitchen and do a quick sweep of the house to make sure all the doors and windows are locked, and the security system is active. Not something I've done before, but with the most precious thing in the world under my roof, I want to make sure everything is secured. By the time I crawl into bed with her and pull her into my chest, I've already missed being with her, and we were apart for less than ten minutes.

She's becoming a necessity, an addiction. One that's settled deep into my skin and bones and become a part of me in the way no one else has. All signs that I'm in love with my wife. She has the power to hurt me more than anyone else on this earth.

Something I'll worry about later.

For now, I'm going to enjoy the curve of her butt, the contour of her waist, the honeyed softness of her skin, the rose-tinged scent of her shampoo, combined with the familiar scent of my soap that smells different on her. She smells like mine, and I know I'm fucked. There's no escaping the fact that I've made myself vulnerable to her.

When Felix's mother left, I swore I'd never allow anyone else into my life. Yes, I was at fault for what happened with her. And no, I hadn't loved her, but it didn't make the aftermath any easier to bear. It pushed me to bury myself deeper in my career. I was confident I'd never let myself be that vulnerable again. Yet, here I am, in love with a woman less than half my age. A woman who's my wife. Who I'm wedded to and have no plans of letting go.

But what if she grows tired of me?

If she leaves me too, what then?

She won't. I'll make sure of that. I close my eyes and drift off.

I'm back in a familiar nightmare. I know I'm dreaming but I'm unable to snap out of it. I'm back in that office on the warship off the coast of Russia that doubled up as our headquarters. I'm the commanding officer in charge of a secret mission to exterminate the insurgents who pose a serious threat to our country. The drones over the hideout of the enemy beam pictures to our screens. I'm watching the scene unfold on screen, but there's tense silence around me.

I've realized that the intel we received is faulty. Our team is on the scene—where they shouldn't be. But so are the enemies to our country.

If I don't call the strike, they'll go through with the plan to detonate the bomb in central London, causing one of the most horrific terrorist incidents in the modern history of the city.

If I do—we'll lose all four team members.

They should not have been anywhere near there, but the information was tainted.

They're also outnumbered. There's at least fifty hostiles spread across that square mile. If our team doesn't die from our missile attack, they're going to be hunted down by the enemy and meet a far more horrific end.

One way or the other, they're not coming out of this alive.

Experience tells me that. And if I don't take out the enemy soldiers, many more people will be injured.

The operator manning the controls grips the edge of the table with white knuckles. He's sweating, despite the air-conditioning in the space. There's silence in the room.

On screen, the sunlight is blinding. The buildings sprawled across the complex seem to be uninhabited, but the drones picking up the body heat of those inside indicate otherwise.

Then a figure emerges from the door. The drone zooms in on him, and the picture reveals he has a portable missile launcher over his shoulder. *Fuck.*

The Fire Control Operator in charge of deploying the missile swears. "You can't do this."

He's the one person on my team who challenges my command. As if I need to be reminded of what's at stake? If I don't follow through, I'll have failed in my duty to my country and to my monarch and to my fellow citizens. I'll have failed to protect them. And if I do... I'll have hurt my own family, irreparably.

It's likely Ryot will never forgive me for this.

The sweat pools in my armpits. My chest tightens. My entire career has led up to this moment. I call upon all of my military experience to help me make the judgement call. I know what I have to do. I push all of my doubts and feelings into a box and bury it in the deepest part of my soul.

"Stand by to engage on my command," I growl.

The tension in the room spikes. The rest of my team is motionless, their eyes riveted to the screen. The scent of sweat and stress, a pungent mix of body odor and something more acidic, deepens. It's the scent of oncoming tragedy. I can taste it on my tongue, feel the electricity in the air. The hair on the back of my neck rises.

"Fire," I bark.

The operator hesitates. This has never happened before. He has never questioned my command. This situation has divided my team. It's going to tear my unit — my family away from home — apart. My heart sinks.

Then with a herculean effort I shove my grief into the same box as my other feelings.

When I speak, my voice is calm, "That's an order, Marine."

There's an edge of authority to my tone that demands action. It cuts through the heaviness in the space. The operator presses the button. The missiles fire. My heart stops then starts up again. *Thump-thump-thump,* the blood booms in my ears.

There's a delay of a few seconds.

Then the buildings blow up, as does our drone.

The picture cuts out.

The operator jumps to his feet; he turns to me. "You took out our own." His eyes blaze, but underneath it is the same sorrow that I tucked away.

"Collateral damage." I keep my voice casual, but my heart squeezes in my chest.

My mind, though, is absolutely clear. I followed the rules to the letter. I did the right thing.

The operator advances on me, an ugly expression twisting his features. His face morphs until he looks like Ryot, who then raises his fist and smashes it into my face. I rear back.

I'm dreaming. I'm still dreaming.

I try to wake up but am unable to break free of the images. Pain, so much pain, filling every molecule in my body and engulfing me. I deserve this. I am responsible for this destruction. I should be punished. I don't defend myself. Don't throw up my arms to ward off his blows.

His features morph again, so he looks like my wife. Raven's bleeding from a wound to her chest, and half her face is blown up. "You did this to me!" She turns her accusing eyes on me.

No! My heart somersaults into my throat. Not my Raven. Not after I realized I love her. I can't lose her.

You're still dreaming.

But the anguish that squeezes my ribcage feels all too real. I deserve this. I deserve to pay for what I did to Ryot. I deserve to lose the love I've waited a lifetime for.

I stumble back. "I had to," I plead with her. "I had to do it. I couldn't not."

"This is your fault." She stabs her finger into my chest.

A sharp pain cuts through my ribcage. The woman I'd give my life for is blaming me for what happened.

And I... I know she's right.

"I know. It's all my fault. And I'm so sorry."

Her eyes flash. "It's not enough."

Her features morph back to Ryot's. "You will lose what is most dear to you." His voice is cold.

There's a finality to it that chills me to the bone.

This is my punishment. I'm cursed to lose the one thing, the person I love the most. I'm cursed to lose *her.*

"No." I shake my head. "No."

"Yes." He cracks his neck. "Only then, will you know my pain."

Sweat beads my forehead and slides down my back. My body is heavy. I'm sinking. It's impossible to breathe.

I shake my head. "Nothing can happen to her."

"Quentin?" Her voice calls from somewhere far away.

No, not my Raven. I cannot lose her.

"Now you'll know how it feels to not want to live anymore." Ryot bares his teeth. "To have the one thing you love the most ripped away from you. To have your future turn into a black hole of despair, to lose every hope and wake up every morning cursing the fact you're alive and she isn't. You deserve this. You dug your hole; now bury yourself in it."

He begins to laugh. The sound echoes inside my head, ripples down my spine, and shreds through my veins, my cells, until every part of my body has turned into an instrument of torture.

I know then, I can't let her into my life. I can't risk losing her. I can't risk something happening to her.

I have to let her go before someone destroys her to destroy me.

Run, Raven. Run from me. Run before I wreck you like I've wrecked everything I have ever valued. My relationship with my family. My son. And now you. Run, you deserve better.

"Run—" I snap my eyes open and see her face hovering over mine.

The curve of her eyebrows, those thick eyelashes, the pain-filled eyes swimming with tears, those bee stung lips forming my name: "Q?" She cups my cheek. "You were having a nightmare."

I grip her shoulders. "A nightmare?" I croak around the constriction in my throat.

A nightmare from which there is no waking. I know what I did. I did wrong by Ryot. I did wrong by my son. And now, I'm going to do wrong by her. I was selfish. I saw her and decided to use her to secure my future. I married her to ensure I got my inheritance. I was drawn to her, then fell in love with her. I allowed myself to become vulnerable to her... Knowing she'll leave me one day. Knowing I'll hurt her like I've hurt everyone else in my life, and then she'll be gone. I'm going to lose her. It's inevitable. Sweat pours down my back, clings to my shoulders.

My heart seems to have expanded to occupy my entire body. I'm one big mass of throbbing, aching, hurt. And she can save me. This one time, I can use her body to get rid of this desperate feeling that grips me. This one time, I can bury myself in her and find solace. And then... I'll let her go.

Then, I'll walk away from her before I further damage her life. She'll be better off without me.

I'll become a distant memory, and she can move on. She can find someone better than me. Someone who'll love her the way she deserves. I swallow the bitterness crowding my throat. Someone who'll kiss her and fuck her and —

"Q, you're hurting me." She swallows.

I loosen my grip on her.

"I'm sorry" — I memorize her features — "so sorry."

Am I apologizing for holding her too tightly, or for letting her go? For the inevitable distance I'm going to put between us... But not yet. I have her in my bed, in my arms, and I can love her... Just for now, I can give her pleasure. I can't undo the fact I married her, but I can bring her to orgasm. I can fuck her the way she deserves. I can make it so good for her, better than anything she's experienced in the past or will from any other man in her future. The thought of anyone else holding her lights a fire in my veins. I flip her onto her back.

"Q," she gasps, "what are you —" She cries out, for I've pushed her legs apart, positioning myself against her opening.

37

Vivian

He impales me in one smooth move. I gasp. I thought I was prepared for it, but when the pain twangs through my center, it takes me by surprise. A short, sharp, burning sensation rips through me.

His gaze widens. The shock in them makes my cheeks flame. I wanted this. Wanted to feel Q inside of me. I was beginning to think I'd never have it. And it feels strange, but also amazing.

Clearly, he doesn't share the sentiment, for he scowls at me. I sense the question in them even before he growls, "You're a virgin?"

I tip up my chin. "The term hymen comes from the Greek, for membrane. There is little to no evidence that it provides any benefits or functionality to your body. Not all women are born with a hymen." I hear my words and realize how absurd my stream of consciousness sounds, but I want him to know how little it matters. How I wasn't hiding anything from him. That I want this, and nothing, especially not a societal construct, is going to stop me from having it.

The lines around his eyes soften. He regards me with a serious expression on his face. "Shh, it's okay, baby. I'll take care of you, I promise." He lowers his head and kisses my forehead.

I swallow. The promise in his eyes when he looks into mine turns my insides to mush. My belly quivers. My pussy flutters, and when I squeeze my inner muscles, his cock swells further.

He's too much. Too big. Too everything.

He stays poised on his arms, his biceps bunching, the ropes of muscles on his shoulders standing out in relief.

There's a tension rolling off his big body, an intensity to the sharp edges of his features, a ferocity to how he watches me, which borders on desperation. There's a tortured look on his face, sweat dampening his forehead running in rivulets down the valley between his pecs. The remnants of whatever horror he saw in his nightmare are gone from his eyes, replaced by one-hundred percent lust. He throbs inside me, stretching my channel, pushing against my inner walls. I feel swallowed, consumed, surrounded by him.

He stays there, jaw hard, teeth gritted. "Do you know what it does to me to find out I'm your first?"

I shake my head, unable to speak. I want to tell him so much. I want to explain how I reached the age of twenty-three without a sexual partner...

But also, I'm glad he's my first.

His lips curl. "It makes me want to fuck you until you can't walk straight.

"Q..." I squirm under him. The earlier pain has receded, replaced by a churning hunger. I tilt my hips, then lock my ankles about his waist. I dig my heels into his back, trying to urge him to move.

He clicks his tongue. "Bad Raven. No topping from the bottom, baby."

"But I want you to fuck me."

"And I will, once I know you're ready."

"I *am* ready," I pout. I sound so whiny, so needy. But I don't care. I want him to get on with it already.

"Q, please. Please, please, please, I beg you."

My words must please him, for the smile disappears from his face. He sets his jaw, then pulls back, balancing at my entrance for a beat. Then another, before he propels his hips and sinks inside me to the hilt.

My groan mixes with his, and he stays there, buried inside me, with his balls resting against my cunt.

A shudder spirals up my body. I can feel him in my throat; I'm not kidding. I make a sound between a sob and a moan, and his blue eyes grow so dark, it feels like I'm looking at an azure galaxy of stars. Sweat trails down the valley between my breasts.

I feel connected to him in a way I haven't with anyone else, which makes sense. It's a feeling I don't have a name for, but I know it has changed me forever.

"You feel so good." His throat moves as he swallows. It's the only sign that perhaps, this is more than a carnal act for him too. And when he captures my mouth with his in a long deep kiss, I'm sure he feels this connection between us too.

Hope blooms in my chest. This is more than fucking... This is my husband making love to me, and he senses the enormity of the emotions that bind us. My heart feels as full as my pussy.

Without breaking the connection of our mouths, he pulls out, then thrusts into me again. My already sensitized channel seems to catch fire. The chafing of his thickness against my walls sends frissons of sensations dancing through my blood. Dragonflies flutter in my belly. Birds take flight in my chest. It's overwhelming how every cell in my body has flowered and is reaching for the sun...

He picks up speed, and I throw my arms around his neck and hold on. Each time he rams into me, my body scoots up the bed. The frame slaps into the wall. He puts the strength of his entire body into the way he pistons into me. Over and over again.

And I love it. And want more of it.

I'll never get enough of his fucking me. Never feel more complete than when he's inside of me. Never feel more powerful than when he's taking from me, and sating his need for me, and pushing me toward that distant place where everything is bright and gold and waiting for me.

Ohgod. Ohgod. Ohgod. I'm burning up. I'm on a spaceship headed from some distant planet. Sex with him is everything I hoped for, and more. Thank God, I waited for him. I'll never feel this way with anyone. Never. Except with my husband.

His cock thickens further, and the next time he pushes into me, he hits a spot deep inside me that sends shocks of rapture dancing across my nerve-endings. I open my mouth to cry out, but no sound emerges. He seems to understand, though, for he wrenches my hand from his neck and slams it into the mattress. He twines his fingers with mine, and the connection, along with how he never breaks the connection between our eyes, awakens something in my soul.

I can't come—not yet; not until he allows me to. He may not have stated it aloud, but his possession of my body demands I ask for his permission.

A warmth seeps into my blood, even as a part of me grows impatient. That darkness inside me ebbs and flows, then submits to him. I feel cherished because he owns my orgasms. I want him to own *all* of me.

I hold his gaze as I hover on the precipice... Waiting... Waiting...

And he understands without my saying a word, for he growls, "Come."

And that's all it takes for the climax to crash into me. When I cry out, he places his mouth over mine, swallowing the sound. My orgasm splinters into a thousand stars, the kaleidoscope of colors ebbing and flowing. As they fade away, I'm dimly aware of him fucking me through the aftershocks before he shudders and yells out his own release.

I close my eyes and float away into the most dreamless sleep I've had in years.

I wake up in the early hours of the morning to find his face between my legs again. As he licks my cunt and sips at my pussy lips and laps at my clit, a honeyed thickness suffuses my senses and turns my brain cells to mush.

The dawn light turns the raven on his back into an ethereal bird of prey as his muscles ripple, or perhaps, that's the imagination of my sleep-deprived, very lust-overwhelmed brain. With the last remnants of my coherent mind, I take in the bricks of muscles on his body, the sheen of sweat on his shoulders, the give of the planes on his back as he continues to eat me out. And when he slides two fingers inside my forbidden back hole, I instantly orgasm. My last recollection is of him climbing up my body and kissing me until everything fades to black.

When I wake up next, the sun is pouring through the windows, and I'm alone in the big bed. My shoulders slump. He left me alone on the first morning of starting our life together as husband and wife?

38

Vivian

I sit up and wince, but ignore it, my body on fire with the need to find my husband. My heart thumps with the irrational terror that he's left me. And then, there are the orgasms. Oh God, I need to see him. I need to feel his arms around me. I miss him so much. My feet don't seem to touch the floor as I race to pick up the shirt he abandoned and shrug into it. I head to the bathroom, take care of my needs, then walk down the stairs.

In the light of day, the place seems bigger, but there's also a warmth to it. The wooden floors, the thick area rugs, the deep sofas, the bookcases, the fireplace, the flowers in a vase on the table in the center of the foyer, which I missed completely yesterday. The flowers are fresh, and there's no dust on any of the furniture. Which means, he has someone who comes in to take care of the house. I walk through the living room and toward the kitchen. The scent of coffee greets me. There's the unmistakable sound of the news being read on the radio, and in front of the range stands Quentin.

He's wearing a pair of grey sweatpants, and his torso is uncovered. Which means, the raven on his back is on full display in the sunlight which pours through the windows of the kitchen. It bathes him in a golden light and turns his shredded physique into that of a pagan king. The kind who'd throw you down and rut into you, fucking you without compunction. The kind who'd protect you and burn the world down for you.

As if he senses my thoughts, he turns and smiles at me over his shoulder. "Good morning," he rumbles.

My pussy quivers. Is there a direct connection from his words to that part of me that makes me feel the need to run over to him and climb his beautiful body like a tree? I lock my fingers together and slide one foot over the other to stop myself from doing that. I settled for, "I missed you."

His eyes flare. He scans my body, clothed in his shirt, and his features soften. "I missed you, too, baby."

The tenderness in his voice lights a fresh trail of heat under my skin. I love his dominance, but I absolutely adore his ability to make me feel so cherished.

A sweep of his gaze down to my feet, and when he meets my gaze again, there's a possessiveness in his, a glint of something feral and dark and wicked, which turns my pussy into a sodden mess. A nervous tension knots my belly. Why do I feel like I'm in the presence of a predator? If I show him the slightest sign of nervousness, I'm sure he'll jump me, and I'm even more sure I'd enjoy that.

I swallow around the dry sensation in my throat and croak, "Did you sleep okay?"

His smile is a flash of white teeth against his tanned skin. "I did. And you?"

Heat flushes my skin. "I did, too, but I wish you were next to me when I woke up."

He scans my face intently, then nods. "Make sure you're next to your wife when she wakes up after a night of fucking. Noted."

"Oh, my God." I blush even more. "You are filthy."

"Only when I'm around you." He looks surprised by his admission. "I'm sorry I wasn't there to wake you up, but I wanted to make you breakfast."

"Breakfast?" My stomach grumbles on cue.

It's his turn to laugh. "I love that you have a healthy appetite, though I have no doubt, the night's activities also contributed to it."

I make a face and mumble, "It's so embarrassing."

"Don't be embarrassed. I love feeding you. Seeing you eat satisfies me in a way I didn't think was possible." He shakes his head, that bemused look back on his face. "Take a seat." He nods toward the island.

I make my way to a stool and slide onto it. He works a complicated espresso machine and brings me a cappuccino, complete with a design in the foam and a dusting of cocoa on top.

When I look at him in surprise, one side of his lips hitches up. "I saw the milk frothing wand at the apartment and since Felix takes his coffee black, I concluded that was your drink of choice."

"Oh." I nod slowly. "It was a gift from Lizzie. She won a competition with her troupe and bought it for me with her prize money. I was so upset with her. I'd rather she spend money on herself, but she wanted me to have something nice, she said, something that wasn't about the essentials of life." I smile in recollection.

"The two of you love each other."

I can't stop the smile that spreads over my face. "We do. I'm lucky to have her for a sister."

"And she's lucky to have you," he says in a serious voice. "You love her."

I nod. "As you do Felix."

I don't know why that just dawned on me, but something about the wistful expression on his face clued me into it.

His eyebrows knit. "Of course I do. I'm aware I may not be demonstrative about it, but I do."

"You should tell him so."

I wish I could tell you that I've fallen for you, too. I wish I could come out and say I love you. I wish you'd say the same to me, for I've seen how you look at me. I've felt how your body feels against mine. How when you fuck me, you do so with your entire body and soul. I wish... We'd cross this unsaid barrier that's still there between us.

He half smiles. "Noted, wife." He returns to the coffee machine and fills a mug with a stream of brown almost black liquid.

A warmth squeezes my chest. I love, love, love it when he calls me wife. Also, I loved his performance on our wedding night. As if he's read my mind, his forehead furrows. "Why didn't you tell me you were a virgin?"

I pause halfway to bringing my coffee cup to my mouth, then decide to take a sip of my cappuccino before I try to answer that one.

"Not that I'm complaining." He seats himself at the island with me and takes a sip from his own cup.

"Of course not." I snort. "And I didn't tell you because, whoever heard of a woman reaching twenty-three and not having done it yet? I was embarrassed."

"And Felix?" His tone is cautious.

When I look up at him, he holds up a hand. "Not that I want to know about my son's sex habits, but"—he shakes his head—"you must admit, it's strange. The two of you were about to get married, after all."

"It's not like Felix didn't want to, but I didn't feel… ready? And when I said I wanted to wait until our wedding night, he agreed. And I was relieved." I laugh without humor. "That should have warned me that marrying him wasn't the right thing to do. Talk about hindsight." I take another sip of the cappuccino.

When he stays silent, I sneak another peek at his face. "What?"

"You have nothing to regret. You have the rest of your life in front of you. It's best to commit mistakes early, so you learn from them. The trick is simply not to repeat them again." His voice is sober. I spot regret in his eyes.

"Are you thinking about the mistakes *you've* made?"

He shrugs. "I made the best choices I could in the moment with the information I had. It hasn't always been the right one." He smiles sadly. "Sometimes, I wonder if I'd make the same choices, and I can't say." His expression turns contemplative. "But that's life. I've learned to live with my decisions, and I'm determined to make up for the fall-out from those decisions."

"Hence, your fight with Ryot?"

He winces. "Nothing I say or do will bring his wife back. And that's one occasion in my life I'd probably make the same decision, given the circumstances. All I can do is do the right thing by Ryot when, or if, the opportunity arises. As for Felix?" he sighs. "I regret not being there for him. I screwed up his life by being absent for such long periods on end. I intend to remedy that."

His confessions stir something primal in my core. "It's not easy to admit to one's mistakes. Some say it requires a great deal of bravery."

He shrugs, then smiles sadly. "It's the least I can do, don't you think?"

That melting feeling in my chest intensifies. "This is why I'm attracted to you. It's not that you're older than me and more mature. It's because you have your shit together. You know your mind, and you don't hesitate to speak it, no matter how difficult it might be. Your confidence and your courage of conviction is very attractive."

"Only my confidence?" His eyes gleam.

I roll my eyes. "Is this where I'm supposed to say I also find your dick impressive, and your sexual prowess?"

"I know that already, but it wouldn't hurt to hear it from you." He chuckles.

"Oh, my God, your insufferable ego." I toss my hair away from my face. "The worst thing is, I find that attractive, and I shouldn't."

His smile widens to a shit-eating grin, and I can't stop myself from laughing. "Stop looking so pleased with yourself."

Our gazes hold. The air in the kitchen thickens. Heat crawls up my spine, and I want to lean over and close the distance between us and kiss him again. My cheeks flush, and for some reason, I feel embarrassed. The man has had his dick and his fingers inside me—not to mention, his tongue—and it's this heated look between us that floors me? *Get a grip, woman!* I clear my throat, then drain my mug. "This cappuccino is very good."

He shakes a finger in my direction. "That's a diversion, but I'll accept it."

"Thanks." I lower my chin so my hair covers my heated cheeks.

"I do have a question for you."

I look at him with curiosity. "Oh?"

"Why did you agree to marry me?"

39

Quentin

Her eyebrows shoot up toward her hair line." What do you mean?"

"It was the money in your account that made you agree to my proposition, wasn't it? You couldn't walk away from it, so you decided to marry me?"

Her features pale. Hurt filters into her eyes, and I curse myself. Since I woke up, I have been trying to figure out how best to start distancing myself. The nightmare still echoes in my head, reminding me that I'm going to lose her. But I didn't mean for it to come out such a callous manner. Especially not after last night, when I made love to her. And it *was* making love. It wasn't fucking. Not when it meant something to both of us. Not when I worshipped her body with mine and revealed the depth of my feelings for her without words.

Which is why I need to change the tone of our relationship.

I'll let her get this close, but no further. I'm in love with her, but she can never know that. I'm bound to hurt her, the way I've hurt those closest to me. It's a matter of time before I hurt her and she leaves, and I don't know how I'll survive it, but it's not about me. It's best I begin to push her away now, before she becomes too attached. It's best I put distance between us, so she'll break up with me and move on to something... Someone better.

This is best for her; this is me being considerate. If she thinks I don't have feelings for her, she'll be happy to walk away from me, right? And she'll still have the money. Her future will be set. So she won't miss me at all.

My heart stutters in my chest. My stomach ties itself in knots. I taste bile on my tongue, and swallow down the bitter taste, then square my shoulders.

"It was the money, admit it. There's no shame in that. It was transactional. You saw the money, and it gave you permission to go through with the rest of the arrangement. You could have walked away then, and I wouldn't have stopped you."

Her gaze widens. "What are you trying to say?"

"That you married me for the money, and because you were curious to find out if the sex would be as hot as I promised. You wanted to explore your submissive side. And then, there's the fact that you were a virgin." I arch an eyebrow. "You realized this was your chance to let an older, more experienced man break your 'hymen'?" I allude to the trivia she spouted earlier. I know it's going to piss her off further, and I'm right.

Her cheeks redden, and her features grow pinched. There's confusion in her eyes though. "Why are you being so hurtful to me? You were so sweet to me. So tender, and now, suddenly, you're this asshole again? What's happening, Q?"

I love it when she calls me that. A warm feeling coalesces in my chest. I ignore it. *You have to push her away, remember? This is what's best for her.*

It's going to mean Arthur doesn't confirm you as CEO of the company. It means you won't get access to your inheritance.

Well, fuck that. I made do with very little as a Marine. I can do the same for the rest of my life. Which is, anyway, going to be bleak without her. So, what need do I have for money if I can't spend it on her?

"Q?" She searches my features. "What's going through your mind? Talk to me. I know there's more to you than this don't-give-a-fuck exterior you like to project."

I stay silent, not wanting to give away my thoughts. Not wanting her to see how much it hurts me to withdraw from her. And at the same time, not wanting to destroy this relationship we've forged since I fucked her.

Perhaps I could wait a few more days?

Perhaps I can be with her a little longer?

And let her fall for you further? That would make it even more difficult for her to leave. That would break her heart even more.

You're doing her a favor by closing off your emotions from her.

My face must reveal some of my thoughts, for she firms her lips. "Guess you're more of a bastard than I thought you were." She drains the rest of the cappuccino, then slides off the stool. "Thanks for the coffee."

She turns to leave, and my vision tunnels.

I can't let her go. I can't allow her to walk away from me; not yet. Not when I still need her.

Perhaps I could stay married to her, but I could hold her at arm's length?

Yes, that's what I'll do. I won't let myself get any closer to her to minimize the possibility of hurting her further. But I can keep her in my life a little longer, right?

Either way, I can't let her leave. Not yet.

"Where do you think you're going?" I bark.

"Why the hell should I stay when you've decided to turn into your glowering, mean, old self anyway? I'm going back to my room; I need a shower—"

"No, you don't."

She scoffs. "Don't tell me what to do."

The defiance in her voice fires my blood. My thigh muscles tighten. My fingers tingle. When she refuses to obey me, it fucking turns me on. I can barely restrain myself from throwing her on the floor and rutting into her.

She heads toward the doorway, when I growl, "Raven, come back and sit your arse down."

Her steps slow.

"Now," I lower my voice to a hush.

She shudders, then comes to a stop, before whirling around and pointing a finger at me. "It's not fair. You use that voice, knowing I can't say no."

"You can say no." I remind her.

"And pay the consequences?" She rubs at her backside, a gesture which turns my cock to granite. *Fuck.*

"Sit." I point to the stool she vacated.

She scowls at me. "Apologize for your earlier remarks. Say you're sorry for saying those horrible things to me. Say you didn't mean them."

I turn the words over in my head. I don't want to lie to her. But I'm not ready to let her go. God help me, but I want to spend a little more time with her. Guess I'm conforming to my role of being a selfish bastard. I'm going to hell for allowing her to get closer to me, for developing deeper feelings for me, but I'm helpless.

Once more, can I hold her in my arms and kiss her lips and feel her heart beat in sync with mine? Once more, can I bring her to orgasm before I tell her the inevitable?

I let my features soften. "I'm sorry I hurt you baby, truly. It devastated me to say those words. It made me sick to my stomach to realize I was causing you pain." That much is true.

"So why did you do it? Why did you act like such a dick?" she cries.

Because it's the only way I can protect you. Because as much as I want to be with you, I can't. You're the woman for me, but I'm not right for you.

"Q?" She prompts. "What's on your mind? Why don't you tell me what you're worried about? Isn't that what being married is about? Aren't you supposed to share your concerns with me?"

"My only concern right now is to feed you," I manage to say without revealing how much it hurts me to maintain a level of detachment between us.

She throws up her hands. "Why are you hiding your true feelings again? You're such a macho guy, it drives me crazy when you don't have the courage to speak your mind."

My wife is right, of course. I'm a coward. Shouldn't I be able to bare myself to her? She's my soulmate, so why can't I reveal my vulnerabilities to her? Why am I so scared of her reaction to my fears? And they *are* fears. But they're informed by the events of my past. They're informed by how I've hurt everyone close to me. How I'm hurting her even now.

And by sharing more with her, she'll only get closer, and then when she leaves me it'll hurt her even more. No, it's best to keep her at arm's length... to the extent I can.

She purses her lips and looks at me closely. "Promise you won't become so cold again? Promise you'll tell me what's worrying you? Whatever it is, we can work through it together."

I want to, so much. I want to tell her what she wants to hear, but I cannot lie to her.

Instead, I allow myself a small smile and hold out my hand.

She looks at my hand, then back at my face; hesitates.

"Please, baby, can you let this one go, for now? Please, let's not spoil our time together here."

Her features grow mutinous. Her eyes spark at me. Of course she's not buying that. Her feistiness is one of the things I love about her.

Fuck, fuck, fuck, how could I have fallen for her so quickly? Knowing what's in store for us. Knowing she's going to leave me.

I lower my hand to my side and curl it into a fist. *How could I let this happen?*

She must see the play of emotions across my features, for the fight goes out of her. "Oh, Q." She closes the distance to me, and when I open my arms and widen the space between my legs, she steps into the gap and hugs me tightly.

I pull her closer into the 'V' between my thighs, then wrap my arms about her and tuck her against my chest. She melts into me and sighs. "Your hugs are almost as drugging as your fucking."

"Thank you, baby. Thank you for letting this one be, for now."

She shakes her head. "You're so annoying, Q. And so, so sexy, it makes my head spin just to look at you."

That makes two of us.

"You make me feel things I haven't before. You confuse me so much half the time, I don't know if I should slap you or kiss you."

"You can do both." I run my fingers down her hair.

"No doubt, so you can punish me for being bratty?"

"And you'll love every minute of it."

"You know me so well," she huffs out a laugh.

And you me. And *that* is the crux of the issue.

"This doesn't mean I've forgiven you for behaving like a total ass."

"I haven't earned that yet, but I will." I lean back and kiss the top of her head. "I still need to feed you."

I set her to the side, avoiding the questions still in her eyes, coward that I am.

40

Quentin

I slide off the stool and busy myself making her and myself omelets, each with toast and hash browns.

I grab the cutlery, set our places on the island, then slide a loaded plate in front of her before placing one in my place.

I also grab a bottle of olive oil from the kitchen counter and place it on the island between the plates.

"What's that for?" she asks.

I stifle a chuckle and say with a straight face, "You'll find out soon enough."

Her gaze narrows, but then I move to the fridge and bring out a small but perfectly created cake and hear her gasp in delight. I place the cake on the island, then return to my seat on the stool opposite her.

"Cake for breakfast?" She claps her hands in delight.

The excited note in her voice makes me smile again as I approach her.

"It's our wedding cake," I murmur.

"Wow, it looks —" She clears her throat. "It looks exquisite."

"Eat first." I take my seat.

She butters her toast and scarfs down half the omelet before she raises her head to find me watching. "What?"

"I forgot what it's like to be young enough to have an appetite like that."

"I don't know, your appetite seems fine to me."

"Is that a compliment?" I smirk.

"Whatever." She rolls her eyes. "By the way, what are you listening to?" She points her fork at the device on the far end of the island, which is streaming the radio channel in the background.

"BBC Radio 6."

"You listen to the BBC?"

"This channel plays eclectic music."

"I thought only the 'older generation' listened to the BBC." Her lips twitch, and I know she said that to rile me about our age gap, but I'm not falling for it.

"Of course, you're not listening to it on a radio—"

"It *is* a radio station." I frown.

"I mean, you're not listening to it on one of those antique, broadcast-player thingies."

Now I'm an antique, am I? Still, I stop myself from getting pissed off about it and lean my elbow on the table. "You're referring to a transistor radio, I take it?"

She nods vigorously. "That's it."

Of course, she doesn't know what a transistor radio is. And I'm sure she's never used a rotary dial phone, or a dial-up internet connection, or a dot matrix printer. Never have I felt our age gap more than now. "Have you seen one of *those* devices?" I ask in a normal tone.

"My dad listens to the BBC on an old school one." Her smile is guileless but, no doubt, she noticed my discomfort at her earlier comment and is pressing home the point. *The brat!* Mentioning me in the same breath as her father hits a little too close to home. This time, I can't stop my wince.

"I mean, it's okay. To each their own," she continues with a mischievous glint in her eyes. "Not that I'm comparing you to my father. I mean, that would be too easy and would suggest, right away, that I have daddy issues." This time, it's she who winces. "What I mean is, I know you're—"

"Closer in age to your father than you." I roll my shoulders in a bid to disperse the ache that's settled between them.

"But I've never thought of you as in the same age range as him, even if, chronologically, you are. You're very different from him. You don't feel that much older than me, most times, especially when — "

"I fuck you?" I use the F-word, knowing it will distract her from the reminder of one of the biggest insecurities I have when it comes to our relationship.

I also want to make her blush. I feel victorious when her cheeks blaze.

She shakes her head and seems to get control of herself. "That's a diversion, but I'll accept it." She points her fork at me.

Why that little — ! "You shouldn't point your fork at me, young lady." As soon as the words are out, I squeeze my eyes shut and groan aloud. "I walked into that one."

"You did." She nods, satisfaction dripping from her voice.

When I open my eyes again, she's watching me with a small smile. "For the record, I never did think I had daddy issues. But I like that you take care of me. I feel secure with you, know what I mean?" She pops a shoulder.

"I'm so glad you do." My heart swells with happiness. I'd fucking do anything to protect her. I'd burn the world down to keep her safe. And even when we're not together I'll... I'll look out for her. The happiness I feel threatens to fracture, and I force my thoughts back to the present.

"For the record, I have no fatherly feelings toward you, either. If anything, I feel fucking young here" — I slap my chest and wave my hand down my body — "and everywhere else it counts."

"Oh, really? I hadn't noticed." She widens her gaze at me, that sassy expression back on her face, the one which makes me want to throw her over my lap and spank her. My dick thinks it's a very good idea, and when she bats her eyelashes at me, my heart flutters. *Fuck, I'm such a goner.*

We look at each other for a few seconds. The silence stretches. And seated here, over the remnants of our breakfast — which I cooked for my wife with the low hum of the radio in the background and the sun pouring in through the windows, bathing everything in a golden glow — I feel closer to contentment than I've ever felt before. Something I'm sure I'll never feel with anyone else.

A heavy sensation coils in my chest. My pulse rate spikes, and I swear, I can feel my palms begin to sweat. I shake my head to clear this strange sensation which grips me. *Love — it's love. I'm in fucking love with her.* I bat the emotion aside, then clear my throat.

"I listened to pirate radio stations when I was at university. Got hooked onto them. Then worked, briefly, at one," I offer. I've never spoken about this part of my life, but it feels right to share this with her, and for once, I don't hold back.

She blinks her eyelids as if coming out of a trance. "Weren't they outlawed?"

"You're right, but some of them went underground. To this day, they operate without licenses in inner city areas or from ships in international waters." Some of that old excitement I felt when I worked with one of them bubbles to the surface. I forgot how good it felt to be part of something bigger than me, something that had a cause and purpose. It's a feeling I had when I was part of the Marines. "It's a very effective platform to promote independent voices, especially serving niche cultural or social needs not supported by mainstream platforms."

I break off when I notice her staring at me with a strange look on her face.

"What?" I snap.

"Umm, nothing." She looks away, smothering a laugh.

I find myself flushing. *Jesus Christ.* When was the last time I felt at such a loss for words? "Raven," I say in a warning tone, "out with your thoughts."

She rolls her eyes. "Just thinking there's a nerd inside you after all. No wonder I'm attracted to you."

"Nerd, hmm?" Somehow, I'm pleased by the compliment. And I know her enough to realize this *was* a compliment.

She nods. "I hadn't realized that you were a rebel when you were younger, and more idealistic than you are now. I'd give anything to have met you then."

"Hmm." I scowl at her, trying to figure out if she's joking or is merely trying to pander to my ego when she dips her chin. "Also, you're hot when you get all stern and formal."

"You think I'm hot?" I smirk.

"I'm here, am I not?" She tosses her head. "And you know you are, so stop wanting to hear it from me."

"I'll never get bored of hearing it from you," I say softly.

This time, it's she who blushes. She looks down at her plate and digs into her breakfast. So do I. For a few seconds, there's only the clinking of our cutlery against the plates. Then she asks, "Then what happened?"

"What do you mean?" I finish off my omelet and use the remaining toast to mop up the remaining bits on the plate.

"What happened after the pirate ship escapades?"

I place my knife and fork in my plate. "I realized, I loved the sea more than the illicit thrill of broadcasting illegally. So, I joined the Marines."

Her features take on a shrewd expression. "Why not join the Navy?"

I hesitate.

"There's something else, isn't there??"

I incline my head. I've gotten so good at fooling people with the lack of expression on my face, it's a shock to realize someone can look past the mask I normally wear.

She holds my gaze, and it's as if she's seeing into my soul.

I crack my neck. "The pirate radio station I worked at? I also owned it."

"You did?"

"I bought a ship with the money I made off the stock market and set up a FM transmitter on it. My closest friend, Danny, joined me on the ship moored off the shore of the UK in international waters. We spent our days working out, drinking, and talking about what we wanted to do with our lives—in between broadcasting punk and grime rock from obscure bands. He wanted to be a Marine. As for me, I knew my path was set. This was my last attempt at rebelling before I joined my father's company."

I swallow, knowing I'm coming to the difficult part.

"Go on," she urges me in a soft voice, which almost undoes me. No one has ever looked at me with such empathy.

For that matter, I've never shared this story with anyone else, but her lack of judgement invites me to confide in her, and I can't stop myself. I look away to gather my thoughts.

"One night, we were horsing around, as we normally did, and drinking. We drank our way through most of the alcohol on the ship that day. Danny was in great form. He'd enlisted and was leaving to join basic training in a few days. I knew I was going to miss him. But I was also envious about how confident he felt that this was his path. It was, maybe, three a.m. in the morning. The wind had picked up considerably that night, and we were both very drunk."

"He decided he had to piss off the bow of the ship. It took him a few tries before he made it there. He was weaving on his feet, barely able to stay upright. I thought it was funny. I kept laughing, until tears filled my eyes. When I blinked them away, he'd disappeared."

She gasps.

"I was too drunk to move. So drunk that when I tried to get to my feet to search for him, I kept falling. It took me three tries before I made it to where I'd last seen him. I looked overboard but couldn't see him. The waters were too dark. I managed to call the coastguard for help, then jumped off the ship to search for him."

"Did you... Did you find him?" she whispers.

I shake my head. That familiar heaviness knocks at the backs of my eyes. I swallow around the ball of emotion in my throat. "They never found him. I was arrested for running a pirate radio station. Arthur had to come bail me out. He also paid enough money to make it all go away. He refused to let me attend Danny's funeral, and I'll never forgive him for that. And when I told him I was joining the Marines in Danny's memory, he never forgave me. He wanted me to join the Davenport Group and learn the ropes. He had dreams of making me the CEO, since my older brothers weren't interested."

"So that's why there's bad blood between the two of you?"

"Well... It didn't help that my nephews followed my example, and all of them, except one, joined the Marines. Of course, you wouldn't know that when you hear Arthur boast about how there's a tradition of serving in the military among the Davenports. He spun it as a PR story to boost the company's reputation."

She shakes her head. "He's a canny old man."

"He is." I half smile. "If it weren't for the fact I was searching for a purpose when I returned from the Marines, and I realized I did want to leave some kind of legacy for my son, I never would have agreed to join him. I also realized that by helping to grow the business and claiming my inheritance, I could use the money to further the cause of military vets. It's what Danny would have wanted." My heart feels heavy, my guts churning with that familiar guilt I've carried with me since he died.

"So, that's why you like listening to the radio?"

I frown. "What do you mean?"

"It makes you feel close to Danny."

I stare at her, my thoughts in a whirl. I never made that connection, but she's right. It's a connection I have with Danny that nothing can sever. When I listen to the radio, it feels like he's speaking to me from the beyond. It never occurred to me. It took my wife to connect the dots and point something so obvious out to me.

"Q, you okay?" she asks in a hesitant voice.

I nod slowly.

"You miss him." She swallows, her gaze filling with compassion "I am so sorry for your loss."

"It was a long time ago." I glance away, not wanting her to see how her words disturb me, yet are so healing. *How can she see me so clearly? How can she read what my subconscious has been trying to signal to me for years, when it never occurred to me? How can she know me so well in such a short time?*

Her eyes gleam with unshed tears. She lays her fork and knife on the island, then slips off the stool and walks around to stand between my legs. "I'm sorry."

Her sweet voice is like a steady rain that wears down the barriers I've placed around my heart. *How could I have let her get this close to me? Why is it I'm unable to walk away from her, knowing I'm setting myself up for a fall?* I can't...

I can't bear to think of a time when she leaves me. And she will. One day, she'll wake up and realize she could do much better than me. She'll leave me, and I won't be able to go on. It's bad enough that I'm in love with her. I can't let this passion for her turn into an obsession. I cannot allow her to get any closer. I cannot get more invested in this relationship. That would hurt her, and me, more.

When she cups my cheek, my entire body seems to leap to attention. My fingertips tingle, but I resist the urge to reach out and touch her. Instead, bastard that I am, I lock up my emotions once more in that deep, dark place inside. And in an attempt to deflect her from showing more compassion for me — which would be my downfall — I twist my lips.

"Aren't you going to kiss me and make it better?"

She rises on tiptoe and presses her mouth to mine. It's sweet and honeyed and tentative. And it's so right... And so wrong.

I don't want her love and sympathy and tenderness right now. What I want is lust and avarice and the need to feel her skin on mine. I want to treat her like the submissive she is. I want to bury myself inside her tight holes, so it drowns out all other thoughts in my head.

My muscles tighten, and when she licks my lips, it's like a signal to my body. I grab her hips and spring to my feet. She gasps, begins to pull back, but I hitch her up. She instantly wraps her thick legs around my waist. Her bare pussy pushes into my crotch. I can feel the heat of her center through my sweatpants, and all of the blood drains to my groin. I lean into her and cover her mouth with mine.

I want her so distracted she forgets to feel sorry for me. I want her so filled with endorphins from the orgasms I'm going to wring from her that she'll forget to look at me with sympathy. I don't want her concern, or her warmth, or her gentleness. I don't want her to learn any more of my secrets. I don't want her understanding. I want to reduce our connection to that of a Dom and sub. I want her to see me as someone who awakened her body to the pleasures of BDSM, and nothing more. I want to distill our relationship to purely the physical, so when I leave her, while she'll be upset, but she'll be able to move on.

A tightness grips my chest at the thought.

I'll awaken her desires, and she'll, no doubt, seek another Dominant. Another lover who'll take advantage of her lush body and her giving nature. The thought sends a ripple of anger up my spine. It's going to be difficult to let her go, but I'll cross that bridge when I come to it.

For now, I'll focus on her mouth, her body, the curve of her hips, the way she melts into me. For now, I'll focus on her pain and her pleasure.

41

Vivian

He nibbles on my lower lip, and when my lips part, he thrusts his tongue inside my mouth. He deepens the kiss, until I melt into him.

He sucks on my tongue, and draws from me, until I whine and press myself closer. Then he slows the kiss. "Remember our wedding cake?"

"Wh-what?" I flutter my eyelids open.

"The wedding cake, baby." A wicked look comes into his eyes. I know then, he's talking about something filthy. Something naughty. Something kinky involving a wedding cake? *Ooh.* A thrill of anticipation tightens my muscles. I manage to keep the eagerness off my features—if he realizes I'm looking forward to it, no doubt, the bastard will stop himself from sharing it with me. I know his games enough to not reveal my excitement —so instead, I scowl. "What about it?"

"You're going to be wearing it."

Excuse me! Did he just say—? Nah, not possible. I don't need to pretend the surprise which makes me stutter, "Y-You mean, eating it, don't you?"

The smirk on his features widens to a grin. "I mean, wearing it," he clarifies.

"Wait, what?" I center my scrutiny on his eyes. There's an evil gleam there, combined with a hint of humor. Whatever this idea is, I'm not sure about it. "What are you up to?" I scowl.

"Gonna introduce you to a new kink, baby."

"A new kink?" I swallow. OMG! The thought of discovering a new kink with my new dominant husband lights up my nerve-endings like it's the fourth of July and Christmas and my birthday, all rolled into one. But also, a new kink involving a cake? Umm… I'm not sure about that.

"Ever heard of cake sitting?"

"Eh?" My frown deepens.

"It's exactly what it sounds like."

No… What? He doesn't mean — I gasp as he lowers me onto our wedding cake.

"What the hell?" I writhe and try to push off the gooey, mushy mix, which rubs up against my butt and gets into the holes and crevices where it has no business being. "What are you doing, Quentin?"

"What better way to enjoy my wedding cake than by licking it off my wife's pussy."

The flesh between my legs convulses, and my belly bottoms out. Those filthy words of his kindle fiery stings of delight through my blood. Goosebumps pepper my skin. *He's going to eat me out? He's going to smear my wedding cake in between my legs and slurp it up with that wicked tongue of his?*

"Raise your arms," he orders.

His bossy voice ignites a million little fires in my blood. As if he senses it, silver flames roar to life in his gaze.

But I'm not prepared for the alacrity with which he pulls off the shirt I'm wearing and flings it aside. I squeak. The air hits my breasts, and my nipples tighten into rigid points. He reaches out and tweaks one, and I whimper.

He glances down at my core. "Part your legs."

I do. The cake squishes and gives. The icing sticks to my skin. It's soft and wet and cool and smushy… and strangely, erotic. A buzzing sensation permeates my skin. It's exacerbated by the fact he's staring down at my pussy.

He flattens a palm to the space between my breasts and applies pressure. I lay back, and when he balances the soles of my feet on the edge of the island, I feel dirty and exposed, and way more aroused than I should be.

It might have to do with the way his features flush, or the way his breath quickens and his nostrils flare. "Fuck, if you could see yourself,

Raven. Those pink pussy lips covered with cake, and your swollen clit wearing a crown of cream—not even my most erotic dreams could compare to this."

He sinks to his knees, and when I try to squeeze my thighs together, he wraps his big palms around them, so I have no choice but to hold them apart.

He lifts his gaze to mine and, without breaking the connection, begins to lick the cream up the side of my inner thigh, then the other. I shudder, my bones turning to jelly. Each time he comes close to my pussy, only to move away, I whine. He laughs.

The vibrations travel up to the knot in my belly, which tightens. "Damn you, Q," I huff, then groan when he blows gently on my pussy. It sets off tiny sparks of lust though my body. I writhe and push up my pelvis, chasing his wicked tongue.

"What do you want, baby?"

"You know what I want."

"Say it aloud."

I open my mouth, but before I can speak, he drags his whiskered jaw up my inner thigh. Sweat breaks out on my brow. I slam my palm down onto the platform. "Ohmigod, please, please, Q."

"Please what?"

"Please eat me out, please put your tongue inside my—"

I cry out as he licks up my pussy lips, then curls his tongue around my clit.

Also, did those filthy demands come out of my mouth? He's changing me already. Turning me into a woman who revels in her need for the more explicit when it comes to sex with him. He attacks my flesh with gusto, and when I think I can't bear it anymore, he stuffs his tongue inside the puckered hole between my ass cheeks.

"Quentin!" He's done this before, and it still shocks me that it feels so good. I don't think the innocent me from a month ago could have fathomed how erotic it is when he licks up the cleavage between my ass cheeks. And I like it. I like it so much. More than I want to admit. I want to hate how much I like it, especially since it's a part of my body that should not be a source of such pleasure. But how can I, when it feels so good?

I squeeze my eyes shut, focusing on the sensations. My pussy clenches down, and my toes curl. The vibrations race up my legs, coalescing in my center. "Oh God, I'm going to—"

He removes his tongue. I sense him reaching over to grab the bottle of olive oil. He uncaps it and pours a thin stream between my arse cheeks. *What the —?* So that's what he needed it for? He's nothing, if not well-organized. I know what he's going to do next, but I can't stop the shudder when he returns. The next moment, something big and blunt nudges at my back hole. I crack open my eyelids to find him hovering over me. Sweat beads his shoulders, and his eyes are the pale blue of a chilled mountain stream.

He kicks his hips forward and slips past the ring of muscle. I open my mouth to cry out, but no sound emerges. He's filling me up in a way nothing has done before. The burning sensation is half-pain, half-pleasure. It ebbs away to be replaced by something thick and dark, an edgy heaviness that tugs at my nerve-endings and stings my flesh. Yet, below that is a tightness which winds my body, squeezes down on my pussy, and turns my chest into a maelstrom of sensations I can't quite comprehend. He pulls out of me, stays balanced on the rim for a second, then pushes in with enough force, the entire island seems to shudder. He bottoms out, touching that sensitive spot deep within me. It sets off reverberations that sweep up my body.

"Hold on," he growls.

I barely have the chance to register his words when he begins to fuck me in earnest. The sucking sound my body makes when he pulls out, followed by the slap of his balls against my butt as he pistons in, is a filthy, yet erotic, soundtrack. He holds my gaze, an order in his eyes to keep mine open. And I oblige.

I'm being consumed by him, surrounded by him, fucked by him. I feel like I'm losing myself and I'm unable to stop it.

"I want you to come as much as you can, show me how much you like it, like the good girl you are," his words drive me over the edge. And when he brings his hand between us and pinches my clit, I instantly orgasm.

I hear someone screaming and realize it's me. As my climax wracks my limbs, he pulls out. He squeezes his cock from base to tip, and with a groan, spills his cum across my breasts, stomach and pussy.

The sight of his fierce gaze, combined with his hoarse cry, is my last recollection before I give in to the darkness.

I'm dimly aware of him gathering me in his arms, of him moving. Then the spray of warm water on my body. I half open my eyes and realize he's holding me up in the shower. I cuddle into him, let him dry me, then lift me up and put me to bed.

He slides in next to me and pulls the covers over the both of us. He turns me on my side, then curves his body around mine.

Then he kisses the top of my head. "Was it good for you? Did you like it, baby?" His voice rumbles up his chest, sending pleasant reverberations across my skin.

My eyelids flutter down, but I manage to nod. "I loved it," I mumble truthfully.

He tucks my head under his chin, wraps his heavy arm about my middle, and by God, I think I could come all over again from this feeling of security engulfing me. Then the needy part of me, the part that wants to make him happy, rises to the fore and I ask, "Was I a good girl for you?"

He chuckles, the sound so delicious, it settles in my bones, and in my cells, and in those secret crevices on my body only Q knows. "You've been such a good girl, and you took me so well. You deserve to be held and snuggled as you sleep."

A smile curves my lips. I'm about to drift off. Perhaps, it's being in this half-asleep, half-awake state that loosens my tongue enough to remark, "I think you'll look even more devastating if you grow out your crew-cut."

I sense his surprise, then he rumbles, "Would it make you happy if I did, little Raven?"

"Very much." I yawn. He sounded so... tender there. Like he'd do anything I ask of him. Damn, these orgasms not only make my pussy very happy but they also confuse my brain. "Goodnight, Q," I whisper.

I am aware of him wishing me goodnight in that deep, dark voice of his as I drift off to sleep.

For the next three days and nights, Q makes love to me. Yes, he also fucks me with a relentless attention to detail, where he ensures every hole in my body is his. But in between, there are occasions where he takes me slowly, tenderly, while looking deeply into my eyes. There are occasions where he ties me up again, other occasions where he bends me over the settee in the living room and fucks my ass. Then, there's the time he screws me against the glass walls of his conservatory with the rain pattering against it on the other side. And there's the other time in the kitchen, in his garden among the jasmine flowers, on our bed, in the bathtub again, the time he simply throws me down on the carpet in front of the massive, lit fireplace and makes me orgasm as soon as he enters me.

My body is an instrument he's tuned to respond to his slightest command. I lose count of the number of times he makes me come.

I get used to this floaty, bubbly feeling that fills my blood. I get used to the ache between my legs that signals I'm well fucked. I forget to wear clothes—why should I? When he's going to tear them off me. Good thing we're so well stocked up and he's a good cook because I'm in a sexual haze and about all I can manage is to eat the food he puts in front of me before he fucks me again.

If there are times when I spot him watching me with a strange look in his eyes, I put it down to him getting used to the idea of us being married. After all, it's difficult to think of anything else when he follows it up with trying out another sexual position. The days meld into nights. When I wake up on the morning of the fourth day, the sun is bright outside.

I realize I'm alone in bed—which hasn't happened since that first morning here. My heart somersaults into my throat. A ripple of apprehension zings up my spine. For some reason I panic even more than I did the last time... then turn to find he's watching me. There's a tray of food on the bed stand next to me. His brow is furrowed, his jaw hard.

But in his eyes, there's worry.

Also, he's shaved—which he hasn't for the past few days. And he's wearing jeans and a chambray shirt. He's only worn a pair of grey sweatpants and kept his torso bare all the time we've been here.

"What's wrong?" I sit up in bed. "What time is it?"

"It's three p.m."

"Three p.m.?" I gape. "You mean I slept away the morning?"

I expect him to smirk and say something to the tune of he no doubt wore me out with his ministrations. Instead, he straightens and places the breakfast tray on my lap. "You need to eat."

"But I want to know why you're dressed?" I cry.

"And I'll tell you, but eat first." The command in his voice insists I obey him. Besides, the scent of the food tickles my nostrils and makes me realize how hungry I am.

I dig into the pasta, and the tangy flavors of tomatoes, combined with the acidity of sautéed garlic and the creaminess of mozzarella cheese, coat my palate. "This is so good," I groan. I polish off a few more mouthfuls, then look up to find him watching me with heat in his eyes.

"What?" I snatch up the napkin from the tray and wipe at the edges of my mouth.

He shakes his head. "I like seeing you eating the food I cook." There's a hint of possessiveness and satisfaction in his voice.

"You're a caveman."

"I like taking care of you."

"I like you taking care of me." I dip my head, not sure why I feel so shy. "In fact, one of my favorite images is of you wearing an apron and cooking for me. It's so sexy."

His smile widens at that. Once again, I expect him to say something that'll build on the sexual tension simmering between us, but when he doesn't, I realize whatever is on his mind is worrying him more than he's letting on.

I concentrate on the food, and when I'm done, drain the glass of water. He removes the tray to the bedside table and stands. When he holds out his hand, I take it, and he urges me to my feet.

He runs his gaze down my body and his jaw tightens. "I wish I could stay but I need to get back to town."

"You do?" My stomach sinks.

"Karma West Sovrano—"

"The designer?" I frown.

He nods. "She's my friend Michael's wife."

"Summer told me." I nod. "She's recovering from the birth of her second child."

He doesn't seem surprised that I know that. He runs his fingers through his hair, and a worried look enters his eyes. "I got a call from Summer that Karma's taken a turn for the worse. It's serious enough that I'd feel better if I go to see her."

42

Quentin

"How is she doing, Summer?" My wife runs ahead of me into the waiting room. She reaches Karma's sister Summer, and the two embrace. I'd told her she could stay or I could drop her off at my townhouse in London, but she insisted on coming with me.

I walk toward the other corner of the room where Sinclair is standing by the window. Summer and my wife follow me, talking in low voices.

"Is she any better?" I ask Sinclair.

He turns to me with a grim look in his eyes. "She was doing well after the delivery. But a few days ago she developed an infection in the lining of her heart which had to be treated with antibiotics."

I swallow. Summer had given me the barest details on the phone. I hadn't realized how serious the situation was until now.

Since I followed the ambulance the last time Karma was admitted to hospital and kept Summer company until Sinclair and Michael arrived, I've felt a responsibility for Karma. She's the little sister I never had. While I haven't known the Sovranos or the Sterlings for very long, I am more at ease with them than with my own family.

I'll confess, I was a little annoyed by Summer's call. Especially since

I'd told myself I only had the few days of my honeymoon with my wife before telling her the marriage was over. So, to have that time cut short was not something I wanted. Now that I realize how unwell Karma is, I'm glad we came.

Perhaps this is fate intervening to remind me I'm not allowed to have such happiness. I shouldn't have let that interlude with her go as long as I did. I said one more day, but it's stretched out into a week. I don't deserve her. And the longer I stay with her, the more difficult it's going to be when the inevitable happens.

I turn to Summer. "I'm sure your sister is going to pull through."

Summer smiles wanly. "She was doing better. We were sure she was going to be okay. Then—" She swallows and tears fill her eyes. "Then this morning, she had trouble breathing. We called Weston, and he told us to meet him here at the hospital. They administered stronger ones through IV, hoping that would do the trick. They gave her steroids to help with the swelling, and a breathing treatment, but then... Then she suffered a heart attack." Summer chokes out the words, then manages to get control of her emotions.

Sinclair pulls her closer before adding, "Weston's in there with her and Michael right now."

Weston, a.k.a. Dr. Weston Kincaid, is one of the top heart surgeons in the country. He and Sinclair went to the same school and have been close friends most of their lives.

Sinclair cups Summer's cheek. "All I can think is that if it were you in there, baby, I would be devastated."

My pulse rate spikes. My heart somersaults into my throat. If it were Raven in there, I would be moving heaven and earth to find a way to cure her. If it were her, I would be going out of my head with worry.

I wouldn't be able to see her in such pain. I'd never be able to live with myself if something happened to her. It would shatter me completely. I wouldn't be able to go on with my life.

I realize, now, I've let her get too close to me. I'm already in love with her. I was stupid to think that counted for nothing and that I could stop her from getting even closer.

She's already under my skin, has carved out a place in my heart, and has burrowed her way into the very cells of my body. I might not have a tattoo with her name on it, but her essence is etched into my flesh and bones.

I'm going to spend the rest of my life knowing I'll never meet a woman like her again. No one else will ever be enough. That's the price I'll pay for letting my heart take the lead this time.

I've never been more conscious of my own mortality than I am in this moment. I'm not young anymore. I have more years behind me than ahead of me. Meeting my wife gave me a new lease of life. But I'm committing her to a future where she's bound to lose her husband when she's still in her prime. *How could I have been this selfish? How could I put her through this?*

It's best I break things off with her before it's too late.

My wife must read some of my thoughts, for she pales. She takes a step in my direction, but I move back. She frowns, opens her mouth to ask a question, when Dr. Kincaid steps into the waiting room.

He's wearing scrubs, and his eyes are shadowed. As one, we walk toward him. I wrap my arm about my wife, and Sinclair pulls Summer into his side.

Dr. Kincaid's features are stoic. He glances between our faces, then shakes his head. "I'm sorry. She didn't make it."

Raven gasps.

Summer stares at him in disbelief. "No, no, no, no. How is this possible?" Her features crumple.

The blood drains from my face.

"Oh, Karma." Summer turns her face into Sinclair's chest and begins to sob.

Sinclair tucks her head under his chin and rubs her back. His look is filled with anguish as he makes eye contact with me. A tear slips down his cheek.

"She was a fighter until the very end." Dr. Kincaid sets his jaw. "As we were trying to stabilize her, she suffered a second heart attack. We couldn't resuscitate her."

My wife swallows, then grips my fingers tightly. "This is so unfair."

I hesitate, then pull her in closer, and she wraps her arms about my waist.

"Michael's going to need help to get through this." Dr. Kincaid drags his fingers through his hair. "It doesn't seem like he's going to leave that room anytime soon."

"How long"—I clear my throat—"how long can you let him be in there before—"

"Before the hospital moves the body? Normally, three to four hours. I could stretch it to six, maybe, while I get the paperwork completed." He sighs. "This is a bloody mess."

"Can I see her?" Summer says through her tears.

"Of course." He addresses his words to Summer and Sinclair. "It might help Michael to have Sinclair there. I've notified his brothers. They're on their way."

"I can't believe Karma is gone. I never met her personally, but I've loved her designs. I've watched so many videos of models showcasing her creations on social media. As an artist myself, I thought she was unique in her approach. I loved her choice of colors and patterns... There was something about a Karma West Sovrano design that marked it out as unique. " She stares out of the window on her side. "I knew she was unwell, but I didn't realize how serious it was." She swallows. "Why is life so unfair?" She turns to me. "Why did it have to be this way?"

No answer I give will be sufficient right now. I opt to tuck her into my side. She nestles in, with her cheek pressed into my chest.

We're in my car. I called my chauffeur and asked him to pick us up earlier to drive us to the hospital. Instead of returning to our country home, we both decided it made more sense to return to our townhouse in Primrose Hill. This way, we'll be close to the Sovranos, and to the Sterlings, and we'll be nearby to attend Karma's funeral.

"It feels wrong to be attending Karma's funeral instead of seeing her in person." I stare out of the window. *Her funeral? Jesus.* It's difficult for me to get my head around that. "The last time I saw Karma was when she'd collapsed and Summer called me for help. I followed her ambulance to the hospital. Once they'd stabilized her, we were allowed in her room. She was in pain but remained calm throughout. Michael, on the other hand, was beside himself with worry when he arrived. He was still upset that she had insisted on carrying the child to term. She said it meant everything that she was able to give him another child. She wanted that child so much."

I remember feeling envious about their closeness, how they only had eyes for each other. Then, there was me, someone who'd never managed to hold down a relationship in my life. At my age, I was sure it wasn't in the cards for me.

Then I met her. *And you're going to let go of her?*

I have to, eventually. I have to, before I do something stupid.

Before I do something to hurt her and alienate her like I've done with every relationship in my life...

Or God forbid, something happens to her, like it did to Karma. Another person I let into my life; another person I lost.

If I valued my own sanity, I'd turn my back on her. If I wanted to make sure she remains safe, I'd leave her now. But not yet. Not when she needs me emotionally. Not when I need her, too.

Just a few more days. I can stay with her a little longer.

I run my fingers down her hair, and she sighs. "I can't stop thinking of her kids. They won't know the love of their mother. And Michael—"

"This is going to break him." I pull her closer. "If it had been you in there, I wouldn't have survived." That's how much I've fallen for her. That's how much a part of me she is. That's how difficult it's going to be when she leaves me.

She looks up into my eyes. "That's a very nice thing to say, but—"

"I mean it." I peer into her features. "Ensuring you're taken care of is the number one priority in my life. As long as I'm alive, you'll never lack for anything." I swallow. "That much, I promise. *And even if I'm not with you, you'll never have to worry about money ever again. You'll be able to paint without worrying about anything else.*"

Her forehead furrows, and a touch of panic comes into her eyes. "I don't understand. Why are you talking like this? Why are you acting like you're going somewhere, Q?" Her eyebrows knit. "What's wrong?"

"It's a shock, losing Karma like this, is all. To see a young life cut short is nothing short of tragic. I've seen enough of it on my missions, and you'd think it would get easier with time, but it doesn't." I swallow.

"I'm so sorry, Q. Of course, it's not easy for you. What can I do to make it better?" Her gaze grows earnest. "Tell me, please."

I lean in closer and murmur against her lips, "You can kiss me."

43

Vivian

He distracted me with that kiss. I knew that's what he was trying to do, and I let it happen. In my defense, that kiss was sweet and tender and life affirming. Warmth bloomed in my chest and spread to my extremities. My fingers tingled, and my toes curled. My heart began to race, and all thoughts fled from my head.

I held his face between my hands and deepened the kiss, and he let me. For the first time, he let me lead the kiss. It filled me with a sense of power that was heady. A part of me was also taken aback, and a kernel of worry was born inside me, but I pushed it away. I crawled into his lap, and he held me and continued to kiss me and nibble on my mouth all the way home. Then, he led me into our bedroom and made love to me.

It was slow, and intense, and he made sure he made me climax thrice before he came. I fell asleep in his arms, and the next day. I woke up to find him gone.

I didn't see him all that day, nor the day after. Last night was the third night we've been apart since we returned to London. I waited up until two a.m. but fell asleep before he came home.

This morning, when I wake up, there's a dent in the pillow, which shows he came to bed. But he was gone before I woke up, which means he's getting very little sleep.

I swallow down the mounting panic which bubbles below the surface of my thoughts. This isn't a sign of anything but his grief over Karma, I tell myself sternly. He's not avoiding me on purpose. He's not. Besides, he texted me a few times and apologized that he wasn't around. He also made sure our belongings were returned from his country home, so it's not like he hasn't been thinking of me.

He insists he has work to catch up on after the couple of days he was away, which is fair enough, I suppose. Of course, he has a business to run which takes up his time. But it would be nice if he also made time for me. We *are* newly married. Isn't this the time husbands can't get enough of their wives? Isn't this when every night is supposed to be a fuckfest? And our honeymoon has shown me how much he wants me. So why is he staying away from me?

Then there's our conversation before he kissed me in the car which I can't get out of my mind. His words hinted that he foresaw a future when we weren't together. Of course, there are no guarantees in any relationship, but my subconscious tells me there's something more behind his keeping his distance from me.

At the same time, I don't want to come across as too needy, so I've decided to give him space. Still, a part of me is a little angry, and also sad, that our honeymoon ended so quickly.

Less than ten days into our marriage, and I'm rattling around his empty house on my own. I know he has business to attend to; but he could, at least, spend the nights with me? I need to talk to him, but damn, if I'm going to have this conversation over the phone. On the other hand, damn, if I'm going to wait around here for him to turn up.

I reach for my phone when it buzzes with an incoming video call.

"Zoey!" I accept the call. "How are you?"

"Hey, how are you doing? Did you hear about Karma?" Her features fill the screen.

I swallow around the ball of emotion in my throat. "Q got a call when we were on our honeymoon at his country estate. We left and came straight to the hospital. We were there with Summer and Sinclair when the doctor broke the news."

Zoey sniffles. "It's so sad. She was so gifted, so talented and now—" She shakes her head. "Those poor kids of hers. My heart goes out to them."

I feel my own tears well up and blink them away. "Yeah, it's such a tragedy. I had no idea she was that sick. And to think, she took time out to leave me that video message." My heart squeezes in on itself. I manage to get my emotions under control to ask, "Have you heard anything about the funeral?"

"Not yet. I didn't want to bother Summer with my questions. She has a lot on her plate right now," Zoey murmurs. "I also didn't want to bother you, in case you were still in honeymoon land, but I couldn't stop myself from checking in to find out how you're getting along, you know?"

"We're okay... I guess?" It seems wrong to complain about how my husband is keeping his distance from me, when Karma's kids have lost a mother.

"Uh, oh" — Zoey's forehead furrows — "trouble in paradise already?"

"Eh, nothing like that..." I hesitate. "Maybe he's been busy with work since we got back, is all."

"But doesn't he come home at night? You two are sharing a bed, aren't you?"

"We are" — I sigh — "but he's gone before I wake up, and by the time he returns, it's so late I've fallen asleep." Damn, my woes seem so insignificant compared to what Karma's family is going through. It makes me want to see my husband and be with him, and have him cuddle me and hold me even more. I hunch my shoulders. "I guess, I miss my husband. But I'm allowed, aren't I?"

Zoey's eyes round. "Wow, are you in love with him?"

"More like in lust," I mutter under my breath. *Gah, did I say that aloud?* My cheeks redden, and I toss my hair over my shoulders. "So, what's going on with you, anyway?"

She accepts my change of subject. "I come bearing huge news. Huge." Her lips curve in a big smile. "Remember my friend, the gallery owner in Soho who I sent the pictures of your paintings to?"

I nod.

"She loves them. She wants to do a showing in four weeks."

For a second, I'm not sure I heard her correctly. Then I register what she's saying, and my heart jumps into my throat. "Wait, what?" I splutter. "What did you say?"

"You heard that right, babe," she says with satisfaction. "She wants to do a showing of your paintings."

My pulse rate spikes. A fierce burst of joy crowds my ribcage. "She wants to do a showing?"

Zoey nods madly.

"Of my paintings?"

"No, of mine," she deadpans. "Of course, your paintings, dummy. I showed her the pictures of your paintings I took on my phone, and she loved them. Turns out, one of her other artists can't make it, so his slot is yours."

Goosebumps pop on my skin. Excitement floods my veins. "Oh my god, oh my god, this is unbelievable!" This is the chance I've been waiting for. Something not even money can buy. A chance to prove myself. This is what I hoped, and secretly prayed for, for so long. Then it sinks in. I wipe the smile off my face. "Did you say within four weeks?"

She nods. "Twenty-eight days."

"Jesus, that's very little time." I knit my eyebrows, and her face falls.

"Is it too little time to get a few more paintings ready? You had a good number in the flat the other day that I saw…"

I nod slowly. "I have about twenty, I think."

"She needs at least twenty-five," Zoey adds.

"Twenty-five?" I gasp. "So, I have to create another five?"

"You said you can create entire paintings overnight."

I laugh. "That was one painting. An outlier. It's never like that, normally."

"You did it once; you can do it again," she says with a confidence I don't feel.

"Can I?" I hunch my shoulders.

"Of course, you can."

"I… I'm not sure…" I begin to pace the floor of the living room.

"But you have to try, right? Didn't you say you've been wondering what to do with yourself while your husband is busy at work?"

I pause, struck by her words. She's right. I've been moping around the house when I could have been painting. For some reason, I hadn't even thought about it. How strange. I've been wanting the mind space to paint, and now, when I have it, I'm not using the time wisely? And if I missed out on this opportunity, would I ever forgive myself?

"What do you say, can you do it?" Zoey pushes her glasses up her nose. "Or should I tell her—"

"I'll do it." I nod. "Tell her I'll do it."

Perhaps, it's the relief of not having to earn a daily wage, or maybe, it's the knowledge that I'm married, beginning to sink in. Or maybe, a part of me has been unlocked by Q's dominance. Or maybe, it's Karma's sudden death that shifted something inside me. Maybe, it's that I subconsciously feel my husband pulling away and I can't understand why. More likely, it's a combination of these factors, along with the deadline that Zoey's gallery owner friend imposed on me, but when I sign the contract, she sent me, a familiar excitement grips me.

Adrenaline laces my blood. That tingling that starts at my fingertips and extends to my heart, and then to my head, the one that tells me I'm ready to start painting, has me marching into one of the guest bedrooms that Q told me I could use as my studio.

He had my paintings moved in there, along with my art supplies—and new ones he bought for me, which I notice now as I stand in front of the easel. I allow the painting to take shape on the canvas, let my thoughts turn to the man who's at the forefront of my mind and guide my fingers.

I dip my brush into the paint and slash it across the canvas in one bold stroke. *Where the hell is my husband?* I load the brush again, and the trembling of my hand sends a spray of crimson across the black.

I step back and brush my hair out of my eyes to examine the effect. For some reason, I can hear Q's voice in my head, telling me to let go. I fling my arm out, and another spray of crimson splatters like blood. *My bleeding heart would look like this canvas.*

I dip my brush in purple and splash the purple over the crimson. *And those are my desires, bubbling to the surface.* Yellow for the need. Green for the yearning I feel for him. Pink for the tenderness I glimpse in him. Black for the darkness that connects us. Blue for his eyes. I set down my brush, then pick up my palette knife and begin to etch out an outline.

I paint into that night and the next day. I end up sleeping on the daybed in the room and break to eat when I'm hungry. I'm almost done with my first painting. That's not bad, considering I haven't painted in so long.

I look away and toward the window. It's dark outside. Gosh, another day has passed, and I haven't seen my husband yet. Where the hell is he? The need I bled out all over my canvas has me trembling. The idea of heading off alone to my cold, lonely bed brings tears to my eyes. No way. I'm not waiting another night.

I square my shoulders. No way, am I waiting another night, only to find I've missed him again. I throw down my brush and take off the apron

I've been wearing over my clothes. I rush to our bedroom, jump in the shower, then pull on a dress that comes to mid-thigh. I throw a jacket over it, pair it with ballet pumps, then rush out of the house. The car and chauffeur he's put at my disposal is parked outside.

It's nearly nine p.m. by the time I arrive at his office.

I take the elevator to the penthouse and walk down the deserted corridor. I haven't been here before, but my name was on the list and the security guard downstairs told me where to find my husband. I reach his door and push it open. The room is empty.

I walk in, my feet sinking into the plush carpet. The spicy scent of woodsmoke and pine, which is so very Q hangs in the air. It's as if I'm surrounded by him. I walk toward the desk that takes up almost the entire back wall. The swivel chair behind it is empty. I glance around the room, then slip into the chair.

It's so big, it overwhelms me. I sink into the plush leather. The seat is warm, which means he must have vacated this chair recently. I place my arms on the armrest and close my eyes. There's so much of him in this space, I can almost pretend he's right here in the room with me. My nipples tighten, and my pussy clenches.

Oh god, I miss my husband. I wish he were here with me.

If he were, would he squeeze my breast? I bring my hand to my breast and squeeze it. Would he touch me between my legs where it hurts?

I flip up my dress, thankful I decided to eschew my panties, then slide my hand under and cup my pussy. Sensations sizzle out from the contact. The hollowness in my core grows, and I squirm. I squeeze my thighs together, but that doesn't help.

I could stuff my fingers inside my throbbing pussy, but the girth would be nowhere close to the size of his fingers or his dick. Perhaps, it'll alleviate some of this emptiness inside, though? I brush my fingers against my entrance when I hear a groan.

Was that me?

No, it sounded too masculine.

It sounded like—

I snap my eyes open. Wait... Wait... Another groan... This one deeper, more insistent than the first.

I whip my head in the direction of the sound and notice the door to the ensuite bathroom is ajar. Is he in there?

Is there... Someone with him?

I swallow, then slip off the chair. I head toward the bathroom, when another guttural noise reaches me. That sounded almost painful. I wince, reach the door, and push it further open.

The sound of wet flesh hitting flesh reaches me.

It's so explicit, there's no mistaking what it is. Heat flushes my skin. *Is there someone with him, and are they doing what I think they are? Does she have her hands and her mouth on his cock?*

I shove the door open all the way and barge in.

And come to a stop because there's only one person in here, and it's my husband. With his cock in his hand.

He's pushed his other hand into the bathroom tile to balance himself. He's standing in profile to me, which means... He's in the shower stall, but the shower is not running. The door to the stall is open, indicating he was about to step out but stopped halfway. Judging by the wetness of his body, he's also just finished. The shower, that is.

As for his other business, his shaft is long and thick and stands upright, and when he squeezes it from base to crown, liquid gleams on the head.

My cheeks flush. Oh, my God. He's jerking off.

I've missed him all these days. I was sure he was avoiding me, his wife. Apparently, he also decided to take care of his needs on his own instead of fucking me? Instead of commanding me, his submissive, to get down on my knees and suck him off, he's using his hands to give himself relief.

I should leave.

No...

Anger squeezes my chest. I take a step forward with the intention of telling him off, when he throws his head back and begins to pump himself harder.

The squelching sound is impossibly loud in the space. It arrows straight to my clit, which throbs. As if of their own accord, my feet carry me closer. My gaze is riveted by the sight of his cock growing thicker. As I reach the open door to the shower, I can make out the thick veins that stand out in relief on the underside of his shaft. He continues to stroke himself from base to crown, and again. Each time he reaches the head, more cum oozes out from the head.

My scalp tingles, and my throat dries. My stomach is so heavy, it feels like I've swallowed a stone. I watch closely as he continues to wank off, his shaft growing more purple by the second.

For a second, I'm jealous that he could give himself so much pleasure. Then the tendons of his throat pop and he growls, "Fuck, Raven, fuck." I know he's thinking of me as he jacks off.

I allow my knees to hit the floor, and when I look up at his face I gasp, for his eyes are open. His blue eyes are filled with lust. But the expression on his face is one of agony and an impending ecstasy. It's how he looked when he came inside me.

When his stomach muscles convulse, I know he's close, and before I can stop myself, I arch up and close my mouth around his cock.

44

Quentin

As my climax spills out of me, she sucks it down. With her cheeks hollowed and drops of my cum clinging to her lips, she's the most beautiful thing I've ever seen. She's perfect. My wife wearing the evidence of my desire is a sight I'll never forget.

I reach down and wrap my fingers about her slim throat.

Her breathing speeds up. The pulse under my fingers spikes. She continues to suck me off, but her gaze is on mine. When she's done, I urge her to her feet and kiss her, enjoying the taste of my cum in her mouth. I reach under her skirt and between her legs and stiffen. "You didn't wear panties?"

She tips her head. "Does that make you happy?"

"It makes me" — I wrap my other hand about her hip and boost her up — "fucking horny."

She gasps as she wraps her legs around my waist. I press her back into the wall, so my dick stabs between her legs.

"Again?" she gasps.

"And again, and again." I fit myself at her entrance, then impale her. She groans; so do I.

"You're so fucking tight, baby."

Her inner walls ripple around me, and I almost come again. I grit my teeth, press my forehead to hers and draw in a breath, another. I stare into those stormy green eyes of hers and find myself drowning all over again. I stay there, thickening further, pressing against her inner walls.

It's only when she digs her heels into my back that I begin to move. I pry her fingers off my shoulders and pin them to the wall. I pull out of her and thrust back in.

She gasps, "Do it again," and arches her back. I bend and close my mouth around her swollen nipple, and she cries out.

That sends me over the edge. I kick my hips forward and bury myself to the hilt. When she whimpers, I know I've hit that space deep inside of her. She tilts her hips and tries to get even closer. That's when I begin to hammer into her, over and over again, until she wails and her body shudders as she comes. Her eyelids flutter down.

"Eyes on me," I order.

She cracks her eyelids open, and I hold her gaze as, with a groan, I empty myself inside of her. She slumps, and I catch her and hold her close. Chest to chest, the beating of her heart synchronizes with mine. When I pull out of her, my cum trickles out, and I push it back in.

"What are you doing?" she moans.

"Making sure every drop of my cum finds a home with you."

She bites her lower lip. "That's filthy. And I should find it dirty, but I don't."

A hot sensation stabs at my chest. It's incredible how much she's changed, and how she's learned to indulge her fantasies without any trace of embarrassment turns me on even more.

"There's no need to hide your sexual perversions with me. There's no reason not to revel in your kinks, baby."

She half smiles. "I didn't realize I was looking for permission—"

"Until now."

She nods, then cups my cheek. "You're spoiling me."

"Of course, I'm spoiling you. Who else would spoil you?" Darkness sweeps over my mind. I hadn't wanted to fuck her. I stayed away from her, hoping to wean myself off of her. I hoped to put distance between us so I could work up the courage to tell her I was leaving her. But one look at her on her knees in front of me, and I wasn't able to stop myself from fucking her. The connection between us is stronger than ever.

At this rate, I'll never be able to leave her. And I must, or risk hurting us both in a way that ensures the kind of pain from which we'd never recover.

I lower her to her feet, then walk out of the shower cubicle to grab a washcloth and wet it. I return, wipe between her legs, and throw the washcloth aside, then straighten her clothes. "You should go."

"What? Why?" The light in her eyes fades. "Aren't you coming with me?"

When I don't reply, her lips turn down. "But I've missed you, Q."

I've missed you, too. I want to tell her that, but my tongue seems unable to form the words. Instead, I dry myself with a towel before dropping it in the laundry basket in the corner. I open the door set into the wall next to it which leads to a built-in closet. I pull on my pants, and a button-down shirt.

I sense her moving toward me and know I have to stop her. If she touches me, I won't be able to stop myself from fucking her again. And I can't afford to do that. Not now. So, I scowl at her over my shoulder. "What are you doing here anyway?"

She pauses halfway across the bathroom. "Shouldn't I be the one to ask those questions, considering I haven't seen you home in the last four days?"

A flush heats the back of my neck. She's right to ask, not that I have any answers for that... At least, none that I'm prepared to give her. So instead, I pretend to be occupied with buttoning up my shirt. "Do you need anything? If it's about your painting supplies—"

"Thanks for ordering them, but that's not what I need right now."

"Oh?" I tuck my shirt, zip my pants, then turn to face her. "What else do you need?"

"You." She closes the distance to stand in front of me. "I need you, Q. I need my husband."

My heart fucking hurts, but I keep my emotions off my face and school my features into a bored look. "I fucked you already, didn't I?"

She winces. "That's not what I meant. And you know that. You weren't like this on our honeymoon. What's happening, Q? Why are you pulling away from me? Why are you trying your best to hurt me?"

Because I want you to realize I'm not good for you. I'm not right for you. I want you to realize you married the wrong man. A man who'll never love you the way you deserve to be. A man who's going to hurt you even more. Because I want you to hate me, so when I leave you, I can do so without breaking your heart.

She searches my features, sadness writ into hers. "I thought, especially after what happened with Karma, you'd realize life is short. That you'd cherish every moment we have together."

The disappointment in her features cuts me to the core. I take a step in her direction, intent on soothing her, then stop myself.

"Why should I, when what we have is not a real marriage?" I make sure my voice is cold when it feels like someone has gouged a hole in my chest.

She looks stricken. The color fades from her features, and she swallows hard. Then her eyes flash. "How dare you! How dare you insinuate what we have isn't genuine? And after everything we've done together!" she spits out.

My entire body feels like I've turned to stone. Sweat pools under my armpits. I move toward the dressing-bench in the closet and take a seat, then begin to pull on my socks, so I have something to do with my hands instead of pulling her into my arms. "Just because I taught you to enjoy kink, and gave you a few orgasms, doesn't mean what we have is real."

She gasps. "I can't believe you said that."

"Believe it." I slide my feet into my shoes, then rise to my feet. "Now, if you'll excuse me—"

"No, I won't." Her eyes spit sparks at me. "Not until you tell me why you're working so late every day? Why are you avoiding me? What are you not telling me?"

Rage turns her cheeks into a shade of dusky pink which stops me in my tracks. She's magnificent, my Raven. My wife. And I'm forcing myself to do this.

"Not everything I do is about you." I slide my hand into my pocket and look her up and down, managing not to show any emotion. "You forget, I have a business to run. Which necessitates putting in hours in the office when needed."

"So you can add to your billions?" she scoffs.

"My money certainly was a key reason you decided to marry me." I watch her keenly, waiting to see what she'll say next.

She swallows; some of the anger on her face dissipates. "I needed the money when we met. But it's not the only reason I married you, and you know that."

Don't say it. Not now. I don't want to know if you have feelings for me. Don't make this more difficult than it already is. Give me a way out. Tell me you hate me for fucking you the way I did. Tell me you can't wait to get away from me. Tell me, before I'm forced to break your heart, because I'll never be able to forgive myself if I do.

I shutter my features and pretend to have a polite interest. "Do I?" I ask in a toneless voice.

"I thought"—she swallows—"I thought you cared for me. I thought you wanted more. I thought you said we had something special. That even though you felt terrible about hurting Felix, nothing could stop you from marrying me. That you wanted a future together."

My heart stutters. She's right on all these accounts but I can't admit that to her. Instead, I ensure my expression remains stony. "It's true I wanted to get Felix on board before we married. And I have *you* to thank for making that happen. As for the rest, you thought wrong. The only reason I married you was to ensure my role as CEO within the Davenport group is confirmed."

And because I love you and need you in my life, but I don't dare tell you that.

She draws in a sharp breath. "How can you say that? How can you pretend whatever happened between us doesn't matter when I know it did. I've seen that look in your eyes when you're inside me. I've seen you watch me when we're in a room together. You can't take your gaze off me."

I raise my shoulder. "What can I say? I'm a good actor. I needed to convince my family our connection was genuine. Seems I also convinced you in the process."

"I don't believe you." She shakes her head. "I don't."

My wife knows me too well. *Fuck. Why is this so difficult? Why does it feel like I've aimed a gun at my temple and am about to pull a trigger?*

I wall off the churning sensation in my guts and lift my chin. "It's true. I saw you and wanted you. I went into this marriage thinking it could be more than an arrangement of convenience, but—"

"But—?" She swallows.

"I realize now, I was fooling myself. I don't want a relationship that will tie me down."

"You don't?"

I set my jaw and inject scorn into my voice when I drawl. "Someone in my position, and with my life experience... You didn't think you could satisfy all my needs, did you?"

The blood drains from her face.

She's watching me closely, watching my mouth make the words like she has to confirm to herself it's me who's doing the talking. *I'm sorry, baby. So sorry.* But it's for the best.

"You… You don't mean it," she chokes out. "The Quentin I know is not someone who'd walk all over my heart. Your gruff demeanor hides the more vulnerable parts of you." She takes a step forward. "That's it, isn't it? I make you feel a lot. You look at me and realize you can't run from your emotions anymore. It makes you feel exposed and raw and emotionally naked. Well, guess what? Welcome to the land of the living."

A tension grips me. I grit my teeth so hard, my jaw muscles protest. *What is she talking about?* That makes no sense. I'm not scared of feeling, and I do feel emotions. Only, I had to lock them away so I could do my duty. *And even there, you failed them. You couldn't protect Ryot's wife.*

But I can protect Raven now. Because I love her, I can push her away. I can do this for her, so she gets the life she deserves. I draw on that coldness inside me which allowed me to make decisions on a mission.

"Nothing you say will make me change my mind." I narrow my gaze on her.

She flinches.

"My mind is made up. Our relationship is one of mutual advantage. And I've done my part." My voice emerges cold and hard, while my entire body shrinks from my words.

"What do you mean?" she cries.

"Your sister's future is set. Your father has been accepted into the trial for the experimental treatment at Johns Hopkins."

"He has?" Her features light up.

And despite the fact I've locked away my emotions, a soft sensation seeps into my chest. *Jesus, I love this woman.*

All the more reason you need to distance yourself from her.

Her lips curve. "That could be potentially—"

"Lifesaving—" I nod. "If it succeeds, it will change the quality of his life for the better moving forward."

"That…" She locks her fingers together. "That's incredible, thank you."

"So, there's no reason for us to stay married anymore," I manage to say the words without faltering. In fact, I sound positively convincing.

"And what about your role as the CEO?"

"Arthur emailed the company. He confirmed my position as CEO of the group company. There is no need for this charade to continue."

Of course, I'm not accepting the role. I already told Arthur I'm stepping down and he should give the role to one of my nephews. But there's no need to tell her that, yet.

The smile fades from her face, then she marches over to me and stabs a forefinger into my chest. "Pardon me for not believing this bull crap you're spouting, but you care for me, Q. I've seen it in your eyes. I've seen it when you fuck me. I've seen it when you hold my gaze as you come inside of me. It's why you remember I like cappuccino and made my coffee exactly the way I enjoy it. It's why you went so far as to note the kind of painting supplies I use, and why you bought me more that matched my specifications. Besides, you all but told me that you love me. You" — she juts out her chin — "you, *do* love me."

"I don't." I look her up and down, managing to infuse disdain into my perusal of her body.

From the corner of my eye, I see her raise her arm, but I don't budge. Don't avoid what I know is coming. And when her palm connects with my cheek, I welcome the burn. I relish the sting, knowing if I were to look in the mirror, I'd see the shape of her fingerprints on my face. I want her mark of possession on my body.

"That's for being such an ass." She shakes the hair back from her face. "But you should know, I'm not falling for the act."

"Eh?" I frown. "What do you mean?"

"You're saying the words you think will push me away from you, but it's not going to happen. I might be your submissive in bed, but in real life, I can go toe-to-toe with you. I'm not going to let you wear me down. I'm a painter. The one thing I am is patient, not to mention, persistent. Every painting has a rhythm, a code I need to understand to unlock its secrets, and I think I'm beginning to understand yours. That's what's making you run scared." She scans my features. "Am I right?"

A strange sensation tightens my chest. *What the fuck? What is she talking about?* I've been trying my best to make her see I'm all wrong for her, but I don't seem to be getting through. If anything, it seems to have the opposite effect. I shake my head. "You're wrong. But what-fucking-ever. If you want to spin stories in your head, who am I to stop you?"

I turn to leave, when she calls out to me, "Q?"

I stop.

"You think if you ignore me and put distance between us, I'm going to give up on you, but you're wrong. You think you can push me away but I'm not going anywhere. I'm going to be waiting for you to come back and apologize to me for being such a douchebag, and I'm going to enjoy every moment of it, I promise you."

45

Vivian

"Whoa, you slapped him?" Zoey blinks rapidly. "And how did he react to that?"

"Like he always does." I glare at the painting in front of me. "He turned and walked away. But this time I made sure I had the last word." I say with satisfaction.

I returned home last night, on my own, then twisted and turned until I fell asleep around two a.m. Doesn't matter what I do, I never seem to be able to stay awake later than that. And my husband hadn't come in by then. I set an alarm and woke up at six a.m., but the bed was empty. And this time, there's no dent in the pillow.

Which means, he never came home.

I still can't believe he said those things to me yesterday. I don't believe he thinks our marriage isn't real. I refuse to accept it. Not when I remember the orgasms he gave me last night, and how hot he looked jerking off—another kink uncovered, apparently.

Only good thing? The pain he inflicted on me resulted in an inability to sleep. As soon as I got up, I started painting. Angst and a broken heart are the best muse, and don't let anyone tell you otherwise. I didn't pause until Zoey walked into my room at noon. I didn't stop painting, though, not even when I narrated the incidents from last night to her—except the part about Q jerking off and how he took me after that in the shower, that is. Thinking of it sends another pulse of longing through my body. I press down on the brush in my hand with enough pressure that it cracks.

"Ugh!" I walk over to the trashcan in the corner and drop the paintbrush in it. "Maybe I'm fooling myself. It's all well and good for me to pretend he didn't mean what he said, but maybe he did. Maybe this was all a farce to him. Maybe everything he did was an act, as he claims?"

But no, it can't be. Not when the intensity with which he fucked me branded my soul forever. Not when he looked into my eyes when he made love to me, and I saw his soul in his eyes. Not when he handled my body like he'd memorized exactly what I like...

I shake my head. "I could have sworn he'd fallen for me, but maybe that was me being delusional." I walk over to stand in front of my unfinished painting again. "I went into this marriage, knowing it was an arrangement, but somewhere along the way it's turned out to be very real —for me, at least."

"Because you're in love with him?"

I stiffen, then scowl at her over my shoulder. "Is it that obvious?"

"Only to me." She walks over and squeezes my shoulder. "How are the paintings coming along?"

"It's all crap. I was being too ambitious to think I could have everything ready in such a short period of time." I tear the canvas off the easel and fling it aside.

"Hey, don't do that." Zoey grabs the canvas and eases it back on the easel. "This thing is heavy."

"That's probably because the painting on it sucks."

She laughs. "You're selling yourself short. I think you have something here."

I stare at the outline of the face I've begun to draw but haven't been able to continue with. "I thought I'd broken my dry streak. I managed to complete one painting. Then I started this one and couldn't keep going."

She pats my shoulder. "You'll figure it out."

"Right." I roll my shoulders, trying to work out the tightness in them. "Meanwhile, I'm going to spend days here unable to go forward, something I hate."

"Maybe you should get out of the way and let yourself paint?"

"Is this the advice you give to all your authors?"

She laughs. "Something similar. I'm not a writer or a painter myself. But I have spent time around enough creatives to know that, often, you are your own worst enemy. Often, the best words or the best brushstrokes arise when you stop judging yourself and let it flow. Don't hold back, Vivian." She squeezes my shoulder. "Don't let your fears hold you back."

The buzzing of a phone reaches us, and she pulls it out from her bag. "It's Summer." She answers the FaceTime call.

"Hey, you."

"Hey, guys." Summer smiles wanly.

"You okay?" I take in her wan features. She looks like she's lost weight since I last saw her.

"I'm holding in there." She half smiles. "But when I think of Karma's kids..." Her chin trembles.

"Oh, honey," Zoey cries.

"Is there anything we can do to help?" I swallow.

She shakes her head. "You guys are doing a lot by being there for me. I'm upset because Michael doesn't want to hold a funeral for her."

"He doesn't?"

She shakes her head. "He's thrown himself into work and refuses to meet his brothers. He's also decided not to hold a funeral. Instead, there'll be a private burial, with only him in attendance."

"That's unusual."

Her forehead scrunches. "He's not allowing himself to mourn. He's moved, with the kids, out of the Primrose Hill house he shared with Karma. He's not answering his brothers' calls. Sinclair is the only one who's managed to speak with him, and only because he staged an intervention at the office. He said—" She squeezes her eyes shut. "He said Michael's not in good shape. He's barely eating; he's lost weight. Only good thing is, he's hired a nanny for the children, but he doesn't want to see them. And he's refused to let me into their new place, so I haven't seen the kids at all! It's like he's shut himself off from the world." A tear runs down her cheek, and she dashes it away. "I'm sorry, I didn't mean to offload on you guys like that. Karma was the person I'd call first but"— she shakes her head—"I need to get a grip."

"It must be so difficult for you. I can only imagine how you must be coping. If something happened to my sister, I'd be wrecked, too," I offer.

She rubs at the moisture on her cheek. "Enough about me. Distract me. How are things going with you and Q?"

I shake my head. "Honestly? Not great."

"When I saw the two of you at the hospital, it seemed like he only had eyes for you."

I lower my chin. " I thought so, too." I swallow around the knives that seem to be stuck in my throat. "I thought this thing between us was real. I thought he loved me. Maybe he does love me, but it seems like he's running scared. He's trying his best to push me away. He's trying to hurt me. He's trying to see how much I'll take before I snap and leave him. I think he's doing it so he doesn't have to break up with me." I shake my head. "In short, it's a mess."

"What are you going to do about it?" she asks.

"What do you mean?" I curl my fingers into fists. "What *can* I do about it when my husband seems to not want anything to do with me?"

She inclines her head, a considering look in her eyes. "You know, the one thing I've realized is that time is fleeting. One day, you're a little girl taking care of your sister in foster care; the next, both of you are grown up and having babies of your own. I'd give anything to have one more conversation with Karma. To hear her laugh. To go to her favorite bakery on Primrose Hill High Street and split a chocolate cookie, but it's not going to happen. And that's the worst thing. I took it all for granted, and it is gone. I knew Karma had a heart condition. I knew chances were she wouldn't grow old with me, and yet… Somewhere along the way, I forgot that everything could change in the blink of an eye."

I rub at my temple. "I sense you're trying to tell me something."

Summer smiles through her tears. "All I'm saying is, don't let self-doubt hold you back. Don't be afraid to go after what you want."

46

Quentin

I flicker my gaze over the features of my sleeping wife. Every night, after working until the early hours of the morning, I make it home, but do I sleep? No. I prefer to spend the time watching her.

I take in the way her cheeks are flushed, how her lips are parted, how her hair is a halo around her shoulders. She's on her side, with her face turned toward me.

The first time I watched her sleeping, I spent the night in the chair next to her.

The next night, I sat on the bed.

On the third, I lay down on my side and watch her until the first rays of the morning light came through the window. My wife sleeps deeply. My climbing into bed didn't register with her.

A strand of hair has fallen over her face. I reach over and tuck it behind her ear, then freeze when she mumbles something under her breath. She falls silent, her breathing evens out, and I allow my muscles to relax. I don't want her to find me in bed with her. I don't want to fall asleep next to her. If I did, I'd wake up wrapped around her, and my dick, which is already erect by her proximity, would not take no for an answer.

She moans in her sleep. That's never happened before. She must be dreaming. Her sleep camisole leaves very little to imagination, with her full breasts pushing the material tight across her chest, the shape of her nipples outlined by the fabric.

I sweep my gaze down to where her camisole has ridden up, revealing a strip of pale, creamy skin. And below that, her panties ride high on her legs, showing off the thick spread of her thighs. I swallow hard. The crotch of my pants — I didn't bother to undress so I don't get too comfortable — is too snug. I adjust myself. Then, unable to resist the allure of the woman next to me, I reach over and slide my fingers under the gusset of her panties. *Jesus, she's soaking wet.*

She's sleeping, and unaware of what I'm doing. I should... put distance between us. I should get the hell out of this bed before I make her come in her sleep.

I begin to pull away, but she moans, then spreads her legs apart. The lips of her pussy glisten with her arousal, and just like that, all thoughts of leaving vanish from my head. She's my wife and she's turned on. She moans again, then squirms in her sleep. And when she widens the space between her thighs, I don't hold back.

I tease her slit, then slide two fingers inside her. Goosebumps pepper her skin. She turns her head in my direction, but her eyes are closed. I resist the urge to lean in and kiss her. If I do, she'll definitely wake up. Instead, I ease my fingers in and out of her, in and out.

Her pussy clenches, then ripples around my fingers. My dick extends, and fucking hell, I can't hold back. I shove my other hand down my pants and squeeze my cock from base to crown. The pain cuts through the noise in my head and helps me focus. I add a third digit inside her, and she groans.

Her breathing grows heavy, but her eyes are closed. *Thank fuck.* I weave my fingers in and out of her, while also jerking myself off. My movements speed up, the moisture squeezes out from between her legs. Jesus, this woman... She's so fucking sexy, it slays me. The pressure at the base of my spine builds, and I know I'm not going to last long. I curve my fingers inside her and am rewarded by a shudder that sweeps through her. She pants, her mouth open in a silent cry. Watching her come sends me over the edge. I swipe my cock from base to crown one last time, and my balls explode.

I come and come in my pants like a teenage boy, then lay there with my fingers inside her pulsing pussy for a few seconds. I pull my fingers from her wet channel and suck on them, then scoop up some of my cum and paint it on her lips. She licks it off, then turns over on her side.

I pull away without waking her, then roll off the bed, head toward the ensuite bathroom, and step into the shower.

That orgasm should have relaxed me, but looking at my hard cock, you wouldn't know it. I need her more than ever, and not only in a physical way. I want her with me, next to me, by my side, in my life.

But I can't have that. I *will not let myself* have that.

I'm torturing myself by having her here under my roof. I'm setting things up to hurt her even more by being unable to break things off with her.

Whatever happened to the bravery I was known for in military strategy? Come up with a ballsy plan to keep ahead of the enemy? I'm your man. Want to structure an audacious acquisition to grow the Davenport Group's profits? I'm one step ahead of you there. But shoring up my courage to tell my wife that I want to leave her, and I lose my balls.

I switch off the shower, grab a towel and dry myself, then walk out with it wrapped around my waist. I walk into my closet, and dress quickly. With a last look at my still sleeping wife, I head out of our bedroom and for the office.

The door to my office flies open. "I'm so sorry, Mr. Davenport, I tried to stop her."

I look up to find my assistant red-faced and on the heels of a young girl who's barged in.

She looks like my wife but is not my wife, because I recognize her from the picture my wife showed me of her and her sister. She's thin, almost painfully so, and is wearing tights and an oversized sweatshirt with the words "Royal Ballet School" on it.

She marches over to my desk and slams down an oversized backpack with various badges pinned onto it. "You have some nerve making my sister unhappy," she fumes.

The soft American twang to her accent, not to mention the way her eyes dart arrows at me, reminds me of Raven.

A sharp tug winds itself around my heart. I ignore it and nod at the girl. "Lizzie, good to meet you."

"It's *not* good to meet *you*, Mr. Asshole Davenport. Or should I say Mr. Butthead Davenport?" she snaps.

Behind her, my assistant draws in a sharp breath.

I wave at her. "It's okay, Mary."

"But, but..." she splutters.

Guess she's never been exposed to temperamental artistes. Trust my wife to change one more thing.

"It's fine. Lizzie's my sister-in-law." I rise to my feet and nod toward my assistant. "You can leave us."

Mary sniffs, then turns to go.

"Oh, Mary, could you send in some" — I turn to Lizzie — "ice-cream?"

"What?" She blinks.

"Do you prefer cookies?"

"Cookies?" Her eyes light up, then her shoulders slump. "Can't. Diet. Ballet, and all that."

"A no-sugar, no-carb, buckwheat, organic, dark chocolate-chip cookie, with very little calories?" I nod in Mary's direction.

She looks at the girl, then back at me, before sniffing again, then turning and walking out.

"If you're trying to weasel your way into my good books, it won't work." She plops herself into her chair. "Also —" She stabs her thumb over her shoulder. "Why are you keeping her on? Don't you *lifestyles of the rich and famous* bosses prefer shapely assistants who cater to your every need?" She uses her hands to demonstrate the shape of a curvy woman.

"If you mean Mary, she's been with the company for thirty years. She came with this office and is only a year from retirement. She's given her life to this company. Why would I let her go? If anything, I plan to reward her loyalty and ensure she's set up for the rest of her life, so she can enjoy her retirement with her grandkids."

Lizzie regards me with a strange look on her face.

"As for your second question, I only have eyes for my wife," I state.

She scoffs, "Is that why you made her cry?"

I squeeze my fingers around the edge of my desk. My heart threatens to cleave its way out of my ribcage. *How could I have done that? How could I have caused her pain?* "She... cried?" I ask in a hoarse voice.

"Oh, she didn't say it was because of you; she's too loyal to you. But when I called her this morning, her eyes were red-rimmed. She said she's been painting non-stop and not sleeping much in preparation for her exhibition."

"I'm aware she's getting her paintings ready for her showing." I also know she's been putting in long hours and not taking out the time to eat. Which is why I told my housekeeper to bring Raven's food to her studio at mealtimes, to ensure she eats.

It's why I decided to spend my nights at the office, sleeping on my pull-out couch so she won't be disturbed by my presence. She's going to crush this showing; I have no doubt. "She's brilliant. And soon the world will recognize that, too."

Lizzie nods slowly. "She is. And I'm so pleased she's getting her due."

"The two of you are close."

She levels a look at me, a very knowing look. A look which makes her seem older than her eighteen years. A look I recognize, since I've seen fellow Marines with that similar look in their eyes after their first tour, when they've had to grow up quickly. Both of these girls have been through a lot in their young lives. I tend to forget that my wife faced challenges very early on which granted her more life experience than many of her peers have. It hasn't made her cynical though, unlike me with my own past.

"Vivian stepped into my mother's role after she passed." Lizzie folds her arms together. "She became my de facto parent, especially since my father was busy trying to hold down a job and provide for us. Then, after my father fell ill, Vivian stepped into the role of breadwinner, as well. She's a brilliant painter and loves poetry, as I assume you already know."

I nod.

"She's so talented"—Lizzie's features soften—"I was sure she'd be a well-known painter by now. She even got admission to the Royal Academy of Arts but decided not to join."

Again, I'm aware, thanks to my friend, the private detective. But nothing like hearing about her past from someone close to her.

"I was gutted. I begged her to reconsider, but she was firm. The money my mother had left us would cover a year of education for only one of us, and she was determined I would benefit from it. She said I had to learn ballet while I was young enough to pursue it, while she could paint at any time in her life." Lizzie laughs. "My sister can be persuasive. It was an argument I couldn't turn down."

I nod slowly. "I'm sorry the two of you had to go through that. I'm sorry you felt the lack of money, and that she had to sacrifice the opportunity to study so you could follow your passion. I'm sorry your father fell ill and couldn't get the care he needed. But I hope"—I clear my throat

—"I hope I've helped to ease some of your lack since I married your sister."

"I wasn't convinced you were good for her. I thought she was moving from one unwanted marriage to another. She and Felix were never right for each other, but moving from the son to the father? You can imagine how that looked from the outside."

I stiffen. Neither sister pulls any punches, apparently.

I nod slowly. "I'm aware of how Vivian will have to go through life with people judging her for marrying me."

No one dares point that out to me, of course. Because I'm a man, and because I have the money to shut them down. But Raven doesn't have that luxury. She has me, though.

"And if anyone dares say anything about her, I'll destroy them so fast, they won't know what hit them."

She seems taken aback, then a small smile curves her lips. "How many people are you going to track down? There will always be somebody who'll point a finger at you and be judgmental."

I lean back in my seat. "It doesn't matter how many people I have to silence, whether it's through money or otherwise, I have the resources for it."

Her eyes round. "I'm going to pretend I didn't hear you say that, though I appreciate the sentiment." She pushes a fingertip into her cheek. "It seems you care for my sister."

"Of course I do."

"Do you love her?"

It's my turn to be taken aback. I'm tempted to tell her it's none of her business, but this is Raven's sister we're talking about. Someone she's very close to, someone who deserves the courtesy of an answer to her question. I nod slowly. "I do"—I clear my throat—"I love her."

She sits up straight. "Why don't you tell her so? What are the two of you arguing about? Why are you trying to put distance between the two of you?"

"She told you that?" I frown.

"We're sisters; we gossip. We know about each other's lives. We like to share the intimate details."

What the —?

She must see the slight look of panic on my face, for she scoffs. "Not *those* intimate details. But you made her cry. I noticed that as soon as I saw her swollen eyes. Besides, she's more reticent than usual when it came to details of her marriage. She insists she's happy, even though she doesn't sound it. It's why I realized something's up between the two of you. But it seems the two of you haven't been open with each other. You love her. She loves you. What's the problem?" She throws up her hands.

The look of exasperation on her face draws a chuckle from me. "It's not that simple." I rub the back of my neck.

Mary comes in with a plate, on it, there are two cookies. Thank God for the respite. It gives me a little time to figure out what I'm going to tell her. She places the cookies in front of Lizzie. "Enjoy, dear." She turns and leaves.

Lizzie breaks off a tiny piece and places it on her tongue. Her face lights up. "Oh wow, that's so good." She takes a piece and chews on it before nodding at me. "You were telling me why it is that you feel the need to stay away from my sister and break her heart, even though you love her?"

I squeeze the bridge of my nose. "It's complicated." I rise to my feet and begin to pace. "I figured I should give her space."

"Space?" she asks in a disbelieving voice.

"She has a big exhibition coming up and needs to focus on her paintings. It's... Best I stay out of her way."

"Bull-fucking-shit." She pushes away her plate. "I might be young, but I wasn't born yesterday. Any fool can see the two of you are made for each other." She holds up her hand. "I confess, I was skeptical about the marriage. But she sent me pictures of the two of you at your country home where you took her for your honeymoon, and you both looked so happy. And whenever she texted me, she sounded so upbeat. She told me she was no longer working at the pizza parlor but was focusing on her painting, and I knew she'd made the right decision. It doesn't hurt that you have the cheese to support her career."

Cheese? I frown, then smooth out my forehead. *Oh, money.*

"She also told me that you got our father onto a trial at Johns Hopkins, which could see a huge shift in his quality of life. For the first time in her life, she's able to focus on herself and her painting. You made that possible, and I'm grateful to you for that—" she hesitates.

"I sense a 'but' coming on," I murmur.

"—but you're still an ass."

"Thanks?" I roll my shoulders.

"That's all you have to say?"

I try to find a more comfortable position in my chair, and when that doesn't work, I rise to my feet and begin to pace. "The fact that I love your sister is the reason why I need to stay away from her."

"I don't understand."

"If I let her get closer, I'll end up hurting both of us."

"What do you mean?" Her eyebrows knit.

"I've hurt every person I've ever loved. Why should this be any different? If something happened to her, I'd never forgive myself. Besides, it's only a matter of time before she realizes she could do better than me. She deserves someone closer to her age. Someone who'll be with her for most of her lifetime. It's only a matter of time before she looks at me and regrets that she married me." I shake my head. "No, it's best I spare her that pain. It's best I put an end to this craziness, before it makes it worse for either of us."

"Oh, my God! Are you hearing yourself?" She slaps her palm on the desk. "Can you see the flaw in what you're saying?"

I turn on her "Explain."

"Who knows what's going to happen in the future? You are so convinced you're going to hurt her, and she'll leave you, you've decided to cut your losses and hurt her anyway by leaving her now. In fact"—her frown deepens—"it seems to me, you've decided to fulfill your own prophecy by leaving her first."

I scowl at her. "I have no idea what you're talking about."

"I mean, you're being very selfish."

My scowl deepens. "I'm trying to do the very opposite. I'm trying to be selfless. I'm trying to walk away before things get too messy."

"They're already messy." She throws up her hands. "The two of you are in love with each other."

She's right. It's because we're in love that our lovemaking is so explosive. It's because we're in *love* that my need to dominate her is so all-consuming. It's because *I'm* in love that the thought of not having her in my life ties my guts in knots and turns my heart inside out. "That doesn't mean anything," I choke out.

Am I telling that to her or to myself? My words come out defensive and sound pathetic, even to me.

"You don't believe that." She stabs her finger in my direction. "In fact, you already know you're not going to be able to leave her, which is why, based on the little bit Vivian told me, you're trying to make her hate you enough that she'll leave you."

I stiffen. Is that what I've been doing? Perhaps, subconsciously, I did, but having it called out like this... It turns my blood to ice, and my stomach seems to bottom out completely. "Oh shit."

"Yeah, it's a shit show, and you're responsible for it. You made her unhappy. You kept her at a distance, hoping she'd make the decision for you and leave—since you didn't have the balls to break it off. Not that I blame you—my sister's a catch." She firms her lips. "What you don't understand is that my sister is committed to you. She's not leaving you. And you treating her badly won't make her give up on you. If anything, it's going to make her double down and do everything possible to save this relationship."

She's right. Raven's parting words to me indicated as much.

"So, you have a choice to make. Are you going to torture her forever? Or are you going to love her the way you should because she's worth all that and more?" She looks at me with an expression of disgust. "Are you going to confirm my opinion that you're a sad excuse for a man? Or are you going to prove me wrong?"

To have this slip of a girl call me out on my mistakes should be laughable, but it's not.

She's pointed out my idiocy, and I can't unsee it.

"You're right, I *am* pathetic." I squeeze the back of my neck. "I thought I was doing her a favor, but—"

"But from what I can see, you were trying to manipulate her into leaving you, so you could keep your conscience clear."

She's right. Again.

How could I have done this? How is it that I didn't see how my actions were unfolding? Did I become so insecure about myself, was I so weighed down by the mistakes of my past, I was about to commit the biggest mistake of them all by leaving her?

"Fuck." I hang my head. "Fuck, fuck, fuck." A searing pain burns my insides. A heaviness weighs down my chest. Every breath I take hurts my lungs. I feel like I've swallowed broken glass, and it's tearing up my insides. *What am I going to do?*

"How do I make this right?" I raise my chin and swallow around the lump in my throat. "How do I make this up to her?" I frown. I must find a way to undo the damage I inflicted on our relationship. I must atone for my mistakes and rebuild the trust between us. "I *can* make it up to her, right?"

"I suppose." She sniffs. "Maybe, if you show her how much you love her, and if you grovel enough?"

"Grovel?" I ask cautiously.

She rolls her eyes. "You know, the part where you throw yourself on her mercy and ask her for forgiveness?"

I nod.

"And on your knees, no less."

"For her, I'll do anything." This shit is hard... But that's because it's real. This is as real as it gets, and I'm not going to back away from the hard stuff this time.

She tosses her head. "And tell her how unworthy you are of her love and of having her in your life."

"Okay." I nod again. It's all true anyway. I plan on telling my Raven exactly how much she means to me and that I'll do anything, so she forgives me for my assholery. "Yes, that's good."

She drums her fingers on my desk, then shoots me a canny look. "Of course, you'll have to figure out what she *really* wants and give it to her as a grand gesture. Can you do that?"

47

Vivian

Lizzie messages me again to say she's off on another of her tours. I'm not sure what to say to her, so I'm using the excuse of the showing to stay quiet and not reply.

When the phone buzzes with an incoming video call from Zoey, I accept it at once. I need to vent to someone, and I know Zoey will understand.

"I know he cares about me, that bastard. I wish he'd stop lying to himself about it." I throw down my paintbrush and begin to pace the floor of my studio. "He's running scared. He knows he's on the verge of telling me how he feels about me, and he's afraid."

"If there's one thing that scares most men, including your husband, it's talking about their feelings. I bet he's worried about being seen as weak. I'm sure he wants to open up to you but doesn't know how to handle all the touchy-feely stuff. It's not unusual," Zoey offers.

"But what if he doesn't come to his senses?" Panic curls in my belly. "He told me I couldn't convince him otherwise. What if he believes that?"

She scoffs, "I've seen the way he looks at you. The man's head-over-heels in love with you."

It's my turn to laugh. "Umm... I'm not sure about that."

"I am."

"He cares for me, I know that, but love? If he loved me, he wouldn't hurt me like this."

"Or maybe, it's because he loves you that he can't stop himself from pushing you away?"

I walk back to stand in front of my canvas and stare at the painting. "A part of me wants to believe you. In fact, it makes sense that he hurt me so much because he's actually in love with me. But another part of me worries I'm losing him."

"And what are you going to do about it?"

"Eh?" I lift my gaze from the colors on the canvas to the phone screen. "What can I do about it?"

"You can finish your painting and go through with your showing, proving to him that your life goes on without him."

"I intend to." I set my jaw.

"On the other hand"—her voice grows cautious— "you could also *not* wait for him."

"What do you mean?"

"You could march into his office and demand he come clean to you about his feelings." She purses her lips.

"Isn't that risky?" I hunch my shoulders. "What if he insists he doesn't care about me?"

"What if he doesn't?" She scrutinizes my features. "What if you were persuasive enough that he doesn't have a choice but to come clean."

"Hmm..." I balance the phone on the table next to my easel, then pick up my paintbrush.

"You've never struck me as the type who's waiting for your future to come to you."

"I'm not." I dip the brush in the paint, then begin to fill in the part I outlined earlier.

"If you were, you'd be stuck trying to make ends meet in the pizza parlor. Not that there's any shame in that, but you took the opportunities that came your way—"

I continue painting.

"So, are you going to wait for him to get his head out of his arse or—"

"Or am I going to stand here painting a profile of him, like a lovesick moron?" I complete her sentence for her.

"You're painting him?"

I throw down my paintbrush in disgust, then angle the screen toward the canvas.

There's silence then she whistles. "Wow, that's impressive."

When I don't speak, she clears her throat. "It's him you've been painting."

It's not a question; not when the features taking shape on the canvas show a man with thick hair, blue eyes, a hooked nose, and those high cheekbones — not to mention, that beautiful throat, the wide chest with the tattoo of the bleeding heart and the drops of blood which I've painted to rain over him. The background is filled with explosions. Do they hint at the war scenes he lived through? Or do they represent the anger I feel with him now? Or are they symbolic of the little flares that seem to go off whenever we're in the same space?

Or perhaps, it's how I see him?

A man at war with himself, trying to come to grips with his past, while yearning for a future where he doesn't have to hide himself and who he is anymore. A man trying to make peace with the part of himself he lost on the battlefields. We know how much being in combat changes the lives of the families of those who die. We know how the survivors struggle to cope with the aftermath. Yet, we send our young onto the frontlines to further the political aspirations of those in power. Will we never learn?

Until I met Quentin and started painting again, I didn't realize I had so much to say through my craft.

"It's stunning," Zoey's soft voice cuts through my thoughts.

"I don't know what it is" — I clear my throat — "but I couldn't stop myself from painting him."

Her forehead furrows. "Your other paintings for the exhibition — "

Once more, I flip the camera and point the screen in the direction of the paintings lined up against the wall.

She inhales a sharp breath. "Wow."

"Is that a good or bad wow?"

"Can you zoom in?"

I do, then pan across the paintings.

"Well?" I shift my weight from foot to foot. "What do you think?"

"They're good." Her voice rings with sincerity. My muscles relax a little. Not that I'd want to make any changes to my paintings once they're done, but she's the first person I've shown a sneak peek of the collection, so I was nervous.

"I'm calling the collection, 'The Pitiless Wave.'"

"Poe?" She arches an eyebrow.

"Poe." I half smile.

"Hmm."

"What?" I turn the screen back to face me.

"Is he coming to your showing?"

"I wasn't sure if I should invite him, but having spoken to you now, I think I should." I was worried if he came, he'd see my paintings and discern all my secrets. He'd see that painting I made of him and know how much in love with him I am. He'd see the name of the collection and know I haven't stopped thinking of him all this time. I realize, it's only right he know everything.

I have to be honest with him, if there's any chance for us to be together. It's going to mean baring my soul to him. Then again, considering how I gave myself up to him in bed, I don't think there's anything about me this man doesn't know. Going into this relationship. I knew I was exposing myself completely.

I had to give myself up and submit to him, then find myself all over again.

I never imagined my husband, while so dominant in our power-play, would shrink from offering me a chance to see his soul, as well. I'm disappointed that he hasn't been half as honest with me. I'm also angry he hasn't come to see me yet. That he'd keep his distance, knowing how much he's already hurt me? I'm so damn angry. And you know what? I'm not going to let him get away with it. I'm going to fight for us. I'm going to make him fight for us.

I tilt up my chin, then set my jaw. "I'm going to confront him."

48

Quentin

"You wouldn't know a good thing if it bit you in the arse," my son growls at me from the other side of my desk.

Funny, I've tried to get him to come into the office and take interest in what we do here but couldn't get him within a mile of the office. Today, for the first time ever, he's here. And for what? To chew me out over how I treat my wife?

It's been three days since that discussion with her sister, which was very enlightening. I intend to see my wife, apologize, and beg for her forgiveness, but I'm having difficulty formulating my speech. Yep, for the first time, I'm at a loss for words. I wrote down what I was going to tell her, then tore it up and threw it away. Many times. I want to do something —something to back up my words, to show her how much I mean it. And so far, I've had zero ideas.

What should I do to woo her?

What do you give a woman who has enough money in the bank to buy herself anything she wants? And her sister and father are taken care of. How else can I show her how serious I am about getting back together?

I've gone around in circles in my head. I decided to shut myself up in my office and cancel all my meetings and calls until I think this through and come up with a plan.

I didn't go home, either, because I needed to mull over my mistakes. I need to do something that will blow her mind. I need to... show her how much I love her. I need to be with her. I only have to tell her I love her. I know she loves me and yet... confessing my love to her is proving to be so bloody difficult. To expose myself completely like that feels like I'm making myself too vulnerable. And what if it's already too late? What if I've pissed her off so badly, she'll never forgive me?

I've never been this indecisive in my life. She's reduced me to a man who barely knows his mind anymore. Speaking of... "How do you know we had a fight?" I scowl. "Did you —"

"Find out about it? Arthur told me. And before you ask, he heard about it from Sinclair."

I frown. I called Sinclair out of desperation, and to brainstorm ideas for how to make things up with my wife. He was taken aback, at first. Then, he laughed and welcomed me to the club of men who realize their lives are nothing without their women. Then, he congratulated me on becoming an honest man. Then, he told me to kindly fuck off and figure things out for myself. He added that, if I love her, I'll be able to. No pressure there. Then, a thought strikes me. "Arthur's been talking to you?"

"He's concerned about you.

I make a rude noise.

My son laughs. "Now you know how it feels to be in my shoes."

"What do you mean?" I scowl.

"You and Arthur are cut from the same cloth. Like Arthur, you only talk to me when you want something from me."

"That's not true —" I begin to protest, but he holds up his hand.

"Don't bother to deny it."

I clamp my lips shut. There's no winning with my son. And anything I say will be used against me. It's best to shut up and let him say his piece. When I stay silent, he scoffs, "Nothing to say for yourself?"

I throw up my hands. "When I tried to defend myself, you shut me up. Now, when I stay quiet, you get pissed off. What would you like, son?"

His frown deepens. "I wish you wouldn't call me that."

"I wish Arthur weren't my father, either, but we can't always get what we want, can we?"

He slowly straightens to his full height. "*Except* you got her. You don't realize how lucky you are."

I do, actually.

He leans forward on the balls of his feet. "From what I hear, you're breaking her heart, and you don't fucking care."

The band around my chest tightens. My belly ties itself in knots. *I care more than you realize. More than anyone realizes.* But I'm going to make sure she does.

"Language," I say in a mild tone, more to get him off the topic, then wince. I've heard men Felix's age swear using the kinds of words I wouldn't. I've seen men his age shoot to kill without displaying any emotion. And here I am, scolding Felix for using a four-letter word. I'm not only duplicitous, I'm turning into my father. I squeeze the bridge of my nose. "Fuck, I am turning into him, aren't I?"

"Glad it's sinking into your thick skull," he says with satisfaction. He throws himself into the seat opposite my desk and moves around until one of his long legs is thrown over an arm.

"Why are you here?"

"To gloat when you make a fool of yourself of course." He flashes me a pleased smile.

"What do you mean?" I frown.

"Jesus, you're so full of shit."

"I don't need my own son insulting me."

"I'll do more than that, considering you're acting like a dickhead."

Anger lassoes a chokehold around my neck. "Watch where you're going, boy."

He scoffs, "You don't scare me, old man." He lowers his feet to the ground. "I told you if you did anything to make her unhappy, you'll have to contend with me, so here I am." He narrows his gaze, "How could you hurt her like this? Don't you ever learn from your mistakes?"

"The fuck you talking about?"

He levels an accusing look at me. "My mother left you because you weren't attentive enough to her."

"Is that what you think?"

"Isn't that the truth?"

"The truth"—I rub the back of my neck—"is more complicated than that."

"The truth—" I begin but a new voice interrupts me.

"The truth is that I am happy to find you both here."

I whip my head in the direction of the door, and so does Felix.

He gapes at the woman standing in the doorway.

Her dark hair is pulled back in a chignon. Her lips are painted a dark red, and there's a pinched look to her features. She's thinner than I remember, and there are new lines around her eyes and mouth. She walks forward, and the skin on her thigh flashes from between the slit in her skirt. She pauses on the side of the desk between me and my son and looks between us.

"I hadn't expected a family reunion, but... Never too late." Her smile is almost genuine.

And I'd have believed it if I didn't know her better.

Fucking hell. I knew this was going to happen when Arthur told me he'd announced my upcoming nuptials in the newspaper. I knew she'd hear about it and turn up to piss all over my life, the way she has the last few times. Always, *always* when something of significance occurs.

Good thing my wife isn't here. If the two of them came face to face, it'd make matters between Raven and me more complicated.

"M-mother?" Felix's Adam's apple bobs. Once more, he seems younger than his years. His blue eyes, so like mine, are fixed on the woman like he's seeing a ghost. And with good reason. He hasn't seen her since the day she walked out on him when he was two-years-old.

"You grew up handsome, Felix." Her features soften as she takes him in. "I see you've still got that piece of hair that won't lie down."

Felix reddens. He runs his fingers through his hair, trying to smooth it down, but the tuft of hair he pulls back springs forward again.

Her throat moves as she swallows. "Aren't you going to give your mother a kiss?" she chides him gently.

He has a dazed look on his face as he gets to his feet, closes the distance to her and pecks her cheek. He pulls back and stares at her, no doubt, trying to make sense of the situation.

I, on the other hand, have no doubt the mother of my son is back to create trouble for me. "What do you want, Shiloh?" I bark.

Shiloh turns her gaze on me, and an admiring look comes into her eyes. "You certainly took care of yourself, Quentin. You're more handsome than when I last saw you."

"And your heart is every bit as ugly as the day you left us," I bite out.

Her face falls. "I... I'm back."

"You're not needed here. Like you weren't needed the last time you decided to pay me a visit. What happened? Did the money I transferred to your account run out?" I growl.

"She paid you a visit?" Felix jerks his chin in my direction.

"She did. And it wasn't the first time, either. Each time she approached me, it's because she needed money. Each time, I offered to take her to you, but she refused. She's had no interest in seeing you." It's going to hurt my son to hear this, but I can't keep the truth from him anymore.

Felix's face falls.

Shiloh's expression grows mutinous. "Is it necessary to tell him that?"

"It's the truth."

The color drains from Felix's face. "Is... Is it, mother?"

"Tell him," I scowl at her.

Shiloh throws me a venomous look. But when she turns to Felix, her expression turns soft again. "I'm sorry. It was too difficult for me to look at you. It brought back too many memories, and I knew I wouldn't be able to cope with seeing you."

"Too difficult for *you*?" He shakes his head. "Are you kidding me? You left me when I was a toddler. Now you're back, and I learn that there were opportunities for us to have met but you never took them?"

She takes a step in his direction.

He holds up his hand. "Do you know how many times I have dreamed of this meeting? How many times I imagined the moment I'd come face-to-face with my mother? The number of times I looked at your picture and wished I could see you in real life? I was sure there was a reason you never came to see me. In fact, I was sure he"—Felix nods in my direction— "paid you to stay away."

What the— I open, then shut my mouth, deciding to stay quiet. Felix has enough to deal with.

"Turns out I was wrong." Felix narrows his gaze on her. "Though apparently, he was paying you, after all."

"I had no other means of income. I am your mother. He"—she glances at me then back at her son— "he owed me."

"Any debts I owed you have been paid off." I cross my arms across my chest. "I have nothing left for you."

"You have billions." She waves a hand in the air. "What's a little more? If you could send me an allowance until he turned twenty-one—"

"You gave her an allowance?" Felix looks shocked.

"—you could continue paying me for a few more years." She flutters her eyelids. "Just until I get back on my feet."

"My answer is the same as the last time you asked. Read my lips. It's a 'no.'"

A sly look comes into her eyes, then she blinks, and it's gone. As slippery as ever, this one.

"I..." She swallows hard. Her features take on an expression of sadness, one I don't believe at all.

"I want to make amends," she pleads.

"A little too late for that. Next?"

Her chin trembles, and if I didn't know her better, I'd almost believe she's contrite.

"I... I'm sorry I left you. I... I didn't have a choice." She wrings her hands.

"Bull-fucking-shit, and if you think I'm buying your nonsense—"

"It... It's not nonsense. You didn't care for me the way you did for your career. You... found out I was pregnant, and you never came home to see me during the pregnancy."

Nothing I haven't heard before, and yet, the ring of truth to it squeezes my guts again. "I was on a mission." I set my jaw. "The fate of the country—"

"And of most of the free world depended on you." She tosses her head. "Good to know your excuses haven't changed."

"It's not an excuse; it's the truth." But if I had to do it all over again, I wouldn't make the same choices. I'd ensure I didn't neglect my son. I'd make sure to be there for him emotionally through his growing years.

Felix flinches. I see the anguish on his features and curse myself. I wish he didn't have to listen to this conversation, but it might be for the best. He's grown up. It's best he listens to what his mother has to say. It's best he sees her true colors himself.

The father in me wants to save him from the truth. But the soldier in me knows he needs to face the reality of the situation.

So, I shove aside my feelings and glower at the woman standing in front of me with a pleading expression on her face.

"You knew who I was when you met me. You knew my duty to my country came first."

"You mean, your duty to building your career and feeding your own ego?" She huffs.

"Good to know your arguments haven't varied after all these years." I bare my teeth.

She draws herself to her full height. "I did not come to be insulted by you."

I place my fingertips together. "No, you came to demand more money. And I've already told you, I'm not giving you any."

Felix shakes his head. "I can't believe that you never wanted to meet me. You had no interest in seeing me grow up? You had no curiosity about how I was, or how I looked, or how I was faring?"

She lowers her chin, but not before the guilt in her expression is evident.

"Oh, my God." He rubs his forehead. "All this time, I made up this fantasy about you returning someday to claim me. Fuck! How could I have been that naïve?"

"Felix." She takes a step in his direction.

He moves back. "Don't... Please. I... I need to figure this out."

"I'm sorry"—she swallows—"truly. I'm sorry I left and couldn't deal with being a mother. But I'm back and I want to make amends." She blinks rapidly. "Uh... Also, I came because I need you both to hear this from me." She hunches her shoulders and nervousness lurks at the edge of her gaze.

For the first time since I've known her, she looks uncertain. She glances away, refusing to meet my gaze, and the hair on the nape of my neck rises.

"What is it? What the fuck have you done?" I growl.

"Good old Quentin, so quick to pass judgement on me." She half laughs. "Sometimes, I'm not sure why we even got together."

"Don't stall. Whatever it is you're here to say, spit it out already," I snap.

Sweat lines her forehead. She looks from Felix to me, then back to Felix. "I... I had an affair when you were gone."

So, my suspicions were right. I set my jaw. When I stay silent, she shuffles her feet. "There's more." She looks away then back at me. "Felix... Uh, he's not your son."

"I'm not sure I heard that right." I begin to laugh, then I see the look on her face and realize she's serious. "What the fuck are you talking about?"

"You're joking." Felix pales, gazing at his mother with a trust she never earned. I want to go to him and shake him, so he sees her true colors. Though the way Shiloh is going, I don't need to do anything.

"This can't be true." He shakes his head. "Tell me, mother. Tell me it's not true. This is your way at getting back at Quentin, right?"

She stays silent.

His face falls further. He turns to me with an uncomprehending look on his face. "What... What is she saying, Dad?"

He called me *Dad*. He hasn't called me that since he was a teen. A heaviness squeezes my chest. A thick sensation coats my throat. I want to go to him and put my arms around him and console him. I take a step in his direction, but he's looking at me with such shock, my heart slams into my ribcage. It feels like a gun has gone off in my chest.

I can't believe she'd do this to him. I can't believe she walked in here and set off that emotional bomb without any warning. Typical Shiloh, never one to consider how the repercussions of her actions would affect our son.

I turn on her. "Tell us everything. Don't hold anything back, you hear me?" I snap.

She nods, then swallows hard. "Felix was born six weeks premature." She addresses this comment to me.

I frown. "How does that—" I join the dots in my head. "Are you telling me you knew you were with child the time I visited you between tours? Which was the only time I was home, and which is when I assumed you fell pregnant?"

She nods, then lowers her chin to her chest. "I... I couldn't tell you."

"So, you let me believe I was the father?" I clench my jaw.

"I didn't know what else to do. I was confused. No one else knew. It seemed best not to bring it up."

"All this time"—Felix shakes his head—"you let *me* believe he was my father?"

"I *am* your father." I glare at him. "You're my son, whether we're blood-related or not. This doesn't change anything, you understand?"

Felix's lips are set. He runs his fingers through his hair. There is a serious look about his eyes, one that suddenly makes him seem more mature. My son is turning into a man in front of my eyes. "That's very decent of you, but it doesn't change the fact that I need to find out who my biological father is." He jerks his chin in Shiloh's direction.

"Who was he?"

"He was a chef. I met him when I went to his restaurant with my friends. It was supposed to be a one-night stand, but lasted a month. We broke up when he moved away."

I squeeze the edge of my desk with such force, the wood cracks. "Why are you telling me this now?"

"I thought"—she squares her shoulders—"I thought I owed it to the two of you to know the truth." She moves toward me. "I thought"—she reaches out to cup my cheek, and I'm in shock from what she revealed, so I don't move away—"I thought we could try again, to be a family."

A tremor of disquiet ripples down my spine. Something draws my attention to the doorway. I glance up to see Raven standing there.

49

Vivian

Ohmigod! Who is that woman? Why was she touching his face? Is she... is she someone he slept with? And how dare he let her put her hand on him? And why didn't he pull away?

How could he do this to me?

My heart plummets to my stomach. Anger tightens the band around my chest.

He must see the play of emotions on my face for he jumps back. He heads in my direction. No, no, no, I'm not doing this now. I can't face him. Not after that scene.

I turn and dart away, down the corridor. I hear his footsteps behind me. Oh no, he's right behind me. I reach the elevator and slap the button to open the doors. Come on come on. The elevator door slide open. I jump in. Then press the button to close them.

He skids to a stop in front of the elevator and shoves his leg between the doors. They spring back, he steps inside. My pulse rate shoots through the roof. My guts churn. I step back to put space between us until I hit the back of the cage.

"It's not what it seems."

He faces me with his back to the elevator doors. I ignore him and stare at the indicator above his head. Except my body is very aware of him. He seems to suck the oxygen out of the small space, so when I draw in a breath, my lungs burn.

"Raven, give me a chance to explain, please."

Tears prick the backs of my eyes. There's no mistaking the concern in his voice, but I can't unsee that scene. He's my husband, *mine*.

"She touched you," I say in a low voice. "She had her hands on you, and you weren't doing anything about it."

He stiffens. "I was too shocked by what happened. If you hadn't entered, at that moment—"

"I'd have never seen it, and you wouldn't have told me about it," I choke out.

His silence confirms I'm right. My heart somersaults into my throat. My chest feels like the freaking Himalayan Mountain range has collapsed on it. My shoulders sag. He's not denying it.

I... came here to confront him and fight for him, for our marriage. And now... I wonder if I was mistaken.

I thought he cared for me, that he wasn't able to voice his affection for me because of his upbringing and everything that happened with him in the Marines. But now...? Now, I wonder if I should have believed him.

Maybe he meant every last word when he said he didn't love me. That he was simply saying the words needed to convince me to do what he wanted, and only because he wanted to save his inheritance and consolidate his position in his father's company.

"I was going to say, if you hadn't entered then, I'd have pulled away. I was about to ask her to leave, anyway."

"More lies," I huff.

"They are not lies." His voice is unperturbed.

It's as if he's trying to talk sense into an errant child. *How dare he treat me like that?* "I'm not a child."

"I've never treated you like one." He raises his hands. "Look, clearly, I'm not good with words when it comes to you—"

"That's putting it mildly."

He shuffles his feet. "I... I admit I made a few mistakes—"

"A few?"

"Okay, a lot of mistakes when it came to us, and I want to put them right."

If he'd said that ten minutes ago, I'd have jumped into his arms.

That was before I saw him with her.

"Who is she?" I burst out. "Why was she touching you?"

He sighs. "If you look at me, I can explain."

"I'm sure you can. You have a rationalization for everything."

"Because I didn't do anything wrong."

I scoff, "So, why do you look so guilty?"

"How do you know that, when you refuse to look at me?"

Goddamn, I hate it when he manages to turn every argument in his favor.

"Raven, look at me," he growls. The command in his voice sends a shiver down my spine. His presence is so big, so solid, so alluring. I find myself leaning in toward him and stop myself. Damn, why is it that I find it so difficult to disobey him? I take a few steps back, until my back hits the elevator wall.

"Raven." His tone holds a warning.

I so badly want to raise my middle finger at him, but that'd only bring our age difference into focus. The fact that he's twenty-six years older than me has never felt vaster.

The seconds tick by. *Come on, come on.* Only two more floors to go until we hit the first, and then— Then he moves. He slaps his big palm on the panel, and the elevator shudders to a stop.

"What the hell?" I yell. "Why did you do that?"

I meet his gaze, and... Big mistake, for the impact is like having the Tundra dump its snow on me. A chill envelops me. I'm covered in ice, without any warm clothes to shield me from the elements. My stomach bottoms out, my pulse rate seems to slow. Heat flushes my spine, and the combination of so many contradictory sensations makes me wrap my arms about myself. It's a protective gesture, one he registers, for his jaw firms. A muscle tics at his temple. He holds up his hands.

"Please... listen to me, baby."

"Don't..." I shake my head. "Don't call me that—not now."

He squeezes his eyes shut, then nods once. And when he opens them, there's torment and a bleakness in them. He rubs the back of his neck, and it's a gesture that's so unusual for him, I pause.

It hints at the confusion he's experiencing... Another first. The Quentin I've come to know is an authoritarian; someone who's very confident of who he is and what he wants. Someone who's assertive and self-assured; someone who'd never hesitate to speak his mind. He looks away, then back at me, and this time, I glimpse sadness in his features.

Even before he says it, my intuition warns me. In fact, from the time I saw the two of them together in his office, I suspected it, so when he tells me, "She's Felix's mother," I'm almost not surprised. But then he says, "She revealed that Felix is not my son."

"What?" My jaw drops.

"She had an affair while I was on a tour of duty. She became pregnant, didn't know what to do, and decided to pass him off as mine."

"Oh, my God." I press my knuckles into my mouth. "That must have come as a shock."

A muscle tics at his jaw. "I knew she was unhappy, but I assumed that was because she was taking time to adjust to being a mother. I suspected she was unfaithful, but it never crossed my mind that he wasn't mine. Not that Felix isn't *mine*." He rubs the back of his neck. "He is, in every way that counts." He shifts his weight from foot to foot. "I can't blame her for what happened. It was my fault. I should have been more present. I was too busy running away from daily life."

"You were devoting your life to the service of your country." I shouldn't want to defend him, but I can't help myself. Q has his faults, but his service to the cause of keeping us safe is not one I'll ever question.

His lips twist. "I was pandering to my need to feel important by focusing on my career. It was a classic escape mechanism—"

I begin to speak, but he raises his hand. "You and I both know it, so don't deny it. It's why, as soon as my feelings for you became too much, and I realized how vulnerable it made me feel, I hurt you. I wanted you to get angry with me and leave—"

"—but I didn't."

"And I hoped you wouldn't." He shuffles his feet. "But also, I wanted you to, because I'm bad at relationships. If it was inevitable you'd leave me at some point, I preferred it happen sooner than later."

He's been thinking all this, and he didn't share it with me? Why didn't he? Why has he been keeping his misgivings to himself all this time? I peer into his face, trying hard to make sense of what he's saying. "So, you were self-sabotaging?"

He laughs, the sound humorless. "You could say that. It wasn't until Lizzie marched into my office and told me off—"

"Hang on, Lizzie told you off?" I stare at him in amazement.

He nods. "And how. She made me realize how selfish I was being. How I was trying to manipulate you into breaking things off because I wasn't able to do it myself."

I rub my forehead, feeling dizzy. My little sister Lizzie faced down my very scary husband—who's more than twice her age and weighs, at least, four times her weight—and gave him a piece of her mind? I don't know what to make of that.

"And when I learned that Felix wasn't mine, everything became clear."

Something in Q's voice prompts me to look up. "How do you mean?"

"I realized how much I love him. I realized...how much I love you."

I blink slowly. "You love me?" I try to keep the skepticism out of my voice but must not succeed because he winces.

He brings his fist up to rub at his chest, then swallows. "I know, I've been an arse—"

"You think?"

He doesn't smile. "I've been more than that. I've been a wanker. I've been selfish, Raven. I hurt you, and for that, I'll never forgive myself." The expression on his face is so tortured, my ribcage tightens. "I understand why you wouldn't believe it, but I'm going to convince you."

"Are you?" I look at him, aware my skepticism is showing on my face. *Hey, I'm allowed to feel cynical, considering how he tried his best to push me away. How he tried to get me to hate him.* And then, seeing him with the mother of his son. Seeing her touching him, and he didn't shake her off? Is there still something there? Does he have feelings for her?

He moves forward and cages me in with his arms. "I'm going to spend the rest of my life making it up to you. I'd kill myself before I hurt you again; this, I swear."

When I don't respond, his lips droop, then he sets his jaw. "You don't believe me?"

"Would you, if you were in my place? You said you wanted to marry me because"—I make air quotes with my fingers—"I was the woman you'd been looking for your entire life, only to turn around and tell me you didn't want a relationship that would tie you down. You said I wasn't enough for you. You said—"

"I'm sorry, so sorry, baby." He takes both of my hands in his. "I was running scared from my emotions. I knew I'd fallen for you. I realized I fell in love with you the moment I saw you walking up the aisle, but I denied it to myself. I knew if I accepted my feelings for you my entire life would change; that I would never be the same again. It made me feel so very vulnerable, and that's something I never felt before. I didn't know how to deal with it.

"And mixed with all that was guilt, too. I knew I didn't deserve you. I was selfish asking you to marry me, when you could be with someone closer to you in age. Someone who'll be there with you for more of your life. Know what I mean?" He stares into my eyes. "You made me feel younger than my years, but you also reminded me my time was ticking down. I have far less life left than you. And that's bittersweet. That, more than anything, made me wonder if you wouldn't be better off without me."

"Oh, Quentin." I swallow. I want to rage at him and tell him I don't believe him, but the sincerity in his voice, the intensity of his gaze, the honesty of his words... All of it gives me pause. "I had no idea you felt this deeply. That all these thoughts were running through your mind. You seem so strong, so dominant, so confident. I never would have guessed you felt so exposed. I didn't realize our age-gap would affect you so deeply."

His lips twist. "Neither did I. And I admit, it didn't, initially. This feeling that hit me when I saw you, knowing you were the one, overpowered everything else. As long as I was acting on instinct, I was fine. But the more I fell in love with you, the more I realized how precious you are to me. The more I realized, if anything happened to you, I wouldn't survive. It shook me."

I want to say something but decide to stay quiet and listen instead.

He kisses my fingertips again. "I don't think I ever got over feeling responsible for Danny's death. And then Karma..." A haunted look comes into his eyes. "She was so full of life. She was one of those people who burned so brightly, anyone in her presence felt lit up from inside. I saw how Michael was around her. And then when she died, how he shattered. He became a shell of the man he was. Not only was it a shock to me to see someone like her being cut down in her prime, but I knew if anything happened to you, if you left me, I'd be worse off than Michael."

He sinks to his knees, still holding my hands. "I knew I wouldn't survive losing you. And that shook me. Worse"—he swallows—"I had to face the reality that I'll be gone before you."

My heart stutters. He's right but... I don't want to hear this. I can't hear this. It's too painful. "Quentin," I begin, but he squeezes my hand.

"Let me finish, baby. I turned a blind eye to this, and that was selfish of me. You'll wake up one day and realize you're married to someone much older, while others your age are living the single life being digital nomads or climbing Everest or going scuba diving... Know what I mean?"

I nod, then shake my head. "Yes and no. I know you're older than me. And that you have more experience and more confidence, and frankly, that's the appeal. And I haven't ever wanted to be a digital nomad, or climb mountains, or go scuba diving. So, I'm not sure what you're getting at."

His forehead furrows. "You have the money. You could do anything you want. You could travel the world. You could work from exotic locations. You could hook up with men your age—" He winces. "You could spread your wings and fly, rather than be with me, and I wouldn't blame you if you did..."

I take in his serious features, the agony in his open gaze, and despite the fact he acted like an asshole, I can't stop myself from feeling his pain.

"I've never wanted to do that." I half smile. "All I've ever wanted is my family to be happy—maybe even one day, have my own—and not to worry about paying my bills. And having a home with a studio where I could paint. I was, and still am, a nerd. I prefer reading poetry in my downtime. As for men?" I raise my shoulder. "The only one I've wanted is you. That's why I married you. It wasn't only for the money," I add in a hurt voice.

"I know, baby, and I'm sorry that I insinuated otherwise." He weaves his fingers through mine. "I want to take care of you and your family. It's my pleasure and privilege to do so. You know that, right?"

I nod slowly.

He must sense the hesitation in my gaze, for he sighs again. "I did a number on you, didn't I?"

I nod. "I... I am going to need time to get my head around everything you're saying."

"Take all the time you need, as long as I can make it up to you in the meanwhile." He holds my gaze with his. "And so, being not so young, yet dipped in folly, I fell in love with melancholy."

I half smile, feeling my heart melt further, despite not wanting to. He can be persuasive, my husband. "Did you adapt Poe's words to help you plead your case?"

"It's called creative license." He doesn't smile back.

"He's probably turning in his grave." I try to look away but can't.

"He knows it's for a very good cause." He peruses my features. "He, more than anyone, realized love is the other name for longing and pain, and being beautiful and tragic at the same time."

"Are you comparing us to one of his poems?"

"Deep into that darkness peering, long I stood there, wondering, fearing, doubting, dreaming dreams no mortal ever dared to dream before," he murmurs.

Liquid longing infuses my veins. His quoting Poe will always be my undoing. He must see the response on my features, for he nods. "Let me make it up to you, baby, please."

"You tried to distance yourself from me." I bite the inside of my cheek. "You tried to make me hate you. You tried to force my hand, so I'd leave you, but I'd have never done that. That's not me. I don't give up easily. All you ended up doing was torturing me. It made me feel so, so, unwanted. You were so horrible to me, Q."

He squeezes my hands, which he's still holding in his. "I'm so goddamn sorry, baby. I thought I was doing you a favor by leaving you alone, but not only could I not make myself walk away, but I ended up hurting both of us. I'm —" He squeezes his eyes shut. "I'll never be able to forgive myself for putting you through that. But I hope you'll give me a chance to make it up to you. Please, Raven. Give me a chance. I promise you, this time, you'll see my love through my actions."

When I see the earnestness in his eyes, when I see how open he's being, that he's bared himself fully for the first time, and knowing that wasn't easy for him, that traitorous heart of mine softens even more.

"Okay," I say softly.

His shoulders slacken with relief. "You won't regret this, baby, I promise you."

"You'll have to prove yourself."

"I will," he says with vehemence. "You'll see."

"You'll have to win back my trust."

"That's going to be the sole aim of my life. I'm going to make you fall in love with me, all over again."

I frown. "I never said I loved you."

"But you do," he says with that familiar arrogance that makes me both chuckle and also, want to slap him.

I settle for tipping up my chin. "So confident," I huff. "I'm not going to make it easy for you."

"Can't wait." He smirks.

And that should piss me off, but all I feel is a familiar tug in my belly. I've missed his smirk. I've missed him holding my hand. I've missed this single-minded attention only Q can bestow on me that makes me feel like I'm the center of the universe. Which is why saying this next thing is so difficult, but I do it because I owe it to myself.

"I have one condition," I add.

His shoulders bunch. A wary look comes into his eyes. I'm sure he's going to say I can't put conditions on our relationship, but he nods. "Go ahead."

"I need some space, so I can focus on getting my paintings done for the show."

His face falls. "You want me to keep my distance from you?"

No, I don't. But it's best for me, for now. "Only until the showing, so I can focus on my painting and hit my deadline."

His chest rises and falls. A myriad of emotions race across his features. I'm sure he's going to say 'no' to this. But then he slowly nods. "Okay."

OMG, I did not expect him to agree to that.

"Okay, good." I breathe out in relief.

But then he adds, "I have a condition, too."

Of course, he does. I manage not to roll my eyes, "What's that?" I ask.

"Kiss me." He looks deeply into my eyes.

It's still an order. Q's in charge when it comes to anything sexual. And yet, his tone is soft, and there's a pleading quality to his voice that sends my pulse rate into a tizzy.

My heart stutters. My thighs clench. A familiar heat squeezes my belly. The heat from his body overwhelms me, and oh god, I want him to kiss me. I do. And if I do, I'll find myself already giving in to him. It's best I don't. It's best I try to keep some distance from him... I suppose.

When I hesitate, his face falls.

Then he squares his shoulders and nods again. He begins to move away, when I close the distance to him. I rise up on tiptoes, grip his arms and raise my face to his. Our lips touch, hold. For a few seconds, we breathe each other in. I feel the softness of his lips. The tenseness of his muscles as he holds himself back, as he lets me explore his mouth and nibble on his lower lip. And when he parts them, I slip my tongue inside. A groan rumbles up his chest. I shiver, throw my arms about his shoulders, and plaster my breasts to his chest. His entire body grows rigid. I rub up against the hardness that pokes into my belly, and he growls, "I need to kiss you properly, baby."

I half laugh, then nod. Instantly, he tilts his head and closes his lips over mine. And his kiss... Oh my god, the feel of his hard mouth on mine, the way he slides his tongue over mine, the way he robs me of my breath and drinks from me like he's starving and thirsty and needs to taste me to

survive — I can feel it all the way to the tips of my toes. Prickles of electricity dance across my scalp.

I've missed my husband so much. Missed the way his body covers
mine and his weight pushes into me and holds me immobile. The way the
band of his arms around my body makes me feel secure. My nipples
pucker, my pussy clenches, my thighs hurt, and yet he doesn't let up.

He hauls me closer, so we're stuck from thighs to hips to chest, so I
can feel the thickness of his erection throb against my lower belly, and feel
my breasts squashed against his chest and his pecs turn into hard ridges of
steel. He runs his hands down my back to my butt and squeezes.
Instantly, more moisture squeezes out from between my legs. I groan into
the kiss, and there's an answering rumble from him.

Then he tears his mouth from mine. We stare at each other, my breath
coming in pants. His nostrils flare. His blue eyes are stormy with desire.
The jut of his chin, the muscle that tics below his cheekbone — all of it is so
familiar and so sexy. The lines radiating from the edges of his eyes deepen.
"I love you. And I'm going to show you how much."

50

Vivian

Husband: I love you!

My heart flutters. I'll never tire of him telling me this.

I haven't seen him since that mind-blowing, panty-melting kiss in the elevator, a week ago. He's been sending short messages like this one at least twice a day, and OMG, each time I read them my entire body lights up.

Husband: You are so talented, baby!

He promised to show me how much he loved me, and clearly, this is his way of honoring my need for a little space.

Husband: You are the most beautiful woman in the entire world.

He surprised me again. I miss him, of course, but I'm equally happy to have this time to focus on my craft.

Also, he uses punctuation in his message. OMG, how cute is that?

Husband: Not a moment goes by when I don't
think about you. I can't wait to see you again!

Gosh, I had no idea the man could be so romantic. I am swooning.

His housekeeper continues to cook for me. Only now, she insists on knocking on my door to get my attention. As I get deeper into the flow, as I feel my muse take over, I begin to ignore the knocks. There've been times when I've skipped meals until hunger forces me to open the door and retrieve one of the trays. Painting day and night without any disturbance is a luxury I've never had before.

And he gave me that.

He gave me the mind-space to create. And ensured I have all the materials I need for it. He ensured I could use this room as a studio. I don't have to worry about my sister or my father. I check in with both most days, but the last time I called, my sister told me she was going on another European tour with her troupe. Q had arranged to have my father, and his carer—who was now also his girlfriend—flown to Johns Hopkins for the medical trials he got on. When I called him, he sounded happy and excited. He'd responded better than expected to the medication and said he felt so much better already.

It means I can continue to focus on my craft. I have Quentin to thank for that. I am grateful to him. But a part of me is uncomfortable with it. That, with his money, he can change my life in the space of a month, is something I'm still coming to terms with.

And then, that kiss in the elevator. It was different from the way he kissed me before. The way he looked at me when he said his actions are going to show me how much he loves me—it was that look in his eyes that made me realize how serious he is about us.

And his texts are proving it. Is that why I miss him?

He no longer sleeps here; I know that because the pillow next to me remains undented every night. So, he's sleeping in his office, or he's moved into a hotel.

After a few days, I started sleeping on the couch in my studio. It's big enough to double as a bed, and it means I don't have to waste time walking up the corridor to our bedroom. It also means, I'm not distracted by thoughts of Q and his scent, which surrounds me in the bed we shared. Now, I have less than a week to go, and the tension within me is building.

I can feel it in the way I've been painting nonstop for the last god-knows-how-many hours. In the way the colors leap from my brush and take a life of their own on my canvas.

There's a knock on the door; I ignore it. It's probably the housekeeper.

A few minutes... Or is it hours later? There's another knock.

"Go away," I yell. My head spins, and my fingers cramp with fatigue. I shake them out, roll my shoulders, and push through the exhaustion. I'm on a roll, and nothing can stop me. I must keep going until I finish.

I dip my brush into the paint and continue to splash the colors on the canvas. *Keep going. Don't stop.* This is the last canvas, and my most important one. I have to complete this in time for the showing. My phone buzzes from somewhere in the room. I ignore it. It stops, then starts again.

I growl, then march to where I've left it face down on the couch and shove it aside. It hits the floor, then bounces once before sliding away.

I head back to my canvas and continue painting.

There's another knock on the door. I don't answer it. One more knock. I block out all noises, focus on my painting. My stomach growls; I ignore the hunger pangs. My throat is parched, and my head hurts. My eyelids flutter down; I shake myself awake. Dip the brush in the paint, press it down on the canvas. And again. And again. A *few more strokes, just a few more.*

The door bursts open. The brush slips from my fingers, and my knees give way. I don't have the strength to turn my head. The floor comes up to meet me. I squeeze my eyes shut and brace for impact, which never comes. Instead, something hard and ungiving bands around me. I'm lifted up, and when I open my eyes, I see him.

"Q"—I swallow—"what are you doing here?"

He says something, but the words fade away, then darkness overwhelms me.

When I come to, I'm in my room, in my bed, under the covers. I try to sit up, but a firm grip on my shoulder stops me.

"Rest," a hard voice rumbles from above me.

I look up into those piercing blue eyes of his. Anger smolders in them. I flinch, and a shutter lowers over them.

"You need to eat." The lines around his mouth seem deeper. His jaw is tight. He seems upset with me. The tendons of his throat stand out in relief. He's barely keeping a grip on his temper, I realize.

"Why are you angry?" I sniffle, hating myself for the weak tears that overflow my eyes.

His features take on an agonized expression. He wipes away my tears with his thumb. "Not angry at you, baby; angry at myself for not being around to take care of you."

"I missed you." The words are out before I can stop myself. It's my turn to flinch. I must be feeling weaker than I realized to let those words slip out.

His features soften. "I missed you, too, Raven."

"Oh." I swallow around the ball of emotion in my throat. "I didn't realize I'd miss you so much when I asked you to stay away. I didn't realize you'd actually honor my request, either."

He seems taken aback, then barks out a laugh. "That was the hardest thing I've ever done. The number of times I called Mrs. Harmon to ask about you, the number of times I asked her if you'd eaten—" he shakes his head. "It's a wonder she hasn't quit yet."

"I knew you were keeping tabs on me through her. It should have made me angry but, if I'm being honest, it also made me feel cherished."

"And I do cherish you, baby. More than anything else in my life." He cups my cheek. "When you asked for space to focus on your painting, I knew you were also asking for time and a little space to work things out in your head. This showing is so important to you, and I thought it best to allow you to focus on it. Now, I wonder if I made the wrong decision. Now, I wonder if I shouldn't have insisted on taking care of you while you painted." He drags his gaze down my body, then back to my face. "You've lost weight. You haven't been eating or sleeping—some of which, I know, is because you're in creative flow, but if you don't keep up your strength, you'll never be able to do your craft justice."

His words send a thrill of warmth coursing through my veins. There's no mistaking the worry in his features, or the caring nature of his words, or the anger which smolders in his eyes. Before I can say anything else, the door to the bedroom opens. His housekeeper walks in and hands him a tray.

"Thank you, Mrs. Harmon." He nods at her. "You may leave now."

She turns to me. "I hope you feel better soon, Mrs. Davenport."

I blink. Eh? She's referring to me? I'm Mrs. Davenport... Of course, I am. I *did* marry Quentin. But no one's called me that before. "Thanks," I mumble. She leaves the room and the door snicks shut. Then, there's a spoonful of food in front of my face.

"Open," he murmurs in a husky voice.

I part my lips, and he slides a spoonful of liquid into my mouth. The aromatic taste of spices, mixed with the heavier composition of the broth and the creamy addition of yogurt, fills my senses. "Mmm." I chew on the pieces of vegetable and meat, and swallow. "This is delicious."

"Mulligatawny soup. It's my mother's recipe."

"Mulliga-what?" I stumble over the word.

"It's an old Anglo-Indian recipe. My mother's father was from the sub-continent. He was a soldier in the British Army."

That's the first time he's willingly shared something of his past. I stay silent as he feeds me another spoonful, and am rewarded when he continues, "She took after her mother in her looks, with fair skin and blue eyes. She was self-conscious about her heritage, probably because she was bullied about it in school. She preferred not to have anything to do with that side of her family. But whenever we boys didn't feel well, she'd make us Mulligatawny soup."

I swallow another mouthful. "It's very tasty."

"This one has chicken broth and vegetables, a dash of yoghurt and is flavored with curry powder. That's a blend of spices like cumin, coriander, turmeric, fenugreek and pepper," he adds.

I stare at him. "You're very knowledgeable about Indian food."

He hesitates. "I went through a phase in my teens when I researched Anglo-Indian history, including the food. I was curious about my heritage, especially because my mother refused to talk about it. Then I joined the Marines, and that became my life."

"You Davenport men take after your maternal grandfather in your tradition of serving the country, it seems."

His gaze widens. He looks at me in surprise. "I never thought of that before." He continues to stare at me, and my cheeks heat.

"What?" I murmur.

"You're beautiful," he says with absolute seriousness. It's not patronizing; he means it.

I lower my eyelashes. "Thank you. Also, I'm hungry."

He smiles, then continues to feed me the rest of the soup, stopping only to break off the bread and butter it before popping it into my mouth. By the time I'm done eating, sleep tugs at my eyelids. When I refuse more food, he places the tray aside, then pulls the covers up around my shoulders.

"Please don't ask me to stay away from you. I can't. Not anymore." He kisses my forehead. "I promise, I won't interfere with your process, but I'll rest easier knowing I'm here to look after you."

I don't think I can keep my distance from him, either. I don't want to spend another day without seeing him. I want him. I draw in a breath. "Okay." I yawn.

"Okay." The tension exits his big body.

I close my eyes and try to fall asleep, but I'm very aware of him moving around the room. He switches off the lights, then the bed dips. The covers rustle, and I realize he's slipped onto the bed with me. He must stay on his side of the bed though, for he doesn't touch me.

I try to will myself to sleep, but it eludes me. I turn on my side away from him, close my eyes, but the heat from his body is too alluring. I can sense his presence, the solidity of his bulk, but he doesn't touch me. I sigh. Then turn on my other side, facing him, and flinch.

His blue eyes gleam in the semi-dark, a predatory glint in them. He's on top of the covers, in his pants and shirt, but no jacket. He's sprawled against the pillows with his left arm folded behind his neck. His biceps stretch the sleeve of his shirt, which he's folded up to reveal his veiny forearms. His burly shoulders dwarf the pillow, and the darkness of his hair is stark against the white bedclothes.

"Couldn't sleep?" His low, hard voice reaches out to lasso around me.

I shake my head.

"Want to suckle my cock until you fall asleep?"

Oh god! Saliva pools in my mouth. That... Why does that sound so filthy and so naughty, and so hot? Why does that sound so appealing? And why am I not more horrified by the suggestion? I squeeze my thighs together and nod.

"Is that a yes, baby?" he asks softly.

"Yes, please," I choke out, trying not to sound too eager, and failing.

He reaches down and releases his zipper. The harsh sound pumps a burst of liquid heat through my veins. My nipples hurt. My toes curl. I lower my gaze to his crotch just as he pulls out his cock. Long, thick, and veiny, with precum glistening at the crown, it's the most beautiful thing I've ever seen. When he pats his thigh, I scramble over, then slide down until my head is cushioned there.

"Open," he commands.

I do, and he slips his fat shaft between my lips until it throbs against my tongue. He holds my head in place, so I'm able to suckle his dick without much effort. He strokes his fingers down the length of my hair, and when they snag on a knot, he gently undoes it. The caress of his fingers through my tresses soothes me. And the feel of his cock, throbbing in my mouth, is reassuring in a way I can't explain. Why does this make me feel so cherished? Why does this make me feel so secure that my muscles relax, and my mind stops going around in circles? Why does this... My eyelids drift down, and this time, sleep takes me under.

When I wake up, I'm on my side of the bed, tucked under the covers. Also, I'm alone. And naked. Guess he took off my paint-splattered clothes? I stretch, feeling more refreshed than I've felt in a long time. I swing my legs over the side of the bed, and head to the ensuite bathroom. I brush my teeth, then shower and pull on a fresh T-shirt and jeans. Allowing my damp hair to dry naturally around my shoulders, I pull on a thick pair of socks and head down to the kitchen. The smell of coffee and the scent of frying bacon has me salivating by the time I reach the island. He's wearing a fresh suit and jacket, seated at one of the stools. BBC Channel 4 plays in the background. He has a cup and a plate with the remnants of his breakfast in front of him. He's also reading the Financial Times—"Uh, you're reading the paper?"

He looks up at me and surveys my features. "Good morning to you, too."

"Good morning." Heat flushes my cheeks as I remember how I suckled his cock until I fell asleep. Another kink unlocked. I'm going to be thoroughly corrupted in no time, and you know what? I am not complaining at all. The gleam in his eyes tells me he knows exactly what I'm thinking. My blush deepens. "The newspaper." I point at the broadsheet in a bid to change the topic. "You're holding it."

"That's what you normally do when you read it." *Whew! He accepted the diversionary tactic.* Also, there's a thread of sarcasm running through his words, which is so very Q.

I resist the urge to smile. "You have a *real* paper—in your hands."

"As opposed to?" He inclines his head.

"I mean, you're the first person I know who prefers to read a hardcopy of the newspaper."

"O-k-a-y?" The quizzical expression in his eyes makes my lips twitch.

He sets his newspaper aside and heads to the espresso machine.

"Everyone I know gets their news from social media. Or else, they consume their news online." I seat myself on the other stool.

"Of course, they do." He works the espresso machine; a few minutes later, he returns with my cappuccino. He sets it in front of me.

A warm glow envelops me. I feel so cared for when he's around. "Thank you." I find myself blushing again, then duck my head and sip the hot beverage.

He chuckles and takes his seat, then slides some of the bacon onto the plate in front of me, along with some hash-browns. He pours me a glass of orange juice, then surveys my features as I drink it. "Feeling better?"

I nod, wipe the back of my hand across my mouth, and place the now empty glass down. "I'm sorry I fainted."

"Not surprising when you haven't eaten in days."

"I'm not normally like that. But sometimes, when I'm in flow, I forget to eat. But I'm done with the paintings, so it's all good."

"Hmm." He continues to study me as I fork some bacon into my mouth.

"How come you were home yesterday?"

"Zoey called me. She's been trying to reach you the past three days. When you didn't answer your phone, she got worried and called me. Followed closely by Mrs. Harmon, who told me you hadn't collected your food trays for over twenty-four hours."

My cheeks heat. "I'm sorry I bothered you."

"Your health is the most important thing in the world to me, Raven."

A weird embarrassment steals through me. Probably because I'm remembering how I hadn't been able to fall asleep until I suckled his cock.

"You have nothing to be ashamed of," he rumbles. *Damn, is he reading my thoughts now?* I continue to eat without meeting his gaze. He cups my cheek with his big hand, and I have no choice but to meet his eyes. There's a softness to his features. The tenderness in his touch turns my pulse into a vibrating top. This...this fondness in his voice, this affection in the way his skin clings to mine, this devotion in his eyes, this... This is everything. This is better than how I anticipated it could be between us.

This... Is this true love? Is this how it feels to be with your soulmate? This meeting of the minds, of feeling in tune with him, of knowing I don't have to speak for him to read my thoughts. Of being confident that he knows what I need before I do. Of owning me without saying a word. Is this...

Is this true dominance—when he anticipates my needs and makes sure I have what I need without my realizing I ever required it? If this is it, then it feels all-consuming, overpowering, all-desiring. It feels dizzying and exhilarating. I want to jump into his arms and kiss him and have him kiss me back. My head spins, and yet, he continues to gaze into my eyes like I'm the only woman in the world for him.

This... is what I was missing. This is what I was looking for, and now that I have it... I realize it's even better than what the poets wrote about. I yearned for it. I have it. I need time to get used to it.

So, instead of throwing my arms around him, I look away. "Quentin"—I swallow—"I... I need to get my paintings shipped for the showing."

His forehead furrows, then a knowing glint comes into his eyes. "I know a diversion when I see one, baby," he says in a gentle voice.

I flush again. "It's not—" I begin to speak then stop myself. If we want to make this relationship work, I need to be honest. "You're right. It *is* a diversion. I... You can be overwhelming, Q, and I'm processing everything that's happened between us, while also trying to get my paintings done in time." I set down my fork. "I just... am trying to figure things out in my head, you know?"

His features soften. The lines radiating out from his eyes deepen and his lips curve slightly. He reaches over and takes my hand, "Take all the time you need, I'm not going anywhere."

51

Vivian

My husband surprised me again. He's been so patient, so understanding, it's hard to reconcile this tender side of him with the dominant, macho, alpha he is. I realize, I might have misjudged him. There are more facets to Q than I appreciated. After he asked—no, begged me not to ask him to stay away, and I agreed, he's been sleeping in our bed the last few nights. But he hasn't touched me, except to spoon me.

I woke up when he slipped into bed last night, then sighed in contentment when he pulled me into his arms. And I woke with the evidence of his arousal stabbing into the small of my back. I knew he was awake, and for a few seconds, I was sure he was going to make love to me. But he pushed my hair aside, kissed the curve of my shoulder, wished me a good day, and got out of bed. He bathed and left me with another kiss on my forehead.

Oh, my God, I felt so desired. I felt his restraint, and that turned me on even more. In a daze, I made it to my studio to find he'd left me a cappuccino in an insulated tumbler. I almost burst into tears with his thoughtfulness, then indulged myself by sipping the cappuccino slowly.

Why does it feel like our relationship has evolved? That he's even *more* in tune with my desires? It makes me feel cherished, but also… Nervous? I place the tumbler aside, then walk over to my easel to survey the last painting I created. This is the final one I need for the show.

It's also the only one that isn't Quentin-themed. An abstract in blue and black, with wing-shaped shadows hidden between the layers of colors, it's the darkest painting I've ever created, and the most personal. I wasn't sure what it was meant to be, only that I felt compelled to splash colors onto the canvas. Now that it's done, I can see it in perspective. I know what it is. I don't want to sell this one, but I committed to the gallery owner to deliver twenty-five paintings, and this is one of them. I can't go back on my word.

There's a knock on the door, and when I turn, it's to find Lizzie popping her head around. "Can I come in?" She beams at me. I wave her in, and she walks over and hugs me. "So good to see you!"

"You, too." I squeeze her shoulders. "How was the tour?"

"Great!" She steps back, and there's a sparkle in her eyes. One I recognize. It's how I feel when I've completed a painting and I know it's good. It's that sense of complete satisfaction at having emptied everything you have into your creation. That sense of having plumbed the depths of your subconscious and given it shape, knowing it's not yours anymore.

We smile at each other, and then Lizzie hugs me again. "Marriage suits you."

"Thank you." I bite the inside my cheek. "I heard about you confronting my husband, by the way."

She seems a little taken aback, then she holds up her hands. "I'm sorry if it felt like I was interfering… Which I was. But when I realized how unhappy you were on that phone call, and I could tell you'd been crying…. And while you didn't let slip much about the details, I gathered enough from our various conversations to realize your man was being bull-headed. He needed a talking to, and—"

"You decided you were the person to give it to him?" I half smile.

"Something like that." She squeezes my shoulder. "I hope I didn't make things worse. I mean, clearly, I didn't because you're here all smiling and glowing. And I'm sorry if you feel I overstepped, but you've done so much for me Vivi, and I couldn't stand by and see you unhappy. I had to do something about it."

I take in her nervous tone and the anxiety in her features. I do think she overstepped, but that's Lizzie. She's impetuous and spontaneous and she meant well. Besides, whatever she told Q seems to have changed his mindset completely. "I am grateful for what you did, but"—I wag my finger— "don't do it again."

"I won't, but I don't think I'll need to, going by that dazed look in your eyes."

"Dazed look?" I scoff. "Must be from all the painting."

"Oh, is that what we're calling it nowadays?" She waggles her eyebrows.

"Oh, shut up"—I pat her cheek— "and speaking of... Being on tour seems to suit you. Must be all that sweating during a performance, hmm?"

She laughs; so do I. Then she shifts her weight from foot to foot. "I may have... uh... met someone."

A burst of happiness blooms in my chest. I feel so happy and I want Lizzie to feel the same. "How wonderful!" I throw my arms about her. "Tell me all about it." I pull her over to the couch in the corner, then head to the small refrigerator in the corner.

"Wow, all the comforts of home." She accepts the bottle of water I offer her.

"Quentin insisted, after he found out I hate to leave the studio when I'm working. He keeps it stocked with water, juices and healthy snacks, so I never starve."

"That's very considerate of him."

I nod. "He knows how to calm me down and anticipate my needs before I do. And he's so caring. Oh my god!" I'm swooning, but I can't stop myself.

She flashes me a knowing smile. "He's one hot silver fox."

You have no idea. I clear my throat. "Anyway, I'm done with the paintings. I can relax."

She glances at the one on the easel. "That's very different from your normal style." She rises to her feet and moves toward it. She surveys it closely. "It's edgier, and evocative, and sexy; yet also, haunting. There are depths to it... It feels like every time I look at it, I could find a new meaning."

"I do like it." I walk over to stand next to her. "I wish I didn't have to sell it."

"So don't."

I shake my head. "I'm contracted to give all twenty-five of the paintings for the show."

She shoots me a sideways glance "You could afford to buy it, you know?"

I scowl. "What are you talking about?"

"Pay the gallery owner and buy it for yourself."

I laugh. "That's insane. I painted it. And you're saying I should buy it back for myself?"

"You have the money, don't you?" Her phone buzzes. She pulls it out of her pocket; her hands fly over the screen. There's a smile on her face. "I have to go. Someone's waiting for me."

"Is that the boyfriend?"

She rolls her eyes. "Too early to call him that."

"But it's headed there?"

She blushes a little. "We'll see."

"You haven't told me anything about him yet," I remind her.

"Let's save some of the gossip for next time, shall we?"

Hmm. Why do I get the feeling she's hiding something? I open my mouth to ask, but she leans in and kisses me on my cheek. "No more questions; I'll tell you when I'm ready."

Okay then. Guess I'm not the only one who needs a little space.

She turns to leave.

I call after her, "See you at the exhibition."

"You haven't seen Quentin, have you?" I lock my fingers together, cursing myself for asking the question which has been buzzing in my mind all day. It's been five days since he first left me the cappuccino in an insulated tumbler. He's taken to leaving it for me on my bed stand so it's the first thing I see when I wake up. Every night, he sleeps with his big body curled around me. But no matter how late I stay up, I haven't managed to catch him. I've been sleeping in, thanks to the relief of getting all my paintings out the door.

I woke up today, determined to talk to him. But it was already two p.m. by the time my eyes opened. Damn, I missed him again. I've missed hearing his voice, missed his chuckle, his devilish smirk, that spicy male scent of his, and that tenderness in his eyes. I miss how he anticipates my every need. More than anything, I want to kiss him and be held by him when I'm awake—instead of only when I'm asleep. So, I'm disappointed that I slept in so late. On the plus side, I feel like a new person. By the time I make it down to grab something to eat, it's three p.m.

Mrs. Harmon looks up from the casserole she's been putting together in the kitchen and shakes her head when I asked if she's heard from Q. "Afraid not. Are you sure he hasn't messaged you?"

I begin to shake my head, then realize I haven't checked my phone in the past few days. I often get that way when I'm painting. I forget about the world. I head to my studio and, after scrounging around, find the device under an unused canvas. I bring it to our bedroom and plug it in. As soon as the battery is charged enough, I switch it on. A stream of messages pops up.

I have a few from Zoey and Summer. They're worried that they haven't heard from me and ask me if I'm okay? I reply and let them know that I'm fine.

I also have one from Lizzie, letting me know she'll be stopping by.

Then, seven from Q.

> Husband: This made me think of you.

There's a picture of a pink rose in full bloom attached to the message. My heart flutters. A warmth steals over my cheeks. Oh my god, was Q walking in a garden somewhere? The picture seems to imply that, for the rose is part of a bush. It's not in a vase. My big tough husband took time out to go to a park? OMG, he's changed so much.

> Husband: And her unmatched loveliness of looks.
> And the rare splendor of her locks, were mine.

I can hear his dark voice reading out Poe's words in my head. I shiver.

> Husband: I dreamed of you last night. I wish I were
> there with you right now.

Oh my god, I press my hand into my chest. I can't get over how open he's with his feelings.

> Husband: I miss you, baby

A giddy sensation takes ahold of me. It feels so good to know he missed me too.

> Husband: Miss you

Little sparks of happiness flare in my chest.

> Husband: Have I told you lately how much I miss
> you, wife?

Those sparks of happiness grow into bubbles of fire that float through my blood stream.

The last message pops up.

> Husband: Get dressed, I'm taking you shopping.
> Be at the front door by 5 p.m.

Ooh, shopping? He's never taken me shopping before. To be honest, I've never been shopping with friends, because... Until I met Q, I never had the money to spend on myself. And even if I had, I didn't have friends to go out with. And when I took Lizzie to the mall, I preferred spending money on her. To have my husband taking me shopping... It's a dream come true. It's something I never thought could happen to me. I glance at the time on the screen of the phone and squeak. I have under two hours to get dressed. Just enough to primp myself, and slough off the fuzz on my legs and underarms. Not my pussy though. Since Q had told me he adores it unshaved, I haven't touched it.

By the time I finish shaving, then take a long soak in the tub, followed by slathering lotion on my limbs and blow-drying my hair, I have half an hour to go. I run into the closet and, of course, can't decide what to wear. With ten minutes to spare—which is how long I dawdled—I pull on a skirt and blouse, then slip my feet into a pair of low-heeled boots. A brush of mascara and lipstick, then I grab my coat and bag and rush to the front door.

When I pull it open, it's to find a car idling at the bottom of the steps. It's the Cadillac Eldorado, and Q is standing next to the passenger door. He tracks my progress, and the intensity of his gaze liquefies my knees and turns my pussy into a mushy, soggy mess. I manage to make it to the bottom of the steps without tripping. When I reach him, he draws his gaze down my face, to my body, and all the way to my feet. By the time he reaches my face again, I feel like I'm about to dissolve into a hot puddle of need at his feet. His eyes gleam in appreciation. "Hello, beautiful," he says. Then he holds the front passenger door open. "Get in," he commands.

Instantly, my already erect nipples turn into bullet points of lust. Ugh!

That dominant tone of his never fails to strike a chord with that slut inside of me who wants him to have his wicked way with me.

I slide into the seat and fasten my seatbelt, without revealing how horny I am. When he enters his side of the car, I turn to him. "Where are we going?"

"If I told you, it wouldn't be a surprise." He flashes me a wicked grin that spikes my pulse rate further. Then, he steps on the accelerator and roars down the driveway. On the short ride into the city, he plays music — classic rock, which I happen to love. I pull topics out of the air to avoid the one topic I don't have an answer for yet. I can see the question in his eyes, but when I deflect by talking about the weather, he accepts my lead with a knowing glint in his eyes.

We discuss the last soccer match, which Arsenal won — a team we both support. He tells me about a new pub that's opened in Primrose Hill, and which he wants to take me to. By the time we come to the news headlines, we're pulling up in front of Selfridges.

It's a department store in the city I used to want to go to, but never could afford. Oddly enough, I can afford it now, but it hasn't crossed my mind to go. He slides out of the car, comes around, and opens my door. He helps me out and tosses his key to a waiting valet. When we walk in, there are no shoppers around.

"Where is everyone?" I wonder aloud as he guides me to an elevator and presses the button for the top floor.

"I had my team book the space so we could shop in privacy."

"Oh—" I swallow my surprise as the doors close. In the silence that follows, my heartbeat is so loud, it drowns out all other thoughts.

He must notice the confusion on my face, for he links his fingers with mine. "You okay?"

"Yes... No..." I shake my head. "I don't know. It's just... I feel a little befuddled."

"Why is that?"

The doors slide open, and he guides me down the carpeted hallway to where a woman in a pencil skirt and jacket is waiting for us. "Mr. and Mrs. Davenport? This way please." She shows us to a circular dressing room which might have been transported straight out of the set of Pretty Woman. There are mirrors taking up one corner of the room, and next to them a platform, meant for whoever's getting dressed. Next to it, is a rack of dresses. There's a couch near us, which Quentin drops into. He pulls me down next to him, and I go without resistance.

"Please give us a few minutes." He gestures to the hostess, who fades away.

This world is one I'm not used to. I may have the money, but not the sophistication or the confidence to use it for myself. It's never mattered to me before, but sitting next to him in this gorgeous room, I've never been more aware of the differences between us.

"What's on your mind?" He takes both of my hands in his. "Tell me."

"It's just"—I wave my hand in the air—"I'm not used to having an entire department store shut down for me so I can shop."

The gesture is typical Q. Since he promised he'd show me through his actions how much he loves me, he's been so attentive. I'm relishing every minute of it. But this? Holy hell, this is huge.

It's not something I ever imagined anyone would do for me. Does he know I'm self-conscious about trying on clothes? I have to try on a few sizes before I find the one that fits my curvy figure. And it's not something I relish doing in a crowded row of changing rooms. To be able to do so without feeling self-conscious is incredible.

It reinforces what I sensed earlier: my husband anticipates my every need and wish with unerring accuracy. It shows how tuned into me he is. To be at the receiving end of all that attention is hugely satisfying, and I admit, arousing...but also, unnerving.

His gaze flits across my features, then he sighs. "You're not used to me doing normal things with you."

"This"—I look around the space again—"is not normal."

He half smiles. "I mean, I never took the time to know you better, to take you on dates, or to take you shopping."

"Is that what you're doing now, getting to know me better?"

"I'm trying to give you everything you might have missed out on when you were taking care of your family."

My pulse rate spikes further. A thousand hummingbirds seem to be flapping their wings in my belly. "No one has ever—" I choke up, unable to finish my sentence.

"That's because none of them were me." He brings my fingers to his lips and kisses the tips. "Let me do this for you. Let me spoil you. Let me give you permission to spend your own money."

I frown. "You mean—"

He nods. "You're a millionaire. You can buy your own dress for your showing. All I'm doing is opening the doors for you to fulfill your potential."

I stare at him, unable to comprehend, at first, what he's saying. Then it sinks in. He's helping me help myself. He's showing me it's okay to take care of my needs. For so long, I've put everyone else before me. I've forgotten that, sometimes, I need to turn that attention on myself. He could buy me the dress. Hell, he could buy out the department store, if he wanted.

Instead, he's making it clear I have the power to make myself happy.

He's showing me I'm not dependent on him anymore; at least, not materially. This is akin to opening the door of a cage and giving the bird a chance to fly away, but the bird doesn't know how and has to be coaxed out. I try to comprehend all of this as I gaze into his eyes.

His smile disappears and he releases my hands, only to curl his fingers around the nape of my neck. He brings me close and presses his forehead to mine. "I want you to be happy. I want you to have everything you desire. The success you so deserve for your talents. I want you... To fulfill your potential."

My heart swells in my chest until it feels too big for my body. A jolt of what I can only describe as happiness thrums through my veins. This man... He's everything I've ever wanted in a soulmate. Everything I hoped to find in a partner I'd want to spend my life with. That he's so supportive of my art is so special and so affirming. He looks into my eyes, and I know this is one of those pivotal moments when our relationship levels up further. "I appreciate you telling me this... So much," I whisper.

That's when the hostess returns. "Are we ready?"

52

Quentin

I watch from a distance as all eyes are riveted on my wife. She bought herself, not a typical short black dress or a long gown with a slit up the side, but what I can only describe as an eccentric, yet very sexy three-piece shorts-suit, which shows off her curves, yet lends an air of edginess to her figure. Combined with the artistically, holes-ridden stockings and platform boots that come to over her knees, and a hat with a veil which falls over her eyes, she looks like a rock queen, wet dream.

Her showing has been a resounding success. All her paintings sold out, and above asking price. There was a bidding war on all but one of the twenty-five. I hadn't expected anything less.

And no, I didn't buy any of the paintings.

I would not deprive my wife of this chance to come into her own power. Over the past few days, as I stepped back and gave her space to focus on her painting, I gradually came to the realization that, not only do I want to care for her and keep her safe, but I also want to see her grow. I want to nurture her talent. I want to nurture her... And it's not the age difference between us bringing out this need in me to see her flourish. It's because I knew she's capable of more.

For too long, she held herself back. For too long, she sacrificed herself for others.

This is her time to shine. Her time to realize her full potential. The satisfaction I get by encouraging her and seeing her actualize her talents is as heady as the rush of having her submit to me in bed, perhaps more so.

I want her to realize how fucking talented she is. Enough that she doesn't need her husband stepping in to buy her paintings.

The twenty-fifth painting—the one I caught a glimpse of in her studio before she fainted in front of it—was sold before the showing opened.

It's the most spectacular of the lot, with buyers ready to pay three times the asking price for it, but she hasn't relented.

My guess is, Raven bought it for herself, and if that's the case, I'm bloody proud of her for doing that.

She has the talent, the ambition, the determination, and now, the name, to make it in her chosen field.

As for me? I'll never stop wanting her. Never stop loving her. Never stop needing her. Never stop... wanting to make her submit to me. But only if that's what she wants. She holds the power in our relationship.

I might be dominant, and I may be older than her, but her happiness is all that matters.

"She's something, huh?" Felix slips into the space next to me. "She's more gorgeous than the last time I saw her."

I shoot him a glance and am about to tell him off, when I notice the expression on his face is one of admiration, devoid of possession.

"She's coming into her own; the look suits her," he adds.

I look at my son in a new light. He's more astute than I've given him credit for.

"It does," I agree.

He turns to me. "How are you doing?"

His question takes me by surprise. When was the last time my son asked after me? *Never?* Another change in the relationship between us. Since the day he walked her down the aisle and pressed her hand into mine—and I should give her *and him* credit for that—the dynamic between my son and me has mellowed. We'll never have a traditional father-son relationship, but I hope it's, at least, one of friends. It doesn't mean we call and text each other daily, but he's agreed to join the family business and work his way up the ladder, which is something I never thought would happen.

And part of this new relationship between us means, I'm going to be honest with him. "I've been better," I admit.

His glance turns watchful. "You look tired, Dad," he offers.

I blink at the rush of emotion that crowds my chest. Since Shiloh's big reveal, he's continued to call me so. Guess that encounter with her did more good than not. It helped us realize we're on the same side.

"I'm okay," I grab him by the scruff of his neck and haul him close for a hug, "Everything's going to be fine."

Someone clears his throat next to us. "What's with the two of you indulging in this very un-Davenportlike behavior?" I step back and release my son, then turn to face Knox's sneering features.

"You mean, why are we hugging each other instead of backstabbing?" I drawl.

"You said it, uncle dearest." Knox glances around the space. "Is there any booze, other than the girly drinks they're serving, you think?"

"I'm sure the bar would be happy to oblige." I nod in the direction of the far side of the room.

He eyes the crowded room with distaste. "So I'll have to walk through that?"

"It might do you some good to rub shoulders with artists," I drawl.

"Artists?" His frown deepens. "A bloody waste of time, if you ask me — your wife not included, of course."

"Of course." I raise a shoulder. "Everyone's entitled to their view-points, I suppose."

He stares at me, a look of amazement on his face. "Going mellow in your old age or something?"

"Or something."

He shakes his head, then pulls out his phone and shoots off a text message.

A few seconds later, a diminutive blonde dressed in a skirt and a jacket, which is two sizes too big for her, materializes by his side. She's holding a cut-glass tumbler with amber liquid in it, which suggests he might have messaged her to bring him a drink? She holds out the glass to him. "Just as you like it, with two pieces of ice."

"You're a doll." Knox takes it without looking in her direction.

She looks stricken for a second, then composes her features. "Do you need anything else before I leave?" she asks in a soft voice.

"Nope, you're dismissed." Knox makes a dismissive gesture.

A hurt look comes into her eyes, then she squares her shoulders and walks off.

Felix and I exchange a glance with each other. "Who was that?" I clear my throat.

"Who was who?" Knox asks without taking his gaze off whoever in the crowd has captured his attention.

"The woman who brought you your drink?"

He looks down at his drink, as if noticing it for the first time, then in the direction of the woman who left. "You mean June?"

"June, huh?"

"She's my assistant."

"Since when?" I frown.

"For a few months now." He shrugs.

"And you brought her to the opening?" Felix asks.

"Of course I did. She knows exactly how I like my drinks, and when I want to eat, and how to get my suits pressed so I never run out of them. She's also very good at guarding my privacy and filtering my work emails so the riffraff doesn't bother me. Couldn't do without her." He throws back the rest of his drink, then looks around. As if reading his mind, she reappears at his elbow and swaps out the empty glass for a full one.

"Thanks, doll," he says absently.

She winces, opens her mouth as if to say something, then shakes her head, and mutters under her breath. This time when she walks off, her shoulders are rigid.

Felix whistles. "Now, that's what I call service."

And if he keeps doing that she's not going to be around for much longer. I drum my fingers across my chest. "She's worked for you for a few months, but I've never met her before?"

"I asked her to accompany me to events recently. She makes my life easier."

"No kidding," Felix says in a dry voice. "She's attractive, too."

"Who?" Knox shoots him a confused glance. "Who're you talking about?"

"June, of course. I mean, obviously, she's dressing to underplay her assets —"

Knox's fingers tighten around his glass.

"—and I'd wager, the glasses on her nose are more to hide behind, but boy, it makes you wonder what's underneath —"

The glass shatters with a crack that's lost in the general din of the crowd. But it shuts Felix up. He looks at Knox's rigid features and takes a step back. "Whoa, no harm done, mate. I was simply voicing what every red-blooded man here is probably thinking."

"Keep your wank-off thoughts and your fucking gaze to yourself, *mate*." Knox pulls a handkerchief from his pocket and wraps it around his palm, before he shoulders his way through the crowd. I watch him as he makes his way over to my wife. He kisses her on her cheek, and whispers something in her ear. She pulls out her phone from her little bag, and whatever she sees there has her glancing past him in my direction.

Guess she knows. It's not a secret. I suppose it was too optimistic of me to hope she'd learn of the news after her show, so she could focus on her event this evening?

Our gazes connect. As always, a hot sensation stabs at my chest. These unspoken conversations that we have when our eyes meet carry a gut punch. I can't quite make out the expression on her features, but whatever he told her causes her to excuse herself and make her way over to me.

"Here she comes." Felix turns and pretends to straighten my tie. I knock his hand off. "Behave," he murmurs with a sly smile on his face. "Or not. I suppose you're old enough to understand the consequences of your actions?"

He turns to greet Raven when she reaches us. He drops a quick peck on her cheek, and with a last look at me, heads in the direction of the exit.

I look down to find she's looking at me with tears in her eyes. "What have you done?"

53

Vivian

My phone buzzed non-stop in the little evening bag I knotted around my wrist. Pretty evening bags and I don't go together. The only reason I agreed to buy it was because its design was part goth-princess, part emo-artist and it, somehow, seemed to complement the outfit I'd chosen for the evening. All those gowns in the boutique, and I hadn't liked one of them. Finally, Q drew the stylist aside and whispered in her ear.

She returned with the clothes I'm wearing now. I was bemused and befuddled. How did he know exactly what I wanted to wear for my opening when I, myself, had no idea? And when she slipped the little clutch over my wrist, I balked. But he coaxed me into buying it, saying I could carry my phone in it. Which put me off the idea further, until he said it reassured him he could reach me wherever I was tonight.

So, I agreed to slide my phone into the bag and hang it over my wrist. And when it didn't stop buzzing all evening, I ignored it. Until Knox showed me his phone.

When he told me the news, I pulled out my phone and, sure enough, there were messages from Zoey and Summer, and our other friends. Now, I understand why they kept darting looks at me across the floor while the critics and reviewers swarmed around me and made a fuss over my paintings. Almost all of which were variations of the same theme.

Ravens and bleeding hearts and his eyes.

Some of them feature the outline of his profile. None of them have enough of his features for people to make a direct connection to him. But there are enough questions from them, asking who the mystery person in the picture is. To which I merely smiled and changed the topic. Easy when you're speaking with a bunch of shallow, self-obsessed, commentators who love to pontificate about their opinions on what I painted. Oh, the irony. And why had it seemed so important to get their approval in the first place?

Now that I have it, I realize it doesn't make an ounce of a difference to how I feel about myself. I'm my own worst critic. I compete with myself, and... for his attention. His approval is what I crave when it comes to my body and my emotions. When it comes to my creative endeavors, though, while his approval makes a difference, my own satisfaction with my work is more important. I also realize how much my art means to me. That it occupies as pivotal a role in my life as he does. And that his role as CEO within the Davenport Group is as much a part of his identity as being a former Marine.

All of these thoughts rushed through my mind as I absorbed the news headlines. And then, I elbowed my way past the woman with the painted face and botoxed lips who'd been insisting I was the future of the artistic community. The owner of the gallery tried to stop me, until she saw the look on my face. Then she beckoned to me to leave and managed the other woman, leaving me to slip past them and make my way through the crowd to him.

I barely notice Felix kiss my cheek before he leaves. I'm too taken in by the purposeful gleam in Quentin's eyes. He knows I found out about what he did. When I open my mouth to ask him again, he places his finger on my lips. I look at him in frustration, then grab his arm and urge him to follow me—out of the gallery, down the hallway, to a storeroom at the end where my paintings were stored before the showing. It's empty now, and temperature controlled enough that the cool air embraces me like a friend when I step inside.

I release his hand and hit the switch on the wall. Warm LED lighting casts a golden glow over him. I beckon him in, then shut the door and lock it before leaning into it. He arches an eyebrow but doesn't say anything. I look at him in frustration, then cross my arms over my chest. It's a defensive gesture, but whatever. The silence stretches.

I may have taken the initiative by bringing him here, but he's not going to make it easy on me. He's waiting for me to tell him what's on my mind, when he already knows what I'm going to say, and... *Gah!* I squeeze my eyes shut and draw in a breath. Another. When I open my eyes again, I'm marginally calmer.

He slips a hand into his pocket, his stance relaxed. He'll stand there until I tell him why I pulled him in here.

I sigh. "You're incorrigible."

His lips twitch.

"And you vex me," I fume.

The smile morphs into a smirk.

"And I shouldn't, but I find that hot."

He chuckles.

"And you shouldn't have done that." I scowl.

The smile fades. He takes a step toward me.

I hold up my hand. "No, let me finish, before I get distracted."

"Do I distract you, baby?" he asks in a tender voice, which is almost my undoing. As dominant as he is, and as much as that turns me on, this caring part of him is what lights a fire in my chest.

"You know you do." I clear my throat. "Why didn't you tell me you were stepping down as CEO?"

His gaze grows wary. "I was going to tell you. But I thought it would be best if I waited until after your show. I didn't want to distract you." He looks from me to the phone in my hand. "Goddam Arthur, I told him not to send out the press release until tomorrow, but he couldn't wait to spin this into another PR story."

He takes a step in my direction, but I shake my head. "No, no, we need to talk about this. Firstly, I'm pissed you didn't speak with me before you resigned."

His eyebrows shoot up.

"Secondly, why would you do this? It's what you wanted," I choke out.

"*You* are what I want."

His voice has a ring of authenticity to it. His features indicate he's giving me his full attention, and the intensity in his gaze, the way he watches me closely and with his entire body and mind and soul, turns that flesh between my legs into a mass of throbbing need. Oh God, he speaks to my mind, my body, and my soul. He speaks to *me*. Always.

"And you're right."

Did he admit I'm right? Did Quentin Davenport, my alpha male, dominant and egoistical to the core husband agree with me?

"Excuse me?" I sound shocked... because I am.

He runs his hand over the hair on his head, hair which he's allowed to grow out of his military haircut because I prefer him this way. Another subtle nod toward taking my preferences into consideration.

"I wanted to wait until after the show to tell you I was stepping down as CEO, so it didn't distract you. I hadn't counted on Arthur, once again, releasing the information publicly and beating me to it. In fact"—he shuffles his feet—"I should have consulted you before I told Arthur." He lowers his chin. "And I promise to do so in the future. I promise to talk over such important changes *before* I make them."

"So, what stopped you this time?" I frown.

"I wanted to surprise you, and I truly didn't think it was so important that I should mention it to you before the first really important showing of your life."

"Oh, Q." I lock my fingers together. "What's important to you is important to me, too. You like taking care of me. Well, I like taking care of you too. But I need you to give me the chance to do so. I need you to trust me enough—"

"I do trust you," he interjects.

"—to share all of your thoughts with me."

"And I will; I promise you, baby." His voice is soft, and the look in his eyes is so adoring, my stomach flutters, and a soft sensation overcomes my chest.

He's so damn charming, this man.

"That is the last time I forgive you for such an oversight," I warn, before I lose myself completely in those deep blue eyes of his.

"That's the last time I let myself commit such an oversight," he says fervently. "You're my better half. My wife. My partner. You're the most important person in my life. I promise to never make a decision affecting both of us without you."

A warmth spreads through my chest. My entire body feels lighter. I never thought I'd hear Q say that. That he'd discuss things with me, instead of making unilateral decisions on issues that affect the both of us? That's true partnership. A real relationship. A real... marriage.

But a small part of me insists he's saying what I want to hear. My husband's a wordsmith, after all. He knows me well enough to say and do things that'll sway me completely, right? *Right?* I shake my head, to clear it. "B-but the CEO position was important to you."

"Not more than you," he interjects.

"Isn't the reason you married me, so you could satisfy your father's stipulation and retain your position as CEO?"

"I married you because I fell in love with you as soon as I saw you, and I didn't want to wait a second longer to make you my wife."

A thousand electric bulbs seem to light up my body. I'll never get tired of him telling me that. *Never.*

"Where you're concerned, I lose my sanity. You're my Raven. My North Star. The compass that guides me. Without you, I'm nothing. Without you, no part of my life makes sense. Everything else fades into insignificance. It's always been you, only you, from the moment I saw you. Everything in my life has been leading me to you. I did the right thing in asking you to marry me as soon as I saw you, but I should have come out and told you why. I was a coward."

Oh my god, that has to be the most romantic thing anyone has ever said to me. If I had any doubt that he loves me, this little speech dispelled that. And it couldn't have been easy for him to say that. It couldn't have been easy to tell me what was on his mind and expose himself completely like this.

"You're not a coward." I half laugh. "You're the most courageous man I know."

"Because I put myself in danger protecting my country?" He shrugs. "That was my duty. But this"—he gestures to the space between us—"this is personal. This is the real thing. This is living with my full faculties, where there are no rules. This is me, by choice, standing in front of you without any words or gestures to hide behind. This is me, coming to you without any barriers between us. This is me, being honest, something I should have been from the beginning."

"And stepping down as the CEO? Was that—"

His features relax. "That was so I could spend more time with you."

"What?" I rear back. Of all the things to say, that... is the most unexpected. "What do you mean?"

"It's simple. I have one goal in my life from now on. And that is to take care of my wife—to please her and make sure I'm there to feed her and attend to her the next time she's in creative flow, focused on hitting a deadline. And when the kids come along, I'll be a stay-at-home Dad to raise them, so you can continue to have time for your craft."

Those thousand electric bulbs in my body turn into laser beams which light up the sky. I have never felt this adored before. Never. I never expected Q to say that. Never expected him to look so sincere, either. *He means it. He does.*

Then the warmth fades away, replaced by doubt. "But becoming a CEO within the Davenport Group was your dream, Q."

"I thought it was, but then I met you." He sets his jaw. "I resent the time spent away from you. Nothing matters more than being with you, Raven." He closes the distance between us. "The more honest I wanted to be with you, the more honest I had to be with myself, too. The more I shared my feelings with you, the easier it was for me to accept my own vulnerabilities and my failings. Remember when I said that I was selfish in marrying you because our age gap meant I wouldn't be around for the latter half of your life?"

"But, Q—"

He shakes his head. "It's the truth. *I* have to face the possibility that there's more of my life behind me than ahead." His gaze deepens. "And I want to spend every remaining moment I have with you."

"Oh, Q." I can't stop the tear that slides down my cheek.

I hate it when he speaks that way, and yet, I know it's a truth I need to face. I can't imagine life without my husband, but Q's being pragmatic for the both of us again. I'd thought Q's biggest fear was intimacy. But he seems to have overcome that and is ready to face one which haunts him as much, if not more... that of his own mortality.

This is true strength. To face your fears is true dominance.

This is my husband. He's fearless and he cares for me.

He wants me. He'll do anything for me, even give up a career that he's been groomed for since he was born.

This is my husband. He's mine. And I love him. I do. So, so, so much.

"I love you, Raven"—he swallows—"I love you so very much."

I allow the tears to come freely. "And I love you."

The next moment I move, and so does he.

54

Quentin

We meet in the middle, and my mouth is on hers, my tongue between her lips. My palms on her hips, slipping down to cup her fleshy butt cheeks and squeezing with enough force that she gasps. I swallow the sound, pulling her closer on her tiptoes, bending my knees enough that my arousal is cradled in the hollow between her legs. I feel myself throb and lengthen and thicken, my cock straining against my pants to be inside her.

She holds onto my biceps, her mouth open, her legs wide apart to accommodate my hips. She's so sweet to taste, so firm and soft and sexy, all at once, in my arms, so perfect, my wife. So beautiful and gorgeous and mine in a way words cannot describe. There's only this effervescent feeling where my heart once was—a confluence of emotion and seething need, and an affection and devotion that overpowers everything else.

She groans into my mouth, and the sound is beautiful and real and anchors me to the present. I soften the kiss. Lick her lips, kiss her chin, her nose, both of her closed eyelids. I brush my mouth across her temple, to her earlobe, which I tug on gently.

She shivers, melts further into me. "Command me," she whispers.

"Take me, break me, hurt me. I want you to... show me how much you love me."

When I hesitate, she flutters open her heavy eyelids. "Please, please, Q, I beg you. I want this."

And I'm unable to give in to the desire that strains my ribcage and weighs down my balls like iron weights. Somehow, the fact that I love her, that my heart beats only for her, that every breath I take is to please her, that my purpose of living is to ensure her happiness, has shifted something inside me. I want her, but her pleasure always comes first.

She must read my thoughts for she slides her hand down to cup my crotch. The growl vibrates up my chest unbidden, and a tiny smile curves her lips.

"In *Boogie Nights*, Mark Wahlberg played a porn star called Dirk Diggler whose penis size is thirteen inches," she murmurs. "You, my husband, would give him serious competition." She squeezes the bulge at my crotch, and I exhale a sharp breath.

"Is that your way of saying, I'm virile enough for you?"

"Especially when you use your Dom voice to command me. On the other hand—" She sinks to her knees so suddenly; the movement breaks my hold on her.

She unhooks my belt and has my zip lowered and cock out so quickly, my body turns into a furnace.

"Raven, fuck"—I allow myself a groan—"you're killing me, baby."

"I want to do this, please." Her gaze turns beseeching, "Please, please, Q."

"You beg so prettily." I cup her cheek.

Her flush deepens.

"You know I love you, baby."

She nods.

"And I've promised to discuss all the big decisions in my life with you before I take them."

Her forehead furrows. She glances down at my cock, and her breathing grows erratic. "Yes, yes, I know. But right now, I want your cock." She reaches for it, but I bat her hand aside.

"I decide when you get to touch me; never forget that. I decide when you get to come. I decide how many orgasms you get. I decide which hole of yours I take for my pleasure; never forget that. I also decide the punishment for your transgressions."

Her lips part, and she pants a little. "Trans...transgressions?" Her gaze widens, partly in fear, partly in anticipation. I continue to glare at her, and she flushes further. Then lowers her eyes.

"Does the thought of being disciplined turn you on, Raven?"

She nods, without raising her eyes. "Yes, yes it does," she says in a small voice.

When I glare at her, she shivers. "I mean, yes, Sir, it does."

"Good girl."

She shivers.

"Earlier, you challenged my decision of stepping down as CEO, and while I'm happy for my wife to do that, and I'm happy to explain myself to her, as my sub, I expect you to pay for your defiance."

A low sound emerges from her lips.

"What do you say?"

"Yes Sir. I understand, Sir." Her words are out even before I complete my sentence.

"Such an eager little Raven."

Her shoulders shudder. Her chest rises and falls. "Sir, please, please, please, I need you." She squeezes her thighs together. "Please, Sir."

"And I want you to have this. Open your mouth."

She shivers and instantly complies. I dig my fingers into her hair and tug so she has to lean her head back. My movements are assertive but I also make sure my hold is soft enough not to hurt her. "I should be taking your smallest tightest hole and making you wait for your orgasm but since time is short, this will have to do. Nod if you understand."

She jerks her chin.

I balance my cock between her lips. "Take me all the way down." I punch forward and slide down the back of her throat. The heat, the wetness, the tightness... It radiates vibrations of pleasure all the way to my brain and down to my feet. My knees tremble—they fucking tremble. "You okay, baby?"

She makes an incomprehensible noise, which judders across my sensitive crown.

"Are you wet?"

She nods, and I pull out, allowing her to breathe, then piston forward and down her throat again. This time, I go deeper, and when she swallows around my shaft, my attention drops to where we're connected.

I grab her arms and position her hands behind her neck, as if she's under arrest, as if her entire purpose in life is to be a willing hole for my cock.

It seems to arouse her further, for her gaze widens, and her breathing grows harsher. She looks at me, a beseeching look in those big green eyes, and I understand her agony.

"Your orgasms are mine, Raven. Understand?"

She manages to jerk her chin, and my groin tightens. My thighs seem to have turned into steel. And when she flattens her tongue against my dick, then grazes her teeth against the skin, I react without conscious thought.

I twist her hair around my palm with enough force that goosebumps pop on her forearms. I hold her in place and begin to fuck her mouth. Once, twice, and when tears slip out of the corner of her eyes and saliva drools down her chin, I can't hold back anymore. I pull out of her, then haul her to her feet. I kiss her deeply, tasting myself on her sweet lips, and fuck, if that doesn't turn me into a possessive, carnal being who's only raison d'être is to bring her fulfillment. I undo the buttons at the waistband of her shorts, then dig my fingers into the crotch of her tights. I tug, and the material tears. She gasps, and when I thrust two fingers inside her sopping wet cunt, her back bows, and her chest heaves. She lets out a low keening cry and begins to flutter around me. I know she's close, but she's not ready to orgasm. Not until I take her to the edge and pull her back, so when she does, it'll grant her the kind of pleasure she'll have trouble forgetting.

She cries out, I grip her jaw. "Not yet. You orgasm when I tell you, and not a second earlier, you hear me?"

55

Vivian

"You will not come until I give you permission." His voice drops a few octaves. The consonants are like bullets slamming into my chest. I shudder, but the reaction mustn't be what he expected, for he hooks his fingers inside my channel. "What do you say?" he growls.

I focus my attention on his stern face and lick my dry lips. "Yes Sir."

"Yes what?"

Oh my god, this man will not be happy until I give him everything. "Yes—" I choke out. "Yes, my orgasms are yours, Sir."

"And?"

"A-and I won't come without your permission," I stutter.

"Good girl."

A shiver springs forth from my core and envelops my body. I'll never get over this absolute pleasure which envelops me when I please him.

He pulls out his fingers and places them against my mouth. "Open."

When I do, he thrusts his fingers down my throat imitating the path of his cock. "Taste yourself," he orders.

Jesus, his bossiness is the ultimate aphrodisiac. I curl my lips around his digits, and the taste of him and me, and of my arousal and his need, nearly makes my pussy clench. He presses down until I'm forced to open my mouth so wide, my jaw cracks. And when he replaces his fingers with his tongue, my knees give way. He grabs me by the tops of the backs of my thighs and pushes me into the door.

The blunt end of his dick teases my opening and I whimper. Warbled words reach my ears. I realize I'm trying to speak but don't know what I'm saying, but he must understand for he releases my mouth. "Not yet."

I almost burst out crying. "Please, please, please, Sir. I need to come. *Please.*"

"Soon." His lips curve in a smile which I can only label as mean. Another layer of need grips my lower belly. My clit is the mythical red button, which the leader of the free world could press any moment to detonate nuclear missiles. My thighs are sore, my slit sobbing and swollen and begging to be put out of its misery. And still, he doesn't enter me, he merely drags his thick shaft between my pussy lips, again and again. I hump myself against the thick ridge, trying to get myself off. He laughs. Of course, he does. I shoot darts at him with my eyes, and that only adds to his general amusement. His eyes gleam like it's all a big joke, and the heat in my belly turns to part-anger, part-arousal. "You're a sadist," I gasp.

"Welcome to my world."

"I should hate you." I allow my features to soften. "But I love you. I love you so much."

"I love you, too, Raven."

With that, he squeezes my hips with enough force that I cry out. The next moment, he's hoisted me up, so my pussy is level with his mouth. He pins me to the wall with one hand, urging me to wrap my legs about his neck, and then he fastens his mouth on my clit. He sucks, and I yell. He continues to lick into my cunt and up my pussy lips, and when he bites down on my clit, the climax squeezes out from between my legs. "Sir, please, please, Sir!" I dig my fingertips into his shoulders, and he snarls against my swollen lower lips.

He releases his hold on my clit, then maneuvers my body so, once more, my legs are around his waist; only this time, he tears at my stockings until my inner thighs are bared. Then he enters me with one swift thrust. I groan, and so does he. I feel every centimeter of his rigid length. He feels about ten feet long, and as broad. It feels like I have the North Pole stuck up my cunt; not that it's actually a pole, but you know what I mean? He's so deep inside me, it feels like he's splitting me in two. He holds me, pinned against the wall, with his palm flattened next to my head. The fingers of his other hand are curled about my hip to hold me immobile. He stares into my eyes, his own crackling with electricity. He stays there, throbbing inside me for a second, another. Heat pours off of him, sweat clinging to his temple. He grits his teeth, then slowly withdraws so I can feel every pull of our flesh. He stays there, balanced at my rim. "Do you want to come?"

I nod.

"Hold on."

He begins to pump into me, putting his bulk behind it. Fucking me with his soul, and his cock, and intention in every angle of his body, and when he hits that spot deep inside me and I cry out, he asks again, "Do you want to come?"

"Yes"—I clear my throat—"yes Sir!"

And he fucks me again, and again and again, the jut of his pelvic bone rubbing my clit with each thrust, until I'm poised, once more, on the crest of that wave threatening to sweep me away.

"Please," I croak, the sound a broken thread that seems to satisfy him, for he whispers back, "Give me your orgasm, baby. Come for me."

And my climax instantly pours out of me. I'm aware I throw my head back and meet with the hardness of his palm, that he must have placed behind my head to shield me. I'm aware of my cum flowing out to bathe his cock, and then with a low roar, he joins me. He holds me as the aftermath jolts me. Holds me against the sweat-stained front of his shirt. Draws his fingers down my hair in long soothing strokes that make me melt further. When my body quietens, he gently lowers my feet to the ground. When he pulls out, liquid dribbles down my inner thigh. We both watch as a trail of white gleams against my skin.

"Jesus," he breathes, then pushes the cum back up my thigh and inside my cunt.

"You're filthy," I manage to not moan when I say it.

"And you're mine." He kisses me deeply, and my heart bangs into my ribcage.

Something drums against my back, then, "Vivian, you guys in there?" A voice cuts through the thoughts in my head. I stiffen, but Q continues to kiss me.

"Viv? Vivian"

I recognize the woman's voice.

I push against his shoulder, and he releases me.

"That's Zoey, she must have come looking for us," I whisper.

"Vivian, you okay?" Zoey calls out.

"I... Yes," I call out, "we'll be out soon."

"Everyone's looking for you; don't take too long." She chuckles. "See you out there."

I straighten my clothes, then glance around. "I need to clean myself."

"No, you don't."

"What?" I frown.

"I want you to go out there with my cum dripping down your legs, so everyone knows who you belong to."

I shiver. That possessiveness in his tone is such a turn on. I'll never get over how much I love that I am his. My husband. My master. My dominant.

I lower my chin, and cast my eyes downward. "It is my honor to wear your cum, Sir."

56

Quentin

She looked at me like she was both turned on and aghast that I'd ask that of her. But when I pulled up her shorts and zipped her up, she let me.

I unlock the door, then kiss her one last time, before I turn her around and urge her forward. I keep my arm about her shoulders as I guide her back to the show. As soon as we enter the hall, applause greets us. She blushes, and I savor her pleasure. I don't take my gaze off her features as she thanks everyone for coming and supporting her art.

Then she turns to me and whispers, "Thank you," before going up on tiptoes to kiss me. Damn, it promptly gets me hard, and when she tries to pull away, I grasp the back of her head and deepen the kiss. By the time I release her, she's wearing that dazed expression I know so well.

There's clapping—from her friends, and whistles—from my asshole nephews—all of which I acknowledge with a wave. She looks like she wants to slap me, then kiss me, all of which I have no problem with. Then she shakes her head and kisses me again, hard. She pulls away, this time, before I can band my arms about her waist.

I wait until the round of congratulations dies down, then whisper, "Ready to get out of here?"

She lets me lead her out of the art gallery, past the waiting crowds and my nephews—minus Ryot, who I haven't seen since our fight—and out onto the sidewalk. When she sees my restored Indian Four parked on the road, she stops.

I walk over to the bike and pat her broad gas tank. It's a classic. One I found for a steal and restored. When I ride, I switch off the thinking part of my brain and allow my subconscious to mull possibilities. And my life is filled with so much potential. When I stepped down as CEO it was the most liberating feeling in the world. It felt like I'd been given a chance to start all over again. Being married to the love of your life will do that to you too. I feel like I've been given wings. I want to fly and soar and explore new horizons. I want to do everything I'd dreamed of but kept putting off. I need to personify this first-day-of-the-rest-of-my life feeling. Which is why I decided to eschew my fleet of cars and take my bike to Raven's showing. Then, there was the hope that she'd agree to be mine fully and I could take my wife for a ride and show her off to the world. It seems more in keeping with this new phase of my life, which is why I opted to ride it here.

"Ooh, a bike?" Her voice is half-excited, half-apprehensive.

"Like what you see?" I grab the helmet from the rack and hold it out.

"Really?" She looks at me with doubt.

"Trust me?" I scan her features. "Do you, baby?"

"Of course, I do," she says without hesitation, and my heart grows so big, it feels like it's taking over my body. She slides the helmet on.

I clip the buckle under her chin, making sure it fits snugly, before I don my own. I straddle the vehicle and kick-start it in one stroke.

She slides up the screen of her helmet, her eyes wide with surprise. "I don't think I've ever seen anyone start a bike this way."

"It's vintage"—I point a finger at her—"and don't say it's like me."

She laughs. "It's definitely more macho to use a kick start than a button start, I'll admit."

"Hop on, baby, let's go home."

When she mounts the bike, I coax her closer, until her crotch is pressed against my butt, and her knees hug the outside of my thighs. She locks her arms about my waist, and when her breasts push into my back, the tension in my body drains away. Having her with me makes everything about the world right. I throttle the bike forward, and she tightens her hold on me. As I weave through the traffic with the wind rushing by, she relaxes by degrees.

"Wow, this... is cozy," she giggles. Her voice comes over the Bluetooth headsets fitted in the helmets. There's a note of nervousness in her tone. Also, a thread of arousal which pleases me to no end. I allow myself a small smile.

"Hold on baby, it's about to get cozier."

I rev my bike, and when the vehicle leaps forward, she squeaks and tightens her grip about my waist. "Lean into me, baby," I urge her.

When I take the next turn, she follows my direction and allows her body to flow with the momentum. "Good girl."

I sense her body shudder, then she pushes her breasts into my back and a groan rumbles up my throat.

With the wind blowing past, and her arms about me a sense of contentment descends. This is better than a dance, and almost as hot as making love. By the time I park in front of my townhouse, the crotch of my pants is tented. The fact that her fingers were less than inch from brushing my cock on the journey over, didn't help matters. She slides off the bike and hands her helmet to me. I lock hers and mine back in the rack, then lock my fingers with hers. "I fucking love you."

She laughs. "We should go on a longer drive if that's all it takes to get that admission from you unprompted."

I wrap my fingers around the nape of her neck and pull her close. "I've never loved anyone as much as you; not even my own son. Does that make me a bad father?"

She cups my cheek and is about to reply, when I shake my head. "Don't answer that. It took my realizing he's not mine to love him completely. Perhaps, it's when we're about to lose the things we take for granted, we realize their value?"

"You'll never lose me."

"I promise, I'll be there for you. I will not make the mistakes I made the first time around. I'm going to spend the rest of my life making it up to Felix. I'm going to make sure I'm a better father to *our* child. I'm going to spend every breath I have left worshipping you the way you deserve to be."

"Oh, Quentin." She steps between my legs and kisses me deeply, and I let her. I let her tease my lips apart and thrust her tongue inside my mouth. I relish the way she digs her fingernails into my shoulders and how she presses her breasts into my chest as she melts into me completely.

When she pulls away to stare into my eyes, I slide a strand of hair behind her ear. "I love you, Raven."

"I love you, Q."

EPILOGUE

A month later

Vivian

"How many people has Arthur invited to his 'Second Coming'?" My husband scowls at the cars parked down the driveway and overflowing onto the street outside.

The second coming is what this event has been labelled by the rest of the Davenports. Apparently, there's a messaging group that Connor, the youngest Davenport, created, so they could talk about the purpose of this event. My husband was added, and he grudgingly accepted the invitation, though he rarely bothers to check it; shocker. The one time he did get on it in the past week is how he found out his nephews think Arthur's going to make a big announcement today, which is why he's invited not only the Davenports, but also close friends. The grapevine is abuzz with speculation that there might be a tabloid reporter in the mix, who'd be getting exclusive access to the event to report the big scoop.

Q eases his bike to a stop and lowers the side stand. I slide off with reluctance. My favorite part of being married is being able to ride behind my husband, clinging to him as he weaves through traffic and leaning into him as he takes curves. The thrill of doing it, with the momentum pinning me to him, my body plastered to his, the wind whipping around us, enclosing us in our own private cocoon as he zooms down an open highway... is almost orgasmic. Though that might have to do with my being able to slide my fingers under his leather jacket and his shirt, flattening them against his taut stomach, and feeling the muscles ripple as he controls the bike.

It's a primal thrill. It infuses my body with adrenaline, which I'm coming down from as I wait for him to dismount. He takes my helmet and locks it in the rack, alongside his. Then, he holds out his hand. "Shall we?"

I take in his much-worn jeans which cling to his powerful thighs, the leather jacket which outlines the breadth of his shoulders, hair slightly overgrown, more than it was when I first met him, and mussed. His cheekbones are sharp enough to cut my heart to pieces, and his lower lip pouty enough that every time I glimpse it, I have an irrational need to bite down on it. The lines around his eyes crinkle as he grins at me. He looks younger, more relaxed, more at ease.

"Marriage suits you, Mr. Davenport." I smile.

"And you, Mrs. Davenport." He locks his arm around my waist and draws me in. I melt against him, raise my lips, and he closes his mouth over mine.

The kiss starts off tenderly, full of promises which I know he intends to keep, full of hope for our future, and happiness, and joy, and every possible emotion that feels right and true and real. Then he swipes his tongue between the seam of my lips, and a jolt of need shoots through my veins. My core clenches; my stomach bottoms out. The sensations zip down to my toes, then back to my pussy, where they hook their teeth into my sensitive skin and elicit a groan from me. A sound that he promptly swallows. He wraps his fingers around my hair and pulls, and the pain bites into my scalp, sinks into my blood, and zooms down to the triangle between my legs. He positions me over his thigh, and I shamelessly begin to hump it, trying to get myself off, trying to— A wolf whistle cuts through my thoughts.

I try to pull away, but Q continues to kiss me. I'm aware of someone approaching us. I slap at his shoulder, and he releases me, but not before he squeezes both of my butt cheeks with his massive paws. The sharp pain spikes my lust, and I almost come. Then he wraps his arm about my shoulders and, turning me around, pulls me into his side. "Son," he holds out his hand.

Felix shakes it, a broad grin on his face. "Seriously, you two, get a room." He laughs.

Q smirks.

I roll my eyes.

In the past month, since Q stepped down as CEO, he's spent a lot of time getting to know his son. The result? There's a noticeable ease between them. There'll always be history between the three of us, but there's an understanding which binds us as family.

"You guys have any idea about what Arthur's cooking up?" Felix stabs his thumb in the direction of the house.

Q raises a shoulder. "Don't know. Don't care. Am here only out of courtesy, and only because Arthur insisted."

He shakes his head. "You're free of his machinations, now that you're happily married, and you're no longer part of the Davenport Group. I admit, I was shocked to hear you resigned as CEO, but the more I think about it, the more I realize you made the right decision. You're a free man." His eyes shadow for a few seconds, then he pulls himself together. "It's time I owned my future. Time I gave shape to my plans and struck out on my own."

Q regards him with curiosity. "What are you going to do?"

He looks between us, and when he smiles, it carries a hint of decisiveness. "You'll find out inside." He nods at us, then continues into the house.

"Should we be worried?" I wonder aloud.

"Nah"—my husband shakes his head—"I trust Felix to make the right decision." A-n-d, that's how much things have changed. A few months ago, I doubt he'd have been able to say that. But Q has put in a lot of effort in building bridges with Felix. "No matter what he decides, his trust fund is in place as a safety net. He'll inherit, as long as he gets married before he turns thirty."

"Is that wise?" I look up into his handsome face. "You're doing an Arthur on him?"

He winces. "Guilty as charged. And I hate to say it, but perhaps there's a method to Arthur's madness, after all. If not for him, I wouldn't have been compelled to act on my instinct and ask you to marry me as soon as I met you." He bends and brushes his lips against mine. "Or perhaps, I'd have done it anyway, but Arthur's ultimatum had a role to play in my actions. There's no refuting that."

"We owe him." I nod.

"Which is why we're here." He blows out a breath "Shall we get this over with?"

"Is the theme... A Mad Hatter's Tea Party?" Knox nods in the direction of the long table set up in the center of the garden.

"Sure could pass for it," I agree.

We're standing in the backyard of Arthur's townhouse. Trees surround the estate, shielding us from early afternoon visitors to Primrose Hill. Knox shuffles his feet, then rolls his shoulders. He continues to scan the group gathered around the table.

"You okay, man?" My husband shoots him a curious glance. "You seem... on edge."

"You need to get your eyesight checked, *old* man," Knox grabs a glass from a passing waiter and takes a sip, only to spit it out. "Some non-alcoholic shit," he growls.

"I can help." The same petite, blonde-haired, bespectacled, curvy woman who hides her curves by wearing a suit two sizes too big, who I saw at the gallery a month ago, materializes at his side. She pulls out a flask and splashes clear liquid into Knox's half-filled glass.

Knox relaxes. "Thanks, doll," he says without looking at her.

She winces but stays silent.

He downs half the glass and sighs in appreciation.

She begins to melt away, but he snaps his fingers, still without looking at her "Don't go, I'll need you to pour." He holds out his glass again.

My jaw drops. *What the fuck?* Clearly, being obnoxious runs in the Davenport bloodline. That is, until these men are put in their place by the right woman. I open my mouth to tell Knox off, but before I can speak, the blonde pipes up, "I don't think you want to get drunk, sir."

Knox frowns. Staring in the direction of the house, he keeps his arm outstretched. The silence stretches. The tension in the air ratchets up, but Knox seems oblivious. He's too busy scanning his surroundings, as if he's looking for something... Or someone?

The blonde purses her lips, then relents and pours a dollop more into the glass. "Thanks." He tosses it back, then looks around as if wondering where to keep it. She takes it from him, and he nods again. "Don't know what I'd do without you, Sierra."

"It's June," she mumbles under her breath, but he doesn't seem to hear her.

He knows her name but purposely got it wrong. Why would he do that? Does he want to rile her up?

I exchange glances with my husband, who shakes his head. Without saying anything, he communicates what I'm thinking: Knox is a cunt. And she's way too good for him.

"Anyone know what Gramps is up to?" Tyler prowls over to join us.

Man's the tallest and the biggest of all the Davenports. His features could be cast from granite. His eyes are cold. His expression is both bored and lethal. Something about these Davenport men. They're not what you'd call handsome... Not when their features have that hint of cruelty which marks them out as men who have few scruples in life. And yet, they have the kind of charisma that makes women throw their panties at them and compels men to turn envious.

While Ryot is the one I wouldn't want to meet in a dark alley—I've seen what he can do—Tyler's the guy who'd come at you with such stealth, that despite his bulk, you wouldn't see him until it's too late. He looms over the rest of us. In a suit and tie, he looks barely civilized for this gathering.

Zoey waves to me from the other side of the garden, where she's talking with Summer and Sinclair Sterling. She's become close to Arthur, who treats her like the daughter he never had. Brody and Connor stand at a distance, smoking, without bothering to hide their cigarettes. Ryot is nowhere to be seen.

Lizzie is talking with Felix. The two have become good friends. I was worried there might be something romantic between them, but Lizzie laughed it off. She hinted, I'm not the only one who has a thing for silver foxes, a comment I chose to ignore.

My father was invited but declined the invitation, preferring to spend the evening with his caregiver-turned-girlfriend. He's happy, and she seems like a genuinely sweet woman.

Tiny ambles into the backyard, making a beeline for the long table packed with foodstuffs. He surveys it, and his ears droop. The mutt looks crestfallen, then walks back to Arthur.

Guess he's unhappy he didn't find any champagne. The dog has a weakness for the bubbly drink, it's true! But since Arthur's diagnosis, Imelda has banned all alcohol and cigars from the house, and to my surprise, the man didn't protest. Is it true love? Watching him walk out with an arm around the woman, who's wearing fatigues today, the pairing seems incongruous. But when she guides him to a chair at the head of the table, he complies. Which is telling.

According to Q, you wouldn't have caught Arthur listening to anyone else before she came into his life. Now, he seems less hard on himself. She takes the seat to his right. It's a signal for the rest of us to take our places.

June turns to leave, but Knox points to the chair on his right. She hesitates, then complies. The chair to his left stays vacant. The rest of us take our seats. There's a general buzz around the table. Otis tops up our glasses with more of the non-alcoholic beverage then stands to the side.

Arthur clinks his knife against his glass, and the chatter dies down.

"No doubt, you're all curious about why you've been summoned."

"Why should we be? We only had to drop what we were doing in the middle of a working day and attend to your summons," Brody growls under his breath.

"Something you want to share with the table?" Arthur arches an eyebrow in his grandson's direction.

Brody shrugs. "It's a working day."

"And I am the patriarch of this family… Still. So, you boys and girls will come when I call." It's a statement which brooks no argument. Arthur glances around the table, the look on his features implying my-word-is-final.

Then Imelda pats his arm. "Don't be a dick, dear."

A titter runs around the table, then there's full blown laughter. Next to me, Q chuckles. Zoey snorts, then slaps a hand over her mouth.

A vein bulges at Arthur's temple. He clenches his jaw. I'm sure he's going into a full-blown meltdown, but as he and Imelda glare at each other, something magical happens. His features relax by degrees and then a reluctant smile curves his features. Imelda's shoulders relax. Something passes between the two of them, then Arthur nods. He turns to the table. "And *that* is why each of you need to find the right woman."

Brody groans. Connor chugs down water from a bottle like it's going out of style. Tyler's expression is as immovable as ever. And Knox? His gaze is focused on the house.

"Is he waiting for someone?" I whisper.

Quentin shakes his head. "Don't think so."

But the seat next to him says otherwise.

"Felix"—Arthur nods in his direction—"you have something to tell us?"

The noise at the table dies down again.

Felix clears his throat. "I'm joining the Marines."

My husband freezes. I shoot him a glance to find a mixture of surprise and pride on his face—combined with a trace of fear.

"You didn't know?"

He shakes his head. "He hinted to me, but no... I didn't think he'd go through with it."

Felix meets my husband's gaze. "I hope to be half as good at it as my father was."

My husband's throat moves as he swallows. Then he raises his glass. "To Felix."

"To Felix." The rest of us raise our glasses. After we've taken a sip—with the blonde topping up Knox's glass again—he places his glass on the table and rises to his feet. He heads toward the house, where a woman steps out onto the porch. She's tall, willowy, and wearing a green dress that reaches below her knees. It's sleeveless, baring her thin white arms. Her dark hair is a waterfall of health that flows down her back. Her eyes are almond shaped, her skin creamy, and so pale the sun seems to be reflected off of it to bathe her in an ethereal light. Knox guides her over to the table and seats her on his left. There's pin-drop silence at the table as we stare at the newcomer.

"Can I do the honors?" Arthur asks.

Knox shrugs. "By all means."

Arthur frowns, then smooths out his expression. "This is Priscilla Whittington, Toren Whittington's sister. Toren and I agree that the best way to resolve our family feud and join our collective fortunes is through an arranged marriage."

"Of course you did," Brody snorts.

Arthur ignores him. "Tor couldn't be here, but he was happy for us to go ahead with announcing—"

"To cut a long story short, Priscilla has agreed to be my wife," Knox cuts in with a bored eye-roll.

I glance at June's face, and she looks stricken.

There's the sound of a glass breaking, and I turn to find Tyler pushing back from the table. He looks between the Knox and Priscilla, then turns and stalks off.

June, on the other hand, seems frozen. It's clear, she didn't see this coming either.

Knox, of course, is oblivious to the drama unfolding around him. He raises his glass in Priscilla's direction. "To my future wife."

TO FIND OUT WHAT HAPPENS NEXT READ *KNOX AND JUNE'S STORY IN THE UNPLANNED WEDDING*

SCAN THIS *QR* CODE TO GET THE *UNPLANNED WEDDDING*

READ AN EXTENDED BONUS EPILOGUE WITH Q AND VIVIAN AND THEIR CHILD?

Vivian

"KFC? You want KFC?" Q's gaze widens.

I stifle a laugh at the look of horror on his face. "I'm not asking you to come with me to a KFC, I only want to order a bucket for myself."

"A bucket?" He frowns.

"It's that container in which you get the chicken pieces —"

"I know what it means, but you want me to get you an entire bucket?"

"Umm, yes?"

"You sure?" He frowns again.

"I'm not normally a KFC kind of girl, but today is one of those days when only a massive nugget injection can satisfy the fowl desires raging within, if you know what I mean?" I flutter my eyelashes.

"If it's a meat injection you're looking for, I can help you with that." He waggles his eyebrows.

I roll my eyes. "At the moment, I'm looking for food."

He barks out a laugh. "You're hungry?"

"I am." I nod. "And since Mrs. Harmon is off today, I figured this was a good time to indulge my craving for fast food." I look at him from under my eyelashes. "Besides, you'll share some with me?"

His forehead furrows.

"Right?"

"If you insist," he says in a doubtful voice. He reaches for his phone, his fingers fly over the screen, and he nods. "It'll be here in fifteen minutes."

Shock. Horror. Apparently, he knows how to use the apps on his phone. Nah, I'm being unkind.

He might be older than me, but when it comes to technology, Q is way ahead of me. It shouldn't surprise me. After all, he did run a multi-billion-dollar empire.

After stepping down from being the CEO of the info-communications division of the Davenport Group, he started his own security agency, which employs many vets who've struggled to find jobs after military discharge.

However, he has a team that runs the company on his behalf. He's insistent that he spend all his time taking care of me and learning to be a good house husband. Q in an apron cooking dinner for me? That's the sexiest sight ever.

He also funds a charity that helps military vets with one of his military buddies. It's his way of actively giving back to the soldiers he served with. He and Ryot haven't settled their differences. Q hopes there'll come a day when Ryot needs his help, and he'll be there for his nephew when that happens.

He begins to set two places at the island where we often eat.

"What are you doing?" I watch with growing surprise as he places cutlery, plates and snow-white napkins next to them. He pulls out an ice bucket and fills it with ice, then he pulls out a bottle of white wine from the cooler.

"We're eating junk food," I remind him.

"Doesn't mean we need to be uncivilized about it."

Guess he has a point.

He pops the cork and pours the crisp Sauvignon Blanc into two glasses. He places the bottle in the ice-bucket, hands me a glass, then holds up his own. "To us."

"To us." I beam at him. Every day with my husband is a celebration. I can't imagine how I ever survived without him. He turns my days into Christmas and my nights into a New Year's Eve celebration. And he takes such good care of me... I admit, I'm spoiled.

We clink our glasses and take a sip. Moments later, the buzzer announces the arrival of the delivery guy.

I eat my way through more than half the contents of the bucket before I notice Quentin isn't eating.

"You're not hungry?" I nod toward the chicken wing on his plate.

He smiles slowly. "Seeing you eat is enough to fill my stomach."

Aww! "I'd never have guessed you're a closet romantic." For all his growly demeanor and glaring looks—especially when he's being the Dom in bed—he has a heart as mushy as boiled smashed peas. I offer him a piece from my plate. He bites off a mouthful and chews I can't stop watching the tendons of his throat move as he swallows.

"It's good," he says with surprise.

"Of course, it is."

He reaches for the wing on his plate and polishes it off.

"I might covert you after all." I laugh.

When we're done, we retire to the living room. "What do you want to watch?"

"Whatever *you* want," he says with an indulgent look on his features.

So sweet! My heart melts all over again. And yes, hubby is often happy to defer to my viewing choice.

"It's going to be another tearjerker romance," I warn him.

He mock groans, "Not a surprise, then?" He kicks back on the sofa with his arm stretched over the back.

I grab the remote, cue the streaming service to show *The Notebook,* and I curl up against his side. He tucks me in close and kisses the top of my head. The heat of his body cocoons me. The feel of his hard chest against my cheek with the thump-thump-thump of his heart a reassuring beat. It's not long before my eyelids flutter down.

It's not a very exciting evening, perhaps, but for me, it's heaven. After taking care of my family for so many years, it's the most amazing feeling to have someone taking care of me. I wake briefly when he carries me to bed. Once he pulls the covers over us and curls his big body around mine, I fall asleep again.

***

I wake up with his heavy arm around my middle and my stomach gurgling. I try to ignore it, but when the burn of bile licks the back of my throat, I scramble out of bed and manage to make it to the toilet bowl before I puke my guts out. Of course, my husband follows me in and holds my hair back while I hang over the ceramic rim. Then, he wipes my face with a damp cloth, flushes the toilet, and carries me back to bed.

He tucks me in, then sits next to me. His eyes are filled with worry.

"It's nothing—" I swallow, wincing at the taste in my mouth. "I'm sure it's nothing," I add again, more to convince myself.

Not that it fools him. "But?" The wrinkle between his eyebrows deepens.

"But—" I sigh. "I should take a pregnancy test."

It takes a beat for my words to sink in. I know the exact moment he registers it because the color drains from his features.

The expression on his face is so shocked, for a second, I'm sure he'll be the next to puke. He swallows audibly and pulls himself together. "Pregnant?" He clears his throat. "You're sure?"

"We haven't been using protection," I remind him.

He pales further, if that's possible.

"Why don't I take a pregnancy test, and we'll know for sure?" I add quickly.

"O-k-a-y." He blows out a breath. Then, without taking his gaze off me, reaches for his phone and his fingers fly over the screen. "It's on its way."

He ordered it via another app.

I nod.

He gets into bed, and I snuggle into him. He holds me against his chest —my favorite place on this earth. I begin to doze and must fall asleep.

※ ※ ※

The next time I open my eyes, the sunlight is pouring in. It's a weekend, and while I've been thinking of painting again for my next showing, I also want to laze around at home and spend time with Q.

That's one of the gifts my husband has given me—the ability to take time out for myself and not be worried about my father's health, or the fees for Lizzie's next term, or if I have enough to pay the rent for the next month. Also, I don't need his money for any of it, either. With what I made from the sales of mypaintings; I could live comfortably for years. I'm finally what I hoped to be — a career artist. I yawn and sit up, then turn to find him holding out my cappuccino.

"Thanks, babe." I'll never get used to him having my cappuccino ready for me when I wake up. It's one of the many ways he spoils me. And I don't feel guilty about it. I'm the luckiest woman ever.

I accept it with gratitude, then chug down a few sips before realization dawns. "The pregnancy test," I gasp.

He insists I finish my coffee first, then hands me a paper-bag.

I slide out of bed and don't complain when he follows me into the bathroom. Not that he'd heed me if I did. I know Q's bossy ways well enough that I don't even protest when he watches as I pee on the stick.

I hand it to him to hold while I right my clothes and flush. I take the stick from him. When I peek at it, the control line has already developed. My instinct tells me I'm not pregnant, and when a few more minutes pass, and still, no second line develops, I know. My heart sinks into my stomach. A heaviness squeezes my throat.

I stare at the single line, not aware that tears are running down my cheeks.

"It's okay, darling, we'll try again." My husband tucks a strand of hair behind my ear.

I can't look at him. I avert my eyes because I want to pretend, I haven't seen that lone pink line on the pregnancy test. It slips away from between my fingers, but he catches it. Then slips it back in its wrapping and places it aside. "Baby, look at me," he pleads.

I shake my head. A heavy anchor seems to weigh down my stomach. My heart feels like it's pushing up against the confines of my ribcage. I can't look at him. How can I, when... I've been hoping, this time, I'll give him the child he wants. A chance for a fresh beginning, to set right his wrongs. To do it right this time around. A chance for me to carry a part of him inside of me. A chance to be a mom.

I didn't think I wanted it so much... Not until I saw the single pink line. Perhaps, I was naive, thinking I'd become pregnant right away. Not that we've had any problem trying, of course. In fact, to call it 'trying' seems wrong, when taking pleasure from each other's bodies is the most natural way to express our love for each other. He scoops me up and carries me into the bedroom, then sits down in the armchair near the bed with me in his lap.

He tucks my head under his chin and rubs circles around my back. "You're young, baby. We have a lot of time to keep trying."

"It's stupid." I sniff. "I don't know why I'm upset. I didn't realize how much I wanted the test to be positive until it wasn't. I didn't realize how much I wanted to be pregnant until I found I wasn't. How can I want something I never had? How is it possible that everything could have changed in the blink of an eye, but didn't?" I rub my cheek against the sweatshirt that covers his chest. "I'm sorry I'm this upset."

"Shh"—he wipes the tears from my cheeks—"it's okay to cry, and never apologize for being upset. It's best you get out everything that's on your mind. And it's okay to be upset. You've been on an emotional roller-coaster. It's normal to feel overwhelmed."

"I feel"—I swallow around the constriction in my throat—"I feel like I've let you down. I—" I gasp as he notches his knuckles under my chin, so I have no choice but to meet his gaze.

"Don't ever say that. You know, I'd love a little girl or boy who looks like you, but if that doesn't happen, I'll be perfectly content with you." He looks into my eyes. "You're more important to me than anything in this world. Felix is my son, and also important to me, but he has his own life. You, on the other hand, are all mine. I intend to spend every waking minute of my life loving you, cherishing you, doing everything in my power to ensure you're happy and thriving and have a smile on your face. And right now, I feel like I'm failing."

"What?" I half laugh.

"You're sad, baby, and I take that as a personal affront. I can't bear to see your tears; you know that." He pushes the hair back from my forehead. "All I want is to see your smiling face every morning next to me… And ideally, kiss you with pussy breath because I made you come, and feel your satisfaction because I made you orgasm before you woke up."

"Just one orgasm?" I murmur.

"Or a few," he concedes with a chuckle. "Us being together and spending our life together is more important than anything else.

"So, a baby—"

"Is important, but not at the cost of your health and happiness."

"Having a child *would* make me very happy," I remind him.

"And I'd love for that to happen, but I'm in no hurry."

I scrutinize his features, and all I see is his sincerity, the love in his eyes, and the concern he has for me. And below it all, his devotion—an almost worshipful note lurking in his expression, which melts my insides.

"I want you to be my child's father." I wrap my fingers around the back of his neck. "I want to feel your child move inside me."

"And I want that for you." He mirrors my hold on him by sliding his fingers about the nape of my neck. He brings me in close and pushes his forehead into mine. "I want you to have everything you desire."

"What if I"—I clear my throat, not wanting to give words to my fear, but also compelled to do so—"what if I can't get pregnant?"

Two years later

Quentin

"Are you ready?" I turn to my wife. There's a strange sensation tightening my chest, one I classify as fear…apprehension…anxiety. Funny, I thought I'd have to calm her down. Turns out, I'm the one who has clammy palms and a dry mouth. I reach for the bottle of water she's holding and chug down some of it. When I lower it and wipe the back of my palm against my mouth, she's watching me with a knowing look.

"Don't be nervous." She slips her slim palm into mine and squeezes. "It's going to be okay."

"I know it will."

"We've wanted this so much."

"We do." We continued to try for a child, but when six more months went by and she still hadn't become pregnant, we decided to stop consciously thinking about it. Instead, we decided to adopt. When my wife mentioned it to me, it felt right.

Whether the child's my blood or not, it doesn't matter to me. I found, as the months passed, I was content to simply be with her. But I've been through this cycle of having a child, and she hasn't.

She's still painting, and her next two shows were more successful than the first. But she confessed to me that it'd begun to feel empty. And then there was the disappointment which occurred with her every period, when she knew she wasn't pregnant. She hid it from me, but I saw the sadness lurking in her eyes. The wistfulness when she saw our friend's children. When she held Sinclair and Summer's child in her arms… When she rocked Michael's motherless children to sleep… When she began to shower her affection on them and wanted to spend more time with them… And when one of them was hospitalized, we rushed over to see them, and she insisted on spending the night with the child in the ward. I saw her getting attached to those kids and yearning to have one of her own to shower her affection on.

She never complained about it. As the months passed and she didn't get pregnant, I saw the light dim in her eyes. I waited for her to raise the issue with me—wondered if she'd like to try IVF or explore other means to help her in this journey. She didn't, and I decided to let things be.

Until one day, I woke up and found the space next to mine in our bed empty. I threw back the sheets and jumped out, heading downstairs. I searched her studio, then the conservatory, which is her second favorite place to be and, not finding her, headed to the kitchen, then my study, and finally, to the living room—where I found her curled up on the couch, sobbing.

I rushed over, sat down next to her, and pulled her into my lap. I held her as she clung to me and continued to weep. Noiselessly. But her shoulders shook, and her body convulsed with the force of the grief pouring out of her.

My heart leaped into my throat, and my scalp tightened. Every cell in my body shrank with the impact of the absorbed sorrow. I rocked her, rubbed circles over her back, and ran my fingers down her hair. I tucked her close and tried to soak up her misery. When she stopped crying, I carried her to the kitchen and made sure she drank some water.

Then, I made her favorite—hot chocolate with mini-marshmallows— and after she'd swallowed half of it, I reminded her it didn't matter to me if we ever had children. She's what matters most to me. I asked her if she wanted to explore IVF. She shook her head and said it felt too intrusive. She admitted she wanted to adopt. And I agreed.

We started the process the very next day. It took us a year to get this far. Now here we are, waiting for our little boy to meet us.

I thought she'd be nervous, but my wife is calm. Whatever haunted her seemed to fade into the background as soon as we started the adoption process. Through all the paperwork and checks and meetings with the social worker, she maintained her graciousness. I'm the one who began to fret with each day that passed. I'm the one who'd balked at the questions asked of us. As they tried to gauge if we'd be good parents. As I had to come clean about the fact I hadn't been the best parent to my first son. It turned out to be therapeutic to talk about the reasons behind it, and it also brought home the fact that I have a chance to set things right this time around. Of course, that'd been my intention, but talking about it makes it all very real.

As the process unfolded, so did my fears and my insecurities. Would I be a good father? Would I do justice to my future child when I'd failed the first time around? As I got more nervous, my wife seemed to grow more serene. I hung in there, managing not to outwardly show my apprehension. Then, we were approved for adoption. And here we are, waiting to see our child, on the settee in the living room of the foster parents' home.

I shift my weight and try to find a more comfortable position. I cross and uncross my legs and don't realize I'm bouncing my knee until my wife stills me with a touch. "It's going to be fine," she reiterates.

I know, deep inside, it'll all work out. But will I deliver on my responsibilities? Will I be the kind of father she expects me to be? I know I'll more than deliver on the material needs for my family, but can I also be there for them emotionally? Can I take care of my wife and my child and ensure they never feel alone? That I'm there for them when they need reassurance? That I love them, and surround them with affection?

"You can do this." My wife places her palm on my joined-up ones and squeezes. "You're going to be the best father ever."

I shuffle my feet. "Considering how I failed the first time around—"

"You won't this time."

I turn to meet her steady green gaze. The love in her eyes, the devotion, the confidence she has in me is humbling.

"How can you be so sure?"

"Because I know you better than you know yourself, Q. You have a big heart. You're generous to a fault. You consistently put the needs of others before yours. And you keep your promises, always. It's why you couldn't step back from your duties to your country. And then as CEO, you had a duty to your employees and to your father. Now"—her lips curve in a soft smile—"now you've made a promise to our child, and I know you'll give up your life before you break it."

There's pride on her face, and affection and tenderness. She fills my life with warmth and intimacy of a kind I've never had before. And now, she's giving me a chance to set right my wrongs. And her belief in me infuses my spirit. It gives me the courage to push aside my doubts in myself and cup her cheek. "I promise to never fail you. I promise I'll put you and our child first. I—"

"Are you my new Daddy?" I turn to find our four-year-old glaring at me. He has his hands on his hips and a frown on his face. "Are you?" He glowers.

There's a pout on his face and he juts out his chin. He's in a hurry to get on with his life. Impatience pours off of him. A feeling of restlessness colors the air around him. My heart swells in my chest. A sensation of peace washes over me. This is why Wordsworth declared, *The son is the father of the man.*

"I am." I twine my fingers through my wife's then sink to my knees. I hold out my other hand. "I'm your Dad."

THE DAVENPORTS CONTINUES WITH KNOX AND JUNE'S STORY IN THE UNPLANNED WEDDING **HERE**

Read an excerpt from Knox and June's story in *The Unplanned Wedding*

June

"Thanks, Norma." My boss nods in my direction without looking at me as I place the bottle of water in his outstretched hand.

"It's June," I mutter, wondering why I bother. I've corrected him a hundred, possibly a thousand, times about my name. Or at least, it seems like it's a thousand times. He's never called me by my given name. Worse, it's a different name each time. That's how much attention he pays toward me — or rather, doesn't pay in my direction. Which is, of course, what I intended when I joined Davenport Group as Knox Davenport's assistant. I'm also his Girl Friday. Which means, I go with him where he goes. In the office, to the gym in the basement of his luxurious condominium building, then back in the elevator with him to his home, where I cook him dinner.

I leave his apartment at seven p.m. each day and am back at seven a.m. each morning to make him breakfast. But not before I call him at five a.m. with a wakeup call. You heard that right—five freakin' a.m. Ugh! Which means, I have five alarms in place to wake me up, starting from four-thirty a.m. until four-fifty-five a.m, and I never wake up before the last one. Then, I only manage to crack open my eyelids enough to call him at five and wish him, "Good F'ing Morning," before crawling back under the covers and sleeping until 6:45 a.m.

The only saving grace is, I need less than fifteen minutes to make myself presentable and take the elevator up to his penthouse apartment. It's also one of the reasons I've hung onto this job for almost a year. Because as his sidekick — sorry, I mean his aide — I'm entitled to the apartment on the floor below his. It means, I have enough distance from him, but I'm close enough for him to call me in case of an emergency. It should also be stated here that, before me, the position was held by a series of men, none of whom lasted more than a few weeks. In desperation, the agency asked for a woman to interview for the role. And they were clear: it had to be someone who could put up with the whims of a dictator who looks like a pagan God—a gross understatement, IMO, for he resembles Adonis himself—and acts like he owns the world. Which, technically, he does, given what he and the Davenports are worth. Oh, also, it had to be someone who wouldn't fall for her boss. That wasn't in the specs on paper, but it was something the recruiter hinted to me on the phone.

They wanted someone who wouldn't complicate the situation by developing a personal relationship with the man. I thought they were joking, until I came for the interview, took one look at his almost too perfect jawline, those high cheekbones, and the piercing silver eyes, and swooned.

Then, there are those scars on his cheek—some kind of war wound, apparently, from when he was a Marine, before he took over at the Davenports. It only accentuates the perfection of the rest of his face and heightens the air of menace clinging to him.

Then he opened those pouty lips and called me by a name that's not mine. And the mystery was broken. He may have fought for his country, but he remains a rich, privileged, born-with-a-sliver-spoon in his mouth, bastard who belongs at the top of the food chain and has no idea how the rest of the population lives. He didn't look at me once as he tossed a few questions at me, yawned through my answers, and dismissed me. I walked out of his office in a rage, certain I wouldn't get hired. Only I did, along with the perks associated with it. And to this day, I'm not sure why.

Not that it matters. To have an address in a post code that boasts more billionaires per square mile than Manhattan, and a monthly salary that helped me pay off most of my student loans within six months, and take care of my siblings' college education, is more than I expected. So, I grit my teeth and hang in there. It also helped that my boss was serious eye-candy.

Whether dressed in a fitted suit that shows off the breadth of his shoulders, or grey sweatpants that encircle his lean waist and hint at the package tenting the crotch, or the gym-shorts he's wearing now, which outline every coiled muscle in those powerful thighs.

He drops down on his palms and feet and proceeds to pump out a hundred push-ups before he springs up and holds out his arm. I slide the bottle of water into his waiting palm. He throws his head back and chugs the contents, then tosses me the empty bottle. I walk over to the recycling bin, drop it in, and grab another from the refrigerator before walking back to him. He's at the push-board bench, pressing weights many times his own. I stand with the fresh bottle of water and a towel, trying not to ogle the way his abs flex, his shoulder muscles bunch, and his thigh muscles ripple each time he pushes up the weights. Beads of sweat glisten on his torso. One slides down his concave stomach toward his waistband.

I gulp. Feel my own forehead moisten. Is it hot in here? I glance around the almost empty gym. The only other occupant is a man on the treadmill, and he's wearing a pair of headphones while focusing on the console in front of him. It's air-conditioned in here, but you wouldn't know it, given the way my palms are sweating. I raise the bottle of water and press it to my heated cheek, and I'm not even working out. Still, I'm dressed in sneakers and yoga pants, combined with an oversized sweat-shirt. Maybe I should take it off? I hesitate, shoot my boss a glance and find his jaw hard, forehead wrinkled as he glares at the weights, he's busy grappling with. The scars on his cheek seem to protrude with the effort.

He looks fierce, like he's fighting a battle or about to start a war. The tendons on his throat pop, the veins on his forearms stand out in relief. And his biceps... Good god, they're as big as my thighs, and I'm not a skinny person.

I love my curves, love dressing to show them off. But also, I want to keep my job. It's why I prefer to wear clothes two sizes too big and tie my hair back in a bun. So far, combined with my eyeglasses, it's helped me stay nondescript. Maybe, it's working too well—my boss has no idea of my name. No idea that I exist. I might be part of the furniture, for all the times he's noticed me... Which, at this stage, is a big fat zero.

So why, why, why am I so drawn to him? Why, oh why can't I tear my gaze off the way his chest heaves and his shoulders swell, and the way his biceps bulge, and the way the muscles of his forearms inflate as he pushes up the barbell with a grunt that rolls over my skin and arrows straight to my clit? Goosebumps pepper my fore-arms. The sweat on my throat dries in the air-conditioning, and I shiver.

Great! First, I'm too hot, now I'm too cold. Maybe I'm coming down with something? Maybe, I need to take a break from the cloud of testos-terone that's pressing down on my shoulders? "I, uh... I'll only be a minute. Just need to... uh... Use the little girls' room." I cringe. *Little girls' room?* Couldn't I come up with a better excuse?

I turn, and promptly trip on a plate weight, which I didn't see. The water bottle in my hand hits the floor, and the towel slips from my fingers.

I throw my hands out to break my fall, then find myself suspended an inch from the floor. The breath whooshes out of me. Then suddenly, I'm upright, and my feet don't touch the floor because two big broad palms are squeezing my waist.

Heat sizzles my back, the scent of sweat and something musky under it—sandalwood?—teases my nostrils. The fine hair on the back of my neck rises and I realize, it's him. He caught me? But how did he even see me? He was on his back, bench pressing, when my feet brushed against the weight. "You... you can put me down," I squeak.

His hold on my waist tightens, then he gently lowers me until my feet touch the floor. Only he hasn't let go of me. Instead, he spins me around to face him. Our gazes meet, and I swear, the world stops. My heart descends to the space between my legs. The pulse blooms there and travels to my fingertips, and my toes, and my scalp, which tightens. Silver sparks light up those colorless eyes, the heat from his body a lasso pulling me toward him. Then my nipples graze his wall-like chest and I realize, we've leaned in toward each other.

A thousand little hummingbirds whirl their wings in my chest. I raise my head; he lowers his. I draw my gaze down the raised scar bisecting his cheek. Then, because I've wanted to for so long, I raise my hand and graze my fingers over the puckered skin. Shock sears his features, and he pulls back so quickly, I stumble. This time, he doesn't right me. He takes a few steps back, then sinks down on the weight bench. I open my mouth to apologize for touching him, when he scrunches up his forehead. "Ah, Melanie, is it?"

What the—! I narrow my gaze on him.

He scrunches up his forehead, then his brow clears. He snaps his fingers. "It's Renée." He nods. "Yep, Renée. Get me an energy drink, will you?"

Remember all those sensations crowding me? Remember how I could have sworn there was an electric connection between us? All of it dissipates in a flash. I shake my head. *What an ass!* "It's June," I snap.

He raises a shoulder. "That's what I said."

I curl my fingers into fists at my sides. "No, you didn't."

"Sure, I did." His tone is condescending. He has a smirk on his face, implying I'm the one who doesn't know my own name.

Anger squeezes my guts. I grit my teeth. "My name. Is. June. I've worked for you for almost a year. The least you could do is remember my name."

My stomach churns, and my vision narrows. Before I can stop myself, I've closed the distance to the fallen bottle of water. I snatch it up and lob it at him. It hits his forehead and bounces off, and it's as if the world stops. Again. *OMG, I did not mean to do that. Okay, I lie; I totally meant to do that.* But I didn't think my aim would be this accurate. Or that he'd freeze, then slowly raise his head and stare at me. And that those grey eyes of his would turn almost silver with rage. Or that his nostrils would flare, and he'd rise to his feet, so I'd tilt my head back, then further back.

He takes a step forward. I gulp. He scans my features, and a furrow appears between his eyebrows. Then his gaze widens. I swear, he's noticing me for the first time. He drapes the towel over his shoulders then prowls closer. He steps over the weight, then stops in front of me. A cloud of heat spools off of his body and slams into my chest.

I gasp. I want to turn and run out of there, but my feet seem to be cemented to the ground.

He holds my gaze, golden sparks flaring in the depths of his eyes as he bends his knees and peers into my eyes. "Run," he growls.

"What?" I gape.

"I'll even give you a head start."

"Excuse me?" I blink rapidly.

He bares his teeth like he hasn't heard me speak. "You have until I count to five." He jerks his chin toward the doorway. "Go."

Knox

"Go, before I change my mind," I bite out.

And what possessed me to ask her to run? She's my assistant, who I haven't paid any attention to until... a few seconds ago. Not until she stumbled over the plate weight—which I left out on the floor—a mistake and a health hazard, which I hadn't worried about because I hadn't clocked her presence.

She's been someone who hovers just out of my line of sight. Someone who's there to fulfill my requests and obey my orders, because dominating women in bed isn't enough, and I haven't allowed myself to take a submissive in real life because... Who'd want to stare at my scarred visage hour after hour? It's why I prefer to never look her in the eye.

That way, I won't have to recognize the look of disgust in her gaze, or the expression of sympathy that follows it, or the questions which hovered just out of reach. But then she tripped, and I acted without thought. I was on my feet and springing toward her. I don't recall placing my barbell back on the rack or swinging my feet to the ground, but there I was, in front of her, just in time to grab her around her waist and straighten her.

And then she raised those big brown eyes up to meet my gaze, and I was a goner. And when she brushed her fingers down the scar on my cheek, the shock of it felt like someone dropping me in a vat of boiling oil, then dumping cold water on me. No one has touched that scar since I was injured. Not even me.

I hate how I look; hate the evidence of my mistakes. Hate my face. Hate what I've become since I left the Marines. I buried my feelings. I swore to never let myself care for anything or anyone again.

And this slip of a woman comes along and rouses emotions I thought I'm no longer capable of feeling. I realize, now, that I want her. I want to push her onto her knees and shove my cock inside her mouth. I want to bend her over and spank her until she begs me for release. I want to defile her and take her every orifice. I want to bury myself in her until I find release.

The intensity of my need punches into my chest like a cannon ball. Worse, something inside me insists I get to know her. To find out all about her. What she likes and hates. What makes her laugh. What she loves to eat and drink and what she likes to do when she isn't working for me and...

What the hell? Where is this compulsion arising from? Why do I want to find out about her as a person before I fuck her? This... is new. This has never happened to me before. This... is something I will not allow, for it leads to my becoming vulnerable. Something I've sworn I'll never let myself be. It's why I'm going on the offensive. It's why I am going to warn her off.

I glare into her face then growl, "Go. Now."

Something in her finally catches on; when I take a step in her direction she turns and bolts toward the exit of the gym.

Adrenaline races through my blood. My heartbeat quickens. Without letting myself think further, I give chase. I jump over the plate weight that tripped her up, then rush past the man on the treadmill near the entrance who tracks my progress with a raised eyebrow. I barrel past him and exit the gym.

I fully expect her to run out of the building but spot her at the elevator. She's stabbing at the button to call the elevator cage. The car arrives, and the doors open. I sprint toward her and careen to a stop as the

elevator doors begin to close on her. I plant my shoulder in the gap
between the doors, and they spring back. I step inside, and she gasps, then
stumbles back until she hits the back of the carriage. The doors swish shut
behind me. I reach over and slap the button for my penthouse, and it
begins to rise.

She looks from me to the indicator flashing above my head, back to
my face, then glances around the space once before wringing her hands
together. I stay silent. So does she. The air between us thrums with
tension.

I drag my gaze down her features, taking in the flush on her cheeks,
the parted lips, the way her eyelids flutter, how her eyes spark with a tinge
of anger. Good. She's a fighter. Not a surprise, considering how long she's
lasted working for me.

She shuffles her feet, and when I still don't say anything, she tosses
her head. "This is stupid. I didn't do anything wrong. It's you who can't
seem to remember my name. I've corrected you so many times, but you
always forget."

"Are you complaining?" I ask with interest.

"No. Yes." She throws up her hands. "Frankly, I don't care. You can
call me by any name you want, as long as you pay my salary on time—"
She raises a shoulder. "I shouldn't care." She says with vehemence, as if
she's trying to convince herself.

"So, it's fine if I call you July?"

"The name's June," she replies, then grimaces.

"You feel more like a July than a June."

She scowls at me. I'm sure she's going to tell me off for suggesting that
which is why I did it, but she purses her lips and all she says is, "And
you're going to be late for lunch at your grandfather's."

It's my turn to grimace. "Do I have to go to that?"

"Arthur's assistant called up and was insistent you be there." She sets
her jaw.

My grandfather never stops meddling with the lives of his sons and
grandsons. His one goal? To see us all settled. He succeeded in alienating
his oldest, who cut off all ties with the family. His middle son—a.k.a. my
father—died in an accident, but not before Arthur managed to get him
married off to my mother. My youngest uncle, Quentin, is the most recent
to fall prey to Arthur's wiles. He ended up marrying the same woman his
own son jilted at the altar. A messy situation all around, but one which
ended with Quentin getting the girl of his dreams.

"Good segue, but it doesn't change the fact that you're going to have to accept your punishment."

Her eyes grow huge. "P-punishment?"

"You hit me with the water bottle —"

"That was a mistake."

"Seemed intentional to me."

She draws in a breath. "Fine. I concede, I did intend to hit you with it, but I didn't expect it to actually hit you." She pauses before adding under her breath. Besides, you deserved it."

I raise one eyebrow and suppress a smirk. Ignoring her final comment, I continue. "Nevertheless, it doesn't change the fact that the bottle bounced off my forehead. Ergo, you need to pay for the consequences of your actions."

She laughs nervously. "You're joking."

"Not at all."

"And what would this punishment involve?"

I reach over and slap the stop button.

June

"You've gotta be kidding me," I cry as the elevator screeches to a halt.

In reply, he slides down until he's sitting on the floor of the cage with his back to the doors and his legs stretched out in front. "So where were we?" he drawls.

"What if I say I'm sorry?"

He shrugs. "It's a start, but it's not enough."

"What do you want then?"

"For you to take your punishment." When he pats his thigh, my jaw drops.

"No way," I snap. One thing about being this man's assistant? There's very little about him I don't know. And that includes his proclivities. I've never seen him bring a woman home, but I know for a fact he's a member of a very elite BDSM club, where he goes every other Saturday and doesn't come back until late the next day.

What happens there? I don't know. Okay, so maybe I researched it and I do know, and it's possible I've been curious about what exactly he does there. And apparently, now I'm going to find out. "I'm, uh, not into that stuff."

"Stuff?" He arches an eyebrow.

"Whatever it is you do at the, uh, BDSM club."

His eyes light up with interest. "So, you're curious about my activities at the club?"

"What? No! Of course, not." Heat sears my cheeks, but I manage not to give in to the embarrassment. "Anyway, aren't there a bunch of laws against this?" I wave at the space between us.

"Probably, but I own the building, and the security, and the security tapes, which will be erased. And then, it's your word against mine. We both know how that's going to pan out."

I firm my lips. Anger churns my guts. Insults tremble on the tip of my tongue, but I refuse to give in to them.

"Besides"—his lips twist—"I'm paying you enough to know you wouldn't want to cut off the source of your income."

"Are you trying to bribe me?" I scowl.

"Am I succeeding?"

My shoulders sag. I need the money. And yes, I could sue him for this behavior, but it's going to be a long drawn out battle, and I don't have the resources to keep it going.

"Of course, you only have to say 'no,' and I'll stop." He yawns.

"You… you will?" I'm, once again, gaping at him, but I can't help it. The way he breaks convention and doesn't care about common decency makes my head spin.

"Sure, all you have to do is be honest, and admit you're turned on right now."

"Oh, my God! How could you even say that?" I cry.

"Because if you took off your panties and held them out, you and I both know they'd be soaked."

I squeeze my thighs together, and the movement doesn't escape him.

"What do you say; shall we put it to the test?"

I shake my head.

"So, you admit, you're aroused."

Don't do it. Don't do it. I nod my head slowly.

"Good girl."

His approval sends a zing of sensations bursting up my spine. *Oh, my God, why does his approval mean so much to me?*

I squeeze my eyes shut. "I can't believe this conversation is happening."

"It's a bit unorthodox I admit"—he nods—"but it's never too late to explore one's affinity for kink."

"What? No! I'm not into kink," I protest.

"Then you don't have to worry that you'll enjoy feeling my palm connect with your arse." He holds out his massive fingers and squeezes them into a claw-like gesture, and I can't take my gaze off of them.

I should be more shocked at the filthiness of his words, but somehow, I'm not. And I don't understand it. Maybe, a part of me always expected that, one day, he'd take notice of me and want to introduce me to the lifestyle. Is that why I finally lost my patience at being ignored by him and threw the bottle? Because I wanted him to notice me? No, no, I'm not that needy... Am I? I shuffle my feet, then tip up my chin. "Uh, you really are going to be late for the gallery opening."

"They can wait." He settles himself back against the doors. He looks comfortable and cool as a cucumber. Unlike me. Sweat pools under my arms and makes me want to hold them out at my sides so I can air dry them.

"I... Uh, I'm really not comfortable with this," I murmur.

He seems disappointed, like he can see through the lies I'm telling myself. I do want to find out what it's like to be spanked by him. But if I do, I'll lose all respect for myself.

He rises to his feet and hits a button on the panel. The elevator begins to move. I slip my oversized specs up my nose and stare at the numbers.

So, that was it—my brush with kink. My brush with finding out how it could be to have him spank me. My brush with finding out how it feels to have him touch me. I should hate him for not noticing me all the time I worked for him, but there's something about finally having his undivided attention that sends a frisson of excitement up my spine.

He probably won't notice me again. I'll go back to being the assistant who fades into the background, and he'll move onto his next weekend at the club and whatever he does there. Everything will go back to normal and... And I'll always wonder how it would have been if I'd let him have his way with me. I'll always wonder how it would have felt to be at the center of his focus. Something I'll never have again.

Live a little, June Donnelly. For once, throw caution to the wind and take this opportunity. Without giving myself another chance to think this through, I reach over and slap the stop button. The elevator whines to a halt one floor from his penthouse. I steel myself then turn to face him. If I expected to see any gloating on his face, there's none. Only curiosity and, dare I say, an expression that's almost understanding.

"I have a few conditions."

"Need I remind you, you're the one who hit me with the bottle?"

I wince. "And I'm going to take the punishment you give me, but only if you agree to my stipulations."

He widens his stance, drawing my attention to his thighs, but I manage to keep my gaze above his crotch.

"Go on then. As you reminded me, we have a gallery opening to attend."

I swallow, then square my shoulders. "One"—I hold up my forefinger—"this will not change our working relationship in the slightest."

"It won't for me. It's you who'll have to watch out for any lingering feelings from our little tryst."

I scoff, "As if."

His eyes spark with what I recognize as challenge, but when he opens his mouth, all he asks is, "What's your next condition?"

"We forget this ever happened."

He cuts the air with his palm, and the confidence in that gesture makes me stiffen. I know, I'm the one who asked that we both forget this encounter, but damn, if I don't want him to remember what he did to me.

"You get one last stipulation. You'd best spit it out before I change my mind," he warns.

"Uh, I want at least"—I raise my middle finger next to my forefinger—"two, no"—I add a third finger—"three orgasms."

Knox

Jesus Christ, this woman. She might have swung my water bottle at me earlier and gotten my attention, but it's only now that I truly notice her. She's nervous, as evidenced by how her fingers shake when she pushes the hair back from her face. But the stubborn set to her chin and the rigidity of her shoulders tells me she's settled on her stance. And while I prefer my women submissive, I also want them to know their mind.

"Done." I hold out my hand.

She stares at it for a second before placing her much smaller palm in mine. An electric current seems to zip out from her touch. I stiffen. So does she. Her gaze widens and she begins to pull back her arm, but I wrap my fingers around her palm and squeeze. A trembling grips her, and her lips part in an O of surprise. Once again, I find myself leaning closer. Goddam, this static electricity that seems to spring to life every time we touch is surely a coincidence. I release her arm, then reach past her and slap the button on the elevator.

It rises up to the top floor and she turns to me. "But—"

"Not today."

"Eh?" She blinks rapidly. "I thought you wanted to punish me?"

"I will, but another time."

"Oh." She seems crestfallen.

"Don't be disappointed. I promise, I'll make it worth your while. I also promise I'll give you all the orgasms you deserve. But—"

"But?" She swallows.

"But if we want to be at Arthur's lunch in time, we need to hurry."

She flushes, then nods. "Of course."

"These documents need your signature." Her fingers move across the tablet, and my phone buzzes. We're in the backseat of my Aston Martin. I got off the elevator at my floor and instructed her to get dressed and meet me at my place in half an hour. And wasn't surprised when I'd showered and walked into my kitchen twenty minutes later to find her already dressed and waiting for me. She's back to wearing a trouser suit two sizes too big for her. She also pulled her hair back in an efficient chignon, and the oversized glasses slip down her nose as she studies her laptop screen.

For a few seconds, I watched her, unobserved. She was focused on whatever she was reading, and a tiny wrinkle appeared between her eyebrows. Her spine was straight, her narrow shoulders at attention as she perched on the stool at the breakfast counter. She muttered something to herself, then made a note in the book next to her. Her fingers raced over the keyboard as she typed something. A tendril of hair pulled loose and flopped over her cheek. She pushed it back, then continued typing.

I approached her on soundless feet, and when she looked up, our gazes met. She instantly flushed but didn't look away. "You have a packed day at the office. We'll need to get back in time for the four p.m. meeting with the sales staff, the five p.m. conference call with the East Coast, followed by the six p.m. review of the creatives for the newest ad campaign, and finally, the seven p.m. discussion with India."

"Best we get started then." I walked past her and headed for the elevator, leaving her to scramble to keep up. By the time the doors to the elevator opened, she was with me.

Never misses a beat, this one. The most efficient assistant I've ever had. And apparently, also a submissive in the making. Too bad my plans don't include her. She runs my office with a ruthless efficiency, which sets me free from the day-to-day and allows me concentrate on growing the business. She's too valuable in her position. Which is why I've given myself one chance to punish her and make her come. And then, I'll never look at her in that way again. But is it worth changing the status quo and risking complicating the work environment? And if I don't, am I going to let her get away with throwing the water bottle at me?

It's not my ego that's hurt... Not only. It's more the fact that she did it, hoping for the consequences of the action. She did it, wanting to be punished, whether she realized it or not. And I admit, a part of me is curious about how she'll take it. It's academic curiosity, is all. I want to see the expressions on her face as she orgasms. Yep, chalk it up to intellectual curiosity.

And why am I spending so much time thinking about it? It pissed me off enough that I barely spoken a word to her on the way here. Not that it stopped her from continuing to work on her tablet, sending emails my way. I preferred to ignore her—easily done, given the practice I've when it comes to her—and we made the trip to Arthur's place in silence.

She follows me in, and I take in the long table set up in the center of the garden in the backyard of Arthur's townhouse. Trees surround the estate, shielding us from early afternoon visitors to Primrose Hill. The table is loaded with food, but no one makes a move toward the table. There's a hush of expectation in the air. Or perhaps, that's my imagination? I roll my shoulders, then continue to scan the group gathered around the table.

"You okay, man?" Quentin shoots me a curious glance. "You seem... on edge."

"You need to get your eyesight checked *old* man." I grab a glass from a passing waiter and take a sip, only to spit it out. "Some non-alcoholic shit," I growl.

"I can help." June materializes by my side. She pulls out a flask and splashes clear liquid into my half-filled glass.

Some of the tension eases from my shoulders. "Thanks, doll." I down half the glass and sigh in appreciation.

She begins to melt away, but I snap my fingers, making sure not to look at her. "Don't go, I'll need you to pour." I hold out my glass again.

"Huh, don't think you want to get drunk, *sir*."

Sir? Did she call me sir? The sass on this woman. It shouldn't affect me, but fuck, if my cock doesn't instantly stiffen, and my balls tighten. I manage to keep my gaze away from her features and my arm outstretched. A few seconds pass, then she relents and pours a dollop more into the glass. "Thanks." I toss it back, then glance around, wondering where to keep it.

My efficient assistant, of course, takes it from me, and I nod. "Don't know what I'd do without you, Sierra."

"It's June," she mumbles under her breath.

Of course, I know it's June. But damn, if I'm going to reveal I remember her name.

"Anyone know what Gramps is up to?" My younger brother Tyler prowls over to join us. Man's the tallest and the biggest of all of us. His features could be cast from granite. His eyes are cold. His expression both bored and lethal.

He looms over the rest of us. In a suit and tie, he looks barely civilized for this gathering.

Tiny, Arthur's Great Dane ambles out onto the backyard, followed by my grandfather. Arthur walks out with an arm around his girlfriend Imelda. She's wearing fatigues today; the pairing seems incongruous, but when she guides him to a chair at the head of the table, he complies. Which is telling. You wouldn't have caught Arthur listening to anyone else before she came into his life. Now, he seems less hard on himself. She takes the seat to his right. It's a signal for the rest of us to take our places.

My assistant turns to leave, but when I point to the chair on my right, she initially hesitates, then complies. The chair to my left is vacant. The rest of the group take their seats. There's a general buzz around the table. Otis, my grandfather's butler tops up everyone's glasses — not mine — with more of the non-alcoholic beverage, then stands to the side.

Arthur clinks his knife against his glass, and the chatter dies down.

"No doubt, you are all curious about why you've been summoned?"

"Why should we be? We only had to drop what we were doing in the middle of a working day and attend to your summons," my other brother Brody growls under his breath.

"Something you want to share with the table?" Arthur arches an eyebrow in his direction.

Brody shrugs. "It's a working day."

"And I am the patriarch of this family... still. So, you boys and girls will come when I call." It's a statement which brooks no argument. Arthur glances around the table, the look on his features implying, my-word-is-final.

Then, Imelda pats his arm. "Don't be a dick, dear."

A titter runs around the table, then there's full blown laughter. Quentin chuckles. One of the women snorts, then slaps a hand over her mouth. A vein bulges at Arthur's temple. He clenches his jaw. I'm sure he's going into a full-blown meltdown, but as he and Imelda glare at each other, something magical happens. His features relax by degrees and then, a reluctant smile curves his features. Imelda's shoulder's relax. That woman has lady balls, but I'm guessing she fully expected to be thrown out of the gathering on her arse. Something passes between the two of them, then Arthur nods. He turns to the table, "And that is why each of you need to find the right woman."

Brody groans. My third brother Connor chugs down water from a bottle like it's going out style. Tyler's expression is as immovable as ever.

"Felix"—Arthur nods in my cousin's direction—"you have something to tell us?"

The noise at the table dies down again.

Felix clears his throat. "I'm trying out for the Marines." He meets Quentin's gaze. "I hope to be half as good at it as my father was."

Quentin seems visibly moved. He swallows, then raises his glass. "To Felix."

"To Felix." Everyone raises their glasses. I toss mine back, and June refills mine without prompting. I throw that back as well, then rise to my feet. I head toward the house, where a woman steps out onto the porch. She's tall, willowy, and wearing a green dress that reaches to below her knees. It's sleeveless, baring her thin white arms. Her dark hair is a waterfall of health that flows down her back. Her eyes are almond shaped, her skin creamy and so pale, the sun seems to reflect off of it to bathe her in an ethereal light.

"Knox." She holds out her hand.

"Priscilla." I tuck her arm through mine and guide her over to the table. She slips into the seat on my left. By the time I'm seated, the table is silent. All eyes are on me and the new arrival.

"Can I do the honors?" Arthur asks.

I yawn. "By all means."

Arthur frowns, then smooths out his expression. "This is Priscilla Whittington. Toren Whittington's sister. Toren and I agreed that the best way to resolve our family feud and join our collective fortunes is through marriage."

He's referring to the fact that the Whittingtons and the Davenports had a conflict going back a few generations, until Toren Whittington helped my half-brother Nathan stave off a takeover of the Davenport group by the Madisons. The only other family Arthur hated more than the Whittingtons.

"Of course you did." Brody snorts.

Arthur ignores him. "Tor couldn't be here, but he was happy for us to go ahead with announcing—"

"To cut a long story short, Priscilla has agreed to be my wife."

Next to me, June draws in a sharp breath. I hear the sound of glass breaking and look up to see Tyler pushing back from the table. His jaw is hard, the skin around his mouth white. He looks from me to Priscilla, then spins around and leaves. Interesting. *So Tyler and Priscilla have some history? Not my problem.*

If he had feelings for the woman, he should have spoken up earlier. When Arthur broached the topic of my marrying Priscilla, I wasn't interested. That is, until he dangled the role of the CEO of a Davenport Group company. The same one that Quentin opted out of when he got married. The same one my oldest half-brother Ed opted out of for the same reason.

Gramps made it a condition of our inheritance that we get married. Getting hitched is inevitable. Might as well be Priscilla. It makes no difference to me. If anything, this is better. Not only will there be no feelings involved, but the old man will owe me if I do this. He'll be beholden to me for helping to bury the ol' Davenport-Whittington hatchet. Something I can use to my advantage. So I said yes.

I raise my glass and glance around the table. "To my future wife.

To find out what happens next read Knox and June's story in The Unplanned Wedding

Scan this QR code to get the Unplanned Weddding

How to scan the QR code?

1 On your phone or tablet, open the built-in cameraapp.

2 Point the camera at the QRcode.

3 Tap the banner that appears on your Android phone ortablet.

4 Follow the instructions on the screen to finish signingin.

WANT TO BE THE FIRST TO FIND OUT WHEN L. STEELE'S NEXT BOOK IS OUT? SIGN UP FOR HER NEWSLETTER HERE

READ SUMMER & SINCLAIR STERLING'S STORY IN THE BILLIONAIRE'S FAKE WIFE

READ AN EXCERPT FROM SUMMER & SINCLAIR'S STORY

Summer

"Slap, slap, kiss, kiss."

"Huh?" I stare up at the bartender.

"Aka, there's a thin line between love and hate." He shakes out the crimson liquid into my glass.

"Nah." I snort. "Why would she allow him to control her, and after he insulted her?"

"It's the chemistry between them." He lowers his head. "You have to admit that, when the man is arrogant and the woman resists, it's a challenge to both of them, to see who blinks first, huh?"

"Why?" I wave my hand in the air. "Because they hate each other?"

"Because," he chuckles, "the girl in school whose braids I pulled and teased mercilessly, is the one who I—"

"Proposed to?" I huff.

His face lights up. "You get it now?"

Yeah. No. A headache begins to pound at my temples. This crash course in pop psychology is not why I came to my favorite bar in Islington, to meet my best friend, who is—I glance at the face of my phone—thirty minutes late.

I inhale the drink, and his eyebrows rise.

"What?" I glower up at the bartender. "I can barely taste the alcohol. Besides, it's free drinks at happy hour for women, right?"

"Which ends in precisely—" he holds up five fingers— "minutes."

"Oh! Yay!" I mock fist pump. "Time enough for one more, at least."

A hiccough swells my throat and I swallow it back, nod.

One has to do what one has to do… when everything else in the world is going to shit.

A hot sensation stabs behind my eyes; my chest tightens. Is this what people call growing up?

The bartender tips his mixing flask, strains out a fresh batch of the ruby red liquid onto the glass in front of me.

"Salut." I nod my thanks, then toss it back. It hits my stomach and tendrils of fire crawl up my spine, I cough.

My head spins. Warmth sears my chest, spreads to my extremities. I can't feel my fingers or toes. Good. Almost there. "Top me up."

"You sure?"

"Yes." I square my shoulders and reach for the drink.

"No. She's had enough."

"What the—?" I pivot on the bar stool.

Indigo eyes bore into me.

Fathomless. Black at the bottom, the intensity in their depths grips me. He swoops out his arm, grabs the glass and holds it up. Thick fingers dwarf the glass. Tapered at the edges. The nails short and buff. *All the better to grab you with.* I gulp.

"Like what you see?"

I flush, peer up into his face.

Hard cheekbones, hollows under them, and a tiny scar that slashes at his left eyebrow. *How did he get that?* Not that I care. My gaze slides to his mouth. Thin upper lip, a lower lip that is full and cushioned. Pouty with a hint of bad boy. *Oh!* My toes curl. My thighs clench.

The corner of his mouth kicks up. *Asshole.*

Bet he thinks life is one big smug-fest. I glower, reach for my glass, and he holds it up and out of my reach.

I scowl. "Gimme that."

He shakes his head.

"That's my drink."

"Not anymore." He shoves my glass at the bartender. "Water for her. Get me a whiskey, neat."

I splutter, then reach for my drink again. The barstool tips in his direction. This is when I fall against him, and my breasts slam into his hard chest, sculpted planes with layers upon layers of muscle that ripple and writhe as he turns aside, flattens himself against the bar. The floor rises up to meet me.

What the actual hell?

I twist my torso at the last second and my butt connects with the surface. *Ow!*

The breath rushes out of me. My hair swirls around my face. I scramble for purchase, and my knee connects with his leg.

"Watch it." He steps around, stands in front of me.

"You stepped aside?" I splutter. "You let me fall?"

"Hmph."

I tilt my chin back, all the way back, look up the expanse of muscled thigh that stretches the silken material of his suit. *What is he wearing? Could any suit fit a man with such precision?* Hand crafted on Saville Row, no doubt. I glance at the bulge that tents the fabric between his legs. *Oh!* I blink.

Look away, look away. I hold out my arm. He'll help me up at least, won't he?

He glances at my palm, then turns away. *No, he didn't do that, no way.*

A glass of amber liquid appears in front of him. He lifts the tumbler to his sculpted mouth.

His throat moves, strong tendons flexing. He tilts his head back, and the column of his neck moves as he swallows. Dark hair covers his chin — it's a discordant chord in that clean-cut profile, I shiver. He would scrape that rough skin down my core. He'd mark my inner thighs, lick my core, thrust his tongue inside my melting channel and drink from my pussy. *Oh! God.* Goosebumps rise on my skin.

No one has the right to look this beautiful, this achingly gorgeous. Too magnificent for his own good. Anger coils in my chest.

"Arrogant wanker."

"I'll take that under advisement."

"You're a jerk, you know that?"

He presses his lips together. The grooves on either side of his mouth deepen. Clearly the man has never laughed a single day in his life. Bet that stick up his arse is uncomfortable. I chuckle.

He runs his gaze down my features, my chest, down to my toes, then yawns.

The hell! I will not let him provoke me. Will not. "Like what you see?" I jut out my chin.

"Sorry, you're not my type." He slides a hand into the pocket of those perfectly cut pants, stretching it across that heavy bulge.

Heat curls low in my belly.

Not fair, that he could afford a wardrobe that clearly shouts his status and what amounts to the economy of a small third-world country. A hot feeling stabs in my chest.

He reeks of privilege, of taking his status in life for granted.

While I've had to fight every inch of the way. Hell, I am still battling to hold onto the last of my equilibrium.

"Last chance—" I wiggle my fingers from where I am sprawled out on the floor at his feet, "—to redeem yourself..."

"You have me there." He places the glass on the counter, then bends and holds out his hand. The hint of discolored steel at his wrist catches my attention. Huh?

He wears a cheap-ass watch?

That's got to bring down the net worth of his presence by more than 1000% percent. Weird.

I reach up and he straightens.

I lurch back.

"Oops, I changed my mind." His lips curl.

A hot burning sensation claws at my stomach. I am not a violent person, honestly. But Smirky Pants here, he needs to be taught a lesson.

I swipe out my legs, kicking his out from under him.

Sinclair

My knees give way, and I hurtle toward the ground.

What the—? I twist around, thrust out my arms. My palms hit the floor. The impact jostles up my elbows. I firm my biceps and come to a halt planked above her.

A huffing sound fills my ear.

I turn to find my whippet, Max, panting with his mouth open. I scowl and he flattens his ears.

All of my businesses are dog-friendly. Before you draw conclusions about me being the caring sort or some such shit—it attracts footfall.

Max scrutinizes the girl, then glances at me. *Huh?* He hates women, but not her, apparently.

I straighten and my nose grazes hers.

My arms are on either side of her head. Her chest heaves. The fabric of her dress stretches across her gorgeous breasts. My fingers tingle; my palms ache to cup those tits, squeeze those hard nipples outlined against the—hold on, what is she wearing? A tunic shirt in a sparkly pink... and are those shoulder pads she has on?

I glance up, and a squeak escapes her lips.

Pink hair surrounds her face. *Pink? Who dyes their hair that color past the age of eighteen?*

I stare at her face. *How old is she?* Un-furrowed forehead, dark eyelashes that flutter against pale cheeks. Tiny nose, and that mouth— luscious, tempting. A whiff of her scent, cherries and caramel, assails my senses. My mouth waters. *What the hell?*

She opens her eyes and our eyelashes brush. Her gaze widens. Green, like the leaves of the evergreens, flickers of gold sparkling in their depths. "What?" She glowers. "You're demonstrating the plank position?"

"Actually," I lower my weight onto her, the ridge of my hardness thrusting into the softness between her legs, "I was thinking of something else, altogether."

She gulps and her pupils dilate. *Ah, so she feels it, too?*

I drop my head toward her, closer, closer.

Color floods the creamy expanse of her neck. Her eyelids flutter down. She tilts her chin up.

I push up and off of her.

"That... Sweetheart, is an emphatic 'no thank you' to whatever you are offering."

Her eyelids spring open and pink stains her cheeks. Adorable. Such a range of emotions across those gorgeous features in a few seconds. What else is hidden under that exquisite exterior of hers?

She scrambles up, eyes blazing.

Ah! The little bird is trying to spread her wings? My dick twitches. My groin hardens, *Why does her anger turn me on so, huh?*

She steps forward, thrusts a finger in my chest.

My heart begins to thud.

She peers up from under those hooded eyelashes. "Wake up and taste the wasabi, asshole."

"What does that even mean?"

She makes a sound deep in her throat. My dick twitches. My pulse speeds up.

She pivots, grabs a half-full beer mug sitting on the bar counter.

I growl, "Oh, no, you don't."

She turns, swings it at me. The smell of hops envelops the space.

I stare down at the beer-splattered shirt, the lapels of my camel colored jacket deepening to a dull brown. Anger squeezes my guts.

I fist my fingers at my side, broaden my stance.

She snickers.

I tip my chin up. "You're going to regret that."

The smile fades from her face. "Umm." She places the now empty mug on the bar.

I take a step forward and she skitters back. "It's only clothes." She gulps. "They'll wash."

I glare at her and she swallows, wiggles her fingers in the air. "I should have known that you wouldn't have a sense of humor."

I thrust out my jaw. "That's a ten-thousand-pound suit you destroyed."

She blanches, then straightens her shoulders. "Must have been some hot date you were trying to impress, huh?"

"Actually," I flick some of the offending liquid from my lapels, "it's you I was after."

"Me?" She frowns.

"We need to speak."

She glances toward the bartender who's on the other side of the bar. "I don't know you." She chews on her lower lip, biting off some of the hot pink. How would she look, with that pouty mouth fastened on my cock?

The blood rushes to my groin so quickly that my head spins. My pulse rate ratchets up. Focus, focus on the task you came here for.

"This will take only a few seconds." I take a step forward.

She moves aside.

I frown. "You want to hear this, I promise."

"Go to hell." She pivots and darts forward.

I let her go, a step, another, because... I can? Besides it's fun to create the illusion of freedom first; makes the hunt so much more entertaining, huh?

I swoop forward, loop an arm around her waist, and yank her toward me.

She yelps. "Release me."

Good thing the bar is not yet full. It's too early for the usual office-goers to stop by. And the staff...? Well they are well aware of who cuts their paychecks.

I spin her around and against the bar, then release her. "You will listen to me."

She swallows; she glances left to right.

Not letting you go yet, little Bird. I move into her space, crowd her.

She tips her chin up. "Whatever you're selling, I'm not interested."

I allow my lips to curl. "You don't fool me."

A flush steals up her throat, sears her cheeks. So tiny, so innocent. Such a good little liar. I narrow my gaze. "Every action has its consequences."

"Are you daft?" She blinks.

"This pretense of yours?" I thrust my face into hers, growling, "It's not working."

She blinks, then color suffuses her cheeks. "You're certifiably mad—"

"Getting tired of your insults."

"It's true, everything I said." She scrapes back the hair from her face.

Her fingernails are painted... You guessed it, pink.

"And here's something else. You are a selfish, egotistical jackass."

I smirk. "You're beginning to repeat your insults and I haven't even kissed you yet."

"Don't you dare." She gulps.

I tilt my head. "Is that a challenge?"

"It's a..." she scans the crowded space, then turns to me. Her lips firm, "...a warning. You're delusional, you jackass." She inhales a deep breath before she speaks, "Your ego is bigger than the size of a black hole." She snickers. "Bet it's to compensate for your lack of balls."

A-n-d, that's it. I've had enough of her mouth that threatens to never stop spewing words. How many insults can one tiny woman hurl my way? Answer: too many to count.

"You—"

I lower my chin, touch my lips to hers.

Heat, sweetness, the honey of her essence explodes on my palate. My dick twitches. I tilt my head, deepen the kiss, reaching for that something more... more... of whatever scent she's wearing on her skin, infused with that breath of hers that crowds my senses, rushes down my spine. My groin hardens; my cock lengthens. I thrust my tongue between those infuriating lips.

She makes a sound deep in her throat and my heart begins to pound.

So innocent, yet so crafty. Beautiful and feisty. The kind of complication I don't need in my life.

I prefer the straight and narrow. Gray and black, that's how I choose to define my world. She, with her flashes of color—pink hair and lips that threaten to drive me to the edge of distraction—is exactly what I hate.

Give me a female who has her priorities set in life. To pleasure me, get me off, then walk away before her emotions engage. Yeah. That's what I prefer.

Not this... this bundle of craziness who flings her arms around my shoulders, thrusts her breasts up and into my chest, tips up her chin, opens her mouth, and invites me to take and take.

Does she have no self-preservation? Does she think I am going to fall for her wide-eyed appeal? She has another thing coming.

I tear my mouth away and she protests.

She twines her leg with mine, pushes up her hips, so that melting softness between her thighs cradles my aching hardness.

I glare into her face and she holds my gaze.

Trains her green eyes on me. Her cheeks flush a bright red. Her lips fall open and a moan bleeds into the air. The blood rushes to my dick, which instantly thickens. *Fuck.*

Time to put distance between myself and the situation.

It's how I prefer to manage things. Stay in control, always. Cut out anything that threatens to impinge on my equilibrium. Shut it down or buy them off. Reduce it to a transaction. That I understand.

The power of money, to be able to buy and sell—numbers, logic. That's what's worked for me so far.

"How much?"

Her forehead furrows.

"Whatever it is, I can afford it."

Her jaw slackens. "You think... you—"

"A million?"

"What?"

"Pounds, dollars... You name the currency, and it will be in your account."

Her jaw slackens. "You're offering me money?"

"For your time, and for you to fall in line with my plan."

She reddens. "You think I am for sale?"

"Everyone is."

"Not me."

Here we go again. "Is that a challenge?"

Color fades from her face. "Get away from me."

"Are you shy, is that what this is?" I frown. "You can write your price down on a piece of paper if you prefer." I glance up, notice the bartender watching us. I jerk my chin toward the napkins. He grabs one, then offers it to her.

She glowers at him. "Did you buy him, too?"

"What do you think?"

She glances around. "I think everyone here is ignoring us."

"It's what I'd expect."

"Why is that?"

I wave the tissue in front of her face. "Why do you think?"

"You own the place?"

"As I am going to own you."

She sets her jaw. "Let me leave and you won't regret this."

A chuckle bubbles up. I swallow it away. This is no laughing matter. I never smile during a transaction. Especially not when I am negotiating a new acquisition. And that's all she is. The final piece in the puzzle I am building.

"No one threatens me."

"You're right."

"Huh?"

"I'd rather act on my instinct."

Her lips twist, her gaze narrows. All of my senses scream a warning.

No, she wouldn't, no way—pain slices through my middle and sparks explode behind my eyes.

READ SINCLAIR AND SUMMER'S ENEMIES TO LOVERS, MARRIAGE OF CONVENIENCE ROMANCE IN THE BILLIONAIRE'S FAKE WIFE HERE

READ LIAM AND ISLA'S FAKE RELATIONSHIP ROMANCE IN THE PROPOSAL WHERE TINY FIRST MAKES AN APPEARANCE, CLICK HERE

READ AN EXCERPT FROM THE PROPOSAL

Liam

"Where is she?"

The receptionist gazes at me cow-eyed. Her lips move, but no words emerge. She clears her throat, glances sideways at the door to the side and behind her, then back at me.

"So, I take it she's in there?" I brush past her, and she jumps to her feet. "Sir, y-y-you can't go in there."

"Watch me." I glare at her.

She stammers, then gulps. Sweat beads her forehead. She shuffles back, and I stalk past her.

Really, is there no one who can stand up to me? All of this scraping of chairs and fawning over me? It's enough to drive a man to boredom. I need a challenge. So, when my ex-wife-to-be texted me to say she was calling off our wedding, I was pissed. But when she let it slip that her wedding planner was right—that she needs to marry for love, and not for some family obligation, rage gripped me. I squeezed my phone so hard the screen cracked. I almost hurled the device across the room. When I got a hold of myself, for the first time in a long time, a shiver of something like excitement passed through me. *Finally, fuck.*

That familiar pulse of adrenaline pulses through my veins. It's a sensation I was familiar with in the early days of building my business.

After my father died and I took charge of the group of companies he'd run, I was filled with a sense of purpose; a one-directional focus to prove myself and nurture his legacy. To make my group of companies the leader, in its own right. To make so much money and amass so much power, I'd be a force to be reckoned with.

I tackled each business meeting with a zeal that none of my opponents were able to withstand. But with each passing year—as I crossed the benchmarks I'd set myself, as my bottom line grew healthier, my cash reserves engorged, and the people working for me began treating me with the kind of respect normally reserved for larger-than-life icons—some of that enthusiasm waned. Oh, I still wake up ready to give my best to my job every day, but the zest that once fired me up faded, leaving a sense of purposelessness behind.

The one thing that has kept me going is to lock down my legacy. To ensure the business I've built will finally be transferred to my name. For which my father informed me I would need to marry. Which is why, after much research, I tracked down Lila Kumar, wooed her, and proposed to her. And then, her meddling wedding planner came along and turned all of my plans upside down.

Now, that same sense of purpose grips me. That laser focus I've been lacking envelops me and fills my being. All of my senses sharpen as I shove the door of her office open and stalk in.

The scent envelops me first. The lush notes of violets and peaches. Evocative and fruity. Complex, yet with a core of mystery that begs to be unraveled. Huh? I'm not the kind to be affected by the scent of a woman, but this... Her scent... It's always chafed at my nerve endings. The hair on my forearms straightens.

My guts tie themselves up in knots, and my heart pounds in my chest. It's not comfortable. The kind of feeling I got the first time I went white-water rafting. A combination of nervousness and excitement as I faced my first rapids. A sensation that had since ebbed. One I'd been chasing ever since, pushing myself to take on extreme sports. One I hadn't thought I'd find in the office of a wedding planner.

My feet thud on the wooden floor, and I get a good look at the space which is one-fourth the size of my own office. In the far corner is a bookcase packed with books. On the opposite side is a comfortable settee packed with cushions women seem to like so much. There's a colorful patchwork quilt thrown over it, and behind that, a window that looks onto the back of the adjacent office building. On the coffee table in front of the settee is a bowl with crystal-like objects that reflect the light from the floor lamps. There are paintings on the wall that depict scenes from beaches. No doubt, the kind she'd point to and sell the idea of a honeymoon to gullible brides. I suppose the entire space would appeal to women. With its mood lighting and homey feel, the space invites you to kick back, relax and pour out your problems. A ruse I'm not going to fall for.

"You!" I stab my finger in the direction of the woman seated behind the antique desk straight ahead. "Call Lila, right now, and tell her she needs to go through with the wedding. Tell her she can't back out. Tell her I'm the right choice for her."

She peers up at me from behind large, black horn-rimmed glasses perched on her nose. "No."

I blink. "Excuse me?"

She leans back in her chair. "I'm not going to do that."

"Why the hell not?"

"Are you the right choice for her?

"Of course, I am." I glare at her.

Some of the color fades from her cheeks. She taps her pen on the table, then juts out her chin. "What makes you think you're the right choice of husband for her?"

"What makes you think I'm not."

"Do you love her?"

"That's no one's problem except mine and hers."

"You don't love her."

"What does that have to do with anything?"

"Excuse me?" She pushes the glasses further up her nose. "Are you seriously asking what loving the woman you're going to marry has to do with actually marrying her?" Her voice pulses with fury.

"Yes, exactly. Why don't you explain it to me?" The sarcasm in my tone is impossible to miss.

She stares at me from behind those large glasses that should make her look owlish and studious, but only add an edge of what I can only describe as quirky-sexiness. The few times I've met her before, she's gotten on my nerves so much, I couldn't wait to get the hell away from her. Now, giving her the full benefit of my attention, I realize, she's actually quite striking. And the addition of those spectacles? Fuck me—I never thought I had a weakness for women wearing glasses. Maybe I was wrong. Or maybe it's specifically this woman wearing glasses... Preferably only glasses and nothing else.

Hmm. Interesting. This reaction to her. It's unwarranted and not something I planned for. I widen my stance, mainly to accommodate the thickness between my legs. An inconvenience... which perhaps I can use to my benefit? I drag my thumb under my lower lip.

Her gaze drops to my mouth, and if I'm not mistaken, her breath hitches. *Very interesting.* Has she always reacted to me like that in the past? Nope, I would've noticed. We've always tried to have as little as possible to do with each other. Like I said, interesting. And unusual.

"First," —she drums her fingers on the table— "are you going to answer my question?"

I tilt my head, the makings of an idea buzzing through my synapses. I need a little time to flesh things out though. It's the only reason I deign to answer her question which, let's face it, I have no obligation to respond to. But for the moment, it's in my interest to humor her and buy myself a little time.

"Lila and I are well-matched in every way. We come from good families—"

"You mean rich families?"

"That, too. Our families move in the same circles."

"Don't you mean boring country clubs?" she says in a voice that drips with distaste.

I frown. "Among other places. We have the pedigree, the bloodline, our backgrounds are congruent, and we'd be able to fold into an arrangement of coexistence with the least amount of disruption on either side."

"Sounds like you're arranging a merger."

"A takeover, but what-fucking-ever." I raise a shoulder.

Her scowl deepens. "This is how you approached the upcoming wedding... And you wonder why Lila left you?"

"I gave her the biggest ring money could buy—"

"You didn't make an appearance at the engagement party."

"I signed off on all the costs related to the upcoming nuptials—"

"Your own engagement party. You didn't come to it. You left her alone to face her family and friends." Her tone rises. Her cheeks are flushed. You'd think she was talking about her own wedding, not that of her friend. In fact, it's more entertaining to talk to her than discuss business matters with my employees. *How interesting.*

"You also didn't show up for most of the rehearsals." She glowers.

"I did show up for the last one."

"Not that it made any difference. You were either checking your watch and indicating that it was time for you to leave, or you were glowering at the plans being discussed."

"I still agreed to that god-awful wedding cake, didn't I?

"On the other hand, it's probably good you didn't come for the previous rehearsals. If you had, Lila and I might have had this conversation earlier—"

"Aha!" I straighten. "So, you confess that it's because of you Lila walked away from this wedding."

She tips her head back. "Hardly. It's because of you."

"So you say, but your guilt is written large on your face."

"Guilt?" Her features flush. The color brings out the dewy hue of her skin, and the blue of her eyes deepens until they remind me of forget-me-nots. No, more like the royal blue of the ink that spilled onto my paper the first time I attempted to write with a fountain pen.

"The only person here who should feel guilty is you, for attempting to coerce an innocent, young woman into an arrangement that would have trapped her for life."

Anger thuds at my temples. My pulse begins to race. "I never have to coerce women. And what you call being trapped is what most women call security. But clearly, you wouldn't know that, considering" —I wave my hand in the air— "you prefer to run your kitchen-table business which, no doubt, barely makes ends meet."

She loosens her grip on her pencil, and it falls to the table with a clatter. Sparks flash deep in her eyes.

You know what I said earlier about the royal blue? Strike that. There are flickers of silver hidden in the depths of her gaze. Flickers that blaze when she's upset. How would it be to push her over the edge? To be at the receiving end of all that passion, that fervor, that ardor... that absolute avidness of existence when she's one with the moment? How would it feel to rein in her spirit, absorb it, drink from it, revel in it, and use it to spark color into my life?

"Kitchen-table business?" She makes a growling sound under her breath. "You dare come into my office and insult my enterprise? The company I have grown all by myself—"

"And outside of your assistant" —I nod toward the door I came through— "you're the sole employee, I take it?"

Her color deepens. "I work with a group of vendors—"

I scoff, "None of whom you could hold accountable when they don't deliver."

"—who have been carefully vetted to ensure that they always deliver," she says at the same time. "Anyway, why do you care, since you don't have a wedding to go to?"

"That's where you're wrong." I peel back my lips. "I'm not going to be labeled as the joke of the century. After all, the media labelled it 'the wedding of the century'." I make air quotes with my fingers.

It was Isla's idea to build up the wedding with the media. She also wanted to invite influencers from all walks of life to attend, but I have no interest in turning my nuptials into a circus. So, I vetoed the idea of journalists attending in person. I have, however, agreed to the event being recorded by professionals and exclusive clips being shared with the media and the influencers. This way, we'll get the necessary PR coverage, without the media being physically present.

In all fairness, the publicity generated by the upcoming nuptials has already been beneficial. It's not like I'll ever tell her, but Isla was right to feed the public's interest in the upcoming event. Apparently, not even the most hard-nosed investors can resist the warm, fuzzy feelings that a marriage invokes. And this can only help with the IPO I have planned for the most important company in my portfolio. "I have a lot riding on this wedding."

"Too bad you don't have a bride."

"Ah," —I smirk— "but I do."

She scowls. "No, you don't. Lila—"

"I'm not talking about her."

"Then who are you talking about?"

"You."

To find out what happens next read Liam and Isla's fake relationship romance in The Proposal where Tiny first makes an appearance, click here

read Michael and Karma's forced marriage romance in Mafia King here

Read JJ and Lena's ex-boyfriend's father, age-gap romance here

Read Knight and Penny's, best friend's brother romance in The Wrong Wife here

Read Dr. Weston Kincaid and Amelie's forced proximity, one-bed Christmas Romance in The Billionaire's Fake Wife HERE

Download your exclusive L. Steele reading order bingo card

Did you know all the characters you read about have their own book? Cross off their stories as you read and share your bingo card in L. Steele's reader group

READING ORDER

1 On your phone or tablet, open the built-in cameraapp.
2 Point the camera at the QRcode.
3 Tap the banner that appears on your Android phone ortablet.
4 Follow the instructions on the screen to finish signingin.

MARRIAGE OF CONVENIENCE BILLIONAIRE ROMANCE FROM L. STEELE

The Billionaire's Fake Wife - Sinclair and Summer's story that started this universe... with a plot twist you won't see coming!

The Billionaire's Secret - Victoria and Saint's story. Saint is maybe the most alphahole of them all!

Marrying the Billionaire Single Dad - Damian and Julia's story, watch out for the plot twist!

The Proposal - Liam and Isla's story. What's a wedding planner to do when you tell the bride not to go through with the wedding and the groom demands you take her place and give him a heir? And yes plot twist!

CHRISTMAS ROMANCE BOOKS BY L. STEELE FOR YOU

Want to find out how Dr. Weston Kincaid and Amelie met? Read The Billionaire's Christmas Bride

Want even more Christmas Romance books? *Read A very Mafia Christmas, Christian and Aurora's story*

Read a marriage of convenience billionaire Christmas romance, Hunter and Zara's story - *The Christmas One Night Stand*

FORBIDDEN BILLIONAIRE ROMANCE BY L. STEELE FOR YOU

Read Daddy JJ's, age-gap romance in Mafia Lust HERE

Read Edward, Baron and Ava's story starting with Billionaire's Sins HERE

ABOUT THE AUTHOR

Hello, I'm L. Steele.

I write romance stories with strong powerful men who meet their match in sassy, curvy, spitfire women.

I love to push myself with each book on both the spice and the angst so I can deliver well rounded, multidimensional characters.

I enjoy trading trivia with my husband, watching lots and lots of movies, and walking nature trails. I live in London.

ACKNOWLEDGMENTS

Edited by: Theresa Leigh (Thank you so much!) and Elizabeth Connor
Cover Design: Jacqueline Sweet

Thanks to Mary Eddins Seale for Meatloaf.

Huge shout out to Li AND Giorgina Meduri You gals are my very own personal cheerleaders and I couldn't do this without you!

And to everyone in L. Steele's Team Facebook reader group, you guys are awesome!

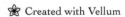 Created with Vellum

www.ingramcontent.com/pod-product-compliance
Lightning Source LLC
LaVergne TN
LVHW012336160225
803895LV00035B/1265